MACGUFFIN

ROY C. BOOTH
JOHN F. MOLLARD

iap
Indie Authors Press

TITLES BY
INDIE AUTHORS PRESS

Synthetic Dawns & Crimson Dusks
First Contact: A Science Fiction Anthology
The Chronos Chronicles: A Time Travel Anthology
Issues of Tomorrow: A Science Fiction Anthology
Altered States II: a cyberpunk anthology
Control Theory
Spooky Halloween Drabbles 2016
Raiders of the Seventh Planet
Blood of Nyx
Corpus Deluxe: Undead Tales of Terror
Spooky Halloween Drabbles 2015
Speculative Valentine Drabbles 2015
Altered States: a cyberpunk sci-fi anthology
Spooky Halloween Drabbles 2014
A Forest of Dreams, a fantasy anthology
British Process Servers Guide
Learning About Love

Forthcoming titles can be found on
www.salgado-reyes.com.

Indie Authors Press

MACGUFFIN

A catalogue record for this book is available from the British Library.

ISBN: 978-1-910910-15-3

1st Edition

Indie Authors Press policy is to use paper that are natural, renewable, and recyclable products and made from wood grown in sustainable forests. The logging and manufacturing processes are expected to conform to the environmental regulations of the country of origin.

London | Chile | USA

London | Chile | USA

ACKNOWLEDGMENTS

FIRST AND FOREMOST, I must say thank you to Roy C. Booth for serving as my writing mentor and co-author on this project. He truly paid it forward with his extensive knowledge of writing, editing, publishing, etc. It's been mostly smooth sailing.

Acknowledgment also to Jorge Salgado-Reyes and Indie Authors Press for choosing to publish this strange little story.

To Faith Kauwe for the third-party edits.

To Druscilla Morgan for the cover. Truly a difficult concept to market.

And finally, to movie geeks everywhere, like myself. This book is for you, about you, and written by you.

Oh, and to Alfred Hitchcock. He's the bomb-dig, yo.

~John F. Mollard~

THIS BOOK IS FOR...

Roy: Cynthia
John: Mom & Dad

CHAPTER ONE

BENEDICT CANYON, WEST OF Hollywood, is a picturesque ravine in the Santa Monica Mountains, overlooking Beverly Hills and Bel-Air.

A three-acre, French country-style estate, at 10048 Cielo Drive, stood on a hillside facing east. It lay secluded amidst thick pine trees, flowering cherry, and split-rail fencing. A black 1964 Porsche 912 sat beside a red 1979 Ferrari 308 GTS before a garage to the south of the main house. A patio, a rustic wishing well, and a kidney-shaped swimming pool lay between.

An attractive young woman swam laps in the pool, as her cell phone rang atop a white towel at the north end. She surfaced and answered the call, "Hello?"

"Um...yes...sorry to bother you at such a late hour."

"Oh, no problem. I love your accent. British?"

"Why, yes, thank you. I'm an old friend of Dr. Milner's: Paul Swan. He told me I could reach him at this number."

"He's doing some catch-up work inside. Let me transfer you."

"Thank you, Miss...?"

"Oh, I'm sorry. I'm Theresa, Larry's fiancée."

"That's terrific. I sure hope Larry got you a beautiful engagement ring. Spared no real expense?"

Theresa pondered the enormous diamond on her left ring finger. "He sure did." She smiled. "The best money can buy."

"Splendid."

"Don't let me keep you. I'll transfer you."

"Wonderful talking to you, Theresa. Hope to meet you in person someday to congratulate you on your impending nuptials."

"That would be marvelous. We'll make sure to invite you to the wedding."

"Enjoy your evening, my dear."

"Goodnight."

Dr. Lawrence Milner sat in his living room, reviewing a stack of medical records, adjusting his glasses. His cell phone rang atop a nearby glass coffee table.

Milner answered the phone on the third ring. "Yes? Dr. Milner."

"Hello, Lawrence."

A look of horror formed on Milner's face. Anxiety set in; his voice wavered. "Swan."

"Forgive me for calling at such a late hour, Doctor. I'm sure you're mighty busy."

"How many times must I tell you, Swan–I can't do anything more for you? Your injuries are too severe. Continued surgery would only make matters worse. The tissues will–"

"Actually Doctor, I've had many a year to gloss things over and grow to appreciate my new...looks. But, that's not the reason I called."

"Wh...what is it you want?"

"The wife and I have decided to renew our vows after forty years, and it would be an honor if you would serve as my Best Man, Doctor."

"I don't...I don't understand what you're asking of me, Swan. I'm not your friend. I'm a plastic surgeon. You're a client."

"I understand you've recently become engaged yourself, eh? A new fiancée? Theresa, is it?"

"Yes, it is. Why do you ask?"

"What is it she does?"

"She's an actress."

"An actress, hmm? Does she have the perfect body? The lush, pouty lips? The flawless skin? The beautiful plump breasts you slaved hours upon?"

"Swan, enough."

"Is she like all the others over the years you fixed and then bent over? Or is she better? Something so good you had to save it all for yourself?"

"This conversation's over."

"I bet she got a lovely engagement ring on top of the deal, too, eh? Too bad she won't be around to enjoy it after tonight."

Milner's voice wavered again. "What the Hell is it you want, Swan?"

"What is it I want, hmm? Let's see–your head on a silver platter as the main course at my wedding; your fiancée's diamond ring on my bride's finger."

Milner checked his phone's Caller ID. "Where are you calling from, Swan? This is my office number."

"Hang up and try phoning the office. No one is going to answer."

"I'm calling the police."

"Be my guest. They won't arrive here in time."

Milner glanced around the living room. "Where the Hell are you?" Undisguised panic now set in.

CLICK. The phone went dead.

In the master bedroom, a ten-paned French door overlooked the exterior patio. Milner turned on the light, popped his head out, and gazed at Theresa in the swimming pool. "Theresa?"

She waved back, mid-backstroke. "Hi there."

"Is–is everything okay out here, darling?"

"You should come in. The water's fabulous."

"I wish I could, sweetheart, but I've got a load of paperwork to do before tomorrow morning."

"Oh, you're always working! When are you ever gonna learn to have a little fun once in a while?"

Milner scanned the patio and the lawn beyond. All appeared secure. "Next time."

"Love you."

Milner ducked back inside.

Theresa swam to the north end of the pool and climbed out. She grabbed her towel and dried off. She walked over and sat down in an Adirondack chair, picked up a glass of ice water with a slice of lemon, and took a sip.

Milner returned to the living room, sat down in his recliner, and resumed his work.

Concentrating proved futile. He grabbed his phone and dialed his office number. A ring came from the loft above, instead. "What the Hell?"

Milner sprang to his feet and climbed the ladder to the upper floor. Fearing the worst, he lunged upward. No one was there. Nothing but a pile of boxes toward the back and a ringing cell phone at Milner's fingertips. "Hah..." he sighed, staring at the little device. "God, you damn near gave me a heart attack!" He picked it up and turned it off. "How did you get up here?"

An ax swung and broke the lower ladder rungs in half, toppling Milner backward.

"Uhhhn..."

Milner landed on the floor with a pronounced thud. His glasses went flying, skittering to a stop under the boot sole of the intruder who crushed them underfoot.

"No..."

Milner glanced up. His eyes set on a shadowy figure in a black satin cape and suit, with a sword scabbard at his side–he sported long, silvery hair, a white *Phantom of the Opera* mask, and a tilted black fedora.

"Swan!"

Swan overturned the couch and whipped out a stiletto knife.

The attack commenced.

Milner lunged and ripped Swan's mask off, exposing a handsome face.

Swan jeered. "You shouldn't have done that! Now you're *reeaally* beginning to piss me off!" He threw Milner into a lamp.

Milner scrambled to regain his feet. Swan closed the gap and stomped down hard on the other man's fingers, breaking them with a horrible brittle sound.

"Aaaahhhh!" cried Milner.

"Tch. You're such a wanker."

Swan hurled Milner over the recliner into the base of a baby grand piano by a bar at the northwest corner of the room.

Milner screamed in pain as the stiletto slashed his Achilles' tendons. "Aaacccckkkkk!"

Swan replaced his mask and fedora. "Keep it down, Doctor. Wouldn't want your girlfriend to hear you squeal like a stuck piglet. Speaking of which, where might I find her?"

Frantic to warn Theresa, Milner crawled toward the master bedroom. "THERESA!"

The noise alerted Theresa outside.

"Larry? Larry, honey, what's wrong?!"

No reply. Only shrieks and banging sounds were audible from inside the house.

Theresa cracked the patio door open and peered inside. She watched Swan grab Milner by the back of the neck and throw him into a wall.

"Unnhhh!"

Swan stabbed him in the rear torso, and Milner crumpled to the floor.

Theresa stood horrified. "LAARRRYYYY!"

Milner looked straight into her eyes. "Theresa!" he gasped. "Get...get the Hell out of here!"

Swan turned his attention to Theresa. "Well, well." He took a bow. "Honey, I'm home!"

Snatching a statue off a wall shelf, Theresa hurled it at Swan's head, knocking him to the floor.

"Aaarrrgghh!"

She again plucked up the statue and continued to hammer Swan while he was down. "Take that, you son of a bitch!"

Swan's wig tore free. The prosthetic applications covering his head peeled away, exposing something gruesome beneath. "Unnhhh..." he moaned, his hands flailing.

Theresa gasped.

Seizing her vulnerability, Swan slugged Theresa in the stomach and grabbed his knife. He plunged the blade into her left thigh to free himself from her barrage.

Theresa's scream filled the air. She dropped the statue and curled up on the floor in a fetal position.

Swan pulled on his wig and hat and got to his feet. "You're a feisty little bitch, aren't you?" he growled. "An actress, huh? Bah! You have no talent. All you have is a body. I'll show you what real acting is about."

Theresa sobbed, holding her belly. "Don't kill me! I'm going to have a baby!"

"Do you think I care about you or your blasted baby? Bollocks! Once I kill you *and* your fiancé, I'll carve out the little chud with a car key, put it in a jar. Later on, feed it to my fish!"

Theresa recoiled in horror. "Y-you're sick!"

"Quit your sniveling. This'll all be over soon."

Angry, Theresa got to her knees and lunged at Swan's legs, sinking her teeth into his flesh.

"Aaarrrghh! You little bitch!"

He grabbed her by the hair, pulled her to her feet, and hurled her face-first through the French patio door.

Swan walked through Theresa's blood and approached the splintered patio door. He picked up a leather doctor's satchel from the floor and exited the house. Bloody footprints trailed behind.

As Swan approached Theresa cowering on the patio, she begged for her life, "NO, NO, DON'T! DON'T KILL ME! NO!"

Theresa forced herself to her feet and hobbled across the patio to the front lawn. Swan toppled her to the ground and kneeled over her on the grass, his knife at the ready.

"I give up! Please, mercy!"

"Woman, I have no mercy for you. Time to end this."

Slashed and stabbed, Theresa died where she fell.

Swan knelt and splayed Theresa's fresh corpse face-up on the grass in the shape of a star, her eyes dilated.

He hovered and admired his work. "Welcome to my Hollywood Walk of Fame, bitch!"

With his knife, he hacked off her ring finger and deposited it into the satchel. He then continued to his next grisly task.

Dr. Milner crawled on the floor by the fireplace for what seemed an eternity and grabbed his cell phone resting nearby. He checked for a signal and tried to dial 9-1-1 with his crushed fingers. "Unh..." The phone managed to dial once before Swan's stiletto knife stabbed him in the back. "Aaaaaahhhhh!"

A police dispatcher picked up the call. "9-1-1, what's your emergency?"

The phone flew from Milner's hands, smashing against the fireplace and shattering into a dozen pieces. The call disconnected as the phone went dead.

The knife protruded from Milner's back. Bleeding profuse, Milner grabbed Swan's overcoat and pulled himself to his knees.

The two adversaries stared each other down.

"W-why are you doing this, Swan? What d-do you want?"

Swan unsheathed his sword from the scabbard and readied to swing. "I told you on the phone: I want your head."

Milner cried out in terror, "OH, GOD, NO, PLEASE DON'T! OH, GOD, NO, DON'T, DON'T–!"

On the front lawn, a ravenous crow pecked away at Theresa Burkhart's corpse. It watched through a window into the living room as Swan severed Milner's head clean from the torso.

The headless body crashed through the coffee table, spraying splinters of glass everywhere.

Like Theresa's body, Swan splayed Dr. Milner's beheaded corpse in the shape of a star amidst the shard remains.

Swan plucked up Milner's detached head and deposited it in his leather doctor's satchel. He then tended to Milner's body as he had Theresa's. Afterward, Swan departed out the front door and fled across the lawn, disappearing into the darkness beyond.

Two whimpering Golden Labs, the surviving family pets, nudged Theresa's body on the grass with their noses and paws. They leaped and jumped around in a panic, barking.

CHAPTER TWO

TUESDAY, AUGUST THE NINTH
EIGHT FIFTY-TWO AM

BY MORNING, 10048 CIELO Drive had become a hotbed of activity involving the LAPD, LAFD, and the media, causing traffic along the narrow drive to bottleneck to a slow crawl. A news helicopter circled overhead—a camera operator balancing himself on the left skid as he filmed the tableau unfolding below—and a fire truck and ambulance raced east toward the scene.

A silver two-door, 1950 Mercury Monterey, sporting the license plate "NUKEM 50," parked nearby.

Once its headlights dimmed and its engine stopped, the Mercury's doors opened, and LAPD Homicide Detectives Christopher "Nuke" Bonaduce and James "Jimbo" Scott stepped out.

Bonaduce, the Mercury's owner, was handsome in an early-40s roguish way, of medium build, and sported short-cropped, sandy-blond hair. His white Maltese Custom Choppers & Hot Rods T-shirt clearly set him apart from the other members of law enforcement on the scene.

In stark contrast, his ten years younger partner, Jimbo Scott, was a total nerd—tall and gangly, with a scrawny, crane-like neck and a protruding Adam's Apple, and otherwise, quite nondescript.

Nuke took off his yellow-tinted, wire-rimmed aviator sunglasses and hung them from the front of his shirt collar. "We must have the right address, Jimbo." He closed his car door and began the short trek down the road to the crime scene.

In the meantime, Jimbo grabbed his antique camera from the car, closed the door, and chased after Nuke.

A horde of onlookers gathered outside 10048's gate, despite yellow police tape cordoning off the site.

Already on the scene were Nuke's other partners, Elvin Lincoln and Billy Hayes. Trying to conduct an interview with them was Gloria Cox, the attractive brunette reporter from KLAX-TV News. Her overweight camera operator, Kenney Brown, filmed them.

Cox stepped in front of Lincoln. "Would it be possible for me to ask you a few questions? Get a statement on camera?"

"Not a chance in holy Hell, sweetheart."

Hayes pushed Lincoln aside and started mugging for the camera, flexing his tattooed Popeye-like arms. "And, if you don't mind, darling, we'd appreciate it if you'd leave us the hell alone and let us do our jobs here. Thanks."

He pushed the camera aside and shoved the mic back into Cox's hands and walked away. She motioned to Kenney to "Cut!" and stormed away in a huff.

Lincoln glanced at Hayes and laughed. "Good one, Marine."

They high-fived one another.

Nuke and Jimbo strode up the drive and approached the gate.

Lincoln nudged Billy in the right arm. "Hey, check it out. Look who's here."

"Huh, they finally made it. And only an hour late, I might add. It's a new record."

Lincoln and Hayes straightened up and put on their best smiles to greet the new arrivals.

"Top of the morning to you, boys," said Lincoln as Nuke and Jimbo approached. "Welcome to Spooky Central."

"We ain't afraid of no ghosts," joked Nuke.

Hayes shook Nuke's and Jimbo's hands. "Hey, Nuke. Hey, Jimbo."

"Hey, Billy," said Jimbo. "How's it going?"

Nuke commented on Hayes' and Lincoln's shotguns, "Stuck on crowd control again, I see."

"Hmm," groaned Lincoln. "I swear it's because I'm black."

Nuke smiled. "Take it up with Captain Dreyfus. Speaking of whom, where is that no-good, old-as-sin, son of a bitch?"

"Inside with the CSI team."

"He's been waiting for you two to show up," said Hayes. "You're only an hour late, Nuke."

Nuke sneered, "Ah, he can bite me. I live in Long Beach. Do you have any idea how long a drive it is to get here every morning? Besides, today was supposed to be my day off."

Hayes shook his head.

"No, I didn't think so. I didn't think so," contemplated Nuke. "Not to mention I had to pick up Jimmy-boy here along the way."

Hayes jeered, "You're so full of it, Nuke."

"Maybe, but I still manage somehow to always get the job done. Which reminds me..."

Minutes later, Nuke and Jimbo arrived at the primary residence where a burly, young police officer led the two blood-encrusted Golden Labs away from the front lawn on a leash.

Nuke and Jimbo approached Theresa Burkhart's body lying face-up on the grass nearby. The scene was beyond gruesome. The killer had chopped off her left ring finger, sliced her mouth ear-to-ear into a Glasgow Smile, and dissected her body at the waist and drained it of blood. Flies buzzed all around.

Jimbo appeared horror-struck. "Jeez! What the Hell happened here?"

"Looks like the Black Dahlia," said Nuke, referring to the brutal 1947 murder of aspiring young actress Elizabeth Short.

Jimbo knelt beside the body and took photographs with the antique camera dangling around his neck.

LAPD Police Captain Richard Dreyfus, 65, approached the duo on the front lawn. "About time you two dunderheads showed up." He took them by surprise.

"Sir!" exclaimed Jimbo, jumping to his feet.

Dreyfus gazed down at the body and sighed heavily. "Such a lovely girl. So young. A terrible shame."

"Who is she?" asked Nuke.

"Theresa Burkhart, an aspiring actress. Her fiancé, Dr. Lawrence Milner, owns the place. A famous plastic surgeon to the stars. Popular with the young starlets, I understand."

"Maybe we can talk to him?" proposed Jimbo.

"Be my guest. If you can find his head."

Nuke appeared stunned. "What?"

Dreyfus pointed to the house. "His body's inside on the living room floor. Somebody cut off his head."

"Jeez! What kind of killer are we dealing with here?" asked Jimbo.

"One with a sword and no respect for human life, that's for sure."

"Do you think it's a serial killer?" asked Nuke.

Dreyfus popped a piece of nicotine gum into his mouth. "Can never be too sure." He pointed to the body on the lawn. "We're checking into how the killer positioned the two bodies."

Looking through the lens of his camera, Jimbo remarked, "The positioning of her body resembles that of a star." He snapped an overhead shot of Theresa's corpse to display its arrangement. He paused, thinking. He lowered his camera and turned to Dreyfus. "Are you suggesting this is the work of the Hollywood Walk of Fame Killer?"

"It's quite possible."

"What are we doing about it?" asked Nuke.

"We're on the phone with the FBI about getting a Behavioral Analysis specialist to assist you."

"Wait, wait, wait! *Assist?*"

"You're getting a new partner, Nuke."

"Whoa! Whoa! I already got a partner, Captain. One, two, three of them: Jimbo, Lincoln, and Hayes. We work as a team."

"Well, soon, you'll have four. Get used to it."

Captain Dreyfus started to walk toward the driveway but turned around to look at Nuke and Jimbo. "Oh, and, uh, I hope you boys both brought your hip boots. The place is a bloody mess."

CHAPTER THREE

QUANTICO, VIRGINIA
TUESDAY, AUGUST THE NINTH
TWELVE FIFTY-NINE PM

THE FBI ACADEMY IN Quantico, Virginia, opened in 1972 on 385 acres of woodland. Today it serves as a secured government training and research facility for new FBI agents and experienced law enforcement officers from such organizations as the FBI and DEA.

During an intense, twenty-week period, trainees endure a series of physically and mentally challenging programs such as Firearms Training, Investigative Training, Practical Applications, Field and Police Training, Behavioral Analysis, and Forensic Science Research and Training, among others.

Located in the main training complex, the Forensic Science Research and Training Center is one of the most fascinating areas on campus. Apart from its reputation as a world-class forensics' laboratory, it also serves as a leading researcher in the fields of genetics, physics, chemistry, and biochemistry. Biometrics is another field, consisting of unique methods for recognizing humans based upon one or more intrinsic physical or behavioral traits.

At the end of a dimly lit corridor of classrooms and administrative offices was a wood-framed door with "BIOMETRIC STUDIES LABORATORY; DR. D.C. FULLER, Ph.D., PROFESSOR; DR. D.M. ROSKOW, Ph.D., ASSOCIATE PROFESSOR" stenciled in black and gold letters on a frosted glass window. Scrawled across the glass was a line of student graffiti: "FULLER IS FULL OF CRAP."

Inside the Biometrics Laboratory, a white-bearded, blue-skinned, British man, Herbert Prentiss, late 50s, sat across from Biometrics Professor Dr. Del Fuller and FBI Special Agent Haley Murch. They sat at a rectangular table holding a small electronic device projecting a magnified image of Prentiss' right eye on a tiny monitor with touch-light panels across the top and sides registering the dilation of the eye's iris.

Fuller, 53, was handsome in a boyish way, brilliant, oddly eccentric, abrasively sarcastic, a tad fidgety, and highly regarded on an academic and professional level.

"Mr. Prentiss, I'd like to introduce myself," said Fuller, shaking Prentiss' right hand from across the table. "My name is Dr. Del Fuller, Professor of Biometrics here at the Academy." He pointed to Murch sitting in a chair to his right. "And this beautiful young lady beside me is Special Agent Haley Murch, who kindly agreed to assist me with this morning's session. Please forgive her appearance. She was running the obstacle course when I called her away suddenly."

At 38 years of age, Murch was a highly intelligent, no-nonsense, athletic beauty. She wore a sweat- and grass-stained gray FBI Academy sweatshirt, black sweatpants, and sneakers. She kept her shoulder-length raven hair pulled back in a ponytail. "Are you familiar with the field of Biometrics, Mr. Prentiss?" she asked affably.

Prentiss remained silent, clearly displeased with his current situation.

Murch shook her head and continued, "It's the science and technology of measuring and analyzing biological data, such as DNA, fingerprints, eye retinas and irises, voice patterns, facial patterns, and hand measurements, to authenticate a person's identity."

Again, no response from Prentiss. Awkward.

Prentiss grew restless in his chair. "Pardon my asking, Doctor, but what kind of test is this?"

Fuller attempted to explain, "It's a combination polygraph/eye retina test. Something new we're testing out. Kind of like the Voight-Kampff test used in *Blade Runner*."

Mr. Prentiss blinked.

"You *have* heard of the film, right, Mr. Prentiss?"

Prentiss shook his head from side to side.

"*No*? Hmpf. Blasphemy."

Prentiss blinked, confused by the reference.

"Sorry, Mr. Prentiss, you must excuse my colleague here," interjected Murch. "He's a bit on the eccentric side."

"I'm sorry–I got carried away. In the movie, the Voight-Kampff is an advanced form of a polygraph test, Mr. Prentiss. It measures contractions of the iris muscle and the presence of invisible airborne particles emitted from the body to determine if a suspect is truly telling the truth by measuring the degree of his empathic response through carefully worded questions and statements."

Murch, glancing down at a dossier file on Prentiss, stated, "So, to begin, I suppose we should have you explain why you were sent to us here by Homeland Security? Unless you have any objections?"

"No objections," said Prentiss. "I have nothing to hide."

"Please, then, tell us."

Fuller quickly perused his own copy of the dossier file. "Says in your police report, Mr. Prentiss, you were arrested during a flight from London to Washington, D.C., for causing an in-flight disturbance. You mind elaborating?"

"Well...as you can obviously see, my skin is blue, which makes it kind of hard for me to blend in. I try to use flesh-tone cover-up when I go out in public, but it doesn't always work. I tend to sweat a lot due to anxiety. So, while I was sitting on the plane, I started to sweat profusely, and my face make-up began to run. When I tried to make it to the bathroom to fix the problem, the passengers on the flight saw blue skin poking through and panicked. They thought I was a terrorist covered in explosive chemicals. Thought I was trying to blow up the plane." He cleared his throat. "Excuse me."

The story both riveted and amused Fuller and Murch.

Prentiss continued, "Upon landing, I was arrested by airport security and put in airport jail. And, now, it's your job to prove to Homeland Security I'm not a crazed psychopath."

Fuller smiled at Prentiss. "You know, Mr. Prentiss, it's too bad the passengers didn't see you emerging from the bathroom colored blue instead because then you could've used the alibi that your skin was dyed blue after accidentally splashing your face with blue toilet sanitizer. That kind of thing happens all the time. I'd have believed that story."

"To Hell with you! I ain't lying! I'm not making this story up!"

Fuller glanced at the experimental machine. Its meter registered green. "I never said you were lying, Mr. Prentiss. The meter reads green. Means you're clean." He moved on to the next question. "All right, moment-of-truth time, Mr. Prentiss." He smiled. "Are you, in fact, a terrorist?"

Murch interjected, "Again, Mr. Prentiss, it's only a question we need to ask to clear your name. Personally, I don't believe you are a terrorist. I believe you're an innocent man."

Prentiss sighed heavily and closed his eyes to ease the tension before answering. "Bullshit. I'm no terrorist."

The meter on the machine registered green instead of red, which elated Fuller. "Surprise! The machine says you're telling the truth, Mr. Prentiss! I knew you were. A no-brainer."

Relieved, Prentiss opened his eyes and sighed. "Thank God."

"All right, hmm?" pondered Murch, looking at the dossier before her. She cleared her throat. "Now that that's been established, Mr. Prentiss, can you explain why you were on the plane?"

"I'm in the process of moving to the States from London because of how people treated me on account of my skin condition."

"Argyria?"

"Yes. My skin turned blue after years of repeated exposure to absorbed elemental silver from drinking an antibiotic-like silver solution to help cure a skin disease."

The machine registered green. Fuller smiled and clapped his hands. "Again, you're telling the truth, Mr. Prentiss!"

Prentiss wasn't so cheerful. He rested his hands on the table in a praying position and stared down at them. "My wife and I had to endure years of taunts like 'Papa Smurf' and 'Blue Man.'"

"Personally, Mr. Prentiss, I don't see any harm in being called 'Papa Smurf' or 'Blue Man.'"

Prentiss shook his head.

There was a series of three knocks at the laboratory door, which caught Murch off guard. "Are you expecting somebody at this hour, Dr. Fuller?"

"No, Agent, this is a private closed session. We're not to be disturbed."

"Must be something awfully important for them to interrupt us like this."

Fuller looked at Mr. Prentiss. "Sorry about the interruption. It'll only take me a moment to scare whoever it is away. It's one of my specialties. Excuse me."

Fuller got up from his chair and went to answer the door. As he approached, there were two more knocks at the door. "Sorry, no soliciting," he joked as he turned the knob, cracking the door open.

"Very funny, Dr. Fuller," an African American man's voice replied.

Fuller smiled. "Well, well, if it isn't *mon frere!*"

"Top of the morning to you too, Del," said Dr. Darren Roskow, Fuller's associate professor, a man in his late 50s wearing a yellow FBI windbreaker over a black suit and polished black leather shoes.

Fuller frowned and looked at his watch. "Can you come back in say, an hour, an hour and a half? We're kinda busy here."

"Sorry, Del, this can't wait. I'm here on orders from the Deputy Director."

Fuller opened the door for Roskow. "Well, then, in that case, please, come right on in."

Roskow stepped past Fuller and entered the lab. "Thanks, Del."

Fuller closed the door behind him. "Sorry about the mess, Darren. The maid quit on us, I guess. Not sure why." He returned to the desk. "Now, what can we do for you this fine morning?"

"I'm looking for Special Agent Murch."

"Well, Darren, you've come to the right place."

Murch looked up from Prentiss' dossier and addressed Roskow, "Yes, Doctor, what can I do for you?"

"Sorry to interrupt your session here, Haley, but Deputy Director Kimble would like to see you in his office ASAP."

When someone important as the Deputy Director requested your presence, Murch knew not to ask questions. She stated simply, "Thank you, Dr. Roskow. Right away, sir," and began to collect her personal effects.

THE OFFICE OF THE FBI Deputy Director lay deep in the bowels of the FBI Academy's Behavioral Analysis Unit's basement. The office is second in command to the FBI Director and leads all prominent criminal investigations.

The tiny room contained a desk, filing cabinets, a fake rubber tree, a leather desk chair, and two guest chairs. Certifications and service awards decorated the walls along with a bulletin board covered in photographs and clippings of ongoing investigations.

Deputy Director John P. Kimble, 58, sat at his desk, sifting through a pack of case materials on his computer. He appeared tired, thin, and haunted. His shirt collar was too big, and he had dark puffs under his reddened eyes. He placed a thick manila envelope on the left edge of his desk as there was a knock at the office door. He glanced up and shouted, "Door's open!"

The clock on the wall to the left of the door read 1:27 PM. The door opened, and Haley Murch entered. "Good afternoon, Mr. Kimble. You wanted to see me?"

Kimble looked at her impassively. "Yes, Haley. Please, sit down."

She sat down. "Thank you, sir. Do you wish to hear more details on our current case? Is that what you wanted to see me about, sir?"

"Truth be told, Haley, I'm deeply sorry to have to pull you away from your team's investigation at such short notice, but a case has come over from the LAPD, and I'm offering them your operational support ASAP."

She smiled. "It's all right, sir, I was taking a short break anyway to help Dr. Fuller on a Homeland Security issue. What kind of case are we talking about?"

Kimble passed her the manila envelope. "A brutal double murder last night in Beverly Hills. A prominent plastic surgeon and his fiancée. Here's a dossier for you."

"You want me to help the LAPD on a homicide case?"

"Correct."

"Excuse me, sir, but, why the urgency?"

"If you gloss over some of the photos in there, you'll understand why I thought of you specifically for the job."

Intrigued, Murch opened the envelope and removed a collection of black-and-white photos of Dr. Milner's and Theresa Burkhart's mutilated bodies and glossed them over.

"Please note how the killer arranged the bodies," said Kimble.

Murch's eyes darted through the photos. "The killer composed the bodies...in the shape of stars." She seemed dismayed.

"Now do you understand my urgency in calling you here, Haley? A while back you did a thesis for your master's degree in Criminology on the Hollywood Walk of Fame Killer. Am I correct? He composed his victims' bodies into stars."

Murch appeared puzzled. "Yes, sir, but, um, that was years ago. I've kind of been out of the loop since then. You think there's a connection?"

"That's for you to determine. Are you game, Special Agent Murch?"

"Yes, sir. Ready and willing."

"Terrific. A plane ticket is waiting for you at Dulles. Go home, pack some things, you leave immediately. A rental car and hotel room have already been set up for you in L.A."

Murch stood and shook Kimble's hand from across the desk. "Thank you, sir."

"No, thank you."

CHAPTER FOUR

LOS ANGELES, CALIFORNIA
WEDNESDAY, AUGUST THE TENTH
SEVEN THIRTY-SIX AM

IN 1939, NOTORIOUS MOVIE executive Harry Cohn, founder of Columbia Pictures, reportedly told actors William Holden and Glenn Ford, "If you must get into trouble, do it at the Chateau Marmont."

The Chateau Marmont, opened on the Sunset Strip in West Hollywood on February 1929, is a legendary castle-like hotel modeled after the Chateau d'Amboise in France's Loire Valley. The hotel features rooms, pool, hillside bungalows, and garden cottages. It has served as the setting for many notable events in the lives of its large celebrity clientele.

At approximately 7:36 AM, a black stretch limousine drove east down Monteel Road at the north end of the hotel and came to a stop in front of the private back gate entrance to bungalow #3.

As the limo idled at the curb, the rear passenger doors opened, and two men in black suits stepped out: Earl and Harve Gittes—the Italian American owners of the Burbank-based For Stars Security, offering protective services to movie and rock stars alike.

Earl, 62, was a quiet, reserved, black-haired, pock-faced tough guy, while his cousin, Harve, 61-year-old, was a balding loudmouth.

Upon closing the car doors, they moved briskly through the gated entryway and walked up the palm tree-lined sidewalk to the front door of the bungalow. As they neared, they could hear The Grateful Dead's "West L.A. Fadeaway" emanating loudly from within.

Harve glanced up at his older cousin and shrugged. "Sounds like somebody's home," he said in his thick Jersey-Italian accent.

Earl only grinned and bobbed his head in response.

Harve knocked on the door. "Hey, wakey, wakey!" After a moment with no answer, he pounded on the door again. "Answer the damn door, you Hollywood prick! I hate waiting on your spoiled, sorry rich ass!" Still no answer. Growing more and more impatient, he pounded his fists on the door again and again. "Come on! Come on! Come on!"

Before Harve could knock again, Earl stopped him with a stern glare and a wave of his right index finger.

Bungalow #3 was one of two identical, adjacent, 1,500-square-foot hillside bungalows, with two bedrooms and baths, a spacious living room, a kitchen and dining area, a private street entrance and carport, and a private garden with direct access to the hotel pool.

Inside the front door, a small entryway led into the dining area and the adjoining living room. The place appeared trashed. A pair of Gucci suitcases lay upturned on the floor by two shredded and stained corner couches. Torn designer clothing hung from a broken flat-screen television beside a shattered porcelain lamp. A set of bongo drums stood by the entryway. Crushed beer cans and broken wine bottles littered the carpet by a coffee table.

Atop the coffee table, a half-empty bottle of Cristal champagne chilled in a bucket of melted ice. A script with *TEENAGE CONFIDENTIAL*, PROPERTY OF PARADISE PICTURES, INC. on the front cover rested nearby. Also of note were a small stash of marijuana in a plastic bag, a rolled-up hundred-dollar bill, and a razor blade beside three neatly cut lines of cocaine. The August 10th morning edition of the Los Angeles Times lay opened to the front page with the top headline, "MURDER IN BEL-AIR: PROMINENT PLASTIC SURGEON AND FIANCEE BRUTALLY SLAIN IN BENEDICT CANYON."

At the end of the main hall, past the kitchen, guest bedroom, and bathroom, was the spacious master suite, where a Jewish male, resembling a young Sal Mineo, slept in the middle of a king-size bed, semi-exposed, beneath gray silk sheets. He stirred from the sound of The Grateful Dead blaring from behind the closed door of the adjoining master bathroom and covered his head with a pillow to drown out the noise.

Inside the bathroom, "West L.A. Fadeaway" played over a radio sitting on the right edge of the sink, as strapping film star Christian Rivers primped himself before the mirror while talking angrily on his cell phone. "Look, Ari, as my agent, your job is to find me acting roles, not to run my personal life!" He paused and sighed. "Yeah, I saw the newspaper headline! I don't understand what the goddamn fuss is! So, every celebrity's living in a state of fear? Big fucking deal! Tell 'em to put in a security system and buy a guard dog!"

Hailing from Dallas, Texas, Rivers was 35 years old, had shaggy brown hair, brown eyes, a goatee, and an uneven smile, and was one of the biggest names in the movie business. He wore only snakeskin cowboy boots and a gun belt over a white bath towel around his waist.

There was another knock at the front door, which, of course, nobody heard due to the loud music.

Rivers continued his heated phone conversation with his agent, "What do I need a bodyguard for, let alone two? A man, a *real* man, can take care of himself, goddammit!" He paused and punched the wall, denting the sheetrock. He scowled as he spoke to his phone. "What...huh? Well...same to you, you..." He hurled the phone into the toilet. *Splash!* He composed himself and scoffed, "*Screw me?*"

He took a drag from a smoldering joint in an ashtray beside the radio, pulled on a tan cowboy hat, quick-drew a prop Colt .44 pistol from the holster on his belt, and admired himself in the mirror. "Hello, handsome!"

He winked and blew himself a kiss. He flipped off the radio and walked into the master bedroom.

Knock! Knock! Knock! Harve pounded on the front door, followed by his aggravated voice, yelling at the top of his lungs, "Uh, Mr. Rivers, sir?"

A minute later, Rivers startled Earl and Harve as he answered the front door stark naked, except for his cowboy boots, gun belt and holster, and cowboy hat over his genitals.

"Jeez!" bellowed Harve, aghast.

Rivers greeted the two cousins with a shit-faced grin. "Well, well, well, if it isn't Earl and Harve, bodyguards to the stars! How's it hanging, boys?" With a cocky smile, he took Harve off guard and clobbered him in the nuts with an open right fist.

Harve howled in pain, his eyes rolling back. "Ow...uh...unh...!"

As Harve keeled over, Earl smiled and shook his head, amused. He said nothing.

Harve spoke through his pain to Rivers, "Mr. Rivers, uh, sir, um, we're here to escort you to the studio."

Rivers checked his watch. "A little early, aren't you? It's only...7:39 in the AM. Pick-up ain't till 8:00 AM."

Harve groaned, holding his groin. "Sorry, boss, but, uh..." He coughed. "...traffic is a real bitch this morning."

"Well then..." said Rivers, moving his cowboy hat from his genitals to his head, giving Earl and Harve an eyeful of male nudity, "...I better move my sorry ass and get dressed, then."

He winked, clicked his tongue, fired a fake shot from a finger pistol, and tipped his hat to the two beleaguered bodyguards. "Gentlemen, if you'll excuse me." He turned and walked back inside, while Earl and Harve returned to the limo.

Minutes later, a fully dressed Christian Rivers, sporting his cowboy boots and cowboy hat, opened the front door of the bungalow and exited, slamming the door closed behind him. He made his way down the sidewalk and out the gate to the limo where Earl and Harve stood waiting.

As Rivers neared the limo, Earl opened the right rear passenger door for him and ushered him inside.

Rivers tipped his hat. "Much obliged there, Earl. At least one of you is earning his keep this morning." He gestured at Harve. "Can't say as much for the other fella whose name escapes me for the time being."

Harve grinned crossly.

"Thank you, Mr. Rivers," said Earl in a New York accent. "Please, watch your head."

"Don't mind if I do, Earl. Don't mind if I do."

As Rivers climbed inside the rear of the limo, Earl and Harve followed and took seats across from him. As Harve pulled the door shut, Earl pounded on the black divider between them and the front cabin to signal the driver.

The driver shifted the gear into "DRIVE" and muttered to himself, "Enjoy the ride. Heh, heh."

The limousine crawled east down Monteel Road, gradually picked up speed, and disappeared around the curve.

CHAPTER FIVE

WEDNESDAY, AUGUST THE TENTH
SEVEN FIFTY-ONE AM

THE POLICE AND MEDIA circus continued outside the gated entrance to 10048 Cielo Drive, while the grounds inside were reasonably quiet as much of the focus of the homicide investigation had now moved inside the primary residence.

In broad daylight, the crime scene inside the house proved merely horrific, as though someone had walked through and splattered buckets of blood everywhere. By the morning of day two, the house seemed empty of police and other crime scene specialists, the few that remained wore special hair and shoe coverings along with rubber gloves.

In the master bedroom, a lab specialist collected blood samples from footprints by the broken patio door. Through the doorway, pieces of a broken Adirondack chair could be seen floating in the exterior kidney-shaped swimming pool. In the hallway between the master bedroom and the adjacent living room, a fingerprint specialist dusted for prints around a human form imprinted into a bloodstained sheetrock wall. On the tile floor, a trail of dried blood led into the living room, as if somebody had crawled or dragged a body.

In the living room, FBI Special Agent Haley Murch addressed a small gathering of crime scene specialists, including Captain Dreyfus and Detectives Bonaduce, Scott, Lincoln, and Hayes, around a body outline within the blood-splattered shard remains of a glass coffee table. "And, based on initial assessments, the LA County Coroner's office places the time of the two deaths somewhere between midnight and 2:00 AM. Police reports from the nearby West Los Angeles Community Police Station indicate a smaller window, somewhere between 12:15 and 1:00 AM."

Detective Jimbo Scott chimed in with a nagging question, "Agent Murch, I'm curious about how the killer left Miss Burkhart's body on the lawn. Her upper torso was dissected from her lower extremities at the waist, which indicates a copycat killing in the style of the 1947 Elizabeth Short case. Can you offer anything about why the killer might have done that?"

"Well, Detective Scott, the Coroner's findings concluded the deceased, Theresa Burkhart, was roughly three to four months pregnant at the time of her death. The killer eviscerated the body in two to remove the fetus from the uterus. Whether or not the act was done as a copycat remains to be seen, but my guess is it was not. The killer is simply toying with us by offering a taste of his creative, demented flair."

Nuke whispered to Lincoln and Hayes, "Next she'll tell us the killer chose the particular date and location by random and not because of its connection to Charles Manson. Cripes, welcome to the Annual Manson Family Reunion. Same date and street." Being the severe TV/movie geek he was, that morning Nuke had chosen to go the Sonny Crockett route by wearing a white Italian sports coat, a black *Purple Rain* T-shirt, white linen pants, slip-on sockless loafers, Rayban sunglasses, and a small amount of beard stubble.

Murch glared at Nuke as he knelt and picked up a bloody shard of glass without wearing rubber gloves. "Detective Bonaduce! Must I remind you to wear the proper protective attire when handling potential forensic evidence?" She reached into her right jacket pocket and pulled out a pair of rubber gloves. "Here! One size fits all."

Nuke smiled at his fellow detectives as he accepted her gift to him. He remarked discourteously to her, "Gee, thanks, sweetheart. Want me to check the boys' prostates while I'm at it?"

Murch wasn't in the mood for any bullshit. She grinned and said coldly, "Put 'em on, Detective! I won't have you tainting my crime scene! It's people like you who allow scumbags and murderers to walk away scot-free!"

Lincoln and Hayes looked at each other and smirked. "Oooh! Ouch!"

Nuke reluctantly snapped the gloves on as Murch straightened her jacket and walked away in a huff.

Dreyfus stepped over and put a hand on Nuke's shoulder, looked down at him, and tried not to laugh. "Love your new partner, Nuke. She's a kitten with a whip and hot to trot. Don't treat her like one of your ex-wives. Land another sexual harassment suit against the department and you're out on your kiester. You don't wanna have to put your name in for yet another job transfer. There can't be too many precincts left in the city who'll take your sorry ass."

"Relax, boss," said Nuke, getting to his feet. "Sit back and watch the master at work." He patted Dreyfus on the shoulder and chased after Murch.

Dreyfus shrugged and bit down on his lip. "Hah. That's what I'm afraid of."

THE BLACK LIMOUSINE DROVE east down Hollywood Boulevard in early morning traffic. In the back, Christian Rivers helped himself to a bottle of Cristal champagne, while Earl and Harve sat across from him at a respectful distance.

"Ah, Cristal. Only the best for the world's greatest and sexiest movie star!" preened Rivers as he popped the top off the bottle and sipped down the foam which poured out.

"That's exaggerating a bit, right?" asked Harve.

"No, I'm not," scoffed Rivers. "I'm on the Hollywood A-List. My flicks have grossed nearly $4 billion worldwide in box office receipts, I make $20 million a picture, and I have lines of fine young fillies lined up around the block for an autograph and a taste of my sweat. Now, you tell me, boys: Am I God or what?"

Harve looked at Rivers, dumbfounded. "You're an asshole. A selfish, self-absorbed, self-centered, maniacal, egotistical, little prick."

Rivers swilled champagne. "Thanks for the compliment, Harve. Remind me later to fire you both."

Without warning, the limo driver, a hunchback with bulging eyes, lowered the electric partition window and muttered to Rivers in a high, raspy voice, "Mr. Rivers...heh, heh...nice to have you onboard this morning. Heh. My two daughters *really* enjoy your movies."

"Christ on a stick! W-who the Hell are you? Marty Feldman's love child? Is the regular driver sick this morning or something?"

"Heh, heh..."

"Hey, I'm not paid to talk with the driver, okay? Especially one with a Peter Lorre speech impediment. So, if you don't mind, please, PISS OFF!"

"Heh...my daughters would...heh, heh...really...heh...love an autograph. Heh, heh."

Rivers sighed loudly. "If I sign one, will you leave me the Hell alone? I need my beauty sleep."

"Anything. Heh, heh."

"Don't ask me to personalize it."

"Heh...would you? Heh, heh."

"Only if your daughters give me the world's greatest blowjob."

"Heh, heh. Unh...?"

Rivers pulled out and autographed a publicity still of himself and handed it across to Earl who passed it up to the limo driver. Rivers hurled the pen into the front seat and closed the partition window. "Dang, the shit I gotta put up with bein' a celebrity and all! When will it ever end?"

As Rivers grabbed the champagne bottle to take another swig, he began to feel ill and lose consciousness. He dropped the bottle onto the carpeted flooring, clutched his throat, and gasped for air.

Earl and Harve grinned back at him.

"Wh-what did you boys...uh...do...do to me?"

"Tranquilizer," smirked Earl.

"*Tranquil...?*"

"A little goes a *looong* way," chuckled Harve.

"Uhnnnn..."

As Rivers collapsed to the floor, "Earl" and "Harve" peeled their prosthetic faces off to reveal their true monstrous and deformed selves: Grendel was a tall, gangly, long white-haired albino with freakish pink eyes. The other thug, Sebastian, had burn scars all over his body, plenty of tattoos, a shaved head, and a buck-toothed grin. They cackled maniacally and threw their masks at Rivers.

Sebastian stomped Rivers in the nuts. "Ain't payback a bitch?"

Grendel pounded on the partition window. "Igor, get us the Hell out of here!"

"You got it...heh...heh..."

Igor stepped on the gas. The limousine sped up, weaving in and around any slow cars in its path.

Along the north side of Hollywood Boulevard between Wilcox Avenue and North Cahuenga Boulevard stood the legendary Casting Couch office building where aspiring actor Rich MacGuffin, aged 41 and rather nondescript, waited on the sidewalk amidst a long line of nearly one thousand other aspiring actors for an extras casting audition.

He glanced up as several angry motorists honked their car horns as the limo ran through a series of red traffic lights and continued east down the boulevard until it became a small dot on the horizon.

AT 8:10 AM, A sullen Haley Murch exited the Milner residence through the broken patio door and walked down the driveway.

Nuke came running after her, yelling, "Hey, hey, hey! What's wrong with you? Why so morose? Was it something I said?"

She stopped and turned to face him. "A man has his head chopped off, and his girlfriend cut in two, and all you can do in there is crack jokes?"

Feeling guilty, Nuke kicked up a cloud of dust. "Sorry, sweetheart. Didn't realize you cared so much." He tried to retain his bravado. "In this line of work, you need a sense of humor. Otherwise, all that blood and death takes its toll on you. It's a freak show. That's why I only do this part-time. I run a customizing business on the side. You know, classic cars, choppers."

Murch wasn't buying it. "A police dispatcher logs several calls from concerned citizens in this area–reports of a male and female pleading for their lives–and nobody lifts a finger to help. Why?"

Nuke turned and pointed west to a large three-acre Mediterranean-style mansion atop the hill behind the Milner property. "See that house there atop the hill?"

She followed his gaze. "Yeah?"

"Well, it's called the Villa Bella now, but about thirty, forty years ago... Does the name Sharon Tate mean anything to you?"

Murch swallowed nervously.

"Yeah, I thought so. That mansion was once the site of the former Tate murder house: 10050 Cielo Drive. Sat mostly vacant for years until the owner had it torn down in 1994. Trent Reznor of the band Nine Inch Nails was the last person to live there. He turned the living room into a recording studio and recorded the Nails' albums *Broken* and *The Downward Spiral* there, along with some early Marilyn Manson stuff."

"That's interesting. I never would have guessed that."

"Darling, in this town, it's our job to know where the bodies are buried. And there's a lot of 'em. I'll give you the tour sometime."

"I'd like that."

"Our two murders here and the Tate murders up there are like twins: Several witnesses in each case heard voices and reported to the police, but nothing could be done because they didn't know where the voices came from as these canyons and foothills play tricks with sounds. A sound a mile away may be indistinguishable at a few hundred feet."

They resumed walking down the driveway in the direction of the main gate.

Nuke continued, "You know the history of the Walk of Fame Killer like the back of your hand, Agent Murch, and I know the history of this city like the back of my hand. To solve this mystery, we're gonna need each other's help."

CHAPTER SIX

A MATED PAIR OF trumpeter swans detached from its bevy and plunged cleanly into the water of a vast overgrown swamp and soon upended and dabbled for food.

A dozen feet away, gentle ripples appeared on the surface of the water. They created a smooth swell, lifting the swans up and easing them down, separating them by a few yards.

The female searched for her mate and, once spotted, started swimming over to him. She froze as the ripples raced toward her. Before she could take flight, she jolted upright and disappeared under the water.

There was no escape for the male either. He too sank down in a final, terrible jerking motion, leaving only eddies and swirls behind.

On the southwest bank of the swamp, a grandiose structure stood atop a sheer rock precipice. Vultures and crows circled a central tower overhead.

The architecture style was early 20th Century French-Norman Revival. With one section built over another, the result was an intricate construction. The edifice loomed thirteen stories tall, covered in twisted vines of ivy. The landscaping included chaparral-covered hills, soaring pine trees, and exotic plants with gardens, stables, tennis courts, a natatorium, and a central rock foundation.

Parked in the courtyard was a vintage, black and yellow 1937 Rolls-Royce Phantom III sedan. A skeleton of a man sat on a bench along a cobblestone footpath, hunched over a yellowed newspaper in his lap, with cobwebs aplenty.

The rusted, wrought-iron front gates at the southwest corner of the property hung from their hinges and prominently featured a crest of the letters "STH" amidst makeshift cardboard signs reading "CLOSED," "CONDEMNED," "KEEP OUT," "ENTER AT YOUR OWN RISK," and, of course, "NO TRESPASSING."

Inside the gates, a ravenous vulture feasted on the remains of a human skull. The vulture plucked out an eyeball and choked it down its scrawny gullet.

The black limousine drove up and pushed the creaky, rusted gates with its front bumper, drove through, and entered the grounds. The limo followed the driveway as it curved to the right around a median of dead trees, shrubbery, and statues. It pulled into the courtyard and parked in front of a cloistered, two-story entryway.

Beneath the terrace, Mr. Swan's harlequin-like muse, Caroline, waited to greet the arrivals. Dressed as a Russian Cossack, her skin was powdered white, and she wore blue eyeliner, pink rouge, and pink lip gloss. In her hands, a clear plastic bag contained Swan's dry-cleaned wardrobe from the Milner-Burkhart slayings.

As the limo idled, the driver's door opened, and the cloaked hunchback Igor stepped forth. He opened the left rear passenger door for Grendel and Sebastian. "Heh, heh...we have arrived...heh...at our destination, Masters. Heh."

"Thank you, Igor," replied Grendel. "We will take Mr. Rivers from here while you dispose of the limousine however you see fit. Leave no trace of evidence behind. Return here immediately once you are finished."

Igor took a bow. "Heh...right away, Master Grendel, sir. Heh, heh."

Igor returned to the driver's seat and closed his door, while Grendel and Sebastian removed the unconscious Christian Rivers. As they pondered what to do next, Igor honked the car horn and backed the car up in the same direction from which they had come.

Sebastian looked up at Grendel. "Now that we got Mr. Rivers here, what do we do with him? It'd be a whole lot easier if we threw him in the swamp and let the master's pets eat him. There'd be no trace left to find."

"As much as I'd like to put this asshole out of his misery, until we're told to do so by the Master, we do nothing. Mr. Swan has special plans for him. For now, though, grab his legs; I'll take his arms."

Grendel turned to Caroline. "Get the door."

With a polite curtsy, Caroline sauntered over to a set of ground-level French patio doors and held them open for Grendel and Sebastian, who carried Rivers' body into a dimly lit basement-level atrium.

"Caroline," said Grendel, "please make your way upstairs and inform Mr. Swan of our new arrival, so he may proceed with his plans."

Caroline nodded and stepped back out into the exterior courtyard. She scaled a flight of concrete stairs to the terrace above and entered into a lavish 1920's-era hotel lobby.

The lobby kept the French-Norman architectural scheme of the hotel's exterior façade. The room was dark and appeared undisturbed for decades, as the plastered walls and ceiling were cracking and crumbling, with thick dust covering everything.

In the middle sat a cobwebbed owl sculpture surrounded by a circle of dead flowers, the centerpiece of the room.

To the right stood a registration desk and concierge station. Behind them was a side aisle with doors at each end. Between were a couple of wooden benches and a giant mural of the hotel in its original heyday.

At the north end of the aisle were two guest elevators. Only the left one was still in decent working condition. The one on the right was "OUT OF ORDER," according to a sign on its right door. The elevator's sliding doors were off their grooves and held open slightly by a plank of wood. The severed cable was visible inside the empty shaft.

Caroline crossed the lobby from the entryway to the guest elevators, pressed the "UP" button on the control panel, and waited for the elevator to arrive.

The needle on the floor indicator above the elevator doors slowly dialed down from number 12 to 1.

The elevator arrived, and its doors opened. Caroline entered and pressed the button for floor 12.

The doors closed.

IN A DIMLY LIT private chamber on the 11th floor, Paul Swan sat before a massive, oak-laden Wurlitzer theater organ. There, in the shadows and shrouded in a white satin cloak, he played Charles Gounod's haunting sonata "Funeral March of a Marionette" to an audience of crows.

THE ELEVATOR ARRIVED AT the 12th floor. The doors opened,

and Caroline stepped out into a hallway illuminated by flickering wall sconces. The décor was much the same as the lobby eleven stories below, including the thick covering of dust.

Caroline wrapped the plastic dry-cleaning bag around her right arm and approached the south entrance to the hotel's after-hours nightclub, the Moonrise Ballroom. She jimmied the French doors open with her free left hand and entered the pitch-black room within.

Guided only by the light from the outside hallway, she made her way over to a nearby stairwell in the floor and disappeared into the darkness below.

IN THE BASEMENT, GRENDEL and Sebastian hauled Christian Rivers' body through a darkened room, past humming boilers, furnaces, and engine turbines, to a metal catwalk and descended a steel staircase into a series of catacombs fashioned out of the earth and lit by torches.

CAROLINE ENTERED SWAN'S PRIVATE chamber via a spiral staircase. As she descended, Swan, still at his organ, turned his head slightly as he realized her presence. "Yes, Caroline, what is it?"

Caroline greeted Swan with a curtsy. "Master—Grendel, Sebastian, and Igor have returned with your new trophy."

Swan smiled at her mention of the word "trophy."

"Good. See to it that Mr. Rivers is treated with the utmost respect and courtesy and shown to his new quarters."

Caroline nodded. "Yes, sir."

She approached a worn leather chair by an old make-up desk and hung the dry-cleaning bag over the backrest.

Cluttering the make-up desk were all sort sorts of kits, wipes, photo morgues, applicators, prosthetics, a desk lamp, and a white *Phantom of the Opera* mask.

On the wall behind the desk was a large vanity mirror. Plastered to the brick walls were vintage horror movie posters. The most prominent one was "*CURSE OF THE WAX PHANTOM*—NOW IN PRODUCTION. A FILM BY JOHN CRAWFORD. STARRING ANTON LEACH & VICTORIA WEST. COMING FALL 1976 FROM PARADISE PICTURES STUDIOS."

Swan turned around and immediately noticed the dry-cleaning

bag. "What did you bring me, my dear?"

"Your suit is back from the cleaners, Master. It took a little extra effort to get all the blood out, but it's clean."

"Aw, thank you, sweet, sweet Caroline. Nobody raised any eyebrows?"

"No, sir. I tried to make things inconspicuous."

"Good. Now run along, my dear. Prepare the afternoon meal."

"Yes, Master."

Caroline took a bow and left the way she came. Swan resumed his organ sonata.

IN THE CATACOMBS, GRENDEL and Sebastian carried Christian Rivers to a dungeon cell. They dragged him inside and shackled him to the rear wall beside a rotting skeleton.

Sebastian sneered, "Enjoy your stay, asshole." He cackled with delight as he and Grendel exited the dungeon and closed its rusted iron door behind them.

Sebastian's laughs echoed down the tunnel as he and Grendel walked away.

SWAN PULLED A CONTROL knob on his organ. It triggered a lift mechanism that hoisted the organ through a trap door directly above in the ceiling. As the organ rose, a panel in the floor beneath slid open to reveal a female corpse in a glass coffin of formaldehyde wearing a late-1960's-era wedding dress.

Swan got down on his hands and knees and pressed his fire-scarred hands to the glass. "My immortal beloved, soon we will be reunited in eternity where our hearts will beat together again in single time."

He stood up from the organ bench and drew a Buckmaster survival knife from a sheath on his belt. He gripped the blade, raised the knife overhead, and sent it soaring across the room, sticking it into the middle of Christian Rivers' agency photo hanging on the Wall of Shame.

Swan fixated on the photograph and scowled, "So, Mr. Rivers, which part of you shall I feed to my pets, hmm?"

As he walked over and ripped the knife free from the wall, he laughed and slashed Rivers' photo into confetti.

Nearby, a glass aquarium sat on a marble pedestal, housing three ravenous piranha feasting on a one trimester-sized human fetus.

CHAPTER SEVEN

FOUNDED IN 1925, PARADISE Pictures Studios was a film and television production and distribution company and one of the Big Seven studios of Hollywood's Golden Age. Its production studios lay east of Hollywood on 415 acres of converted farmland.

Haze Films Productions occupied a two-story, Santa Fe-style adobe office compound ornamented on the front by a giant billboard marquee of a fictional 1920's silent film-era heroine named Evelyn Haze. Other exterior features included an outdoor spa, gardens, and a wishing well.

The interior of the building contained a lobby in the front where 28-year-old, red-haired receptionist-secretary Janine Potts kept her desk.

Lining the walls throughout were expensive framed artworks by the likes of Andy Warhol and Norman Rockwell. There were also posters of films made under the Haze Films Productions banner over the company's nearly 30-year history, including ones for their latest film productions, *Texas Ace Arcana and the Lost City of Atlantis* and *Teenage Confidential.*

In editing suite B, Haze Films' founder and movie producer John Crawford, 63, sat in a swivel chair across from 54-year-old, hot-shot British film director Nigel Guest, reviewing film dailies from *Teenage Confidential* on a 36-inch flat-screen computer monitor.

On-screen: Christian Rivers knelt beside a bathtub in the bathroom of a middle-class, suburban family residence, looking down at attractive 28-year-old actress McKenzie Banks in a bath of bloody water, her wrists slit from a razor blade resting on the bathroom floor.

Nigel Guest turned his attention from the monitor to Crawford and said in his thick British accent, "Don't get me wrong, John, the scene plays good, but Rivers is acting like he was stoned out of his mind that day. We're gonna have to redo all his coverage shots."

35

Irritated, Crawford replied, "Well, I don't think it's going to happen today, Nigel, not with Rivers AWOL."

Nigel lit up a Cuban cigar and retorted, "How dare that son of a bitch pull a disappearing act when we're this close to completion! I'm gonna wring his bloody neck!"

Crawford sighed. "Relax, Nigel. He's probably passed out drunk in a gutter somewhere with some two-bit stripper. Happens all the time. We'll shoot around him for a while until he shows up. I've already informed McKenzie and George about using the cover set."

"All I'm saying, John, is: He better get his act together. He's under contract. He might get $20 million a picture, but that doesn't mean he can do whatever the bloody Hell he wants. We don't cater to him."

"Agreed."

CHAPTER EIGHT

FOUNDED IN 1974 AND operated out of an ACME storage facility in Laurel Canyon, Trauma Films Studios was in the business of making schlock films on shoestring budgets.

A two-car storage garage served as a makeshift soundstage with a banner over the entrance reading "TRAUMA FILMS."

Inside, a small crew filmed a scene on a bathroom set for a horror film called *Attack of the Killer Cockroach*, directed by Trauma's 67-year-old founder, producer, screenwriter, and occasional actor, Lloyd Hoffman.

Hoffman, a tall, lanky, New York City-raised Jew and Yale business major, stood behind a digital movie camera in army green khaki shorts and a red *Magnum P.I.*-style Hawaiian shirt, wearing a pair of headphones and holding a megaphone.

Moving around the set performing various production tasks were three crew members.

On Hoffman's left, special effects guru Max Winston, a 42-year-old Scotsman in Scottish-flag khaki shorts and a black satin "MAXIMUM F/X" crew jacket, struggled to perform the work of two people by operating two remote control units. He didn't appear too happy with his work. "Bloody Christ!"

On the set, an overweight man sat on a toilet reading a newspaper, when the floor beneath his feet began to quake. The man dropped his paper and grabbed onto the bathroom sink and the wall to balance himself. "What the Hell?"

He grew more frightened as the pipes within the walls began to rumble and groan. His eyes bounced around, and he let out a blood-curdling scream. "Aaacccckkkkk!"

The man flopped around on the toilet, clutching his throat, his eyes bulging out of their sockets. One was a bit out of sync with the other.

Off set, Max Winston muttered to himself as he worked his remote controls, "Dammit!"

The man on the toilet, an animatronics dummy of a human actor standing off set with a microphone, collapsed onto the floor.

Max pressed a button on the remote, and a large, mutant "Killer Cockroach" slimed its way out of the man's mouth, revealing a set of razor-sharp teeth.

Lloyd Hoffman stepped out from behind the camera, raised his megaphone, and shouted to his crew, "AND CUT!" He clapped and cheered exuberantly. "That was awesome! We'll print that and move on to the next scene everybody!"

The small crew broke into action and began disassembling the bathroom set.

Max Winston wasn't so cheerful and admitted so to Lloyd, "You sure you don't want a second take, Lloyd? To be safe? You know how I refuse to settle for Ed Wood-level quality?"

Lloyd smiled and shrugged the comment off. "Let me remind you, Max–we're not Warner Brothers. We're not made of money. We make shit. Literally. We're making a movie about a killer cockroach. Think about it."

Max sighed and kicked the ground with his left foot. "Whatever you say, Lloyd? It's just that, as I'm doing the job of two people here, the effects weren't quite in sync with each other."

Hoffman glanced down at the watch on his left wrist–10:23 AM–and looked back up at Max. "Speaking of doing the job of two, where's your assistant, McMuffin?"

"MacGuffin."

"Whatever. Where is he? He's been gone all morning."

"Bruckheimer's holding an extras audition for his two *Pirates* sequels."

Lloyd rolled his eyes in disgust. "Bruckheimer? His films are nothing but glossy, expensive shit! Big budget, no substance! Hell, our shit looks better than his *crrrrap*."

INSIDE THE CASTING COUCH, amidst a lobby full of auditioning hopefuls, actor Rich MacGuffin sat on a well-worn black vinyl couch, reviewing a set of script sides.

A female casting assistant stepped into the hall and consulted her clipboard. "Is there a... Richard MacGuffin here?"

MacGuffin stood up from his chair at the head of the line and shook the lady's right hand. "I'm Rich MacGuffin." He smiled at her, a little too eager, perhaps. "Hi, nice to meet you. I'm here for the audition."

"Yes, I can tell."

HOFFMAN BLEW OFF SOME steam. "Bruckheimer! Son of a bitch!"

Max patted him on the back. "Relax, Lloyd. Mac'll be back for the next scene. You ain't gonna lose him to Bruckheimer. His auditions never work out."

MACGUFFIN SAT IN A metal card chair in a small office and met with a male producer, a female casting director, and the female casting assistant, who all sat across from him at a table covered with headshots and bottles of water. A video camera set up on a tripod behind them recorded the session.

The casting director perused MacGuffin's underwhelming resume. "Mr. MacGuffin, you do realize this is an audition for a major Hollywood film production, not some grade-Z horror film my third-grade sons could make with their cell phones?"

MacGuffin frowned but said nothing.

"I mean, sure, you've got experience behind the camera as a member of some minor-league special effects crew, but you've got damn near zilch as an actor."

MacGuffin started to speak, "Well, I...," but the casting director proved too intimidating, so he chose to hold his peace.

The producer stared MacGuffin straight in the eyes with a shit-eating grin on his face. "Plus, quite frankly, Mr. MacGuffin, your looks are a problem. John Barrymore you're not. I'm afraid you're not what we're looking for."

"Somebody like Christian Rivers," said the casting director.

"Sorry," apologized the casting assistant, crossing MacGuffin's name off on her clipboard.

Dispirited, MacGuffin bit his upper lip and got up from his seat. "Thank you."

As he stepped into the hallway, he glanced back and saw the

casting director drop MacGuffin's resume into a recycle box. MacGuffin sighed and headed for the back exit.

CHAPTER NINE

STAGE 28 WAS ONE of thirty soundstages on the Paradise Pictures Studios backlot. It measured 22,000-square-feet in floor area and stood 32.8' high, with doors measuring 20' wide by 20' high.

For two months, it served as the principal filming location for Haze Films' *Teenage Confidential*, a modern-day re-imagining of the 1955 James Dean classic, *Rebel Without a Cause*, only this time with a young starlet as the teenage rebel.

The day's filming took place within the living room of the Barton Family house set. Actress McKenzie Banks lounged on a couch, smoking a cigarette, as she waited for the next take. Her co-star, Kentucky-born actor George Rowe, 54, stood nearby reviewing his script.

With a commanding presence, Nigel Guest, sitting in his green-backed director's chair, raised his megaphone and addressed the large film crew gathered around him, "All right, people, listen up! This is a take, not a rehearsal! Are my actors ready? McKenzie? George?"

"Yeah, yeah," muttered George Rowe.

"Ready as we'll ever be," said McKenzie.

Nigel reiterated, "All right, let's try not to bugger this one up, okay?" Nobody replied, and his temper flared. "*Okay?*"

John Crawford, carrying a thin manila envelope, rushed over, shouting urgently, "Nigel!"

"Goddammit, John! Can't you see I'm working here? Huh?"

"I have something important to show you!"

"Can't this wait?"

"No, it can't, Nigel! Now calm the Hell down!"

Crawford opened the manila envelope and pulled out a black-and-white agency photo. "I think we might have to shut down production on the film for the indefinite future."

"What the Hell for?"

Crawford held up the photo for Nigel to see. "This came in the mail."

Nigel grabbed the photo from Crawford and examined it. It was a picture of Christian Rivers with his face X'ed out by a bloody star. "What the blooming Hell is this, some kind of bloody joke?"

"I'm thinking it might have something to do with Rivers' disappearance. There's no return address. No postage. It had to have come from within the studio."

"Are you suggesting a kidnapping? Or murder?"

Crawford was beside himself. "I don't...I don't know, Nigel. But it's time we bring the authorities in on this."

"Bloody Hell, John! We can't file a missing person report, now! The shithead hasn't even been missing a couple of hours! It needs to be at least twenty-four hours to declare a person missing!"

"Well, Nigel, the police'll have to make an exception in this case on account of the blood on this photograph."

Nigel put his megaphone down on the ground by his feet and raised his arms and hands in protest. "Fine, John, do what you want, but I'm telling you, Rivers isn't missing. You'll see. We'll be laughing about this whole bloody affair in the morning."

McKenzie Banks listened in on their conversation from the couch. Distressed with the news, she lit up another cigarette.

OUTSIDE THE MAIN GATE of 10048 Cielo Drive, a Duke Skorich Famous B-B-Q truck served lunch to the remaining crime scene personnel on-site.

Haley Murch sat with Detectives Bonaduce, Scott, Lincoln, and Hayes on the grass, as they enjoyed plates of barbecued beef, chicken, and corn while discussing the Milner-Burkhart murder investigation. Murch, being a strict vegan, ate only a salad.

"You in the LAPD know our suspect as the Hollywood Walk of Fame Killer," she explained. "The killer prefers another name: the Hollywood Spectre—a disembodied spirit or phantasm."

"Does anyone even know what this guy looks like?" asked Lincoln.

"Well, about ten, twelve years ago, there was this young actress: Normandy Pike. Although she was stabbed a dozen times in her Hollywood Hills home, she somehow managed to escape and survive long enough to provide a neighbor with a description."

"What did she say?" asked Jimbo.

"Her assailant was male, say late 40s, early 50s, and wore dark, extravagant clothing like a cloaked cavalier."

"A *what?*" asked Hayes.

"A *cavalier*: a swashbuckler or gallant knight–also known as a *caballero*."

"What kind of weapon did he use?" asked Lincoln.

"He carried a sword in a scabbard on his belt, but he used a survival knife to stab her with."

"Did she get a look at his face?" asked Jimbo.

"He had long white hair and wore a wide-brimmed black hat and a *Phantom of the Opera*-style mask to cover his scarred face."

"What do you mean by *scarred?*" asked Nuke.

"Body and facial scarring from severe burn trauma. It didn't appear to affect his motor skills. He was fast and strong."

"His disfigurement could explain why he murdered Dr. Milner here. An act of retaliation for unsatisfactory plastic repair work," said Jimbo.

"What about Milner's fiancée?"

"Simply an innocent victim in the wrong place at the wrong time," said Nuke.

AT 11:52 AM, RICH MacGuffin entered Trauma Films Studios as the *Killer Cockroach* crew set up a bedroom set.

Max Winston sat off to the side, fiddling with a broken remote-control unit. He glanced up in time to witness his assistant's arrival and rejoiced. "Jeez, Rich, it's about time you showed up! Lloyd's ready to have an aneurysm!" He looked over MacGuffin's shoulder and quivered. "Speaking of whom..."

Lloyd Hoffman snuck up behind MacGuffin and tapped him on the shoulder. "MacGuffin!"

Rich nearly jumped out of his shoes at the mere mention of his name.

"Lloyd!"

Hoffman took a whiff of MacGuffin's stench. "Have you been drinking?"

Max egged MacGuffin on. "Bombed the audition, eh, Rich?"

MacGuffin frowned. "Is it that obvious?"

"What happened?"

MacGuffin sighed. "You were right, Max. You're always right."

"Uh, huh."

MacGuffin let out another sigh. "I might be a good actor, Max, but my looks are my Achilles Heel."

"Shyeah. Loser."

MacGuffin looked at Hoffman and snickered. "I hope Lloyd has a writer working on a sequel to *Killer Cockroach* as we speak because I could really use an acting gig right now."

Lloyd smiled gleefully. "In my world of zero-budget filmmaking, my friend, there's always, *always* a sequel. We could call it *Revenge of the Killer Cockroach*. Or, better yet, *Bride of the Killer Cockroach*."

"Who gives a shit what you call it, Lloyd? Make sure you give me a decent role."

Hoffman smirked, lying. "Oh, absolutely."

CHAPTER TEN

AT THE CORNER OF Laurel Canyon Boulevard and Lookout Mountain Avenue in Laurel Canyon stood an unusual property belonging to movie producer John Crawford. The massive wooded retreat called the Treehouse had an 80-foot living room, a floor-to-ceiling fireplace, a bowling alley, and a sunken indoor pool. An attached guesthouse had two trees growing out of its living room. There were artificial caves fashioned into the surrounding hillside and a duck pond. It was a masculine retreat for wealthy men, which Crawford was.

Outside the main cabin, Crawford's daughter, actress McKenzie Banks, sat on a log bench before a campfire, wrapped in a light blue blanket, and stared up at the moon over the West Hollywood cityscape. She appeared distraught with tears running down her face.

John Crawford walked over, carrying a bag of marshmallows. "You know, McKenzie, sitting there in the glow of the fire, you remind me of your mother. She always loved a good campfire. You're the spitting image of her."

McKenzie tried to smile, but she couldn't help but cry. She wiped away her tears with her blanket and tried to compose herself. "What did you really come out here for, Dad? Certainly not to roast marshmallows?"

As she dried her eyes, Crawford took a seat beside her on the log bench and put a reassuring hand on her right shoulder. "I know how you feel about the movie being shut down, McKenzie. Believe me, it's not the first one in my long career as a director and producer."

She scowled, staring at the ground in front of her feet. "You have no idea."

"What can I say, honey? We've considered everything possible to try to salvage the project, but with too much left to be filmed with Rivers, well, there isn't much hope. The studio coffers aren't willing to lend us the extra dough to re-cast and re-shoot. From the start, they

45

never had much faith in the movie. It's a smaller production with not a whole lot of blockbuster potential behind it. Rivers might have enough clout to bring in huge revenues for his big summer action pictures, but he's unproven for this kind of film. I'm surprised he even agreed to star in this movie. It's a drama. Not his usual cup of tea."

"Judy is the best acting role I've ever had. It would have led to better roles in the future."

"I'm sorry I let you down, sweetheart, but this...this is how the business works."

She stood up and glared at him. "It's a screwed-up business!" she snarled and walked away.

Crawford called after her, "Your mother would have been proud of your work in the movie, McKenzie. She loved watching you perform in plays on stage when you were a child. You reminded her of herself when she was a young actress."

McKenzie turned back, albeit reluctantly, and hugged her father.

UNDER A MILE TO the west, Rich MacGuffin lounged on an inflatable mattress in a kiddie pool in the backyard of a three-story, single-family townhouse at 8763 Wonderland Avenue. He drank a bottle of beer and gazed up at the stars. His dog, a one-year-old Golden Retriever named Hitchcock, slept on the grass beside the pool.

MacGuffin took a sip of beer and sighed as he stared up at the sky. "You know, Hitchcock, sometimes I feel like Luke Skywalker staring out at the setting twin suns on Tatooine, dreaming of a brighter future. Alas, while Luke's dreams do come true on the silver screen, whenever I dream, all I ever see is a vast ocean of stars all more successful than I'll ever be."

A shooting star streaked across the starlit sky.

"We're stuck in this hellish reality together, boy. You and me: a couple of shooting stars."

Hitchcock yawned, licked his chops, and went back to sleep.

MacGuffin shook his head. "Okay, *me*."

THE IRON-BARRED DOOR to Christian Rivers' dungeon cell opened, and Caroline entered, carrying a tray of moldy bread and rusty water, which she placed on the dirt floor before the still-unconscious

Rivers, shackled to the rear wall beside the rotting skeleton, also chained up. As Caroline set the tray on the ground, she stepped to her right and to obstruct the view of a surveillance camera embedded in the concrete block wall.

Grendel and Sebastian sat in a small room watching Caroline's every move on closed-circuit television. They glared at each other as their view became obscured.

As Caroline blocked the camera, she removed a bag of table scraps and tucked it under Rivers' right arm, out of sight. She leaned in toward his face and kissed him on the lips for a long moment.

As she pulled away, Rivers' eyes fluttered and crept open. As he looked at her through his haze, Caroline fell backward, startled.

"Forgive me," she whimpered, fearful.

Rivers' left hand grabbed onto her right arm, causing her to shudder. He tried to speak, albeit unintelligible, "Who...?"

Caroline pulled away and dragged herself across the floor to the exit. She crawled out and pulled the door shut behind her.

As she scampered away, Rivers cried out, his voice hoarse, "Wait...don't go."

CAPTAIN RICHARD DREYFUS SAT in his office in the Robbery-Homicide Division of the West Los Angeles Community Police Station, mulling over a Missing Person report on Christian Rivers. In front of him was Rivers' bloody agency photo in a plastic evidence bag. After a moment of hesitation, Dreyfus picked up his antique rotary desk phone and began dialing.

Thirty miles to the south in the city of Long Beach, Detective Nuke Bonaduce, garbed in a pair of black khaki pants and a white sweat-stained wife beater, worked barefoot and alone in his motorcycle shop, Maltese Custom Choppers & Hot Rods, while listening to loud heavy metal music over a set of loudspeakers. As he installed a set of chrome-plated triple trees on a custom bike, his cell phone started blaring the Village People's "YMCA."

Nuke muttered to himself, "Go away, Dreyfus. Can't you see I'm busy here?" He lowered his voice to mimic a Matt Hooper line from Steven Spielberg's *Jaws*, "'I'm not gonna take this abuse any longer.'"

Nuke grabbed his cell phone from a small toolbox on the floor beside him and answered Dreyfus' call in a faux effeminate voice, "Yes, Dick...I mean, Captain...how may I service you this fine evening?"

Dreyfus ignored the bullshit and got straight to business. "Quit jerking off that damn machine of yours, hotshot. I've got a new case for you: a missing celebrity."

Nuke switched back to his normal voice. "You gotta be shitting me, Dreyfus?"

"Nope. I ain't shitting you, Nuke. This is for real."

"If this is a missing person case, shouldn't you be talking to a different department? I only handle robberies and homicides."

Dreyfus held up the bloody agency photo of Rivers. "Granted, this case is out of our jurisdiction. It belongs to the Hollywood boys on North Wilcox. Based on new evidence, though, I managed to pull a few strings with the brass to get you and your team involved on this."

"Must be pretty darn interesting for you to be calling me up at this hour?"

"Trust me, sport. You'll want to work this case. It's something right up your alley. I'll email you the address. See you soon."

Click! Dreyfus hung up the phone.

CHAPTER ELEVEN

THURSDAY, AUGUST THE ELEVENTH
EIGHT ZERO-SEVEN AM

CHRISTIAN RIVERS' PRIVATE HILLSIDE bungalow at the Chateau Marmont swarmed with police cars as Nuke's Mercury drove up and pulled into the bungalow's attached carport. Yellow police tape cordoned off the site.

Inside, forensic specialists and homicide detectives from the Hollywood Community Police Station milled about as Nuke entered through the front door and moved into the adjacent living room, carrying a tray of four coffees and donuts.

The living room was still in the same state of disarray as Rivers left it the morning before. Jimbo stood by the coffee table, taking Polaroids of various items in the proximity as Nuke walked over.

"Hey, hey, Jim-bo!"

"Hey, Nuke."

"So, what can you tell me about the case, Jimmy boy?"

"Well...we're dealing with a missing A-list celebrity named Christian Rivers."

"Sorry, not a fan. Who called in the report? The parents?"

"Mr. Rivers' parents are both dead. Car crash in 2001. He was an only child. No, it was the producer of his latest movie filming over at Paradise Pictures who called in after Rivers failed to show up for work at the studio yesterday morning."

Nuke shook his head and smirked. "Doesn't sound so bad."

"Well..."

Nuke attempted to set a smoldering cup of coffee on the coffee table. "Trade you a coffee for a peek at your crime scene photos?"

Jimbo was quick to grab it with his rubber-gloved right hand before the cup touched the table's glass surface. "Sorry, Nuke– fingerprints–but thanks for the effort."

Nuke patted him on the shoulder. "Relax, Jimbo. I was testing you."

Jimbo realized Nuke was wearing rubber gloves and smiled. "Hey, I see you wore your rubbers this time. Agent Murch will be pleased."

Nuke chuckled. "Yeah, too bad they don't come ribbed for her pleasure."

Jimbo handed Nuke an envelope of his Polaroid photos. "Here. Enjoy."

Nuke smiled as he took the package and sipped his coffee. "Thanks, Jimbo. You're a good man."

"You're welcome, Nuke."

"Now, tell me where I can find my other boys, Lincoln and Hayes?"

"The master bedroom at the end of the hall."

"*Muchas gracias*, Little Kahuna."

"You're quite welcome, *amigo*."

Nuke took the package and made a beeline for the master bedroom at the other end of the bungalow. He entered and approached Lincoln and Hayes, who were busy combing about. "Find anything, boys? Perhaps a pregnancy test from some underage starlet?"

"Can't help you there, Nuke. Sorry," said Lincoln, handing Nuke a collection of snapshots printed on glossy computer paper. "We did find these."

"Wonderful! I love surprises!"

"Looks like they came from some device with a built-in camera and printed by computer. A cell phone seems most plausible. We found a laptop computer and a scanner in the guest bedroom. The Hollywood precinct's tech guys are examining it for any potential evidence as we speak."

Nuke flipped through the collection of photographs. They were of a scandalous nature, featuring Christian Rivers in provocative poses with a male companion. "Honeymoon photos?"

Hayes smirked. "Cute, aren't they?"

As Nuke brushed through the stack, he came across a photo of Rivers playing a set of bongo drums in the nude and a couple shots of Rivers and the male snuggling in bed. "The one beating the bongos with his cock–is that who I think it is?"

"Yep, Christian Rivers," replied Lincoln.

"What about the other guy? Who's he?"

Hayes tossed Nuke a plastic evidence bag containing a leather wallet. "Found that under the bed."

Nuke pulled the wallet out of the bag and flipped it open to reveal a California driver's license belonging to Rivers' male companion. "Bingo!"

"He appears to be the other person in the photos," said Lincoln.

"Juno Calvecchio–do you know who that is, Nuke?" asked Hayes.

"He's an actor. Used to be on that TV show a way back about the math genius who helped the FBI solve crimes."

"Can't say I've seen it," stated Hayes.

"Not many people have. Lasted only six episodes."

Lincoln pulled out the evidence bag with the bloody agency photo of Rivers inside and handed it to Nuke.

"What's this?"

"An agency photo of Christian Rivers. Somebody mailed this to the producer of his latest movie filming over at Paradise Pictures. Recognize the bloody star over his face?"

Nuke appeared stunned by the revelation. "The Hollywood Spectre's calling card. Now I see why Dreyfus was so adamant about wanting us to work this case."

"Speaking of the Hollywood Spectre, Nuke–we paid a visit to Dr. Milner's place of business yesterday afternoon."

"We figured if the Hollywood Spectre were getting plastic surgery, you'd think there'd be a record of some type at Milner's office?" added Hayes.

"You boys find anything?"

"Negative," said Lincoln. "We came up empty."

"Somebody ransacked the office, Nuke," said Hayes. "They stole all the computer hard drives. If anything was there, it's gone now."

"Did you question Milner's employees: his nurses, medical assistants, that sort of thing?"

"We gave them the description Agent Murch provided of the Hollywood Spectre," said Hayes. "None of them were familiar with a client meeting those criteria."

"It's a safe bet the Hollywood Spectre met with Milner in

private, outside the office," said Lincoln.

"What about Milner's residence? Anything on a computer or in a safe?"

"Negative," said Hayes. "We even checked the loft above the living room. Nothing but secret sex tapes and photos of Milner with members of his female clientele."

Nuke sighed. "Well...so much for that idea." He moved to the bedroom doorway.

"Where you going, boss?" asked Hayes.

Nuke gazed down at the wallet in his hands and noted the address on the driver's license. "8569 Holloway Drive: Juno Calvecchio's place of residence. He might be a witness to Rivers' abduction. I gotta get to him before the Hollywood Spectre does first. He needs to be protected."

MINUTES LATER, AS NUKE drove his Mercury southwest along the Sunset Strip in early morning traffic, he talked with Agent Murch via cell phone. "Haley, honey, I hope you don't have anything urgent scheduled for this morning?"

Murch, fresh from the shower in her room at the Highland Gardens Hotel and wearing a red bathrobe and slippers, sat at the front edge of her bed, and dried her hair. She sounded groggy on the phone. "Huh...what do you want, Detective?"

"Well, when you finish drying your hair, can you meet me someplace? I'm working on a new case, and I could really use your assistance."

DRESSED IN A RATTY blue bathrobe, Rich MacGuffin entered his tiny, one-room, basement-level apartment from outside, dropped the morning edition of the *Los Angeles Times* down on his small kitchen table, and poured himself a mug of coffee from a pot.

The décor of the apartment was quite drab: wall-to-wall white-painted concrete blocks and a black-and-white checkered linoleum floor with basic appliances and sparse furniture.

Sipping his coffee, MacGuffin sat down at the table and made himself a heaping bowl of Cheerios. As he poured on milk from a pink-and-white carton, he opened the newspaper and spread it out to read. His Golden Retriever, Hitchcock, ran inside through his doggy door.

As MacGuffin took his first few bites of cereal, the newspaper's front-page headline caught his eye: "FILM STAR MISSING: CHRISTIAN RIVERS ABDUCTED FROM CHATEAU MARMONT; AUTHORITIES BAFFLED." A photo of Rivers ran alongside a half-page article.

MacGuffin experienced a moment of curiosity about the erstwhile celebrity before strange thoughts began to form. He glanced down at Hitchcock under the table by his feet and remarked, "I think today's gonna be my lucky day, boy."

CHAPTER TWELVE

THURSDAY, AUGUST THE ELEVENTH
NINE ZERO-EIGHT AM

NUKE BONADUCE'S MERCURY MONTEREY sat parked at the curb in front of the Hollyview Manor, a two-story apartment complex off the Sunset Strip on Holloway Drive. Nuke leaned against the trunk, a manila envelope tucked under his right arm. He waited as Murch climbed out of her rented, red 2005 Ford Mustang GT convertible which pulled up behind him. "Top of the morning, Miss Haley."

Murch appeared flustered as if everything was happening too fast. "You mind explaining to me what exactly it is you called me here for, Detective?"

"Please, call me Nuke."

Murch rolled her eyes and shook her head in annoyance. "Detective?"

Nuke scoffed, "Gonna play hardball, eh?"

Murch nodded and smiled.

Nuke sneered. "All right, then, have it your way, sweetheart!" He removed the evidence bag containing Rivers' bloody agency photo from the manila envelope.

"What's that?"

"As I said on the phone, darling, I'm working a new case. What I didn't tell you is it might relate to the Milner case." He pointed to the photo inside the bag. "Note the bloody star: the Hollywood Spectre's calling card."

Murch took the evidence bag and examined the photo closer. "I see. Hmm?"

"We identified the victim as Christian Rivers."

"Isn't he a movie star?"

"Yes, and, as it's still early, there's no indication of murder. For now, we're treating it as an abduction. Unlike the Cielo murders, the Hollywood Spectre got sloppy this time. He abducted Rivers from his bungalow at the Chateau Marmont but left behind a witness; a male someone: Juno Calvecchio–he's an actor as well."

"You're saying Christian Rivers is...?"

"Heh," chuckled Nuke. "I've got an evidence bag full of photos to prove it, too." He cleared his throat. "Regardless, Juno Calvecchio is most likely the last person to see Rivers alive before he disappeared, and this apartment complex is where he lives. That's why we're here. We need to get him into protective custody."

Minutes later, Nuke and Murch stood in a dimly lit stairwell alcove outside Juno Calvecchio's first-floor apartment. Behind them was a courtyard full of overgrown potted plants and plastic patio furniture.

"This is it," said Nuke.

"Sure he's home?" asked Murch.

Nuke pounded on the door. "One way to find out."

A moment later, the door creaked open, and Juno Calvecchio poked his head out. "Yes?"

"Juno Calvecchio?" asked Nuke.

"Um...yes? How can I help you?"

"I'm Detective Nuke Bonaduce, LAPD Homicide." He pointed to Murch at his left. "This is FBI Special Agent Haley Murch."

"Uh, can I see some IDs?"

Nuke and Murch removed their wallets and displayed their badges and IDs for Juno to see.

"Holy smokes! Are those things real?"

"No shit, Sherlock!" said Nuke, snotty. "What, you think we picked 'em up at the local Kids 'R' Us? We're here on official business, not to babysit."

"Shit."

Murch tried her best to ease his anxiety. "Don't worry, Juno, we're not here to arrest you. We have a few questions regarding the disappearance of Christian Rivers. Is there someplace we can talk?"

ESTABLISHED IN 1987, THE Quality Café in downtown Los Angeles is one of the most popular eateries featured in Hollywood movies. It was also Detective Nuke Bonaduce's favorite diner in all of Los Angeles County, on account of his intense love for film.

A mountain of pancakes smothered in blueberry syrup and whipped cream sat before Nuke, beside glasses of milk, orange juice,

ice water, and a cup of coffee. He was the only one having breakfast. He sat next to Murch in a red vinyl booth, across from Juno Calvecchio, who fidgeted nervously and sobbed.

Juno wiped his eyes. "The reason I got into acting in the first place was to stay out of trouble like this. When I was eight, I was involved in a street gang back home in the Bronx, and after I was busted for robbery at ten, I was given a choice of juvenile confinement or professional acting school. I chose acting school."

Nuke took his glass of ice water and handed it to Juno, who accepted it and began to drink. "What was the last time yesterday morning you saw Christian Rivers, Juno?"

Juno sobbed and sniffled. "I can't believe this is happening. Hah."

Murch put her right hand on Juno's to console him. "Please, try to relax, Juno. Take your time."

Juno took a moment to collect himself. "The last time I saw him was when the limo was driving away. I watched the whole thing through the peephole in the front door. His two bodyguards always pick him up in a limo in the morning and escort him to the studio. Rivers chooses not to drive. I don't think he even owns a car. Claims he's too rich to have to deal with such nonsense. He expects to be catered to hand to mouth. The dude's friggin' lazy as shit."

"What color was the limo?" asked Nuke.

"Black."

"Did you find anything unusual about the limousine or the two bodyguards?"

Juno shook his head. "Nothing out of the ordinary, other than they arrived earlier than normal."

"How early?"

"Pick-up was set for 8:00 AM. They showed up around 7:30."

"A good half-hour?" said Murch. "That is early."

"Strange, yes, but not implausible," said Nuke. "What time did they leave, Juno?"

"I don't know. Maybe quarter to?"

"When did you leave?" asked Murch.

"Right before 8:00 AM."

"Did you leave by car? A taxi?" asked Nuke.

"I walked home. It's only a few blocks away."

"Yes, we know where you live."

"Do you own a car, Juno?" asked Murch.

"Yes, I do. A 1975 Chevelle."

"Ooh, nice," said Nuke.

Juno shrugged his head. "It's a piece of shit, but it gets me where I need to go."

Nuke pulled out his business card and handed it to Juno. "If you'd like a restoration, I'm the man for the job. I'm not just a detective. I'm also the proprietor of Maltese Custom Choppers & Hot Rods out of Long Beach. My address is at the bottom of the card."

Juno tucked the card away. "I'll have to think about it. Thanks."

Nuke took a bite of his pancakes and sipped his coffee. "So, why were you staying at the Chateau, Juno?"

"We were filming at the studio until late Tuesday night. Anyway, afterward, a bunch of the cast and crew took a studio limo to go partying along the Strip. A few of us wound up back at Rivers' bungalow. I was so wasted; I guess I passed out. When I awoke yesterday morning, the place was trashed, and everybody was gone except for myself and Rivers."

"Did you or any of your party, including Mr. Rivers, partake in any illegal drug use or engage in any sexual activity at any time during the course of the evening?"

Juno grew apprehensive and hesitated to answer. "I...I... couldn't tell you. I... don't remember."

Nuke smirked. "I'd call that a big *yes*."

Murch was growing uneasy with Nuke's questioning. "Where are you going with this line of questioning, Detective?"

"Forgive me, Agent Murch, if I was insensitive, but I'd like to keep the evidence I'm about to show you strictly off the record and confidential. Word of this doesn't get out, understand?"

Murch nodded in agreement. "Mum's the word."

Nuke pulled out a wad of photos and flip through them, motioning to Juno. "Two of my partners did some searching around the bungalow this morning and came across these snapshots in one of the bedrooms." He handed the photos to Juno. "They're pictures of you and Mr. Rivers in intimate positions. You mind explaining your relationship with him to us, Juno?"

Juno scanned through the photos but set them down as they didn't impress him much. "You're asking if he and I were lovers or something?"

"That's one way of putting it. Sure."

Juno chuckled and glanced back at the photos. "Heh. That's funny."

Nuke prodded. "Well?"

Juno shook his head. "No...no, Rivers and I weren't lovers. We're doing a movie together: *Teenage Confidential*. We took these photos as a joke to leave behind for the maid to find once Rivers checked out of the hotel. To have a little fun. You know, so she could sell them to the *National Enquirer* or something. Create a scandal." He took a sip of ice water and chuckled. "No... we're not a gay couple."

"It doesn't matter anyway if you are," said Murch.

Juno handed the photos over to Murch to examine. "If you check those out a little closer, Agent, you'll see two of the others' reflections in the mirror holding the camera."

Murch checked out the photos and turned to Nuke. "He's telling the truth."

"Well, that solves that matter."

Nuke removed Juno's wallet from his right jacket pocket and tossed it to Juno. "Lose something?"

Juno smiled. "Thanks. I was looking for that."

"No problem."

"Are we done then?"

Nuke turned to Murch and nodded. He looked back at Juno. "Not even close, me bucko." He sipped his coffee. "Now, tell us about Christian Rivers, Juno. Did he have any enemies you can think of?"

"Um, I don't know about any enemies, *per se*, but he was famous for rubbing people the wrong way, if you know what I mean. He could be a real pain in the ass at times. I mean, he's got all the money in the world, and it's clearly affected his ego. He's a spoiled child with the run of the mill. A walking media circus. It's almost annoying at times."

Nuke grinned. "All celebrities are annoying, Juno, including you."

"So, what happens now?"

"Well, we need to put you in protective custody for the time being. Right now, you're our only witness. Once the news of your involvement gets out, you won't be safe. As far as I'm concerned, the people who took Rivers are probably aware of you already."

"What do I do?"

"Already got it covered. When we drop you back off at your apartment, Lincoln and Hayes will help you scramble some stuff together then transfer you to an LAPD lockdown suite back at headquarters. Once there, you'll have nothing to fear. You'll be monitored twenty-four hours a day."

Murch added, "Something happened to Christian Rivers along the way to the studio, and he never made it. Now it's our job to figure out what went wrong."

AT 10:23 AM, RICH MacGuffin entered Maximum F/X Studio, a 4,000-square-foot state-of-the-art facility in the San Fernando Valley.

Founded in 1997 by special effects wizard Max Winston, the company did effects for big-budget movies and low-budget independents, with expertise in animatronics, creatures and puppets, props, and make-up effects.

MacGuffin tried sitting down on a couch but landed on the concrete floor instead. He remained seated.

Max Winston was in the middle of sculpting a monster's face out of clay on top of a plaster bust of an actor's face as he noticed his friend's dilemma. "What's your boggle, *hombre*? Lock yourself out of your apartment again?"

MacGuffin smiled gleefully. "Max, I am a certified genius."

"This from the guy who only hours ago was calling himself a complete loser?"

"My problems are over, Max."

"What are you blabbering about, Rich?"

"Christian Rivers has gone missing."

Max shook his head and shrugged. "Yeah, so?"

MacGuffin grabbed hold of Max's face. "Max! I need your help in creating the perfect special effect! I need you to turn me into Christian Rivers!"

Max shook his head. "Are you drinking again? Why would you want to do something as idiotic as that? The authorities don't even know what's happened to him yet. What if he comes back?"

UPON DROPPING JUNO CALVECCHIO off at the Hollyview Manor and placing him into the protective custody of Detectives Lincoln and Hayes, Nuke and Murch walked back to their cars parked along Holloway Drive to the south.

"You handled yourself well, Detective Bonaduce. I'm impressed," said Murch. "I hope you found what you were looking for?"

"Yes, I did. I sure did."

"You mind explaining?"

"Later. I'm sure you have a lot of work to do this morning."

"I need to file a status report with the FBI Deputy Director–"

Nuke interrupted her as he opened the driver's door of his car, "So, Haley, you wanna go out sometime in the not too distant future? Perhaps a ride on the back of a chopper? A Haley on a Harley? Think about it."

Murch opened the driver's door to her Mustang and turned to Nuke. "Lose the attitude, Detective, and maybe I'd consider it." She started the engine, and sped away to the east, leaving Nuke choking on her exhaust.

Nuke's gaze followed the Mustang as she disappeared down the street. Feeling like a little kid with a skinned knee, he muttered to himself, "How many times must I spell it out to you, sweetheart–the name's Nuke? Call me Nuke." He climbed into the Mercury's driver's seat and smiled. "She likes me. It's the only explanation."

That said, Nuke gunned the engine, whipped a U-turn, and peeled rubber west down the street.

Had Nuke not been in such a hurry, he might have noticed Grendel and Sebastian sitting in the front seat of a black-and-yellow Rolls-Royce Phantom III sedan parked across the street with its engine running, watching the entire scene unfold before them.

CHAPTER THIRTEEN

THURSDAY, AUGUST THE ELEVENTH
TEN THIRTY-ONE AM

INSIDE MAXIMUM F/X STUDIO, Max sat in a chair next to MacGuffin on the couch and served as his psychiatrist. "This is the stupidest idea I've ever heard, Rich! I'm not gonna do it!"

"Look, Max, I'm tired of living in a shit-hole apartment, okay? My car is like the Flintstone's car! The floorboards are so rusted out I can see the ground beneath my feet! And I'm tired of casting directors always telling me *no*!"

"I know how you feel, Rich. Sincerely. It's...you're crazy."

"Come on. There's only a few days left of filming on Rivers' new movie. A week or two is nothing. I'd be in and out in no time."

A brief pause.

"Do you have any idea how difficult pulling that off would be?" asked Max. "No, probably not. The make-up isn't the problem. That's the easy part. Without flawless knowledge of your subject, your efforts mean shit. You must get inside Rivers' head, learn his voice, his walk, his mannerisms. Watch as many movies as you can. Interviews. Learn how he writes his signature..."

MacGuffin shook his head. "Doesn't sound so bad."

"People must believe you are Christian Rivers, Rich. People work with him. They know what he's like. I mean, the fans, the media, the bloody stalkers–they'll be hounding your ass like friggin' vultures. You'll need to be on your toes and calculate your every move. Otherwise, it's all over, baby. Your identity will be outed, and if that happens, nobody, and I mean *nobody*, will ever consider Rich MacGuffin for an acting job in this angel town again."

"Come on, Max. Live a little. What is there to lose?"

"My pride, for one. I'm also pretty sure stealing a person's identity is a huge felony."

MacGuffin held out his right hand to Max as a peace offering. "Let's go for it, Max: the brass ring. For me: Rich MacGuffin–your best friend in the world."

Max sighed. "Why couldn't you play the role of an alcoholic, instead, huh? You have the experience. It'd be method acting. You'd be a shoo-in for an Oscar."

"Nah. I'd much rather play Christian Rivers. It's a much meatier part."

Max paused to think things over. Albeit reluctant, he gave in under pressure. "Bah! All right, Rich, I'll do it, but it'll cost you."

MacGuffin smiled and high-fived Max's left hand. "You the man!"

WITH HIS HAIR SLICKED back, MacGuffin sat in a dentist's chair with a white sheet draped around him, while Max applied a thin rubber bald cap to the top of MacGuffin's head, trimmed around his ears with scissors, and glued the edges down with spirit gum adhesive.

Max outlined MacGuffin's hairline on top of the bald cap with a blue skin marker.

He smeared Vaseline on MacGuffin's face, neck, and head, as a separation agent.

With straws stuck up MacGuffin's nose to breathe, Max covered MacGuffin's entire head in alginate and strips of gauze and allowed it to dry.

DURING LUNCH BREAK, NUKE Bonaduce sat in the West Los Angeles Community Police Station's media room and reviewed surveillance tape from the Chateau Marmont on television.

On-screen: Christian Rivers exited his bungalow and climbed into the back of a black limo which drove off. The timestamp in the lower-left corner of the frame read 07:43:16. Nuke scribbled notes in a small notebook: "EARL GITTES, HARVE GITTES, FOR STARS SECURITY."

THAT NIGHT, MACGUFFIN SAT on his bed in his apartment and watched his way through a pile of Christian Rivers movies on DVD. He studied and took notes on a yellow legal pad. His dog, Hitchcock, slept by his side.

SATURDAY, AUGUST THE THIRTEENTH

TWELVE FIFTEEN PM

MACGUFFIN SAT ON A staircase outside his apartment, practicing writing Christian Rivers' signature with a black pen. Hitchcock slept nearby in a doghouse.

IN THE BEDROOM OF her apartment, McKenzie Banks sat in a red beanbag chair and watched a dailies DVD of raw footage of scenes from *Teenage Confidential*, featuring her and Christian Rivers, on a small television.

     Angry, she jumped up, ripped the disk out of the player, flipped off the television, and whirled the DVD across the room and into a framed photograph of her late mother on a dresser, sending it crashing to the floor.

     Frantic, she ran over and picked up the broken picture frame. As she removed the torn photograph and looked at it, she began to cry.

SUNDAY, AUGUST THE FOURTEENTH
FOUR TWENTY-SIX PM

RICH MACGUFFIN SAT IN a make-up chair facing a wall of the FX studio. Max Winston stepped over and whipped off the white drape over MacGuffin's front.

     "How do I look, Max?"

     Max handed MacGuffin a mirror. "Beautiful, Rich. This make-up trial run was a bona fide success. You're a dead ringer for Christian Rivers, right down to the goatee cum-catcher on your chin. Now, let's see if you can fool everybody into believing you're the real McCoy."

CHAPTER FOURTEEN

MONDAY, AUGUST THE FIFTEENTH
EIGHT FIFTY-TWO AM

DEEP WITHIN THE CATACOMBS of Swan's lair, the real Christian Rivers sat on the dirt floor of his dungeon cell, shackled to the wall beside the rotted skeleton. He was alert, although beaten, starved, and dehydrated. He tried to wet his parched lips, but he had no saliva.

Rivers glanced at the skeleton's face and watched as a large, centipede-like creature slithered its way out of the skeleton's mouth and dropped onto Rivers' shirt. Petrified, Rivers watched the monstrous insect inch its way up his torso and crawl into his nose. He thrashed about and winced in pain as blood dripped from his flared nostrils. He began to fade as Grendel, Sebastian, and Igor arrived outside the dungeon door.

Igor unlocked the cell door with a skeleton key and pushed the door inward. He entered carrying a torch which he dropped beside Rivers' feet. "Rise and shine, shit stain! Heh! Heh! Time to meet your maker!" He stepped aside to allow Grendel and Sebastian to enter with a stretcher.

Rivers' eyes widened as the gruesome threesome crowded around him. He tried to speak but was barely audible. "Whatever you're...going to do with me...finish it."

Sebastian sneered. "Oh, we intend to."

"Now, Mr. Rivers, there are two ways we can handle this: the easy way or the hard way," said Grendel.

Sebastian slammed a fist into the side of Rivers' face. *Smack!* As Rivers faded into unconsciousness, Sebastian snickered, "The *eeeeaaasy* way..."

IN THE POLICE STATION'S media room, Nuke Bonaduce watched exterior surveillance footage of Christian Rivers' Chateau Marmont bungalow played at double the normal speed on television. The timestamp at the bottom of the screen read 08:03:24.

Nuke stood at a counter filling a black, Maltese Custom Choppers & Hot Rods coffee mug from a stainless-steel coffee pot. He added cream and sugar and stirred his coffee with a stick. As he took a sip, he glanced over at the TV screen. He dropped his mug. "Son of a bitch!"

On-screen: A white limousine pulled up in front of Rivers' bungalow, and two men in Hawaiian shirts and khaki shorts climbed out of the back, walked through the front gate, and approached the bungalow's entrance. The two men were Earl and Harve Gittes.

Nuke's eyes fixed on the limo's license plate, ANL-709 and glanced down at the video's timestamp, 08:06:48.

SWAN STOOD IN A small, makeshift operating room, preparing for surgery. Garbed in blue scrubs, a surgical mask, and a cap, only Swan's neck, eyes, and hands were visible. The exposed flesh appeared melted and fire scarred. Rusted antique surgical instruments lay on a stainless-steel stand beside an operating table.

Swan's three henchgoons wheeled a semi-conscious Christian Rivers in on a gurney, transferred him to the operating table, and fastened him down with leather straps.

Caroline, serving as Swan's nurse, and dressed in a tight, revealing white vinyl nurse's uniform and fishnet stockings, placed an oxygen mask over Rivers' mouth and gave him a blast of oxygen to revive him.

As Rivers came to, Swan stepped over and smacked him hard across the face. "Wakey, wakey, Mr. Rivers!"

Caroline gave Rivers another hit of oxygen.

His eyes fluttered. "Where...where am I?"

Swan connected an IV line to a bag of saline hooked to an IV pole and inserted a needle into the back of Rivers' left hand.

"Owww!"

Swan laughed. "Relax, Mr. Rivers. The pain you are experiencing now is nothing compared to what you are about to receive." He turned to his three goons. "Boys, that will be all. Leave us."

Grendel, Sebastian, and Igor lumbered away, leaving Swan and Caroline alone with the captive Rivers.

"Who...who are you?" asked Rivers. "What do you want from

me?"

"I know how important an actor's appearance is in Hollywood," explained Swan. "It means everything to their career. I know about it all too well. I myself am an old relic of Hollywood: once revered; long forgotten. I was one of the cinema's golden boys, much like yourself now: handsome, rich, spoiled, the world at my disposal. I had it all, and I lost it all as easy..." He lowered his surgical mask and showed Rivers his gruesome face. "...after *this* happened. My career was as dead as I should've been. After my accident, nobody in the business would ever consider hiring a monster like the one I became. I'm nothing more than a heap of melted remains. I'm as good as dead but very much alive."

Rivers attempted to free himself, but his efforts proved futile against the leather straps binding him down.

"There's no point trying to escape, Mr. Rivers. As you can see, I've taken all the necessary precautions."

Caroline prepared a glass syringe of anesthetic.

"It's taken me some thirty years–half my life–to reach this point," continued Swan. "Living like a disease-infested rat in the gutter, scavenging for food. But soon, my master scheme of things will reach its zenith. I will have my revenge on this town called Tinsel."

"But, why me?" asked Rivers. "What have I ever done to you?"

"You're one of their golden idols. One of the keys to their kingdom. Four billion dollars in worldwide box-office receipts."

Caroline handed the glass syringe of anesthetic to Swan. "Your Propofol, Master."

"Thank you, my dear."

Swan turned back to Rivers. "Others have come before you, Mr. Rivers, and you certainly won't be the last. As long as their inflated egos and million-dollar smiles infuriate me, I'll continue to take their lives, one-by-one. Hopefully, my work here teaches you an important lesson: Beauty is only skin deep. What lies beneath is horrifying."

Swan took the syringe and injected the anesthetic into Rivers' IV drip. As the drug entered his bloodstream, Rivers' eyes rolled back, and his eyelids fluttered shut.

Swan slipped on a plastic face shield and a pair of rubber gloves. "Nighty, night, sweet prince. When you awake, you'll look worse than a friggin' toad. Only there will be no beautiful princess to

66

kiss you on the lips and turn you back into your beautiful, spoiled self."

A devilish dose of laughter erupted from Swan's mouth as he picked up an electric bone saw and dug into his work.

Caroline closed her eyes to shield herself from the unfolding horror.

CHAPTER FIFTEEN

MONDAY, AUGUST THE FIFTEENTH
NINE FORTY-FIVE AM

HUNDREDS OF PEOPLE WAITED at the gate for Paradise Pictures Studios Theme Park to open, as a yellow taxi pulled up to a nearby curb.

The back door of the cab opened, and superstar celebrity "Christian Rivers" stepped out, wearing a ratty, olive-green cargo jacket and a pair of mirrored sunglasses strung around his neck.

He approached the female taxi driver and handed her a black pen and a folded piece of paper. "There you go, darling: one black pen; one autograph. Enjoy."

"Gee, thanks."

"Don't mention it. Anything for a fan."

The driver rolled up her window, and MacGuffin waved after her as the taxi drove away.

He smiled as he pulled on a New York Yankees baseball cap and his sunglasses to hide his new identity, strolled over to the wall of ticket booths and turnstiles, and got lost in the crowd of people.

NUKE SAT AT HIS usual booth inside the Quality Café, eating a huge breakfast of blueberry pancakes drowning in blueberry syrup and whipped cream. Glasses of milk, orange juice, water, and coffee sat nearby.

As Agent Murch approached the booth and took a seat across from him, she couldn't help but stare dumbfounded at his breakfast. "Do you have a complex for this place or something?"

Nuke smiled cheerfully at her with a mouthful of food. "Yes." He sipped his coffee.

Murch rolled her eyes. "What is it you wanted to show me, Detective?"

Nuke pulled out a large manila envelope containing photographs and tossed it to her, spilling them onto the table. "These are screen captures taken from the surveillance footage of Christian Rivers' bungalow at the Chateau Marmont."

Murch glanced through the photographs. "These are photos of the limousine and two bodyguards, Earl and Harve Gittes. I've seen these already. So what?"

"I rechecked the footage to see what time Juno Calvecchio departed, to see if it corroborates his alibi. It does. He left the bungalow at approximately 7:57 AM. Note the photograph and the time-stamp."

Murch pulled out a photo of Juno Calvecchio leaving the bungalow at 07:57:16. "Yeah, so?"

"Well, I happened to stumble upon something else quite interesting as I let the footage run forward a bit. Seems there was another visitor after Juno left, at approximately 8:06."

Murch pulled out a photograph with the corresponding timestamp. "The two bodyguards returned to the bungalow twenty minutes after picking Rivers up. Did they forget something?"

Nuke dug out photos of the limousine and the two bodyguards from the 7:43 AM pickup and showed them to Murch. "Notice anything unusual about the two sets of photos?"

"Two different limos. One's black; the other's white."

"*And?*"

"And, the clothes they're wearing change from black suits to Hawaiian shirts and khaki shorts. So?"

"Two guys in the black limo abducted Christian Rivers. It's like the old movie Western credo: The bad guys always wear black; the good guys always wear white."

"Are you suggesting two sets of bodyguards as well?"

"Bingo."

"Are you sure?"

"I checked it out myself. I called up the agency owned by the Gitteses: For Stars Security. Earl and Harve both deny ever arriving at 7:30 and picking up Rivers. They did show up at 8:06, as they normally do."

"So, who are the other two guys from the 7:30 photos?"

"Not a clue. Some guys posing as Earl and Harve? Your guess is as good as mine."

"Did you run the plates on the two limos?"

Nuke sipped his orange juice. "The second limo's legit. It's owned by Paradise Pictures Studios in East Hollywood. As for the first limo, I knew it was fake right away."

"How do you figure?"

"It has the same license plate number as Marion Crane's white, 1957 sedan in Hitchcock's *Psycho*. NFB are the initials of Norman Francis Bates."

"How do you know that?"

"When I'm not a cop, and when I'm not building choppers and cars, I'm a big-time movie geek. *Psycho* is my all-time favorite. Well, second only to Spielberg's *Jaws*."

"So, what do we do now?"

"I have the boys examining surveillance tapes from all traffic stops in the vicinity of the Chateau Marmont. See if we can figure out where the first limo was headed."

"That's not going to be easy."

"Nothing ever is, darling. Nothing ever is."

MACGUFFIN SAT AT THE back of a tramcar, taking in the Paradise Pictures Studios backlot tour. He stared in amazement at a tour brochure featuring the exterior sets from some of his favorite movies.

The tour guide spoke over the tram's intercom system, "We are now passing down Elm Street. To our left is the Majestic Theatre, a set used in 1974's *Phantom of the Paradise*, starring Jackie Coogan."

A few tourists aboard the tram, mostly Japanese, took photographs or video of the scenery with their cell phones. "Ooh...! Aah...!" they cooed in unison.

MacGuffin chuckled and shook his head in amusement. "Jackie Coogan was in *The Phantom of Hollywood*, not *Phantom of the Paradise*, you dork," he whispered to himself. "And, that's not the Majestic Theatre from *Phantom of the Paradise*. DePalma shot that movie in Dallas, Texas. This is the Majestic Theatre from the 2001 Jim Carrey movie, *The Majestic*. Go back to school and get your facts straightened out. Putz."

The tour guide stood at the front of the tram car and talked into a microphone. "To our right is Stage 28, where director Nigel Guest's *Teenage Confidential* is filming. It is an updated version of 1955's *Rebel Without a Cause* and stars Christian Rivers, McKenzie Banks, and Juno Calvecchio in the roles made famous by the legendary James

Dean, Natalie Wood, and Sal Mineo. So, please, keep your eyes peeled throughout the rest of the tour, as I'm told some of the cast and crew are on-site today. Moving on..."

As the tour guide's voice faded out, MacGuffin found it an opportune time to sneak onto the film set. While everybody on the tram had their heads turned, he slipped off the back and snuck over to the soundstage.

He approached an elderly security guard in a lawn chair, guarding the east entrance. The guard was either hard-of-hearing, suffering from cataracts, or too engrossed in his copy of *Hustler* magazine, as he failed to regard MacGuffin's presence.

MacGuffin glanced at the guard's name tag. "Excuse me...uh...Marvin? Anybody home?"

No response.

MacGuffin rustled Marvin's magazine to gain his attention. "Hell-o?"

Marvin put down his magazine and glanced up. "What the Hell you want, sonny? Can't you see I'm busy here?" His voice was gravelly.

MacGuffin shook his head in bewilderment. "I'm sorry, I'm looking for John Crawford or Nigel Guest."

"Inside."

"You need to see my ID?"

Marvin scoffed and waved his hands. "Do I look like a farthead? No, that's all right, Mr. Rivers, I don't need to see an ID. I know who you are. You're the star of the movie. You are permitted inside."

"You sure about that?"

Marvin didn't reply.

MacGuffin shrugged and pointed to the stage entrance. "Never mind, I'll be on my way now. Okay? Thanks for everything."

Marvin shook his head and watched as MacGuffin entered the soundstage. "Heh. Meddling kids. They think they know everything." He removed a walkie-talkie and spoke into it, "Uh, Mr. Guest, sir? This is Marvin Larkin, Security. You have a visitor, and you're not going to believe who it is."

MacGuffin pocketed his sunglasses as he emerged from a labyrinthine maze of thick black velvet curtains and peered inside the soundstage. To his astonishment, the place wasn't used for filming that day. Instead, a small construction crew kept busy striking a living room/dining room set at the rear of the stage. Awestruck, he whispered, "What is this place?"

The cell phone in MacGuffin's jacket pocket began to play "*The Terminator* Theme." As MacGuffin answered the call, the video image of Max Winston popped up on-screen. "Aloha, Maxwell! How's it going, buddy?"

"That's the question I was gonna ask you, *compadre*. Any problems breaking into the studio?"

A carpenter walked past MacGuffin, carrying a piece of drywall.

"Want some help with that?" asked MacGuffin.

The carpenter snarled and kept on walking. "Go screw yourself, dickhead!"

"Sheesh! Top of the morning to you, too!"

MacGuffin went back to his cell phone. "Max, you still there?"

"Yes, of course. What happened?"

"Nothing."

"So, you made it in okay?"

"Piece of cake."

"Did you find Crawford or Guest yet...?"

Nigel Guest snatched the phone from MacGuffin's hands and hurled it to the ground where he smashed it to smithereens under his right boot heel.

MacGuffin was furious. "Hey! What the Hell, man?"

Smiling devilishly, Nigel grabbed MacGuffin by the throat, slammed him up against a concrete wall, and hissed in his face. "The horns are out now, boy!"

MacGuffin struggled to breathe as Nigel lifted him a foot off the floor. He gasped and scratched at Nigel's hand around his neck. "I can't...breathe."

"Rivers, you no-good, disgusting sack of excrement! How dare you show your pathetic buggering mug on my set after what you pulled last week?!"

"I can...ack... explain."

"Can you now?"

"Let...let me go. Trot out."

Nigel grinned and snarled. "I like watching you squirm, you little maggot pus wad! I bet you're quaking in your booties right about now; you're so happy to see me?"

The foul stench of Nigel's breath made MacGuffin want to puke. "You ever hear of a breath mint? You could really use one." He gasped.

Nigel smiled and released his iron grip around MacGuffin's neck, who collapsed to the ground, gasping for air.

Actress McKenzie Banks stood by the nearby Craft Services table and watched the scene unfold. She appeared sad or angry or both.

CHAPTER SIXTEEN

MONDAY, AUGUST THE FIFTEENTH
ELEVEN ZERO-SEVEN AM

NUKE AND MURCH SAT around Nuke's unkempt desk in Robbery-Homicide. Murch poured over cold case files while Nuke sketched a chopper design on a sketchpad with a pencil.

"Don't you ever get any work done around here?" asked Murch, appalled. "This case file is six months old. This other one is over three years."

Nuke never looked up from his sketch. "Sorry, sweetheart. The maid quit on me."

Murch glanced at Nuke's sketchpad. "Design for a new motorcycle?"

"Something I'm designing for a new client. Helps clear my head so I can think through the details of whatever case I'm currently working on. And this latest one is turning out to be a real bugger."

Murch's mouth twitched upwards on the left, dimpling her cheek. She rolled her eyes. "Why is that? Too many *I*'s; too many *T*'s to cross?"

Nuke hurled his pencil across the room. "For the record, darling, the preferred nomenclature is *chopper*, not *motorcycle*. There's a difference."

"Sheesh. Forgive me for not being politically correct."

Jimbo Scott entered the department and approached Nuke's desk. "Hey, Nuke; Haley. I got something for you." He handed Nuke a file folder.

"These the traffic photos I asked you to get?"

"Yep. Lincoln, Hayes, and I–we figured out where the first limo went."

Nuke poured dozens of photographs onto his desk and sorted through them. "I'm itching to hear this, Jimbo. I love surprises. Go."

"Paradise Pictures Studios."

"What?"

"Hey, that's what the traffic cameras showed us. I'm not making this up."

Nuke scratched his head. "No one's accusing you, Jimbo. I believe you. It's just...Paradise Pictures doesn't make any sense. That's where Rivers intended to go. He's making a movie there."

"I don't understand it myself, Nuke. I mean, Rivers arrives at the studio as scheduled, yet he fails to show up on set for his 9:00 AM call time. What happened in between there?"

"That isn't good logic," said Murch. "I mean, the limo heading to the studio doesn't mean the actor ever arrived or even got out of the limo."

Jimbo shrugged. "I know, but it's all we have to work with. I'm making an educated guess."

Nuke got up from his chair and shook Jimbo's hand. "Good work, Jimbo."

"No problem, Nuke. That's what I'm here for."

"Until next time, Little Kahuna."

Jimbo scooped up the photos and hurried off.

Nuke turned to Murch. "Agent Murch, I hope you don't have anything planned for this afternoon? No autopsies? No manicure or pedicure? We're going to the movies. I'll drive; you buy the popcorn."

SITTING ECLIPSED BY AN enormous oak desk in his Haze Films Productions office, Nigel Guest cut off the end of a Cuban cigar and lit up. With a good drag, he exhaled a series of smoke rings and glanced over at MacGuffin, tied to a wooden chair, looking a bit roughed-up. "Well, well, Mr. Rivers, what am I to do with you, considering you aren't, in fact, Mr. Rivers?"

"What are you saying? Of course, I'm Christian Rivers. Don't be ridiculous."

The office door opened, and John Crawford walked in.

"Ah, John! Welcome, welcome!" said Nigel. "Have a seat. Got some important business to deal with."

Crawford closed the door behind him and took a seat at the edge of the desk and faced MacGuffin. "So, I see. Hmm...?"

"What is this all about?" asked MacGuffin. "Why am I tied up?"

Nigel smiled. "As I told you earlier, I like seeing you squirm."

He opened a desk drawer, pulled out a copy of the X'ed-out agency photo of Rivers, and held it up for MacGuffin to see. "If you are Christian Rivers, perhaps you could shed some light on this?"

"I'm guessing some vindictive fan was having some fun with one of my headshots and sent it to you as a joke."

"I think not."

"Calm yourself down, Nigel," said Crawford. "Let's see what he has to say." He turned to MacGuffin. "Can you explain the photograph?"

MacGuffin shook his head. "No, sorry."

Crawford grabbed the photo from Nigel. "Well, then, allow me the privilege of enlightening you. For the past few days, we've been in contact with the LAPD and FBI regarding your disappearance last Wednesday. We received this photograph the same morning."

"I have no clue what you're talking about."

"Shut up and listen!" said Nigel.

Crawford continued, "If indeed you are Rivers, it is imperative you cooperate. The FBI has been tracking a known serial killer for the past twenty-five years who leaves behind a similar calling card at the scenes of his crimes."

"What does this have to do with me?"

"The killer has abducted several other celebrities besides yourself. They were never heard from again. And, now, out of the clear blue, you show up again, unharmed. You say you're Christian Rivers, prove it."

MacGuffin hesitated a long moment and surrendered his guard. "All right, you got me. Untie me, and I'll show you."

NUKE AND MURCH STOOD at the Paradise Pictures employee gate and questioned a lanky, young, African American security guard named Orlando Nod outside his guard shack. While Orlando perused through the gate's logbook for August, Nuke scribbled notes in his notebook.

"Sorry, there doesn't seem to be any record of Christian Rivers' arrival last Wednesday morning," said Orlando.

Nuke held up a photo taken from a traffic camera showing the black limousine approaching the employee gate. The timestamp in the lower-right corner showed a time of 08:19:36. "This photo captured from a nearby traffic camera's video feed shows a black limousine arrived at this gate around 8:19 AM."

Orlando checked the logbook for verification and again turned up zero. He shook his head. "Sorry. Like I said, there's no such record for a black limousine arriving at that time."

"You sure?" asked Murch.

"Positive."

"But you said you were working here that morning?" asked Nuke.

"I was here, yes. If there was any such arrival, I would know about it and would've written it down in the logbook. All arrivals need to sign in before entering the backlot. It's studio protocol."

Nuke looked at the traffic photo. "Well, this picture doesn't lie. The limo did arrive here at 8:19 or 8:20, so something is rotten in the state of California here. Is it possible you could've nodded off on the job for a few minutes? Did the limo sneak itself in through the gate, right past you, without you knowing about it?"

Orlando stared at his feet for a moment and glanced back up at Nuke and Murch. "Okay, if I tell you something, do you promise not to tell anybody? I can't afford to lose my job here."

"You have my word on it," said Nuke.

Orlando closed the logbook. "There was a car–a black limousine like the one you described–that let itself in through the gate. The driver raised the bar by hand. It drove right on through, and I didn't even know about it until the driver honked the horn once inside the gate. Scared the shit out of me. I even fell out of my chair."

"Dare I inquire what kept you preoccupied long enough for the limo to sneak itself by you?"

Embarrassed, Orlando looked around to make sure nobody was in earshot. "I was reading a porno mag."

"Reading the articles or looking at the pictures?"

"Looking at the centerfold."

"You were jerking off in there, weren't you?"

"Dear God, no. No."

"It doesn't matter if you were. I don't care."

Murch chimed in. "Orlando, did you get a good look at the limo once you realized what had happened?"

"I caught only a brief glimpse of it from behind once it was through the gate."

"Did you notice any passengers in the car?"

"Nah. The windows were tinted."

Nuke stomped his foot. "Dammit!"

"What about a record of the limo leaving the lot after that, Orlando?" asked Murch. "Do you have that?"

Orlando again consulted his logbook only to shake his head. "I don't see...no...no such record. Nothing in the last few days. Sorry."

Nuke tapped his pen on his notepad. "So, the limo never left? That means he's still here. Hmm...?"

"What about a surveillance system, Orlando?" asked Murch. "Can you tell us whom we might get in touch with?"

After getting all the information they needed, Nuke and Murch climbed back inside Nuke's Mercury. Nuke pocketed his notepad and turned the key in the ignition. The engine roared to life.

"What do we do now, Detective?"

"Call in the troops and search this entire place over with a fine-tooth comb, Agent. If the limo never left, it's gotta be around here somewhere. And, where there's a limo, there's bound to be a Rivers."

Murch shook her head. "Again, that's terrible logic, Detective. The logbook system is faulty, so the limo could have left unrecorded as easy as it entered."

"I appreciate your opinion, sweetheart. I do. But, next time, keep it to yourself unless I ask for it. This is my investigation. I operate by the rule of Occam's Razor: The simplest solution to any problem is usually the right one. You sit there and look cute. Okay?"

Murch glared. "Have it your way, Detective. Have it your way."

"Thank you, I will."

Nuke honked the car's horn, and Orlando raised the checkered swing arm for them to enter the backlot. Nuke pressed down on the gas pedal, and the Mercury drove on through.

CHAPTER SEVENTEEN

MONDAY, AUGUST THE FIFTEENTH
ELEVEN TWENTY-FIVE AM

MACGUFFIN TRIED TO FREE his hands from their restraints, but he tipped his chair over backward onto the floor. Crawford rushed over and picked him up.

"For Christ's sake, would you untie me?" asked MacGuffin.

Crawford knelt and untied MacGuffin's hands.

Finally free, MacGuffin leaned forward in his chair and looked into Crawford's and Nigel's eyes. "All right, feast your eyes on me." He placed his hands behind his neck, grabbed onto a fold of his prosthetic make-up, and peeled away Rivers' face to reveal his own.

Crawford and Nigel looked on in disbelief.

"Holy shit!" bellowed Nigel.

MacGuffin threw his mask on the desk and offered to shake both Guest's and Crawford's hands. "Nice to make your acquaintance, Mr. Guest; Mr. Crawford."

The three shook hands.

"That was incredible!" said Crawford.

"What's *your* name, and what do *you* do again?" asked Nigel.

"My name is Rich MacGuffin: part-time actor and apprentice to Maxwell Winston–master of special make-up effects. I'm a huge fan of your work."

Crawford appeared stunned. "Incredible!" He smiled. "Your ruse was sheer brilliance! You looked and sounded like that asshole Rivers! Had me fooled." He shook MacGuffin's hand a second time. "What was your name again?"

"MacGuffin. Rich MacGuffin."

Nigel leaned back in his chair and took a drag off his cigar. "So, Mr. MacGuffin, you mind explaining what the Hell you're doing on this lot and in my office disguised as Christian Rivers?"

"Well, I was thinking: You only have like one or two weeks of filming left on *Teenage Confidential*, am I right?"

"Most of which requires Mr. Rivers presence on set. Yes," said Nigel.

"But Christian Rivers isn't here," said MacGuffin. "Nobody knows what happened to him. For all anybody knows, he's dead. Why not have somebody take over in his place? Somebody who looks like him through the use of prosthetic make-up. Somebody who knows how to talk like him. Move like him. Sign his signature like him."

Crawford nodded. "I see where you're going with this."

Nigel extinguished his cigar in an ashtray on the corner of his desk. "You're saying we should hire you, Mr. MacGuffin?"

"Why not? You got any better ideas?"

Nigel unwrapped a new cigar and cut off the tip. "An interesting gesture, Mr. MacGuffin. Sincerely. One I'm not entirely comfortable with. However..." He lit his cigar. "...it's the best idea I've heard all day. It would mean I could fulfill my obligation to the studio. I can deliver a finished motion picture."

"So, it's a deal, then?"

"Not so fast, sonny boy. Only if Mr. Crawford here agrees to it, as well. I'd be committing fraud by agreeing to this crazy deal."

Nigel turned to Crawford. "So, what's your decision, John? Should we hire Mr. MacGuffin here and finish the movie, or not? I'll agree with whatever you choose."

Crawford hesitated a moment. "This is a big decision to make."

"Well, John?"

"I'm only gonna go along on this, Nigel, because of my daughter, McKenzie. This movie means everything to her and her career. She was heartbroken when we shut down the production. I'm only gonna do this for her love and respect."

"And, John, let's try to keep this a secret between us three. The studio doesn't need to know about MacGuffin. We'll say Rivers is back; that it was all a publicity stunt. We'll release a PR segment to the media. Let them know he's back and that he'll finish the movie."

"But what happens if the real Rivers does come back?" asked MacGuffin.

"If you knew the details about his disappearance, you wouldn't ask that question," said Crawford.

"You sure about that?"

"Positive."

"I assure you, Mr. MacGuffin, Christian Rivers is *not* coming back," said Nigel. "He's dead."

AS STUDIO MAINTENANCE WORKERS sifted through the debris of a burned-out building on the Paradise Pictures backlot, Nuke and Murch talked to Walter Stuckel and Doug Roberts, the heads of Security.

Murch stared at the debris pile. "What happened here, Mr. Stuckel?"

"Arson–about a week ago. This building used to be a security shed used to house the surveillance system. Nothing survived. Not even the backup system. It's gonna take us weeks to get it up and running."

Nuke fretted. "Surveillance, eh? That's interesting. That was one of the things we were going to ask you about. What day did this happen?"

"Sometime last Tuesday evening after the studio closed for the night."

Murch gave Nuke a meaningful look. He nodded.

Nuke removed a photo of the black limousine and handed it to Mr. Stuckel and Mr. Roberts. "Gentlemen...this is a picture of the limousine used to abduct actor Christian Rivers last Wednesday morning."

"Yeah, I heard about that," said Stuckel. "It's a terrible thing."

"Using traffic cameras, we were able to track the limo from the Chateau Marmont to this studio. Our trail runs cold at the studio gate."

"We were hoping the surveillance tapes could help us track the limo inside the lot," said Murch. "Looks like somebody got to them before we could."

"Have either of you ever seen this car around the lot?" asked Nuke.

Roberts inspected the photo closer. "Yeah, I know this car. It's owned by the studio."

"What can you tell us?" asked Murch.

Nuke interjected, "More specific–when was the last time you saw this limo, Mr. Roberts?"

"Thursday night. I was working the graveyard shift. One of the other guys found her abandoned along one of the street façades. She was a mess when they hauled her in."

"Enlighten us, Mr. Roberts."

"Somebody jimmied the door locks with a power drill or something. The windows were all broken out..."

"A good way to hide trace fingerprints," said Murch.

"Anything else, Doug?" asked Nuke.

"Well, yeah...the paint job was all messed up. The seats were shredded. Should I continue?"

"No, that's all right. I surmise whomever took the car made damn sure no evidence remained."

"Did anybody report it to the police?" asked Murch.

"Nah. We figured some of the spoiled movie stars took her out for a drunken joyride. Happens all the time around here. There's a lot of downtime on movie sets. Regardless, we fixed her up good as new in only a couple days. No worries."

"Well, you've got worries now, Mr. Roberts. You've destroyed potential evidence in a kidnapping and possible homicide case."

"Aw, man. I'm sorry. How were we supposed to know?"

"You don't find an arson fire and a trashed limousine in two days suspicious?" asked Nuke.

The anxiety set in for Roberts and sweat started to run. "Are we in trouble here?"

Nuke shook his head and tried to pacify him. "Relax, Doug. Tell us where we can find this car right this moment. We'll need to check it out."

MACGUFFIN AND NIGEL STARED each other down across Nigel's giant oak desk, while Crawford sat at the edge of it and observed quietly.

MacGuffin felt anxious. "Mr. Guest, sir, I don't mean to sound desperate here, but, uh, what kind of pay can I be expecting here?"

Nigel smiled sly and tapped his cigar against the edge of his ashtray to get rid of spent ashes. "It always comes down to money, doesn't it? My kind of man. I like the way you think. Money's good, and I do like to make lots of it. And, that's exactly what's gonna happen to us with this movie. Unfortunately, we can't afford to pay you anything. Mr. Rivers already received his fee. *You*, Mr. Rivers, already got paid. You see where I'm coming from?"

MacGuffin sighed. "I see."

"Sorry to disappoint you. But, if you help salvage this movie, I'll get you a lucrative contract for further endeavors."

"Sounds like a sweet deal."

Nigel smiled. "It's the least I could do, considering. Now..." He put his phone on speaker and pressed a button.

Secretary Janine Potts picked up the line on the other end. "Yes, Mr. Guest?"

"Janine, darling, could you have my driver, Mr. Larkin, swing one of the cars around to escort myself, Mr. Crawford, and, uh..." He nodded to MacGuffin. "...Mr. Rivers, to Stage 28? Also, call Jonesy and have him prep a make-up trailer for us ASAP for an impromptu PR shoot?"

"Right away, sir."

"Thanks, darling!"

Nigel pressed a button on the phone to end the conference call and looked across at MacGuffin. "Welcome to Hollywood, son."

MacGuffin stood up from his chair and shook Nigel's hand across the desk. "Thank you, Mr. Guest!"

"Please, call me Nigel. Now...as your first official duty, Mr. MacGuffin, let's fix your make-up. We got a PR spot to shoot."

DETECTIVE JIMBO SCOTT STOOD beside Nuke and Murch around a now-pristine black limousine in the reserved parking area outside Haze Films Productions' office building.

Jimbo knelt and, using forceps, removed a blue-and-yellow sticker fragment, with the partial letters NFB visible, from the limo's front license plate. He deposited the fragment in a plastic evidence bag, as Nuke and Murch watched close by. "This is definitely the limo used in the abduction. The kidnappers removed most of this fake sticker, but you can still make out the first three letters, NFB."

Nuke smiled at Murch. "Norman Francis Bates."

Jimbo glanced up from his work. "Uh...actually, Nuke, the letters NFB—at least according to the *Internet Movie Database* trivia page on Hitchcock's original *Psycho*—stand for the National Film Board of Canada, not Norman Francis Bates. Also, the numbers 418 on the license plate referred to the regional postal code of an area of Quebec where Hitchcock shot his 1953 movie, *I Confess*."

Nuke frowned. "Hrm."

"Sorry, Nuke. I know you love film trivia. I'm only trying to correct you."

Nuke glowered. "Never contradict me, Jimbo. Focus on the case."

Jimbo stood up. "Right, sorry." He joined Nuke and Murch.

"What did you find, Detective?" asked Murch.

Jimbo removed his gloves. "Um...aside from the sticker, this car is clean. Those maintenance guys fixed her up nice. Too bad for us."

"Do you think you'll be able to recover any prints off the sticker?"

Jimbo removed his cell phone. "It's possible, but the kidnappers likely wore gloves to cover their tracks. We'll need to impound the car for closer inspection. I'll call for a tow truck."

Nuke nodded in agreement. "You do that, Jimbo."

As Jimbo made the phone call, Nuke turned to Murch. "He's great, isn't he?"

"What do we do now?"

"I don't know. I'm making this up as we go."

A black Mercedes arrived and pulled up alongside the limousine.

Nuke rolled his eyes and grinned. "Great, we got company."

The Mercedes' engine cut off, and the driver, Marvin Larkin, stepped out.

Inside the car, Nigel Guest, Crawford, and MacGuffin watched as Nuke approached Larkin, displaying his police shield and ID.

"Who the bloody Hell is this, now?" asked Nigel.

Outside, Nuke confronted Larkin. "Hello, there."

"Did I do something wrong, Officer?"

"I'm a detective, actually. Nuke Bonaduce–LAPD Robbery-Homicide."

"We're investigating the abduction of actor Christian Rivers," said Murch. "You'll have to park your car someplace else. The area around this limousine is a crime scene."

Larkin looked puzzled. "*Abduction*? What are you talking about?"

"Excuse me?" asked Nuke.

"Christian Rivers wasn't abducted. He's sitting in the backseat of my car as we speak."

"What?" asked Nuke and Murch in unison.

The doors of the Mercedes opened, and Nigel, Crawford, and MacGuffin stepped out. Nuke and Murch appeared dumbfounded at the sight of Christian Rivers.

Even Jimbo looked shocked in the middle of his phone call. "Son of a..." Out of reflex action, he bumped his camera and snapped a photo of the scene.

CHAPTER EIGHTEEN

MONDAY, AUGUST THE FIFTEENTH
FIVE ZERO-SEVEN PM

NUKE'S MERCURY, MURCH'S MUSTANG, and Jimbo Scott's red 1995 Volkswagen bug sat in the parking lot of the Red Rabbit Pub, a notorious honky-tonk bar on the Sunset Strip in West Hollywood.

Nuke sat on a stool beside Murch at the bar, drinking a bottle of Heineken, while Murch sipped a strawberry margarita.

A television on the wall behind the bar aired KABC Channel 10's *Los Angeles Eyewitness News Live at 5*. "CHRISTIAN RIVERS RETURNS" was the Breaking News story of the night.

On-screen, Rich MacGuffin appeared in full Christian Rivers make-up. He stood with John Crawford and Nigel Guest outside Paradise Pictures' Stage 28. Crawford and Nigel did all the talking to prevent MacGuffin's secret from leaking out.

"But, no," said Crawford, "the reasoning behind his alleged abduction was intended solely as a publicity stunt for his latest movie, *Texas Ace Arcana and the Lost City of Atlantis*, which opens in a couple weeks."

"Rivers came to us early last week, complaining of fatigue," said Nigel. "*Teenage Confidential* is the fifth movie he's made back-to-back in the past twelve months, and it took a toll on him. He needed a break for a few days."

"And, now that he's back, production will resume immediately. There's roughly a week's worth left of shooting. Much of it involves heavy emotional scenes between Christian and McKenzie Banks."

Nuke pelted the TV screen with a bowl of beer nuts, which scattered everywhere. "A 'publicity stunt' my ass! Son of a bitch!"

The curmudgeonly bartender shouted, "Hey! That was totally uncalled for, hotshot!"

"Sorry, Lou, I was venting."

Lou walked over to the TV and changed the channel to a Dodgers game. "There. That's more like it. Something uplifting."

Murch tugged Nuke's right arm.

"What?"

"What was that all about?"

Nuke sighed. "Right now, darling, I'm all out of apologies. I'm ready to deck that asshole Rivers. I've wasted the last five days working this stupid case. Which, surprise, isn't a case at all, but rather a publicity stunt. More like he was coked out of his gourd in a rehab facility somewhere." He finished off his beer. "Everybody knows Rivers' history with drugs and alcohol..."

"Can't say I keep in touch with such matters."

"...not to mention his predilection for underage call girls dressed as cheerleaders."

Lou brought Nuke a fresh bottle of beer. "Here you go, Nuke. Have a cold one on the house, so you'll chill out."

"Thanks, Lou."

"Don't mention it," he said and walked away.

As Nuke uncapped his new beer, Murch objected, "Are you going to bitch about this all night? You're giving me a headache."

Nuke took a healthy chug of beer and belched. "Sorry, darling, but this whole thing is bullshit. Somebody should have their balls castrated for wasting our time and resources when we could've been working another case. I'm pretty sure that's a crime, and it needs addressing."

Murch glanced around the bar. "Would you calm down? You're making a scene. People are staring."

"Let 'em stare. I'm betting that dipshit Rivers came up with this hare-brained idea right after reading about the Cielo case in the Wednesday morning newspaper."

Murch finished her margarita and wiped her mouth with a napkin. "We questioned him and the others at the studio in-depth about his disappearance. I'm convinced it was all a publicity stunt."

"Bah."

"So, what are you doing about Juno Calvecchio's security detail?"

Nuke set his beer down on the bar. "We're pulling the plug. Hayes and Lincoln are dropping him off at home as we speak. I told them to swing by and join us for drinks when they're done. Gotta celebrate being the bunch of fools they think we are."

"At least everybody gets paid for a job well done."

Nuke said nothing. He finished his beer and tapped the bottle on the counter to get Lou's attention. "Lou, I'll take another brew, and my girlfriend here'll have another frosted margarita. Put 'em on Dreyfus' tab."

Lou wiped his hands on a towel and threw it over his left shoulder. "Right away, Hoss."

As Lou fetched their drinks, Nuke turned back to Murch. "So, Miss Haley, now that things have cooled down around here, does this mean you'll be heading back east anytime soon?"

"I'm staying through the end of the week to see if anything develops in the Cielo case. I don't see how it's going to lead anywhere close to capturing the Hollywood Spectre. The Rivers case seemed such a breath of fresh air. I thought we had something going in the right direction this time...some fresh leads. Alas, it was never meant to be."

"*Que sera, sera.*"

"Whatever will be, will be. *Que sera, sera.*"

Jimbo Scott played a solo game of pool at one of two adjacent pool tables. He racked up a new game and set the cue ball. Jimbo chalked his stick and prepared to break. As he started to line up his first shot, Hayes and Lincoln arrived.

"Hey, hey, Jim-bo!" shouted Hayes.

Jimbo misfired the cue ball and nailed a burly biker in his beer mug, sending shards of glass and beer all over the biker's black leather jacket and chaps.

"GODDAMMIT!"

Red-faced and pissed off, the biker got up from his seat, turned, and glared at Jimbo. "Why you little son of a whore!"

Jimbo stood mortified as the biker moved in. "Oh, shit!"

Hayes had a good laugh.

Lincoln offered his help, "Use some manners, Jimbo. Apologize."

"Easy for you to say, Linc. Stand in my shoes for a change."

The biker raised an enormous fist before Jimbo and growled in his face, "You gutless yellow turd! You're in for a world of hurt!"

Jimbo cringed. "S-s-sorry."

Jimbo took the fist to his face and landed face-down on the

pool table, blood running from his mouth and nose.

Nuke, Murch, Hayes, and Lincoln appeared stunned. "Ooooooh...!"

Hayes groaned. "I bet that hurt."

"You okay, Jimbo?" asked Nuke.

As the biker moved in for the kill, Murch intervened. "Why don't you pick on somebody your own size, asshole?" She wedged her left arm between his thighs from behind, grabbed him by the nut sack, yanked down hard, and flipped him onto his back on the floor.

Nuke stared mesmerized. "Holy shit! I think I'm in love!"

Murch whipped out her FBI badge and flashed it in the biker's face. "I believe he said he was sorry..." She inhaled deeply. "...but I'm just getting started." She exhaled. "You wanna live to see yourself impregnate some hot Betty, or would you like me to give you a vasectomy in front of all these fine people? Your choice. You done?"

The biker nodded his head and croaked, "I'm done, I'm done."

Murch released her iron grip on his nuts and helped the man to his feet. "Walk it off!"

A couple of the biker's fellows helped him to his seat.

Nuke, Hayes, and Lincoln helped Jimbo up and carried him to the bar.

"You okay, Jimmy?" asked Nuke.

Jimbo rubbed his jaw. "You mean getting clobbered back there? Shit, that was nothing. This kind of thing happens to me all the time. The story of my life. I can't help looking like a nerd. I kinda am one. I'm a glutton for punishment."

Lincoln chuckled. "Take a seat, my boy. I'll buy you a beer."

"Sorry, I don't drink."

"You gotta be kidding me?" asked Hayes. "How old are you?"

"Thirty-three."

Hayes shook his head in bewilderment. "Sheesh. You gotta learn to get out more, Jimbo. Gotta sever the umbilical cord sometimes."

"Hayes, you know I'm accelerated. I haven't lived at home since I was fourteen."

"Jimbo, my boy. You don't drink. Fine." said Lincoln. "How's about I buy you a glass of the finest cow juice around?"

Jimbo nodded. "Sounds good to me." He took a seat on a

barstool and slapped his right palm down on the counter to get Lou's attention. "Give me milk… chocolate!"

In an instant, a glass of chocolate milk slid down the bar into Jimbo's waiting hands. "Thanks." He took a sip.

Nuke helped Murch back to her seat and sat beside her. "Give this girl a prize!" he cheered, clapping his hands. "What the Hell was that? You took on the Missing Link and won."

"Some people need to learn some manners."

"They teach you that maneuver in FBI school?"

"They do, but that was my PMS acting up. I'm a girl, and I'm small. I get knocked around a lot."

"I'd love to see what you could do with a taser gun and a can of mace. Buy you a drink?"

She sipped her margarita and smiled. "When I finish this one, you may, Detective."

"Please, call me Nuke."

Murch shook her head and laughed. "That's such a stupid name."

Nuke emptied his beer bottle. "Is not!"

Murch stirred her margarita and ate the strawberry garnish. "So, Detective, what are your plans for tomorrow now that this case is over?"

Nuke pondered the question for a moment. "I don't know. Take a day off, collect my thoughts, work on the new chopper I'm doing? How 'bout you? Any plans?"

"What about that tour of Hollywood you promised me?"

"Serious?"

"What can I say? Celebrity death scenes are beginning to interest me."

A girl after my own heart. So, it's a date then?"

"I guess you could call it that. Yeah."

Nuke handed her his business card. "Swee-eet! Meet me at my shop around noon. The address is on the card. We'll go from there."

"I look forward to it."

"So do I."

CHAPTER NINETEEN

MONDAY, AUGUST THE FIFTEENTH
SEVEN SEVENTEEN PM

RICH MACGUFFIN RODE UP to the rear loading dock of Maximum F/X Studio on a bicycle, carrying with him a bottle of cheap champagne in a brown paper bag. Once he ditched his ride behind an overgrown bush, he walked to a maintenance door and punched in a multi-digit code on the keypad to the right of the door. A green light flashed, and he entered the studio.

MacGuffin ambled his way over to Max Winston's workstation where Max worked on a grotesque-looking mechanical prop.

MacGuffin looked at the prop with a confused expression. "Max, your work is amazing as always. But what the Hell are you making?"

"Well, Lloyd finally handed over the revised script pages from the film's finale. Turns out, he wants the new ending to tie in with the inevitable sequel, so he asked me to create a new prop. The Killer Cockroach now gives birth to Baby Cockroaches. Speaking of which, thanks for loaning me your Torino this morning. It's now a character in the movie: *The Big Yellow Cockroach,* the Killer Cockroach's main mode of transportation besides the sewers."

MacGuffin grimaced. "Sounds lovely. Make sure you wash the car before giving it back to me."

"As if that'll make an improvement?"

MacGuffin picked up the pregnant Cockroach prop, examined it, and scratched his head, pondering, "The Killer Cockroach, who, for all practical appearances, is male, gives live birth to Baby Cockroaches, eh? That's gotta be the stupidest idea I've ever heard."

"I told Lloyd that, and he laughed at me."

"And, what did you tell him after that?"

"Count me out for the sequel. I have much better monsters to create."

"What monsters?"

"Well, you for one. To keep you looking like Christian Rivers is going to take up a lot of my free time, what with making and painting new prosthetic appliances every night. That is if you got the gig. Tell me you got the gig, Rich? Tell me you got the gig?"

MacGuffin pulled out the bottle of champagne and popped the cork. A fountain of foam poured out onto the floor. "Max, you are looking at the star of the new Christian Rivers movie, *Teenage Confidential*."

Max didn't seem too enthused. "Well, duh, I kinda guessed that from the champagne. Talk about a no-brainer. Shyeah. What are they gonna pay you?"

"Well, that's kinda the sucky part."

"See, there's always a catch."

"They can't afford to pay me anything right now, at least not for this job. But, if I'm good enough, they might offer me the lead in the next big movie."

"Oh, yeah, right? Like that's gonna happen?"

"Hey, that's what they said."

"How long do you think the real Rivers is gonna stay missing?"

"They're pretty sure he's not coming back."

"Now, how the Hell would they know that unless they were in on his disappearance from the beginning? Think about it, Rich. Everybody knows the mob runs this town."

"Why would Crawford and Nigel hire a fake Rivers if they wanted the real one out of the picture? Answer me that, Maxie?"

"I don't know. To collect a big insurance claim?"

"Whatever?"

"How do you know they won't try to kill you as well, Richie? Stuff that thought in your pipe and smoke it."

AT 9:15 PM, CHRISTIAN Rivers still lay unconscious and strapped to a gurney in Swan's operating room, as Caroline wrapped Rivers' entire head in cloth bandages.

Swan sat in a high-backed leather chair before an oak desk in the abandoned shell of a former restaurant on the hotel's 11th floor. Before him was a spacious room lined with floor-to-ceiling, red-velvet curtains. A fire burned in a stone fireplace at the opposite end of the chamber.

A white, *Phantom of the Opera*-style, ceramic mask sat on top of the desk. Swan picked it up with his gloved left hand and pulled it on over his fire-scarred face. After adjusting the mask, he pulled on his wide-brimmed black hat.

A heavy steel door slid open behind him, as Caroline entered, pushing a steel dolly with the bandaged body of Christian Rivers strapped aboard.

Once in the room, Caroline pressed a button on a wall-mounted control panel, and a red-velvet curtain rolled open to reveal a glass cylinder. She pressed another button, and the cylinder slid open.

Caroline removed the leather straps from around Rivers' torso and legs and strained as she lifted his body off the dolly. She stepped inside the cylinder, planted Rivers within a rubber body harness, and inserted IV tubes down his throat, into his arms, and into his chest.

Caroline exited the cylinder and slid its door shut, sealing Rivers inside. The cylinder acted as a coffin, only its occupant was still alive, in a state of suspended animation.

Caroline pressed the third button on the control panel, and the cylinder filled with a translucent pink, bactericidal fluid. Oxygen bubbled up from a vent in the bottom, as IV fluids pumped into Rivers' body.

An external breathing apparatus connected to an oxygen tube down Rivers' throat, keeping him alive. The cylinder acted like the bacta tank used to treat frost-bitten Luke Skywalker on Hoth in *The Empire Strikes Back*.

As Caroline departed the room with the empty dolly, Swan marveled at his new trophy.

CHAPTER TWENTY

FOUR STAR WAGONS LINED up at the rear of Paradise Pictures Stage 28 for the cast of *Teenage Confidential.* Actress McKenzie Banks sat on the steps of her trailer reading her script. She watched a golf cart zip around a corner of the soundstage and pull up before a neighboring trailer.

John Crawford stepped off the golf cart's driver's seat, followed close behind by Rich MacGuffin and Max Winston, each carrying a make-up kit.

"Here we are, gentlemen: Mr. Rivers' trailer," said Crawford. "Hope the place isn't too much of a mess. You can clear a space and make yourselves at home."

McKenzie wandered over. "Well, well...who's this?"

Crawford blushed at his daughter's unexpected presence. "Uh...good morning, darling. This is...um...Mr. MacGuffin and Mr. Winston. Rivers hired them to do his make-up for the remainder of the shoot."

MacGuffin and Max shook McKenzie's right hand.

"Nice to meet you, Miss Banks," said MacGuffin. "We're both big fans of your work."

"Especially your horror movies," said Max. "I love horror movies. Love them. My job is special effects. This is my assistant, Rich."

"Have we worked together before?"

Max was starstruck. "Oh...um...no. I...um...we work mainly on grade-Z horror or sci-fi productions. Your films are on a much bigger scale than ours."

"What kind of movies have you done?"

"Well," said MacGuffin, "we're currently doing the effects on a little horror opus for Trauma Films."

McKenzie chuckled. "Yep...that's definitely out of my league."

94

"Well, we're kinda hoping to break into the big leagues as soon as possible. It was so nice to get the opportunity to work on this new movie, thanks to Mr. Rivers. It means a lot to us."

Crawford cleared his throat to get their attention. "Sorry to interrupt you, gentlemen, but...Mr. Rivers should be here shortly. You can set up inside. Take all the time you need. Rivers isn't due on set till 11:00 AM, when we start work on the second scene of the day."

McKenzie appeared confused. "Um...I'm...I don't remember this movie having any special effects."

"Well...it's...it's something new we've come up with, McKenzie. We've revised the final confrontation scene between Mr. Stark and Judy's father: George now grabs a knife and stabs Rivers during the fight."

McKenzie flipped through her script. "I didn't get any revised pages."

Crawford grew impatient. "And, why would you, when you don't appear in the scene in question?" He kissed the back of his daughter's right hand to try to ease the sting from his words.

McKenzie felt embarrassed. "Whatever?" She threw up her arms and stormed off to her trailer.

Crawford smiled and called after her, "See you on set at 8:00, honey."

Max looked at MacGuffin. "What the Hell was that?"

"Sorry about that, gentlemen," said Crawford. "You know how these young girls are. She's emotional. This movie means a lot to her. So, please, try not to mess this up for her."

"Um...Mr. Crawford, sir," said MacGuffin, "if there isn't anything else, Max and I should get started if we're to make Rivers' 11:00 call time."

"While I'm a master of make-up effects," said Max, "this one's gonna require a little extra finesse to make it believable."

"Then, off to work you go," said Crawford. "And, off to work I go."

CHAPTER TWENTY-ONE

TUESDAY, AUGUST THE SIXTEENTH
EIGHT THIRTY-EIGHT AM

THE MOONRISE BALLROOM OCCUPIED the 12th floor of Swan's hotel hideaway. It was spacious, with a 20-foot ceiling, art deco ornamentations, crystal chandeliers, and skylights. A multi-tiered bandstand stood at one end and a dance floor on the other, with two-level aisles on each side.

Swan sat at a candle-lit table for two on the side of the dance floor, as his animatronics jazz band, the Clockwork Oranges, performed Huey Lewis & The News' "Doing It All for My Baby" on stage to an audience of domesticated crows nestled in the rafters and chandeliers.

Swan watched as the glass doors at the south end of the ballroom opened and his beautiful, 29-year-old bride, Victoria, gowned in a vintage, late-60's wedding dress and matching veil, stepped forth, bathed in backlit white mist. Mesmerized by her beauty, Swan exclaimed, "Victoria!"

Victoria crossed the floor and joined her husband at the table. Once the champagne was poured and drank, they toasted their undying love and devotion to each other by spinning a dreamy tango on the dance floor.

Caroline, dressed in a skin-tight, white-and-black-checkered vinyl catsuit, emerged from the stone stairwell behind the stage-left bandstand, carrying a wire cage containing two green lovebirds in one hand and a folded newspaper in the other. She stopped as she spied her master, dancing alone on the dance floor. She ducked down and watched.

Little did Caroline know, a solitary crow sat studying her and the lovebirds from atop a chandelier, with its beady, black eyes.

The once docile crow let out a horrific shriek, alerting not only Caroline and Swan but every other crow in the room.

A murder of crows ensued. They swooped and dive-bombed

Caroline from every nook and cranny. In the maelstrom, she dropped the wire cage on the bandstand and used the newspaper to protect her neck and face. The poor startled girl received many a blow and bruise about her body but nothing as bad as what the two caged lovebirds endured. The crows pecked them to pieces; the cage ripped to shreds.

Even the Clockwork Oranges took a severe hit. Not one of the four puppet musicians on the stage-left bandstand remained standing. The crows either damaged or obliterated them altogether. The three musicians stage-right continued to play their jazzy tune.

Covered in blood and attacking crows, Caroline curled up in a fetal position on the stage and cried out for help, "GET THEM OFF! GET THEM OFF ME! THEY'RE ALL OVER ME! HELP!"

Startled awake from his trance, Swan rushed up the white marble staircase to his raised Wurlitzer pipe organ and played a few notes which made the crows scatter.

He leaped down to the lower level of the stage, grabbed Caroline by the neck, and hurled her face-first into the left bandstand where she collided with the puppet drummer, rolled off the stage, and landed on the hardwood floor below.

Swan stepped down from the bandstand with ferocity, picked up Caroline's limp body, and held his stiletto knife to the nape of her throat, as tears of black mascara rolled down her cheeks.

"Don't...don't kill me!"

"Why were you watching me?"

"I wasn't watching you, Master. I was only bringing you a cage of lovebirds to sit atop your organ. They were your wife's favorite."

Swan pressed the blade tighter against her throat. "MY WIFE IS DEAD!"

"Forgive me, please! I... I'm sorry!"

Apology accepted, Swan released his grip and let her go. As he tucked his knife away and stood up, he surveyed the damage to the stage. "Clean up this mess!"

Caroline cowered on the floor, whimpering. "Sorry, Master..."

Swan walked away, his black cape flowing behind him. As he ambled back up the marble stairs to his pipe organ, he noticed the morning *Los Angeles Times* laying face-up on the stage floor amidst the carnage. A headline grabbed his attention: "RIVERS RETURNS TO WORK AFTER DISAPPEARANCE; ABDUCTION BOGUS."

Swan was livid. He jumped onto the stage-right bandstand and finished off the three surviving puppet musicians.

Grendel, Sebastian, and Igor rushed into the room through the south entrance to see what the ruckus was.

"Master Swan, what's the problem?" asked an urgent Grendel.

Swan hurled the newspaper in their direction, sending pages flying everywhere.

Igor recovered the front page and noticed the headline. "'Rivers Returns.' Heh. Heh. How...heh...how is that possible? Heh. Who's that downstairs in the tank? Heh."

"Yeah, boss, how can this be Rivers when we kidnapped him?" asked Sebastian.

Swan sighed, disgusted with the three of them. "I'm surrounded by imbeciles! Imbeciles!"

"Heh. Imbeciles...heh, heh...that's funny," muttered Igor. "Who's that, Master? Heh."

Swan retorted, "I want somebody's head on a silver platter for this! Nobody meddles in my affairs!" He was furious. Needing to disappear for a while, he rushed to the pipe organ and pulled the knob to lower it into the floor.

"What do you want us to do, Master?" asked Grendel.

As Swan and the organ descended, he bellowed, "KILL THEM! KILL THEM ALL!"

CHAPTER TWENTY-TWO

TUESDAY, AUGUST THE SIXTEENTH
TEN FIFTY-SIX AM

WITH MINUTES TO SPARE before Christian Rivers was due to report to set for filming, MacGuffin exited Rivers' trailer in full make-up and headed to Stage 28 for his first scene.

He became anxious as he approached the rear entrance. It was his first time to appear as Rivers in front of the film crew. How were they going to react to him? Would Max Winston's uncanny make-up job pass muster with the people who spent so much time with the real Rivers? Who knew?

No sense worrying about that now, MacGuffin thought. Showtime was about to begin.

MacGuffin peered inside the soundstage through the back door. The place swarmed with activity as filming continued on the first scene of the day: Teenage rebel Judy Barton confronts her domineering father in the Barton living room.

Nigel Guest sat in his director's chair holding a megaphone and watching the scene play out, as various cameramen and crew members moved about the set. John Crawford watched from Video Village, tucked off to the side.

Nigel appeared thrilled with McKenzie's and George's performances. He raised his megaphone and shouted, "Cut and print! Brilliant work, everybody! Brilliant work!" He turned to his cameramen. "Check your gates!"

Everyone clapped and cheered.

"Take a short break, everybody, while we set up for the next scene! We're moving on to the confrontation scene with Rivers and George!"

The majority of the cast and ancillary crew walked off the set to take a break, while the principal crew rushed to conduct a lighting change and miscellaneous behind-the-scenes business.

MacGuffin walked over to the Craft Services table and grabbed a glazed donut. He stopped at the edge of the living room set, about ten feet from where McKenzie sat on the couch. He felt nervous, mesmerized by her beauty. She didn't acknowledge his presence as she studied her script.

MacGuffin cleared his throat. "Good afternoon, Miss Banks."

She looked up at him. To her, he was her co-star, Christian Rivers. At a loss, she dropped her script on the floor by her feet.

MacGuffin stepped over and attempted to pick it up, while McKenzie reached down to pick it up herself. They met somewhere in the middle and bumped heads.

"Ow!"

"Shit! I'm so sorry, McKenzie!"

McKenzie held her forehead, sat back down on the couch, and stared bewildered at MacGuffin. "Christian! Where the Hell have you been the last few days? We were all worried sick!"

MacGuffin told a fib, "I needed a couple of days away to clear my head. I've been working non-stop for months, and I needed a break."

"It's so like you to wander off and not tell anybody where you're going."

"It wouldn't be a vacation if people knew where I was, now, would it?"

"So, that whole kidnapping story was all a publicity stunt for your stupid action movie, as my father said?"

"Everything in Hollywood is a publicity stunt nowadays, darling."

"I hate you! This movie might not mean anything to you, Mr. Moneybags, but it sure means a Hell of a lot to me!"

"This movie means a lot to me, too, trust me."

"Right, I bet."

"I'm serious. I'm grateful for getting this part. I can't understand why somebody would wanna remake a classic like *Rebel Without a Cause*. Leave it alone, I say. It's a perfect film. I mean, didn't Hollywood learn any lessons after the 1998 *Psycho* debacle? You can't remake something that is already a masterpiece. Make a remake of some crappy film. There's plenty of those to go around."

"Yes, but Nigel's remake isn't shot-for-shot like Van Sant's movie. It bears little resemblance to the original. Hardly what I'd call a remake."

"If you say so."

"The character names might be identical, but everything else is different. I mean, Jim Stark is now a high school English teacher and everybody's favorite guidance counselor; no longer the teenage rebel. That distinction is now given to my character, Judy. She's a teenager who rebels against her abusive father and ends up killing herself. That wasn't in the original."

"No, but Plato is still the same here as in the original. The dialogue doesn't lie. He spends the entire movie cruising for a piece of Stark's ass."

"That's only subliminal. You don't see him actually do it."

"I'll even go so far as to say Juno Calvecchio is as big a closet homosexual as Sal Mineo was. You ever notice they even look alike? I bet that's how Juno got the role in the first place."

"You're such an asshole, Rivers. You know that?"

"I know, man. I'm a huge asshole. Hemorrhoids and all."

McKenzie had enough. She got up from the couch and pushed MacGuffin down onto it.

"Hey, what gives?" he protested.

McKenzie cried, scowling. "Nice to have you back, Rivers! See you on the set for the next scene!" Disgusted, she tossed her script at MacGuffin and stormed away. "Asshole!"

MacGuffin called after her, "For the record, McKenzie, I thought you were great in that last scene!"

No luck. She flipped him the bird and rushed off to her trailer outside the soundstage.

Nigel Guest approached MacGuffin and patted him on the right shoulder. "Nice try, sport. You almost had her."

"What's her problem?"

"Besides the fact she's a woman with raging hormones, she's cold and unattainable but not quite a diva. Yet."

"God, she must hate Rivers to behave so harshly. She's ruthless."

"Her behavior toward you was neither harsh nor ruthless. Being disliked was Rivers' status quo. He was an A-1 prick. You acted like an asshole to her, and she displayed her displeasure. I'd say your performance was a success."

"I wasn't trying to be an asshole to her."

"Too bad. It didn't work. Regardless, it is now time for Mr. Rivers' close-up. Are you ready for your big close-up, Mr. DeMille?"

"Actually, it's the other way around: 'I'm ready for my close-up, Mr. DeMille.'"

Nigel smiled. "That's what I like to hear, champ. See you on set in a few, mate. This is gonna be good."

"Dear God, I hope so."

"You'll be fine, Mac. I'm gonna enjoy seeing you beat the piss and vinegar out of that son of a bitch, George Rowe. I swear this is the last movie I work on with that bloody bastard. All he ever does is bitch, bitch, bitch. He's worse than a woman. Make sure you get in the occasional real jab at him. You know, for payback."

MacGuffin feigned a smile. "Great, I'll try to remember to do that. As long as he doesn't get in a few real jabs at me with that knife you spoke about."

As Nigel took a bow and headed for the Craft Services table, MacGuffin remained seated on the couch and scarfed down his glazed donut. Once finished, he reached down and picked McKenzie's script off the floor, cracking it open to the next scene.

CHAPTER TWENTY-THREE

NUKE BONADUCE SPENT HIS day off at his workbench inside Maltese Custom Choppers & Hot Rods down south in Long Beach. He ran a piece of patterned sheet metal through an English Wheel to shape it into the right side of a custom chopper gas tank. Heavy metal music blared over the shop's loudspeakers.

As Nuke worked, a red Mustang pulled up outside the shop's open garage door. He heard a familiar voice behind him. "How 'bout a ride, Mister?"

Nuke turned to find Haley Murch and smiled with glee. "I'd love to give you a ride, darling. Believe me."

"Sicko! Keep dreaming, Detective, I'm not that easy. You're not going to weasel your way into these pants."

"And, such nice pants they are, too. Do you floss?"

"I'm not going to answer that."

"*Que sera, sera*, darling."

Murch walked over to the workbench and checked out what Nuke was working on. "An English Wheel, eh? Is that a custom gas tank?"

"Yeah. I just came up with the design last night. It's gonna be real slick. A slick tank for a slick person."

Murch glanced past him. "You drive a 1950 Mercury Monterey. Did you customize it yourself, too?"

"No, I bought her at a Warner Brothers Studios prop auction back in the late '90s. She was a studio-produced stunt double for Sylvester Stallone's movie *Cobra*– 'Crime is the disease, I'm the cure.' As a detective myself, it's a motto I live by."

"She's a sweet ride. I'm impressed."

"She sure is, darling. She sure is."

Nuke put down his piece of metal, removed his work gloves, and grabbed a rag to wipe off his hands. "So, Miss Haley, are you ready for Nuke Bonaduce's Tragical History Tour of LA?"

"I made sure I dressed appropriately."

"I must say, sweetheart, you definitely fill that leather out well. Mmm, mmm..."

She rolled her eyes. "God, you're such a pervert!"

"Yes, I am. I'm not sorry, either."

"Actually, it's artificial leather. I'm a vegan. I don't eat or wear anything made from dead animals."

Nuke frowned. "Aw, too bad. Now I know it would never work between you and me."

"*It* would never happen in the first place."

"*Touché*, darling."

"Shall we start this little tour of yours? Where's your motorcycle?"

"It's a *chopper*, baby, not a *motorcycle*. I told you, there's a difference."

"Well...?"

"Not yet, sweetheart. The tour begins upstairs in my apartment."

"I told you, I'm not going to sleep with you!"

"I wasn't gonna show you what I look like in my birthday suit, even though my tattoos really must be seen to be believed. No... I wanna show you my dead celebrity memorabilia collection. It's way cool."

"Okay."

"*Okay?*"

"Okay, let's go."

"After you, milady."

Murch smiled. "Lead the way, *Mon Ami*."

RICH MACGUFFIN SAT SLUMPED on the steps of "his" trailer outside Stage 28. Still in disguise as Christian Rivers, he appeared beaten, bruised, and bloody, with a fillet knife protruding from his gut— all a means of Max Winston's special effects make-up.

He took a bite of a toasted bagel with cream cheese and sighed. "Christ, I gotta be crazy doing this job for nothing. What a workout."

George Rowe came limping around a rear corner of the soundstage and ambled over to his own trailer. He held a bloody napkin to his lower lip and glared at MacGuffin. Rowe disappeared into his trailer and slammed the door.

MacGuffin smirked. "You're welcome, Nigel."

Juno Calvecchio strolled over from his trailer and took a seat beside MacGuffin. He acted animated and energetic, a side effect from drinking one too many cappuccinos. He held a large Starbucks coffee cup in each hand: one for himself; one for "Rivers."

"Christian! It's really you!"

MacGuffin appeared unenthused. "Last I checked."

All MacGuffin needed right then was another annoying interruption, so he did his best to avoid eye contact with Juno.

"Nice to have you back, man! Sincerely!"

"It's nice to feel wanted."

"You wouldn't believe the hellish ordeal I went through with the police and FBI after you disappeared!"

"I can imagine."

"It was insane, man! I was interrogated by this nutcase detective and this no-nonsense FBI chick! They thought you and I were a couple of closet queens after they found the photos at the bungalow!"

MacGuffin feigned a look of mortification. "What a nightmare!"

Only then did Juno remember the second cup of coffee in his hands. "Oh, I brought you a cappuccino. Swiss Mocha, the way you like it."

"Thanks, eh. Don't mind if I do. It's been a long morning."

MacGuffin took the coffee cup from Juno and took a sip.

"You wanna come check out our play rehearsal tonight at the Geffen Playhouse once filming wraps for the night? It's the first time with the full cast."

"What play is that?"

"Christ, you got the memory of a goat! How many times I gotta tell you? It's called *The Desperate Hours*. Bogart and Newman were in the original production. I'm starring in it and directing. We've been hard at work on it for the last month. We open in two weeks."

MacGuffin shook his head. "I'm sorry, what day is it?"

"It's Tuesday."

MacGuffin pondered a quick moment. "*Tuesday*? Hmm? Sorry,

but I can't make it. I got a... I got a thing." A complete lie. "Later..."

Juno frowned. "Yeah, right, a *thing*? I've heard that before. What kind of *thing* would that be?"

"Look, man. I'm sorry, okay, but, unlike you, I do have an early call time tomorrow."

Juno shook his head. "That's funny, it's never stopped you before staying up all night; having a good time with your friends."

"Well, I'm...sorry to disappoint you...you..."

"Juno..."

"Right, sorry...Juno."

"What!? You got Alzheimer's or something?"

"No, I've...I've been doing a lot of soul-searching these past few days, and I've decided it's time to make some serious changes in my life. I need to be more grateful for things. No more reckless behavior. No more drinking. No more fast women. No more drugs."

"You're definitely not the Rivers I used to know. What kind of *drugs* were you on while you were away?"

MacGuffin sipped his coffee, expressionless. "Come what may, my friend. Come what may."

NUKE AND MURCH ENTERED the kitchen of Nuke's second-story apartment, at the back of Maltese Custom Choppers & Hot Rods. It was a shrine to true geekdom, as movie memorabilia and other celebrity-related swag consumed every nook and cranny of the flat.

"Wow, this is where you live?"

"Home sweet home. *Mi casa, su casa*. My crib. My junk museum."

It was almost too much for Murch to take in all at once. "This is incredible! A little messy, but *incredible*, nonetheless."

Nuke shrugged his head. "Again, I'm sorry, the maid quit on me."

They headed into the adjoining living room, which, in reality, was more of a small museum than a living space. Autographs, death certificates, newspapers, books, posters, comics, costumes, *etc.*, filled the room.

A framed handwritten note from famed former prosecuting attorney Vincent Bugliosi caught Murch's eye. "Where did you meet Vincent Bugliosi?"

"Back in Minnesota. Bugliosi is from a small mining town about a half-hour drive from where I grew up. Back in March of '94, Bugliosi gave a lecture about his life and career, what it was like prosecuting Charles Manson, that sort of thing. I attended the lecture and spoke to Bugliosi afterward. That's how I got this little memento. Pretty cool, eh?"

"Bugliosi is a legend. He's a god in the world of law."

Murch noticed a J.W. Gacy painting of the Seven Dwarves hanging nearby. "J.W. Gacy? As in John Wayne Gacy?"

"Don't ask."

"Fine, I won't. I don't think I want to know where you got this."

Murch perused the rest of the collection. She smiled. "It's a pretty impressive collection, Detective."

She noticed a map of Los Angeles County full of yellow place markers on the wall above a computer desk. "What's this map over here?"

Nuke approached her. "Oh, that. It's...something I cooked up late last night while coming down off our little drunken bender. It's a map of our tour today. It's the entire city of Los Angeles and its neighboring suburbs."

"Groovy."

Nuke pointed to the place markers and explained, "I plotted out several points of prime interest using these little yellow place markers: Marilyn Monroe...Ron Goldman and Nicole Brown Simpson...Phil Hartman...River Phoenix...the LaBiancas...Elizabeth Short..."

"The Black Dahlia?"

"That's correct."

Nuke went back to the map. "That, and as you can see, a lot more. Even John Belushi. Oh, yeah, I got a lot planned today."

Once the tour of the apartment ended, Nuke led Murch down the exterior staircase. As they descended, he pulled on a Black Rebels motorcycle jacket, black leather gloves, and a wool biker cap.

"What the Hell are you wearing, now?" asked Murch.

Nuke smiled. "Classic Marlon Brando as the original biker outlaw, Johnny Strabler. *The Wild One*; Columbia Pictures, 1953."

"You are so weird, Detective Bonaduce."

"Please, sweetheart, call me Nuke. Anyway, I suppose we should get cruisin' along on our little tour if we're to make all our stops."

Nuke stepped over to his backyard storage shed and pulled open the wooden double doors. Murch followed close behind.

He turned on the lights, revealing a collection of five custom choppers he kept inside.

"Take your pick, sweetheart."

As Murch glanced over the collection, she immediately took to the fifth bike and ran her left palm across its gas tank. "I like this one."

"Hell, yeah. That's the one I would've chosen myself."

"Looks dangerous."

"It's a replica of Steve McQueen's motorcycle from *The Great Escape*. It's a 1961 Triumph TR6 Trophy Bird disguised to look like a 1940's German BMW R75 motorcycle. The only thing *dangerous* about her is the gas mileage."

Murch walked around and checked out the attached sidecar. "Something tells me this isn't part of the original bike?"

"Nope. I knew you were coming today, so I added it especially for you. Thought it would make the ride a little less terrifying for you. More comfortable. This way you'll have some freedom to move. You won't have to cling on to me for dear life. At the first sign of impending doom, though, I'm pulling the lynchpin. You're on your own after that, darling."

Murch grinned. "Sounds so reassuring."

Nuke picked up and tossed her a helmet modeled after Peter Fonda's *Captain America* motorcycle helmet.

"What is this?"

"It's called a helmet, my dear. You know, for safety. Wouldn't want your brains splattered all over the pavement, now, would we?"

Nuke backed *The Great Escape* out of the shed and climbed aboard. He pulled on his pair of aviator sunglasses and offered Murch a helping hand as she climbed into the sidecar. Once strapped in, she pulled on her helmet.

Nuke kick-started the engine, and the bike roared to life. "Atomic batteries to power. Turbines to speed."

Murch smiled. "Purrs just like a kitten."

"You got that right, sister. This lady's a well-tuned machine."

He nudged the foot clutch and jockeyed the shifter into "DRIVE." He gunned the throttle. "All right, Chewie, let's see what this piece of junk can do."

The Great Escape peeled rubber down the street, leaving a plume of exhaust in its wake.

CHAPTER TWENTY-FOUR

THE CAST AND CREW of *Teenage Confidential* gathered around the Craft Services table inside Stage 28.

Nigel Guest popped the cork on a bottle of Cristal and addressed the congregation, "Ladies and gentlemen, with this toast of bubbly, I consider this a wrap on Juno Calvecchio!" He doused Juno with champagne.

Everyone grabbed a glass of champagne from the table and toasted Juno's impending departure. Everyone except McKenzie Banks.

John Crawford held up his glass and made a toast, "Juno...here's to a great job on this picture! And, here's hoping to see you on the next picture!"

Juno smiled. "Whatever *that* will be?"

As the crowd applauded Juno, MacGuffin grabbed a plate of cookies and cake and a can of soda and slipped away into the background.

At the opposite end of the soundstage, McKenzie Banks lounged on the Barton bathroom set, stark naked, in a bathtub of bloody water, listening to music through a pair of white, plastic earbuds. Her wrists appeared slashed with a little make-up trickery.

As McKenzie hummed along to a tune, MacGuffin entered the set, held up the plate, and offered her a snack, "Care for a chocolate chip cookie or a piece of carrot cake? They're fresh out of the Craft Service oven."

Although McKenzie lay naked and vulnerable in the tub, MacGuffin's presence didn't faze her. She smiled at him and removed her headphones. "Don't mind if I do. Thank you." She helped herself to a cookie.

"Bon appetit, Mon Amie."

MacGuffin helped himself to a cookie and put the plate down

on the lid of the nearby toilet bowl. He took a seat on the edge of the tub.

McKenzie continued to smile. "You sure do like to hang out at the Craft Services table when you're not working."

MacGuffin took a bite of his cookie. "What can I say? It's free food! Can't go wrong there. This is better than the shit in my fridge at home. I'm a Spaghettio's kind of guy. So, how come you're not out there toasting Juno's departure?"

"That last scene was draining. Whenever I do a weighty scene, I like to wind down by shutting myself off and listening to some uplifting music."

MacGuffin nodded. "I know the feeling." He paused. "You're not feeling miserable right now, are you?"

"Oh, no, I'm quite content with myself. Thank you."

MacGuffin smiled. "Well, you're welcome, McKenzie." He wolfed down the rest of his cookie and washed it down with a sip of soda.

"I don't mean to change the subject, but I'd like to congratulate you, Christian, for your great work in the last couple of scenes. I've always felt you couldn't act for shit or were phoning it in. Looks like I was wrong about you."

MacGuffin chuckled nervously and smiled. "This is the first time in a long while I've worked sober. It feels great. A few days R&R is all I needed, I guess."

"I guess, but you still need to work on losing your craving for junk food. You've got the mad munchies."

MacGuffin chuckled. "Speaking of *mad munchies*, it's almost dinner time. Would you like to get away from here for a while and join me for a walk to the commissary? We're not needed on set for another hour or so."

"Are you going to be the male chauvinist asshole you always are? Suppose you're going to ask me for a quickie in your trailer?"

"Why would I do that?"

"You're always trying to get into my pants, Christian. Not to mention all the other actresses you've ever worked with."

MacGuffin smirked. "Well...you do look good naked in a bathtub of bloody water, I must say. Not many people can pull off the look of a naked suicide victim, but you've pulled it off in spades."

"Can you give me about ten minutes to run back to my trailer to wash this blood off and put some clothes on?"

"No problem, McKenzie. Sounds like a plan."

A SHORT TIME LATER, MacGuffin and McKenzie walked around the studio backlot's canyon of soundstages, chatting about MacGuffin's ratty, olive-green cargo jacket which he now wore.

"I can't believe you're wearing a winter jacket on a ninety-five-degree summer day," said McKenzie. "You're gonna die of heatstroke."

MacGuffin chuckled. "It could be a hundred and forty in the shade, and I'd still be wearing this jacket. I love this thing. It's got deep pockets for all my shit."

They passed a black-and-yellow Rolls-Royce Phantom III sedan parked idling off to the side of the alley.

Inside, Grendel, Sebastian, and Igor watched MacGuffin and McKenzie's every move.

"What do you think, Grendel?" asked Sebastian. "Should we follow 'em and nab 'em for the Master?"

"Not yet. The Master's got something special planned for these two."

Juno Calvecchio drove by in his beat-up, blue two-tone 1975 Chevelle. He honked the horn, waved at MacGuffin and McKenzie, and kept on driving.

"What about him?" asked Sebastian. "He was with Rivers at the bungalow that morning. He knows too much. He talked to the police."

Grendel hesitated to answer. He turned to Igor in the driver's seat. "Igor, follow that Chevelle."

"Heh...as you wish, Master. Heh. Heh."

As MacGuffin and McKenzie walked down the alleyway between soundstages, the sedan drove by and followed Juno's Chevelle.

A tour tram appeared from around a corner up ahead, turned down the alley, and headed in MacGuffin and McKenzie's direction.

"Our ride has arrived," said MacGuffin. "You feel like signing a few autographs for the fans?"

"Sounds like fun."

They waved down the tram as it approached.

Realizing two celebrities were in their midst, the tram slowed as the young tour guide addressed her tour group, "Ladies and gentlemen, it appears two of Hollywood's biggest names have decided to bless us with their presence this evening."

MacGuffin hopped up onto the front of the tram car and pulled McKenzie aboard. He grabbed the tour guide's microphone and spoke into it, "Good afternoon, ladies and gentlemen, boys and girls! My name is Christian Rivers, and this lovely lady beside me is my co-star, McKenzie Banks."

McKenzie leaned over the microphone and greeted the tour group, "Hi, everybody!"

Everybody clapped and cheered. Some took snapshots.

MacGuffin continued, "I hope you're all doing groovy this fine evening? I know we are. We're taking a break from filming over on Stage 28. That said, we'd like to buy you all a round of milk and cookies at the studio commissary, to show you our gratitude for going to watch our movies and making them successful, which keeps us employed. Now, McKenzie would like to say something." He handed her the microphone.

She was all smiles. "Anybody want an autograph? We're taking offers!"

Everybody raised their hands.

McKenzie handed the microphone back to the tour guide and took a seat on the floor beside MacGuffin as the tram moved forward.

The fans swamped MacGuffin and McKenzie for autographs, and the two were more than happy to meet and chat with everyone.

CHAPTER TWENTY-FIVE

TUESDAY, AUGUST THE SIXTEENTH
SIX THIRTEEN PM

VITELLO'S ITALIAN RESTAURANT IS a popular dining spot in Studio City, where legions flock to see where, on the night of May 4th, 2001, actor Robert Blake and his wife, Bonnie Lee Bakley, shared their final meal together. It was also where Nuke Bonaduce treated his date, Haley Murch, to dinner, following their afternoon Hollywood Tragical History Tour.

Nuke and Murch sat at the "Robert Blake" table. He dined on the "Robert Blake" pasta dish, while she feasted on the "Bonnie Lee Bakley" Cheese Ravioli.

"The Cheese Ravioli was her last meal, eh?" asked Murch as she slid a forkful into her mouth and started chewing. "Gee, how special. I'm committing a crime against my veganism."

"Everyone's a sinner, sweetheart, at least once in a while."

"It is exquisite, though."

"Well, I'm glad you like it. Sure cost a small fortune."

"It wasn't that much, compared to other restaurants around here."

"No, but you wouldn't believe how difficult it was to get a reservation to sit at this table. I had to bribe the hostess with a c-note. It would've been cheaper to get the 'Sharon Tate' table at El Coyote's."

Murch wiped her mouth with her napkin, smiling half-heartedly. "Enough psycho-babble about dead celebrities and their murdering spouses. I want to hear about *you*. Tell me about Detective Christopher Bonaduce." She sipped her coffee.

Nuke grinned, sheepish.

Murch smiled, holding her coffee cup. "Aw, I've struck a nerve."

"What's there to say?"

"How did building choppers and hot rods come about?"

Nuke hesitated as he contemplated the complexities of his

personal universe. "Well...I was not a good student in school. I spent most of my time working on cars in the school auto shop or catching up on all the latest Hollywood blockbusters at any of the local movie theaters.

"My parents split when I was fourteen. My sister and I moved with our mother here to Long Beach around '76.

"When I was 26 or so, I started a four-year stint as an apprentice builder at Boyd Coddington's hot-rod shop over in Cypress. Once I gained enough experience, I started my own custom car and bike shop, The Maltese Speed Factory, out of Mom's garage in 1992.

"As business grew, we set up Maltese Custom Choppers & Hot Rods in a larger facility. It's quite successful. We're now working on setting up a merchandising branch."

"When did you become a homicide detective?"

"Well, I completed a two-year program in 1995 and became a part-time LAPD police officer that summer. Worked my way up through the ranks, and, in January 1997, I became a detective."

"Where'd the nickname come from?"

Nuke chuckled. "You mean, *Nuke*? A former captain started calling me that years ago on account of my explosive temper and repeated insubordination. Said I have a nuclear personality. Needless to say, the name kinda stuck."

"I take it you're not married?"

"Hell no. I'm a recovering alcoholic. Not something I'm proud of."

Murch shrugged. "I'm sorry. I'm making you uncomfortable."

"Don't be sorry. I'm an asshole...a pig. I wouldn't want to live with me, either."

"You're not an asshole. You're... unique."

"*Unique*, eh? Hmm? Why, thank you. That's the nicest compliment I've ever received. Usually, I'm accused of sexual harassment."

Murch smiled and sipped her coffee. "You're welcome."

"How 'bout you, Special Agent Haley Murch? Tell me about yourself. I've bared my soul to you."

"My story is nowhere near as exciting as yours, believe me."

"Where were you born? Who were your parents? Any brothers and sisters? Where did you go to school?"

"I was born and raised in Seattle, of all places. My parents were both teachers. I'm an only child, unfortunately. School was rather uneventful. I was a straight-A student. The Valedictorian of my class. I also excelled in sports. My favorite was hockey."

"You played hockey? No shit?"

"Yep. That's how I made my way through college, on a hockey scholarship."

"I figured it was either that or you worked as a stripper."

"Sorry to disappoint you, Detective, there are no stripper poles in my academic past. Only ice skates, pads, hockey sticks, and hockey pucks."

"Damn."

"I did a ten-year stint in college. I have a Ph.D. in Criminology and a Bachelor's in Psychology and Sociology. I'm employed as a member of the FBI's Behavioral Analysis Unit. And, no, I've never been married or have any children. My age is classified."

"Interesting."

"*Interesting*, eh? Hmm? This is definitely one of the most interesting dates I've ever been on."

"And, it's only gonna get more interesting, darling."

"Why? What's next on the agenda?"

"One of the greatest love stories ever told."

MACGUFFIN AND MCKENZIE TOOK a leisurely detour along the studio's backlot New York street façade as they walked back to Stage 28 for the rest of the night's filming. They each carried a vanilla-chocolate twist ice cream cone and a soda from the studio commissary.

"Nigel and my dad are gonna be mad about us being late," said McKenzie. "Every minute's costing the studio a lot of money."

MacGuffin smirked. "Eh, who gives a shit? They can take it out of my paycheck." He lapped up a glob of ice cream and washed it down with a sip of soda.

"I want to thank you for what you did back there for all those fans. That was sweet."

"Aw, don't mention it, *Mon Amie*. I'm giving a little of myself back to the community. The fans are the ones who pay to see the movies."

"You have no fears about making a complete fool out of

yourself. I've had a lot of fun with you tonight, Christian."

"I thought you could use a little cheering up. Lately, you've seemed distracted."

"You don't seem to be acting like your normal self these past couple of days. For once, you're acting...nice. Usually, you come off like a real dick; a person obsessed with fame; a spoiled brat who can get anything he wants. It's all about you; to Hell with everybody else. You've changed, Rivers. What's up with that?"

"I guess I've had a lot going through my mind, lately. And, it's not about working on this film."

CHAPTER TWENTY-SIX

TUESDAY, AUGUST THE SIXTEENTH
EIGHT FORTY-SIX PM

NUKE AND MURCH SAT in the back row of the infamous Silent Movie Theater on Fairfax Avenue. They joined a medium crowd of 60-70 people for a screening of director Hal Ashby's 1971 cult comedy classic, *Harold and Maude*. They each had a soda and shared a large tub of buttered popcorn.

WITH FILMING WRAPPED FOR the night, MacGuffin and McKenzie took a taxi to Lake Hollywood in the Hollywood Hills, where they stood at the edge of a lake walk and fed breadcrumbs to a family of ducks floating on the water below. The moon cast its silvery reflection across the wake.

"So, McKenzie, what was your childhood like?"

"Dysfunctional, to say the least."

MacGuffin chuckled. "Huh, same here."

"I never saw a nickel of the money I made as a child actor before the age of eighteen, as my mother squandered it all. I'm still on good terms with my father, though."

"Makes you wonder whatever happened to the Jackie Coogan Law?"

"I'm not bitter about my childhood, though. By not having any money, it kept me away from the party scene. No drinking and drugs for me. I'd say I came out pretty well-grounded."

"Well, that's good. I, on the other hand...well, you know how that turned out."

AT 9:46 PM, THE Silent Movie Theater's exterior doors opened, and a throng of movie patrons spilled out onto the sidewalk beneath the marquee following the 8:00 screening of *Harold and Maude*. A line of people stood behind a velvet rope for the 10:00 PM show.

Nuke and Murch ambled their way through the crowd to the

street curb and walked to *The Great Escape* parked a block away.

"I can't believe you've never seen *Harold and Maude!*" said Nuke. "It's only like the greatest movie ever!"

Murch smirked. "Yeah, I noticed you had an autographed poster on your apartment wall."

"Bud Cort and Ruth Gordon are friggin' awesome!"

Murch sighed, unimpressed. "Yes, they made such a nice couple despite their huge age difference."

"Too bad he had to forever become typecast as crazy after making this movie, and she had to up and die on us in '85. They were one of a kind."

A moment of silence followed.

"So, how come this is playing at the Silent Movie Theater when it's not a silent movie?" asked Murch.

"I don't think any theater that shows only silent films could survive in today's society. There just isn't much of a draw for that type of thing anymore. As Bob Dylan once crooned, 'The times they are a changing.' I'm thrilled to see they've expanded their film repertoire to include just about anything. See a show where a murder occurred. I would, I have, and I do."

Nuke sipped his soda through a straw.

Murch was curious. "Wait. What do you mean, 'see a show where a murder occurred?' What *murder?*"

"Seeing *Harold and Maude* wasn't the only reason I brought you here, Haley. No sir. This place holds a lot of sentimental value to me. This is still a part of our tour. I have things carefully planned out. The Silent Movie Theater was the site of my first official murder investigation as a homicide detective."

"What happened here? Who got murdered?"

"Well...it was the night of January 17th, 1997. The movie showing was the 1927 film *Sunshine*, and it seems the projectionist, a young man named James Van Sickle, was out to collect early on a $1 million inheritance from his male lover of seven years, the 74-year-old theater owner, Laurence Austen. Van Sickle was heavily in debt at the time and desperately needed the money. So, the idiot hires a nineteen-year-old hitman named Christian Rodriguez for $30,000 to kill Austen and candy counter girl Mary Giles and make it look like a robbery gone bad.

"Rodriguez managed to pump three shots into Austen with a .357, taking most of his head off in the process. Killed him instantly. Oh, yeah, it was a pretty gruesome scene to behold. Now...Mary Giles, on the other hand, she was lucky to survive being shot twice in the chest. And, based on her testimony, Rodriguez and Van Sickle were both found guilty in separate trials and sentenced to life in prison without the possibility of parole.

"Every year since, on the anniversary of the murder, January 17th, the theater screens the same murder-night shorts and *Sunrise* in tribute to its founder, Laurence Austen."

"Damn!" exclaimed Murch. "That does sound pretty gruesome. Hope our next stop isn't as terrible?"

Nuke smiled. "It's not that bad, I assure you. Sure, somebody died, but it's not terrible."

"Where's our next stop?"

"You'll see. I've saved the best for last. It wouldn't be Hollywood without it."

MACGUFFIN AND MCKENZIE TOOK the taxi to Wonderland Avenue in Laurel Canyon. He led her up a sidewalk to his ground-level apartment behind the townhouse. His Golden Retriever, Hitchcock, lay inside its doghouse and barked at its master's return.

"Quiet, Hitchcock," said MacGuffin. "I brought a friend home, boy. This is McKenzie."

McKenzie knelt and gave Hitchcock a friendly scratch behind the ears. He appeared quite enamored with her. "Yes." She smiled at him. "You like that, don't you, boy? Don't you?"

MacGuffin kept his eyes on them as he unlocked the door to his apartment. "I think he's made a new friend."

"He's cute."

MacGuffin held the door open for McKenzie. "After you."

"My, you're quite the gentleman."

McKenzie stepped inside and checked out the room, chuckling in amusement at the lackluster décor. "Well...it's...it's an apartment."

"I hope you weren't expecting the Taj Mahal?"

McKenzie smirked. "Actually, I kinda was."

MacGuffin sighed. "I know, I know. It...it ain't much to look at, but I call it home. I don't spend a whole lot of time here. Usually, when I'm working, I stay at the St. James Club or the Chateau Marmont or wherever the studio allows me to stay. I'm even banned from a few places due to some creative behavior."

"Would you care to elaborate?"

"Oh, you know...tossing TV's out the windows, or furniture, riding my motorcycle down the hallways, attacking the lobby Christmas tree for no apparent reason, passing out naked and drunk in the hallways, playing the bongo drums in my birthday suit..."

"Ah, yes, I've heard from Juno and several others on the crew about your fascination with the bongo drums."

"Oh, they totally rock!"

McKenzie chuckled. "Your apartment is fine. It's fine. It's...I find it unbelievable that a millionaire movie star would live in such a craphole apartment."

MacGuffin thought for a second, trying to come up with a suitable excuse for his living situation. "It helps me hide from the paparazzi."

He entered the apartment, followed by Hitchcock who scampered over to the bed mattress and plopped down in the corner for a nap.

MacGuffin shook his head and smirked. "I swear, Hitchcock, that's all you do around this place: sleep."

He turned to McKenzie. "Um...anyhow...uh...make yourself at home. Help yourself to the fridge. I hope you like Yoo-Hoo. That's all I ever eat."

McKenzie stepped over to MacGuffin's computer desk and found a movie script laying by a laptop. The cover read *REGISTER DOGS: A Screenplay by Richard MacGuffin and Maxwell Winston*. "What's this script by your computer here?"

MacGuffin felt trapped as he remembered his real name appeared on the script cover. He came up with a quick lie to cover his tracks. "*Register Dogs*: The story of a group of disgruntled ex-service workers who unite to strike back against their former masters of retail slavery. A couple friends of mine wrote that. You met them this morning outside my trailer."

"Oh, right, they did your make-up."

"Yes...yes, they did. Anyway, the script is an independent feature film project I'm thinking of financing. I'm working on a little script polish in my spare time to get it up to my standards. I might star in it as well as executive producing."

"Any female roles in it? I'm always looking for the next project."

"There are two female roles, as a matter of fact. I'll let the boys know you're interested and get you an updated copy of the script for you to look at."

"Thank you."

CHAPTER TWENTY-SEVEN

TUESDAY, AUGUST THE SIXTEENTH
TEN TWENTY PM

NUKE AND MURCH SAT on the steep, rough terrain beneath the 45-foot high letter "H" of the historic "HOLLYWOOD" sign, situated on the southern face of Mount Lee in Griffith Park, in the Hollywood Hills area of the Santa Monica Mountains. They stared awestruck at the miraculous view of the city and Lake Hollywood beyond.

"The view at night is stunning from up here," said Murch.

Nuke scoped out the red satin thong protruding from the back of her faux leather pants. "It sure is," he smiled. "I told you it wouldn't be Hollywood without the Hollywood sign."

"I'm surprised by the absence of any 'No Trespassing' signs, considering the authorities are so keen on keeping people away from the sign."

"There's a lot about this city that doesn't make a whole lot of sense to me, darling."

"Isn't this illegal?"

"Well, yeah...there's a security system with motion detectors and closed-circuit cameras all over the place, but I really don't care."

"Detective!"

"Hey, sometimes you gotta live on the edge, darling. If not, you're taking up too much space."

"What if the police show up?"

"What're they gonna do, arrest us? They can't do that. I'm a cop, and you're a fed. We'll say we're here investigating a possible suicide jumper. It's not the first time somebody's leaped to their death from the Hollywood sign. Do you know who Peg Entwistle was?"

"Not a clue."

"She was a real person, all right, but she's since become more of a metaphor for everybody who's ever flocked to this city with hopes of stardom in television or the movies; a symbol of the dark side of the Hollywood dream. The fact is few people who do make the journey ever make it in the industry. Most of them just go back where they came from, while others, like Peg Entwistle, stay and suffer the disillusionment."

"Who's she?"

"She was a New York stage actress, who, like many others before and after, came to Hollywood hoping to set her sights on the silver screen. Unfortunately, the call she was hoping for never came. And, then, one night in September 1932, she made a fateful trek from her uncle's home on Beachwood Drive to the Hollywood sign, once her beacon of hope and dreams but now a symbol of failure and rejection. At only twenty-four years of age, Miss Entwistle climbed fifty feet up a workman's ladder to the top of the letter 'H' and made the giant leap. She plunged to her death, forever to be dubbed 'The Hollywood Sign Girl.'"

"How sad."

"Ironically, her uncle received a letter addressed to her the following day from the Beverly Hills Playhouse, offering her the lead role in a play. And, get this, it was about a woman driven to suicide."

Nuke stood up and leaned against the base of the letter "H."

"Thank you, Detective," said Murch.

"For what?"

"Thank you...for the tour, I mean. It was a beautiful day. I had fun."

Nuke gasped. "You're welcome, Haley. Hope I didn't annoy the piss out of you with my vast knowledge of Hollywood filmdom? Most people would've bailed hours ago."

"It's not like that at all. I... I don't know a thing about movies. I've never had an interest. Movies have always...dare I say...bored me. I've always been more into sports; that kind of thing."

"So, why did you choose to tag along for the ride, then?"

"It was a tour of celebrity death sites. I like stories of crime and death. The forensic aspect of it all. To catch a killer. Catch a thief. It's what I yearn to do. The celebrity part means nothing to me."

"I love this town. It's the whackness of it all that does it for me."

"*Whackness?*"

"In life, and in death, everything in this town is done with a little extra dramatic flair to it; even by those who aren't celebrities. It's all one big show."

Nuke removed his cell phone.

"What are you doing?" asked Murch.

"Come over here and stand beside me. I want to take a picture to prove to the boys at work I was really here."

"I don't know..."

"Hurry up, will ya? Before the police show up."

Murch sighed. "Oh, all right." She got up and stood close beside Nuke. "I can't believe I'm doing this."

"Well, believe it, you are doing this."

Nuke raised his phone in front of him. "Say cheese."

Nuke and Murch looked into the camera and smiled, as Nuke snapped a picture of the two of them in front of the letter "H."

UP NORTH IN THE San Fernando Valley, Max Winston kept busy at his effect's studio, mixing up a large batch of dark brown sludge in a bucket. He dumped in a couple of tubs of Cool Whip and folded in some powdered hot chocolate mix. Behind him was a small buffet table, complete with *hors de oeuvres* and a large bowl of strawberry punch. There was also a blender filled with lime-flavored margarita mix.

The loading dock door at the back of the shop opened, and in walked MacGuffin and McKenzie Banks, still on their pseudo-date.

MacGuffin shouted, "Oh, Maxwell!"

Max looked up and stretched out his arms. "Mr. Rich...er...Mr. Rivers!"

MacGuffin appeared perturbed. "Hey, now. No name calling."

"Sorry, bro. A little Freudian slip there."

MacGuffin glared at Max and gave him a "What the Hell?" look. McKenzie chuckled.

Max shrugged his shoulders. "Sorry, man."

MacGuffin took a quick glance around the studio and smiled. "Max, you've outdone yourself. Are you throwing a party without inviting us?"

"Oh, putting together a little celebratory feast for the crew for a job well done. The picture wrapped tonight, and the last special effects are in the can."

Max put down his bucket of brown goo then smiled and

winked at McKenzie. "So, Mr. Rivers, are you not going to introduce me to your lovely friend this evening, or do I have to start smothering her with affection?"

"Oh, gee, I'm sorry. Max, allow me to introduce you to my young friend here: McKenzie Banks."

Max gave her a friendly kiss on the back of her hand. "Again, pleased to meet you, Miss Banks. I'm still a huge fan of your work. Welcome to Maximum F/X Studio. *Maximum* as in *Max*, my first name. We're a small business here struggling to stay afloat in this dog-eat-dog business of fierce competitors. Mostly, we work on grade-Z horror pictures. It's a fun gig, most of the time. Doesn't pay as much as you'd think, though. Sometimes, we're not paid at all. It's all part of the game."

McKenzie's eyes scanned around the studio and saw all kinds of strange props, most from the *Killer Cockroach* movie. "What movie are you working on, now?"

"A little piece of cinematic shit we're calling *Attack of the Killer Cockroach*. This punch bowl gag is from the movie's big finale which we shot all day today. The sequence takes place at the school prom. Seems the Cockroach is hiding out in the punch bowl. Some horny teenager gets his hot date a glass of punch, and the Cockroach pops up and starts biting him.

"Next, the school bully–this big, fat disgusting blob–grabs the Cockroach and throws him into the blender and turns him into a margarita."

"Fortunately for us," said MacGuffin, "Max has decided to boycott any further *Killer Cockroach* movies. Instead, he's moving on to greener pastures: He's doing the effects for *The Lethal Teenage Mutant Aardvark Strikes Back*. In this new sequel, the anthropomorphic aardvark in question finds out a movie is being made in Hollywood about his life. Problem is somebody forgot to pay him for the use of his likeness in the film. You can guess where the story goes from there."

Max sighed and shrugged. "The movie's going to be an absolute piece of shit, I'm sure. The only reason I'm doing it is to work beside the great Lloyd Hoffman. He's the man behind Trauma Pictures. Any effects expert in town would give his left nut to work with him. He's a legend. Now, if you two will excuse me, I need to go

126

to my room to get ready for the wrap party."

He walked over to a cage elevator which led upstairs to his studio apartment. Before he departed, he looked at McKenzie and asked, "Miss Banks, if it's no problem, can I get your phone number so I can ask you out sometime?"

"It would be my pleasure."

"Stay gold, Pony."

With the push of a button, the elevator sprang into action, and in a flash of light and a cloud of smoke, Max Winston disappeared upstairs.

MacGuffin smiled at McKenzie. "A nice guy, isn't he?"

McKenzie swooned. "Yes. Yes, he is."

CHAPTER TWENTY-EIGHT

TUESDAY, AUGUST THE SIXTEENTH
TEN FORTY-SEVEN PM

NUKE AND MURCH RODE *The Great Escape* into the parking lot of the Highland Gardens Hotel on Franklin Avenue and parked the bike in front of the sidewalk leading to the main entrance.

Minutes later, they walked down the first-floor hallway.

"Don't worry about your car," said Nuke. "I'll take you back down to Long Beach in the morning to retrieve it."

"Where are you going to spend the night?"

"It's all right. I'll crash over at Jimbo's. He's got an apartment in Silver Lake. There's plenty of room. I do it all the time."

"You don't need to do that, Detective. My hotel room is a double occupancy. It has two beds. You're more than welcome to spend the night."

"I wouldn't want to impose."

"It's no problem, really."

Murch stopped at room 105. "Here we are, the infamous death suite."

Nuke appeared excited. "I can't believe your superior at the Bureau set you up in the exact same hotel and in the exact same room where Janis Joplin overdosed on heroin and died in 1970."

Murch unlocked the door with her key card and turned the door handle. "I think Deputy Director Kimble was trying to impress me. He's kinda got a crush on me. He's never admitted it directly, but I sense a subtle tug of sexuality going on."

"Relax, I wasn't trying to scare you by revealing this hotel's sordid history to you. I'm sure even weirder things have happened here than someone dying from a heroin overdose."

"Huh? Name me one?"

As Murch entered the darkened room and flipped on the lights, Nuke followed like an obedient lapdog, pulling the door closed behind him.

Murch slammed Nuke up against the door, flung off his biker cap, and whipped off his leather jacket, all before he could comprehend what was going on.

"Uh...what are you doing?"

She peeled off his T-shirt. "Do you ever shut up?"

"Uh..."

She put a finger to his lips to silence him. "Shhh...surrender yourself to me." She unbuttoned his jeans and stripped him down to his black silk boxers.

"I thought this was forbidden?"

She looked deep into his eyes, seductively. "I know you've wanted this since the first time we met and... I guess I've wanted it as bad as you."

"But I thought you said...?"

She shushed him again with her finger. "It doesn't matter what I said before. That was then, and this is now."

"But—"

"Shut your trap, Detective, and take me. You make me so wet."

"Please, call me Nuke. What's so hard about that?"

She grabbed his crotch. "You are...rock hard."

He lost control and, tangling his fingers in her hair, he brought his mouth wildly into hers.

She sighed and pulled away. "I can't believe I'm doing this."

"Neither can I, sweetheart."

A few more kisses and she removed her red, faux-leather jacket and black dress shirt until only her red satin bra remained.

Staring at Murch's plump breasts, Nuke couldn't believe his eyes. "Nice rack."

She kissed him again, her tongue in his mouth, and his in hers.

"Guess that's what they call 'swapping spit?'"

"How about *swapping* something else?"

Nuke liked the sound of that idea.

A moment later, Murch cracked open the hotel room door and deposited a "Do Not Disturb" sign on the outside door handle. She pulled the door shut and locked it.

THE STREETS AND SIDEWALKS around the Geffen Playhouse on Le Conte Avenue in Westwood Village appeared sparsely populated.

That evening's play presentation of *The 39 Steps* had concluded, the theater cleared and closed for the night, as the marquee lights dimmed.

Plastering the back-exterior wall of the playhouse were posters and flyers for various upcoming stage productions and rock concerts, including a poster for the play *The Desperate Hours,* due to open in two weeks.

Juno Calvecchio exited the rear stage door, stepped into the alleyway, and started in the direction of Weyburn Avenue to the south where his car was parked.

His smoking-hot and openly gay Latino personal assistant, Blake Williams, chased after him, shouting, "Juno!"

Juno stopped and turned to face him. "Yes, Blake?"

Blake ran up to Juno, embraced him, and kissed him on the lips.

A few seconds later, their faces parted, and Blake asked, "What time are you gonna be back?"

"I shouldn't be long. I'm going home for some dinner and a quick shower. It's been a long day. 1:00 AM at the most."

"All right, see you then, Juno. If you need anything, give me a call on your cell. I'll be here with the rest of the troupe."

"Will do." Juno blew Blake a friendly kiss and smiled seductively. "See you later."

As Blake waved goodbye and walked back to the stage door, Juno disappeared around the southwest corner of the building.

Weyburn Avenue, at the south end of the playhouse, was quiet as Juno made his way to his blue Chevelle parked along the curb.

As he unlocked the driver's door and was about to climb inside, a beautiful, young brunette approached, waving a black-and-white agency photo of him.

"Excuse me, Mr. Calvecchio?" she asked in a squeaky, prepubescent voice.

"Ack, you scared me!"

"Sorry to bother you. Can I trouble you for an autograph?" She handed him the photograph and a silver paint marker.

"With pleasure," said Juno, smiling rather ungraciously. "Anything for my adoring fans."

Juno sat down in the driver's seat of his car and signed his signature at the bottom of the photo. As he wrote, he remarked, "The play doesn't open for another two weeks, but already you're lining up outside the theater like some die-hard *Star Wars* fan. You know, you people really need to get a life. I'm not famous. I'm nobody."

She smiled. "You're not a *nobody*. You've been nominated for two Saturn Awards."

"*Nominated*, yes; *won*, no." He glanced back at the photograph and asked, "What's your name, darling?"

"Caroline."

"Sweet name, just like in the Neil Diamond song."

Juno went on to scribble the message, *Sweet Caroline–Good Times Never Seemed So Good–Juno Calvecchio*, and handed the photo and marker back to Caroline. "Enjoy!" he told her; a bit more gracious this time.

"Indeed, I will."

She grinned and watched as Juno climbed into his car and sped away with a squeal of his tires.

MACGUFFIN AND MCKENZIE WALKED up the sidewalk, deep in discussion, to the main entrance of McKenzie's apartment building: an old, white, four-story at 650 N. Detroit Street, off Wilshire Boulevard.

"Your mother was an actress, eh?" asked MacGuffin.

"Yes," said McKenzie. "Her name was Victoria West."

MacGuffin shook his head and shrugged. "Sorry, I can't say I'm familiar with her."

"You probably aren't. She stopped acting when she became pregnant with me and didn't work again for another ten years afterward. She gave up her career to raise me."

"Does she still act? Anything I may have seen?"

McKenzie sighed. "No... she...she passed away."

"I'm sorry."

"It's all right. I got over it years ago."

They arrived at the building's main entrance, with a door that resembled a castle's drawbridge, and McKenzie unlocked the door for them to enter.

"This is cool," remarked MacGuffin about the doorway. "It's almost like a castle."

"It's one of the things that attracted me here."

131

She pulled the glass entrance door open, and the two of them entered a small mudroom housing mailboxes for the residents. She led MacGuffin through another entry into the first-floor foyer.

"Which apartment's yours?" asked MacGuffin.

"I'm up on the second floor—number 202."

They went up a flight of green-carpeted stairs and stopped before the first door on the left.

"How long have you lived here?"

"Um, a little over a year and a half. I moved in sometime in January of last year." She unlocked the door and led MacGuffin inside. "Make yourself at home."

The place was spacious, a double occupancy, and sparsely furnished with beanbag chairs, movie and television ad clippings featuring McKenzie, fashion magazines, and nude body paintings on the walls.

MacGuffin took one look around and couldn't help but crack a smile. "Interesting apartment. Who does your decorating?"

"My roommate, Perrey Maran. She's a model, an artist, *and* an actress. She has some wild tastes."

"Are you expecting her to return anytime soon? I thought maybe we could talk a while longer."

"I believe she's in New York for some big fashion show. We have the place all to ourselves."

SOME THIRTEEN MINUTES AFTER leaving the Geffen Playhouse in nearby Westwood Village, Juno Calvecchio's blue Chevelle turned west off Alta Loma Road, drove down the broad, dark alleyway behind the Hollyview Manor complex on Holloway Drive, and pulled into a one-stall carport beneath his two-story apartment building.

The car's engine sputtered and died, and the head- and taillights faded, followed a moment later by Juno climbing out of the driver's seat. He shut and locked the car door, set the car alarm, and exited the garage, humming Piero Umiliani's popular 1968 song "Mah Na Mah Na" to himself as he went.

Once outside, he pressed the button on his garage door opener, and the garage door closed behind him.

CHAPTER TWENTY-NINE

WEDNESDAY, AUGUST THE SEVENTEENTH
TWELVE FORTY-FIVE AM

NUKE AND MURCH ARRIVED at the Hollyview Manor on Holloway Drive. A police barricade cordoned off a three-block radius; yellow crime scene tape was everywhere. Police, Fire, and Rescue specialists and crime scene investigators scattered about doing their various jobs.

The sidewalk between carports R6 of Juno Calvecchio's apartment building and R7 of the adjacent apartment building to the east was now the scene of Juno's brutal murder. His body, covered in a blood-soaked white sheet, lay face-up on an incline of driveway, in a pool of blood trailing ten feet to a nearby sewer drain. Beside the body was a package of cupcakes and a clipboard with play rehearsal notes. A pair of eyeglasses sat near Juno's feet.

Nuke and Murch knelt beside Juno's body and listened intently to Captain Dreyfus and Hayes and Lincoln's assessment of the situation, while two eyewitnesses stood waiting nearby.

"Now, according to our two witnesses here, the deceased returned home at approximately 11:40 PM," stated Dreyfus, consulting his steno pad. "Apparently, he had been rehearsing a play at the Geffen Playhouse due to open in a couple of weeks."

Nuke lifted the white sheet with his rubber-gloved left hand to reveal Juno Calvecchio's exposed upper torso, a single knife wound to the middle of his chest. A team of paramedics had turned his body over onto his back and cut away his shirt and jacket to attempt resuscitation.

Nuke closed the deceased's eyelids. "What a waste." He shook his head in disgust.

Two paramedics from Fire Rescue Unit 7 walked over and placed Juno's corpse into a black plastic body bag and loaded it into the back of a waiting ambulance for a quick trip to the L.A. County Coroner's office.

Hayes continued the crime scene assessment for Nuke and Murch, picking up where Dreyfus left off, "The deceased parked his car in the private carport behind us and was heading to his first-floor apartment when he confronted a man wielding a large knife."

Eyewitness Raymond Erickson stepped forward to tell them what he heard. "I was walking my dog about a block away when I heard a young man screaming, 'Help! Help! Oh, my God!' I could see everything clear as day because the streetlights were on. I heard the man scream, and then I saw him collapse to the ground and a man running east from the scene toward Alta Loma Road."

The other eyewitness, Nancy Mitchell, added, "I also heard the victim screaming, but I didn't see anything because I was upstairs."

Erickson continued, "When I saw the man collapse, I rushed right over and tried giving him mouth-to-mouth. The color in his face was fading fast. The blood was pouring from his chest. I was joined by several bystanders. It didn't matter what we did, the stab wound to the heart was fatal. After five or six minutes of gasping, Mr. Calvecchio drew one final breath and slipped away."

"What about a possible motive?" asked Murch. "Was it a mugging or robbery?"

"You can rule out robbery, Agent Murch," said Dreyfus. "We found his wallet on him, twenty-one dollars in his left jacket pocket, some change in his left pants pocket, and eighty-five cents on the ground under the body. He also had a gold pocket watch on a chain in his pocket and a gold ring on his left index finger."

"What about drugs?"

"Nope," said Lincoln. "No drugs were found on him, in his car, or his apartment."

"Then, what is the possible motive?"

"The Sheriff's department is guessing it was gay-related; perhaps a hate crime. They found several restaurant receipts on him and two cards with names of different males and phone numbers on them. They also found gay porn in the apartment: magazines, sex manuals beside the bed, a leather vest and pants in the closet, a load of candles. The victim also shaved his chest hair."

"How do they figure this to be a 'gay thing' and not Hollywood Spectre-related?" asked Nuke.

The group dispersed, leaving Nuke and Murch standing around

with the two witnesses.

Nuke looked at Murch. "I don't buy it, Haley. Juno Calvecchio may have been gay or even bisexual, but that's not what got him killed."

"Who knows? It could be a case of him being in the wrong place at the wrong time."

Nuke turned to Mr. Erickson and asked, "Sir, you said you saw a man running from the scene. How good a look did you get of him? Could you describe him?"

"I got a real good look at him. As he was running away, he looked directly at me and cackled maniacally. My presence didn't seem to faze him any." Erickson thought to himself for a moment and added, "He was a tall, middle-aged man, stooped over, wearing a thick black overcoat, a black top hat, and carrying a fancy cane with a silver handle. And, the one thing I remember most vividly was his face. He was ghoulish with a pasty-white complexion and long, silvery hair. Exactly like Lon Chaney in *London After Midnight*."

Nuke nodded his head in acknowledgment. "I know exactly what you mean, Mr. Erickson. I have the movie poster back at my apartment."

Jimbo ran over carrying three plastic evidence bags containing pieces of a prosthetic mask, a silver wig, and shreds of an agency photo of Juno Calvecchio. Winded, he said to Nuke and Murch, "I think I may have found something."

"What you got, Jimbo?" asked Murch.

"Pieces of a mask, wig, and photographs. Found 'em in a dumpster about two blocks away."

Murch took a look at the new evidence and stated, "This could provide a possible link between tonight and the Cielo case."

"How can you be so sure?" asked Nuke. "There isn't one of those so-called calling cards anywhere in sight."

"We'll have to take these back to the lab for closer inspection. I don't know; maybe we can find some DNA evidence from the prosthetics."

LATER THAT EARLY MORNING, Swan entered his private trophy room and approached the wall of red-velvet curtains. He pressed the button on the wall-mounted control panel, which opened the curtains and unveiled a cubical Plexiglas cell, where inside lay a sleeping Christian Rivers, still encased in his cloth bandages. Swan tapped on the glass and screeched, "Wakey, wakey, Mr. Rivers. It's time for some entertainment."

Rivers stirred.

Swan removed a bloody photo of Juno Calvecchio from under his coat and slapped it up against the glass for Rivers to see. "Consider yourself one of the lucky ones, Mr. Rivers. You're still alive..." He pointed to Juno's photo. "...unlike your little friend here."

Rivers stared wearily at the photo and shrieked angrily, his voice raspy, "Juno! What did you do to him?"

Swan took great pleasure in the moment, cackling maniacally. "I put a knife through his heart until he stopped kicking. My boys even filmed it for my viewing enjoyment. It was all so amusing to watch. He squealed like a little girl as he begged for his life. 'No! Don't kill me! I'm too young to die!' How pathetic."

Rivers sprang to his feet and lunged toward Swan, his fingers ready to rip into Swan's fire-scarred flesh. "I'M GOING TO KILL YOU, YOU SICK SON OF A BITCH!" he shouted, right before smacking into the glass so hard he nearly knocked himself out cold.

Swan chuckled. "Try all you want, Mr. Rivers. There's no escape."

Bruised, Rivers stepped back and took a seat on the floor; his legs bent before him. "You bastard!"

"Sticks and stones may break my bones..." Swan pulled out a folded copy of the August 16th edition of the *Daily Variety*. "If you think the murder of your friend here was bad, Mr. Rivers, wait till you see this next item I have for you. You're gonna *love* it. You'll *really* want to rip somebody's throat out after seeing this."

He unfolded the newspaper to the front page, which prominently featured a color photo of MacGuffin in make-up as the faux Rivers, alongside John Crawford and Nigel Guest, outside the Haze Films office building, beside an accompanying press article, and held it up against the glass for Rivers to see. "Recognize the person in the photo?"

Stunned, Rivers once again approached Swan, albeit this time calmer, and pondered his presence in the photo, "How can I...?"

Swan finished his prisoner's sentence, "You mean, how can *you* be in two places at the same time? Gee, Mr. Rivers, I don't know. I'm as perplexed as you. But it does appear that you have a clone."

"Is this part of your master plan, Swan: replacing me with a look-alike as you did my two bodyguards to kidnap me?"

"I wish this were my idea, but no. I planned to eliminate you, period, but now someone has the audacity to pull off this little stunt to complete your last movie. It makes more work for me. Instead of one Rivers, I now have two to dispose of."

"And, how do you plan on getting rid of this other me?"

"Not sure yet, but I'll think of something."

Rivers sneered menacingly. "Here's an idea: Let me out of here so I can kill the bastard myself!"

CHAPTER THIRTY

WEDNESDAY, AUGUST THE SEVENTEENTH
EIGHT THIRTEEN AM

THE CRIME SCENE INVESTIGATION into Juno Calvecchio's murder lasted long into the wee hours of Wednesday morning. Nuke and Murch took off around 3:00 AM to Nuke's apartment in Long Beach for a few hours sleep before returning in separate vehicles to the West Los Angeles Community Police Station at 8:00 AM for a debriefing.

Nuke, Murch, Jimbo, Lincoln, and Hayes sat around the conference room table, discussing the re-opened Hollywood Spectre case. Case notes appeared on a flat panel monitor on the front wall.

Murch placed a reconstructed agency photo of Juno Calvecchio down on the table before Nuke. Instead of a bloody pentagram over Juno's face, the picture itself was slashed in the shape of a star. "You Detectives were looking for a calling card to connect Juno Calvecchio's murder to the Hollywood Spectre killings? Well, here it is."

"Yes, but for what reason was Juno targeted?" asked Nuke. "He may have been a witness to Christian Rivers' alleged abduction from the Chateau Marmont last week, but we all know that ordeal turned out to be a hoax to help garner publicity for the release of Rivers' upcoming movie. Rivers was never involved in the Hollywood Spectre case. So, to claim Juno Calvecchio was murdered by the Hollywood Spectre makes absolutely no sense."

As they talked, Jimbo sat by himself at the far end of the table, deleting old files and photographs from his personal laptop. He opened a file of notes, deemed them worthless, and dragged the file to the computer's recycle bin.

To Jimbo's right and down a ways sat Hayes and Lincoln, directly across from Nuke and Murch.

Hayes cleared his throat. "Um...Agent Murch, you said before one of the Hollywood Spectre's earliest victims was a celebrity?"

Murch nodded. "I believe you're referring to actress Normandy

Pike?"

"Yes, that's the one. Now...besides the latest victim, Mr. Calvecchio, as well as Normandy Pike, who were the Hollywood Spectre's other victims? Were they also celebrities?"

"Sure, most of them, if not all. Why?"

"Celebrity is all about vanity. It means everything to their careers."

"What are you getting at, Hayes?"

"All this information Haley's revealed to us about the Hollywood Spectre: his choice of wardrobe, his use of make-up and masks—it reminds me of someone trained in the theatre."

"Again, what are you getting at, Billy?" asked Lincoln.

"I'm saying, maybe the Hollywood Spectre himself is a former celebrity: a film or stage actor?"

"It's highly possible," nodded Murch. "It's actually an angle I never even considered when researching my thesis."

Jimbo flipped through a slideshow of crime scene photos from the Christian Rivers case on his laptop: pictures from Rivers' Chateau Marmont bungalow and the black limousine at Paradise Pictures. He flipped past photos of the limo's rear compartment, the front and rear license plates with blue sticker residuals, and a picture of Rivers with John Crawford and Nigel Guest outside of Crawford's Mercedes at the Haze Films Productions office. Baffled, Jimbo muttered to himself, "When did I take..." He noticed something strange about Rivers' eyes: One was blue, while the other was brown. "That's funny."

The conversation about the Hollywood Spectre continued down the table, as Hayes requested, "Agent Murch, can you provide us a complete list of victims so we can try to find a link between them?"

"I think there's one in the FBI dossier back in my hotel room. I'll email you all a copy."

"As soon as possible would be nice."

Jimbo pulled up a video of the "Christian Rivers Returns" press release and scanned through it. Once again, Rivers had one blue eye and one brown eye. "Boo-yah!"

Murch concluded her reply to Hayes, "I'll have it to you by tonight, Billy."

"Thanks."

Jimbo stared excited at his laptop's screen and shouted out,

"Hey, guys, I might have something here!"

Nuke rolled his eyes and groaned. "I'm not interested in seeing naked pictures of your mother, Jimbo, unless, of course, she's smoking hot."

"No... that's not it. It's something way better."

Undeterred, Jimbo connected his computer's flash drive to the laptop atop the podium. With a couple swift keystrokes, the files from the flash drive broadcast over the television for everybody to see. He clicked on both the photo of Rivers and the video, so they appeared side-by-side on the screen.

"What are we looking at, Jimbo?" asked Nuke.

"On the left side of the TV screen, you'll see a photograph of Christian Rivers taken during our visit to Paradise Pictures the other day. To the right is a video of the studio's press release announcing Rivers' return from the same day." Jimbo used a laser pointer to highlight Rivers' eyes in the on-screen photograph. "Now, do any of you notice anything unusual about Rivers' eyes in this photograph?"

The four all noticed the problem right away.

"He has two different colored eyes," stated Nuke.

Jimbo smiled. "He has two different colored eyes in the video, too."

Lincoln shook his head in confusion. "So, maybe he's wearing contact lenses for his movie role, and one just happened to fall out?"

"I don't think so," said Jimbo. "I saw a promo for Rivers' latest movie on a billboard back at the studio, and Rivers had brown eyes, his natural eye color. Also, while investigating his alleged disappearance, I read somewhere he doesn't wear contacts and never has. Nor does he wear glasses of any kind, as his vision is perfect."

"So, what exactly are you implying, Jimbo?" asked Hayes.

"I'm saying the Christian Rivers who supposedly reappeared after being missing for five days, presumably at the hands of the Hollywood Spectre, is not, in fact, the real Christian Rivers but an impostor."

Nuke nodded. "Makes sense, considering everything that's been going on."

"If he's an impostor, he's got one Hell of a good make-up job," said Lincoln.

Hayes shook his head and grinned. "Oh, please! Any make-up

artist in town could make somebody look like that. Remember, this *is* Hollywood."

"Yeah, but how do we prove he's an impostor?" asked Lincoln. "We can't just walk up to him and rip his damn face off."

"Why not?" asked Nuke. "That's what I would do. It would be the simplest answer. Occam's Razor."

"Right, Nuke, but not a logical solution," said Jimbo. "I mean, what if, just what if, he *is* the real Rivers? He could hang us all on an assault charge."

"So, what do we do, then?" asked Hayes.

Murch chimed in, "We conduct a Biometrics analysis using this photograph and the press video. No two people, save for identical twins, have the same facial skeletal structure."

"And, Christian Rivers doesn't have an identical twin," added Jimbo. "He's an only child."

"*And*, how do you propose we conduct such an analysis, Agent Murch?" asked Hayes. "We don't have the fancy equipment to do so like they have on *C.S.I.*?"

"I have a friend back at Quantico, Dr. Del Fuller, who specializes in Biometrics. It's an area of study that comprises unique methods for recognizing humans based upon one or more intrinsic physical or behavioral traits. No two humans are completely identical. Fingerprints, face recognition, DNA, hand and palm geometry, and iris recognition, for example."

"Get in touch with him, Haley," declared Nuke. "We need his help on this ASAP."

CHAPTER THIRTY-ONE

"RIVERS" SAT AT A student's desk on a high school English classroom set inside Stage 28, studying a scene from the script, as a flock of crew members prepped for the next scene.

John Crawford and Nigel Guest rode up to the west door of the soundstage on a golf cart, drove right on in, and approached MacGuffin on set.

Crawford shouted to the crew, "Gentlemen, will you please excuse us for a few minutes while Nigel and I have a chat with Mr. Rivers?"

The crew members stopped working and filtered off the set.

"Thank you!" shouted Crawford after them.

Crawford and Nigel walked over to MacGuffin at the desk and took seats atop two neighboring desks.

"Mr. MacGuffin," greeted Nigel, "how in the bloody Hell are you doing this morning?"

"Fine and dandy, Nigel. Cramming for the next scene."

Nigel smiled.

"Eh, don't worry about it," said Crawford. "I'm sure you'll do great."

Nigel remarked, "Your work the last couple days has been sensational. We viewed some of the dailies this morning and even a rough edit of the bathtub scene, including footage of both the real Rivers and you, and I must say, the two performances are quite seamless."

"I also appreciate how few takes your scenes have required," added Crawford. "You're saving us a ton of money."

"At the rate we're going," said Nigel, "we might finish a few days ahead of schedule and under budget."

"So, I encourage you, Mr. MacGuffin, keep up the good work," stated Crawford.

"Not sure how much help I'll be today," said MacGuffin. "It's my first big classroom scene. I'm gonna be dealing with a lot of teenage extras, most of them starstruck girls yearning to rip my...nay, Rivers'...clothes off."

"Heh. The price of fame, my boy, the price of fame."

Crawford sat down in the desk to MacGuffin's left and slid over closer. "First thing's first, Mr. MacGuffin. I'd like to personally thank you for taking my daughter out last night. It's not something she does a lot these days. She's been a bit reclusive ever since her mother died."

MacGuffin shrugged. "It was no problem, really."

"I'm amazed she even agreed to go out with you. She and Rivers hated each other infamously."

"Probably has something to do with all the booze and drugs he did. His trailer is stocked full of it."

Crawford smirked. "Um...there was a little more to it than that, trust me. Oh, yeah, McKenzie hated Rivers. He was a no-good son of a bitch with a capital S.O.B."

"What else are you here to tell me, Mr. Crawford?"

"We were wondering if you were planning to attend Juno's memorial service on Friday. Everybody's gonna be there."

"I'll have to check my schedule, but I don't see why not."

"It's a shame what happened to him," added Nigel. "I'm almost certain he would have been nominated for an Academy Award for his performance. I'm just glad we got his role in the can before he died. It woulda been a trick to finish his scenes without him."

MacGuffin smirked. "Well...you could've let me play him, too?"

Nigel laughed. "Right!"

Crawford pulled out a thick manila envelope and slapped it down on the edge of his desk. MacGuffin eyed the envelope with curiosity. "What's that?"

"Now, when Nigel and I said we were both really pleased with your work on the picture, Mr. MacGuffin, we meant what we said, sincerely."

"And," said Nigel, "because you're speeding things along so nicely and saving us a chunk of dough..."

"...We've decided to cook the accounting books a little and give the left-over money to you," concluded Crawford.

MacGuffin looked puzzled. "But, at the beginning you said..."

"I know what we said," stated Crawford. "I guess we lied." He handed MacGuffin the envelope. "Your payment, Mr. MacGuffin, for services rendered."

"How much is in here?"

"To be honest, we're not really sure," said Nigel. "We just happened to stumble across a couple loose stacks of cash lying around the office."

"He's kidding," chuckled Crawford. "Both he and I each pitched in $20,000 out of our own pockets."

MacGuffin ripped off a sealed corner of the envelope and took a peek inside. "$40,000? Are you serious?"

"Serious as a heart attack, Mr. MacGuffin," replied Nigel.

"I know, forty grand doesn't sound like much," remarked Crawford. "It's small beans compared to Rivers' $20 million-per-picture deal, but at least it's something for your trouble. Be thankful you can go home at the end of the day and not have to deal with all the shit being a celebrity of Rivers' caliber brings. You can be yourself."

"Also," said Nigel, "if we do agree to hire you for the next picture–and I'm betting we will–I guarantee you'll be pulling down a much heftier sum than you are on this picture."

"Even in the event the next movie doesn't get made," added Crawford, "if a contract has been signed, the studio must still fork over the dough."

"You're talking about a Pay-or-Play deal, right?" asked MacGuffin.

"Precisely," replied Crawford. "It can be a pretty sweet deal if it does happen." He removed a movie script from his suit coat and handed it to MacGuffin.

"What's this?"

"The script for the next movie, *Texas Ace Arcana and the Sons of Darkness*. In this new sequel, Texas Ace goes searching for Noah's Ark, meets the son he never knew he had, and uncovers a Nazi plot to resurrect Adolf Hitler. Now, as for you, Mr. MacGuffin, we want you to appear again as Rivers in the title role."

"Inside the script, you'll find a copy of your contract," said Nigel. "Read it over carefully, and make a decision. Production begins in January. It's going to be an awesome time, I assure you."

MacGuffin shook Crawford's hand. "Sweet! Er...I mean, thank you."

"It's our pleasure."

"Thank you, both."

MacGuffin next shook Nigel's hand.

"No..." said Nigel, "...thank you, Mr. MacGuffin, for helping us finish our picture. We couldn't have done it without you."

MacGuffin chuckled. "Christ, I feel like I should give an acceptance speech. 'Yes, I'd like to thank the Academy...'"

Crawford got up from his desk and said to MacGuffin, "Don't spend the money all in one place, now."

MacGuffin pocketed the envelope. "Thanks, I'll try not to."

As Crawford and Nigel were about to leave, Crawford added, "Oh...one last thing, Mr. MacGuffin. The big premiere for Rivers' latest blockbuster is being held next Tuesday night at the Rialto Theatre in South Pasadena. The film cost the studio a fortune..."

"$250 million," said Nigel.

Crawford continued, "So, we expect to see you on the red carpet as Christian Rivers."

"What's the movie called?"

"*Texas Ace Arcana and the Lost City of Atlantis*," said Nigel.

"What do you do at a premiere?"

Crawford started to explain, "Well...you arrive in a limo right in front of everybody: the fans, the paparazzi–"

Nigel interrupted, smiling, "With a smoking-hot actress or model on each arm."

Crawford continued, "You walk the red carpet, mingle amongst the crowd, sign a few autographs, take a few pictures, do a bunch of interviews–"

Again, Nigel interrupted, "You enter the theater, say something flashy to the audience before the picture rolls, you take a seat in the back, watch a few previews..."

"We're premiering a teaser trailer for *Teenage Confidential* at the premiere to whet the fans' appetite for a Christmas release," stated Crawford. "Also, a Christmas release means the movie will be eligible for awards season."

Nigel concluded, "Once the previews end, the lights will dim, and then you walk out the back door and go home."

"Wait," said MacGuffin, "we don't get to watch the movie?"

Nigel shook his head. "Well, err...I suppose you could if you want, but that's not normally how it's done."

"So, Mr. MacGuffin, can we count on you to be at the premiere next Tuesday night?" asked Crawford.

"I don't know. Is there any money in it for me?"

Crawford and Nigel each had a good laugh.

Nigel lit up one of his signature Cuban cigars and shook MacGuffin's hand. "Now you're getting the hang of it."

CHAPTER THIRTY-TWO

MURCH STRODE TO HER Mustang in the parking lot of the West Los Angeles Community Police Station. She leaned against the trunk and removed her cell phone from her coat pocket. As she dialed a number and waited for someone to answer, she looked over at the cars driving past the station. "Pick up the damn phone, Fuller! Anytime would be nice..."

The time on the east coast was 1:37 PM, as Dr. Del Fuller's cell phone rang four times before he answered it. "You better be a fickle broad, or I'm hanging up," he joked.

Murch's voice answered back, "Del?"

Fuller sat at a patio table outside his favorite small-town diner, Alice's Restaurant, on the main street of Plainfield, Virginia, fifteen miles south of Quantico. He wore his usual white dress shirt, black tie, and black dress pants. His black suit coat rested on the backrest of the white plastic patio chair to his left. In front of him on the table sat a human skull partially covered in glued-on pencil erasers. "Well, well, if it isn't a blast from the past–my most favorite student."

"Hope I didn't catch you at an awkward moment?"

"Nonsense. I'm having my usual grilled cheese and Cherry Coke at Alice's Restaurant and scaring off some of the local patrons with one of my pet skulls. You know, nothing to write home about."

Murch chuckled.

"So... Haley...how may I service your good looks and generosity this fine afternoon? May I interest you in a Voight-Kampff iris scan to verify how emotionally in love you are with my vast intellect of the forensic universe?"

Murch smiled. "Perhaps later, when I'm back at the Academy."

"Where are you hiding?"

"Los Angeles."

"Ah, yes, the City of Angels. I've heard of it. Been there many a time myself. What are you doing way out there? Shouldn't you be working on a case with the BAU or training how to thwart a bank robbery in progress at Hogan's Alley or something?"

"Not today. Deputy Director Kimble has me operating as a special liaison with the LAPD on a murder investigation. Speaking of which, I have a special favor to ask of you."

"A *special favor*, eh?" groaned Fuller. "Haley, Haley...you know how the Bureau frowns upon intimate relations between agents and members of the Academy faculty. A sex scandal just wouldn't look good on my resume."

"Ha, ha, I forgot you were so funny, Fuller."

"I know, I'm a regular stand-up comedian."

"Look," said Murch, "I'm not calling to ask permission to jump into bed with you, Fuller. I'm calling because I need you to run an analysis for me."

"You got my attention, Haley. Whatcha need?"

"If I emailed you a photograph and video clip of a celebrity who's a person-of-interest in our investigation, how long would it take to run it through facial recognition?"

"All depends on the quality of the source material. A sharper image would produce a faster result. Otherwise, I'll have to outsource the documents to the math geeks at MIT or Caltech and have them create a special algorithm to enhance and sharpen the materials. That could take days."

"I'll say scratch the video clip. It's not Hi-Def. It's highly pixilated. The picture is good, though."

"Eh, send me everything you have, anyway. We could get lucky. I'll run a check with the National DMV database. That ought to give us a name and a picture ID. Email the documents to my office in about an hour. I should be done with lunch by then."

"Quit dicking around, Fuller, I need those results ASAP!"

Fuller pondered Murch's offer. "A celebrity, eh? Hmm? God, how I hate those people and their inflated egos. Spoiled rich bastards. I wouldn't mind having one of their bank accounts, though. Money never sleeps."

Murch sighed. "Well, I don't think the celebrity in question is, in fact, a real star at all, but rather an impersonator."

"You mean a person wearing prosthetic make-up?"

"You read my mind."

"Ooh, sounds like a challenge."

"As is the investigation we're conducting. Our killer has eluded capture for nearly thirty years."

"And, you think this pseudo-celebrity is somehow involved?"

"It's a distinct possibility."

"In my field of expertise, Haley, I'd call your suspect a red herring."

"Maybe he is, maybe he isn't."

"Oh, *he* is."

"Look, can you help me out or not?"

"I'll try my best, Haley, but I ain't a miracle worker. I'm a busy man."

"You're the best person in the field, Del. You're the only person I know I can trust."

"I know. I know. And, I'll make an exception in your case because thinking about your raven-colored hair makes me all hot-and-bothered."

"God, you're disgusting."

"I know I'm the king of the friggin' world in your eyes, and I ain't afraid to admit it. Give me a day or so to work my magic. See what I can come up with. Okay?"

"Thank you."

"You'll owe me for this," said Fuller after a calculated pause.

"I don't want to know what you have in mind."

"I kind of have a Catwoman fetish. Anything skin-tight and made from PVC vinyl will suffice. The kinkier, the better."

Murch rolled her eyes and shook her head. "We'll talk later. Goodbye, Del."

"I accept your challenge, Haley Murch," confirmed Fuller. "Talk to you later, Princess."

CHAPTER THIRTY-THREE

WEDNESDAY, AUGUST THE SEVENTEENTH
TWO FORTY-SEVEN PM

IN HER ROOM AT the Highland Gardens Hotel, Murch sat at a bureau desk with her laptop computer and briefcase sprawled out before her and transposed a list of Hollywood Spectre victims from a master file in her briefcase. She then emailed the list to Billy Hayes' LAPD account.

Next, she removed a flash drive from her coat pocket and connected it to her laptop. She opened a new email window and typed in Dr. Fuller's address.

DR. FULLER STOOD BEFORE a high-tech computer station in the Biometrics Laboratory of the FBI Academy and scanned a high-res copy of Jimbo's Christian Rivers picture into the system for analysis.

Once the photo appeared on the computer screen, Fuller sat down in a swivel chair and, using a stylus pen, dragged the picture and dumped it into a facial recognition software program. "We're ready to rock 'n' roll."

BILLY HAYES APPROACHED JIMBO Scott at Jimbo's desk. "Mr. Jimmy...I got a special job requiring your utmost attention."

"Whaddaya got for me, Billy?"

Hayes handed Jimbo a folder. "*Bon appetit.*"

"Is this the list of the Hollywood Spectre victims?"

"Yeah. Haley sent it over."

Jimbo opened the file, pulled out a single piece of paper, and perused the list of names. "Funny," he said, scratching his head, "the Hollywood Spectre has eluded capture for thirty years, you'd think there'd be more names than this."

"These are only the confirmed cases, Jimbo. They *found* the bodies. I'm betting there's lots more."

"I wonder what connects all these names? Why these people?"

"Recognize any of them?"

Jimbo scanned the list. "A few of them were actors—Juno Calvecchio, Normandy Pike, Sadie Corre, Peggy Ledger, Tony Then, Peter Hinwood, Perry Bedden, Terry Ackland—but the others were people like Dr. Lawrence Milner and his fiancée, Theresa Burkhart: high-profile names who worked outside the entertainment industry."

"Nuke wants you to focus your attention solely on these names until you find any possible connection, even if it's only between one or two of them. Think outside the box."

"I'll give it my utmost attention."

MAX WINSTON'S MAXIMUM F/X van pulled up in front of the infamous exterior to the fictional *Melrose Place* apartment complex. In real life, the complex was the El Pueblo Apartments, a two-story, eight-apartment, Mediterranean courtyard-style building at 4616 Greenwood Place in Los Feliz, a short distance from Hollywood.

Max Winston sat behind the wheel of the van and smiled at the sight of the apartment complex. He turned and found MacGuffin in the front passenger seat. "Are you sure about this place, Rich?"

"What about it?"

Max sighed. "Come on, Mac, the El Pueblo Apartments: The real-life façade of the fictional *Melrose Place* apartments—are you kidding me?"

"Something wrong with that?"

"No, not unless you find it a bit eerie that Suzan Struthers, the daughter of Manson Family murder victim Rosemary LaBianca, used to live here at the time of the killings in 1969."

"Really? Awesome."

"Oh, yeah, this was one of the LaBiancas' final stops before they returned home the night they died. They stopped here on their way back from Lake Isabella to drop off Suzan before heading on their way. Suzan, her brother Frank, and Suzan's boyfriend found the LaBiancas' bodies the following night. Rumor has it, Suzan once dated a biker associated with Manson. She also now believes Tex Watson is a changed person and should be released from prison. She's a freakin' whack job."

"Nice try, but that was nearly forty years ago. I don't care what you say, Max; I'm not swayed that easy. I'm taking a tour of the apartment."

"Okay, but when somebody comes looking for your head, don't say I didn't warn you."

Max killed the engine, and he and MacGuffin exited the van and started walking up the sidewalk to the apartment building.

CHAPTER THIRTY-FOUR

THURSDAY, AUGUST THE EIGHTEENTH
FIVE AM (PST)/EIGHT AM (EST)

A RINGING CELL PHONE awoke Haley Murch from a sound sleep in her hotel room. She glanced at the time on the clock radio. "Dammit, Fuller, it's 5:00 AM. This had better be good."

Fuller stood within a skywalk in the FBI Academy's main complex, overlooking the quad, as he talked with Murch. "Haley," he said, his voice sounding urgent, "the computer's facial recognition software ran the photo of Christian Rivers and came up with a hit from the California Department of Motor Vehicles. And, as you suspected, the person in the photo is *not* the real Rivers."

"Then, *who* is *he*?"

OVER THE NEXT FEW minutes, Murch got in touch with Nuke, told him the big news, and asked to meet him at the West Los Angeles Community Police Station by 7:00 AM to go over Dr. Fuller's Biometrics analysis report with him.

NUKE AND MURCH SAT at Nuke's desk in the police station's Robbery-Homicide Division. With his feet propped up on his desk, Nuke examined a color printout of MacGuffin's driver's license. A cup of coffee sat nearby. "So, this is our impostor, eh?"

"At least according to the facial recognition analysis, it is," replied Murch.

Nuke sipped his coffee. "Richard M. MacGuffin? Hmm? An interesting last name. Very Hitchcockian."

"What do you mean?"

"Alfred Hitchcock popularized the term 'MacGuffin' to describe a plot device used to set a story into motion and drive it through to its third act, but which ultimately proves irrelevant to the overall story."

"That's an interesting parallel."

Nuke continued to look at MacGuffin's driver's license photo. He may have liked MacGuffin's name but not his appearance. "Christ, if I had a face like his, I'd want to cover it up, too. It's frightening."

Murch examined a copy of MacGuffin's employment records. "This report lists his occupations as an actor and a special effects assistant."

"Probably needs the effects gig because he can't get an acting job. If I were a casting director, I wouldn't hire him for anything based on his good looks. He looks like a friggin' psycho."

"That's a little harsh, don't you think?"

"No, I'm telling it like it is." Nuke sipped his coffee. "Does that thing list an address for his place of residence?"

"It lists several. This guy sure moves around a lot."

"Figures. Anything current?"

"It doesn't specify."

"We'll have to check them all, then."

"That'll take a while."

"What's the problem? You got a hot date or something?"

"No, my schedule's wide open."

"Good, so is mine. Buy you breakfast?"

"Let me guess, the Quality Café?"

Nuke smiled. "You read my mind, sweetheart."

"And, such a lovely, albeit predictable, mind it is, too," added Murch.

CHAPTER THIRTY-FIVE

FRIDAY, AUGUST THE NINETEENTH
NINE FORTY-SEVEN AM

NUKE'S MERCURY PULLED UP behind the Maximum F/X van parked at the curb in front of the three-story townhouse at 8763 Wonderland Avenue.

Nuke indicated the "FOR RENT" sign as he removed his yellow aviator sunglasses.

"Looks like we lucked out again," frowned Murch.

"What's the next address?"

Murch caught a glimpse of the Maximum F/X emblem on the side of the van parked out front and pointed it out to Nuke, "Look at that logo."

Nuke glanced over her right shoulder. "Maximum F/X? So?"

"Rich MacGuffin works for Maximum F/X."

"You think he's still here?"

The apartment door opened, and a startled Max Winston exited, hauling out a dolly loaded with boxes. "You bloody scared the piss out of me!"

"Are you the current resident of this apartment?" asked Nuke.

"Me? No. I'm helping a friend move his stuff out."

"Your friend, his name wouldn't happen to be Richard MacGuffin, would it?"

"Why, yes, yes it is. Why are you asking?"

Nuke and Murch displayed their badges. "We're here on official business," replied Murch.

"Damn," groaned Max.

"Would you happen to have an address where we might find him?" asked Nuke.

A STAINED-GLASS WINDOW high above the altar of the Hollywood Temple Beth El reflected the late-morning sunlight upon Juno Calvecchio's closed casket before a sparse crowd of mourners in black. The pews contained John Crawford, Nigel Guest, Janine Potts, and McKenzie Banks, various members of the *Teenage Confidential* cast and crew, as well as Juno's family and friends, including Juno's personal assistant and boyfriend, Blake Williams.

The officiant stood at the pulpit and chanted the *El Malei Rachamim* prayer to the standing congregation, "...God, full of mercy, who dwells in the heights, provide a sure rest upon the Divine Presence's wings, within the range of the holy, pure and glorious, whose shining resembles the sky's, to the soul of Juno Calvecchio, for whom charity was pledged to the memory of his soul. Therefore, the Master of Mercy will protect him forever, from behind the hiding of his wings, and will tie his soul with the rope of life. The Everlasting is his heritage, and he shall rest peacefully upon his lying place, and let us say: Amen."

The officiant concluded his prayer and exited. The pallbearers then carried the casket down the middle aisle to the front of the chapel, through the front doors, and down the steps to a silver hearse. The mourners followed.

Minutes later, a line of black limousines trailed the hearse in a funeral procession down Lakeview Avenue through the Hollywood Forever Cemetery to a freshly dug gravesite.

The small group of mourners stood around as a lowering device gently placed Juno's kosher casket at the bottom of the open grave.

As the casket came to rest six feet down, the mourners recited the Kaddish prayer. Upon completion, several people approached the open grave and tossed in handfuls of dirt, flowers, and mementos. Of those gathered, the one notable absentee was MacGuffin, a fact which John Crawford, Nigel Guest, and McKenzie Banks were quick to note.

CHAPTER THIRTY-SIX

MACGUFFIN LOUNGED ON AN inflatable raft in the El Pueblo Apartment's rear courtyard swimming pool, drinking a glass of iced tea. His dog, Hitchcock, lay beside him on a towel, as did MacGuffin's cell phone which began to play *"The Terminator* Theme" ringtone.

"Go away, Max! I'm only laying here with my eyes closed, trying to get some sleep!"

Max Winston sat behind the wheel of his van in late-morning traffic on Mulholland Drive, trying to reach MacGuffin by phone, but all he got was MacGuffin's voicemail: "Please, leave a message." *Beep.*

Max left a message, "Rich, I know you're there! Answer your damn phone!"

MacGuffin smiled as the ringtone ended. "Ahhh, silence."

His newfound peace and quiet were short-lived, as his phone rang again. "Max, you're killing me!"

Out of frustration, MacGuffin answered the call, "Max, how many times do I have to spell it out to you? Leave me alone!"

The voice that replied back was not Max Winston's. It was McKenzie Banks'. "Christian?" She sounded confused.

MacGuffin shook his head and did some quick thinking. "Uh...no... sorry. This is Rich...Rich MacGuffin. Remember me? I'm Rivers' make-up assistant."

"Yes, of course."

"Is this McKenzie?"

McKenzie called from a limousine parked graveside at the Hollywood Forever Cemetery. "Yes, it is."

"Hold on a second, darling. Let me get Rivers for you. He's in the other room."

MacGuffin placed McKenzie on hold and picked up the call a moment later in Rivers' Texan accent. "Whassup, little lady? How you doing?"

157

"Dandy. And, you?"

"Groovy, groovy. It's all good on this end. No worries."

"Missed you at Juno's funeral today."

"*Funeral?* That was today? Crap! I'm sorry! I... was...uh...I've spent all day yesterday and most of today moving into my new apartment. It's been crazy busy here."

"It doesn't matter anyway. There wasn't much of a turnout. His family and some of the film crew. It's not like he was a big-name star or anything."

"Again, I'm so sorry I wasn't there."

"It's all right, don't beat yourself up. That's not the reason I'm calling."

"It isn't?"

"No."

"Why are you calling?"

"I wanted to ask if you needed a date for your movie premiere."

"Uh, what movie premiere?"

"Silly! The *Texas Ace Arcana* premiere at the Rialto in Pasadena next Tuesday night. The one with the red carpet."

"Uh..."

"Is something wrong?"

"No, don't be silly. I'm honored to take you, McKenzie."

"Thank you."

"See you on set tomorrow?"

"The final day of shooting. As always."

"Goodbye, *muchacha*."

"Bye."

MacGuffin turned off his cell phone and leaped up in celebration. "Whoo-hoo!" Unfortunately, he lost his balance and fell backward off the raft into the pool. "Oh, shit!"

Hitchcock managed to keep his balance and remained on the raft. He yawned and went back to sleep.

Minutes later, MacGuffin walked back to his second-story apartment with Hitchcock following close behind.

As he went to unlock the door to apartment 7, his cell phone rang again. "Dammit, Max! Can't you see I'm busy here?" He answered the phone, "*Ma-ax*, old buddy! How's it going?"

"Rich, quit messing around! I've been trying to reach you for a half-hour!"

"Well...*sorrr-ree*. Didn't realize you cared so much about my well-being. I was in the pool with Hitch. What's up?"

"While I was at your old apartment, a couple of–"

Nuke and Murch walked up the stairs to the second-floor balcony and approached MacGuffin outside his apartment door.

"Rich MacGuffin?"

MacGuffin looked at Nuke and Murch, skeptical. "Um, Max... I'll have to call you back. Somebody's here."

"Rich–"

Click! MacGuffin closed his cell phone, turned, and confronted Nuke and Murch. "*Yes?*"

"Are you Richard MacGuffin?" asked Nuke.

"That's my name. Who's asking?"

Nuke and Murch displayed their badges and IDs. "The LAPD and the FBI," said Murch.

MacGuffin swallowed hard. "Oh...shit."

"Is there someplace we can talk?" asked Nuke.

"Whatever it is, I didn't do it."

Nuke tucked his wallet away, smiling. "Oh, you did."

MACGUFFIN SAT ACROSS FROM Nuke and Murch inside the Quality Cafe; his eyes fixated on the enormous banana split sundae on the table before Nuke. Nuke wolfed it down with a cup of coffee as he interrogated MacGuffin. Murch observed, drinking only coffee. MacGuffin got nothing to drink: one of Nuke's interrogation tactics.

"Tell me, Mr. MacGuffin," asked Nuke, "were *you* at all involved in the abduction of actor Christian Rivers?"

"Of course not! Are you crazy?"

Nuke smiled with glee, taking a bite of his sundae.

MacGuffin sat back in his seat and rested his hands on the edge of the table. "I don't even know Christian Rivers." He sighed and looked away. "Never even met him."

"Then, why have you been posing as him for the past week?"

"How do you know about that?"

Nuke removed the Rivers photo and handed it to MacGuffin. "A Biometrics facial analysis proved positive that you are, in fact, the person in this photo; not Mr. Rivers."

"Well, then...looks like you caught me red-handed. I've impersonated Christian Rivers since reading about his disappearance in the newspaper."

"For what purpose?"

"I'm a struggling actor. I thought it would help me make the Hollywood A-list. I'm a nobody who can never catch a break in this Tinsel Town on account of my looks. I'm like the spawn of Mickey Rourke."

"Hey, Mickey Rourke was one handsome dude before he turned to professional boxing in the early '90s. Messed his looks way up."

"Yeah, but he always has an acting career to go back to on account of name recognition. Didn't you see *Sin City*? He was awesome in that."

"You bet your ass I saw that. Mickey Rourke was Marv, all right. Like in the comics."

"Wait, you read comic books, too?" asked Murch under her breath.

"Shh, we'll talk about that later," whispered Nuke.

"See? That's the problem. *Me*? I have nothing. Nobody knows who Rich MacGuffin is. I did what I did because I was desperate."

"You do know you're in a lot of trouble, right? What you're doing is fraud. A little something called identity theft. You're looking at five years in prison and/or a $250,000 fine. However..."

A brief pause.

"*What*?"

Nuke helped himself to another scoop of ice cream as he thought to himself. *How should I know? I'm thinking.*

"What *are* you thinking, Detective?" asked Murch. "I'd like to know myself."

Nuke took a sip of coffee, paused again, and drummed his hands on the edge of the table. Murch and MacGuffin stared at him with confused expressions on their faces.

"Would you quit stalling?" asked Murch.

"Sorry...ice cream headache," smirked Nuke. "You, Mr. MacGuffin, can avoid jail time and becoming some gross hulkabitch's bitch for five years if..."

"*If...?*"

"*...if* you agree to help us find and catch our killer."

"What kind of killer?"

"One who preys on celebrities like Christian Rivers. Haley here will brief you at the station. She's the one who created the killer's profile."

"Is there any way for me to help you and avoid becoming a victim myself?"

Murch looked at Nuke. "Yeah, how would we ensure his safety?"

"Nobody said this was going to be easy, sweetheart."

Nuke turned back to MacGuffin. "But, it'd be a lot easier...cleaner...and less painful...than spending five years in San Quentin with Jabba the Slut."

MacGuffin swallowed hard. "I've heard enough. I don't wanna go to jail. What do I have to do to help you?"

"All I'm asking is that you go about your normal routine. Report to work tomorrow as usual, or whatever it is you do."

"I'm due on set tomorrow."

Nuke sipped his coffee. "Fine, go about your business."

"It's the final day of shooting on Rivers' latest movie."

"Even better. The killer will be all the more eager to seek you out, then. You've pissed him off with this whole Rivers routine of yours."

"Great."

"Regardless, when he does seek you out, and *he* will, we'll be right there to slap the cuffs on him."

CHAPTER THIRTY-SEVEN

MACGUFFIN DROVE UP TO Paradise Pictures' employee gate in a mint, two-door, Ford-red 1958 Plymouth Fury, flashed his studio ID to the guard, drove through the gate onto the backlot, and pulled into a parking space next to a white limousine outside the Haze Films Productions building.

MacGuffin approached the secretary Janine Potts' desk, where she sat polishing her fingernails. MacGuffin smiled. "Top of the morning, Janine."

"Good morning, Mr. MacGuffin. How may I help you?"

"Are Mr. Crawford or Nigel present as we speak?"

"They're in the editing suite."

"No problem. I can wait. Can I use the bathroom?"

"It's right down the hall. Help yourself."

MacGuffin strode past Janine's desk and traipsed down the hallway to the executive offices. Locking himself in the bathroom, he removed his jacket and shirt to reveal a radio mic taped to his chest.

"Testing. Testing," he said, tapping the mic. "Can anybody hear me? Hello? Is this thing working?"

The covert earpiece plugged into MacGuffin's left ear crackled to life as Nuke replied back, "Loud and clear, kid."

"What is it you want me to do?"

Nuke and Murch sat at a table in the middle of the studio commissary, as Nuke communicated with MacGuffin via walkie-talkie.

"Business as usual, Mac," said Nuke. "Give a little whistle if you need us. We're on-site in case you need anything."

"That's a big ten-four, Nuke."

"Over and out. Ten-four."

In the Haze editing suite, Crawford and Nigel worked on a scene as MacGuffin arrived.

"Ah, Mr. MacGuffin," greeted Crawford, "so nice of you to

join us this morning. Have you made up your mind yet about the contract?"

"It's a tempting offer, Mr. Crawford. Show me a pen, and the contract is all yours!"

Nigel smiled. "I like the way you think."

TEN MINUTES LATER, CRAWFORD removed a fountain pen and a bottle of ink from his top desk drawer and handed the pen to MacGuffin. "Forgive my old-fashionedness, Mr. MacGuffin. I tend to reserve this pen's use for special occasions like this."

"A *special occasion* it is, indeed."

Nigel placed a contract on the desk before MacGuffin. "You've had ample enough time to review the details of the contract, Mr. MacGuffin. Hope everything is to your liking?"

"It's fine. I'm not greedy."

"Then, please, sign," said Crawford. "Janine will notarize the contract and have it delivered to you ASAP."

"Sound good?" asked Nigel.

"Let's do it."

MacGuffin made the contract official by signing his name on the dotted line.

"Terrific," said Crawford.

MacGuffin handed the fountain pen back to Crawford. "Now it's official."

"Indeed it is," said Nigel. "Now the studio has no choice. They must pay you even if the picture doesn't get made. Pay-or-Play." He took the contract, rolled it up, and stuffed it inside the left breast pocket of his suit coat. "No matter what, in the end, it's still a pretty sweet deal. Congratulations, Mr. MacGuffin. You are now an official cast member in my next movie." He shook MacGuffin's hand. "The story will appear in tomorrow's *Daily Variety*. Now, if you'll excuse me, I have a film to finish. See you on set in a few."

ABOUT FORTY MINUTES LATER, MacGuffin sat inside Christian Rivers' trailer behind Stage 28, in the middle stages of applying his Rivers make-up, as he talked with Nuke over the wireless mic. "... No. No sign of anything weird. This place is as secure as Fort Knox."

Nuke and Murch sat in the studio commissary as Nuke chatted

into his walkie-talkie. "Well, it's still early, Rich. Haley and I are gonna hang around a few more hours in case anything transpires. Lincoln and Billy will take over at three until you're done filming for the night. If nothing goes awry, we'll have to come up with a Plan B. Who knows when you'll set foot on this studio lot again?"

"January. I signed a contract to appear as Rivers in Nigel Guest's next blockbuster."

"Well, we'll see about that."

"What if nothing happens?"

"Then, we're shit outta luck."

There was a knock on MacGuffin's trailer door. "I'm gonna have to let you go, Detective Bonaduce. Somebody's at the door."

"Who is it?"

MacGuffin peered through a set of horizontal blinds. "Somebody dressed in a postal service uniform. Looks like the mail guy."

"All right, talk to you later. Keep in touch. Remember, anything weird."

"Can do, Nuke. Bye for now."

MacGuffin stepped over to the trailer door.

A tall and lanky mailman stood outside as MacGuffin opened the door, his make-up half-finished, a prosthetic cheek appliance hanging from his face.

"Yes, what is it?" asked MacGuffin.

"Special delivery for Mr. Rivers."

"Well, he's not here at the moment, but I'll sign for him anyway."

MacGuffin signed own his name on the mailman's clipboard and accepted a letter-sized manila envelope addressed to Rivers. "What is this, a copy of the contract?"

"Have a nice day."

"Thank you. I'll make sure he gets this."

The mailman hopped on a flimsy bicycle and teetered away, as MacGuffin ducked back inside the trailer and closed the door behind him.

MacGuffin sat down at his make-up desk and stared at the address on the envelope. "C. RIVERS." MacGuffin chose not to open the envelope. He held it up to his nose and smiled. "The contract: The sweet smell of success. All I need now is a frame to put you in."

CHAPTER THIRTY-EIGHT

SATURDAY, AUGUST THE TWENTIETH
ONE PM

AS THE CAST AND crew of *Teenage Confidential* prepared for the last day of principal photography, MacGuffin arrived on set in full Rivers make-up. He found his talent chair sitting off to the side and planted his script and jacket upon it. As he did, Crawford and Nigel approached, drinking glasses of champagne.

Nigel smiled. "There's our boy, John. The Million Dollar Kid."

Crawford handed MacGuffin a glass of champagne. "Here you go, son. Enjoy a glass of Cristal to celebrate this final day of filming and for signing the new deal."

MacGuffin took a sip of champagne and swirled it around his mouth. "Mmm...that's good. It would be even better if it were $20 million like the real Rivers commands."

"Not this time, unfortunately. The next project is an ensemble affair. Nobody is getting paid their usual salary. It would be way too expensive with all the A-list talent we're lining up."

"Notice John referred to it as *A-list talent*, Mr. MacGuffin," said Nigel. "Bet that makes you happy as a pig in shit?"

"It does."

"*A-list*, it's why you're doing what you've been doing these past several days. You're in the big leagues now."

MacGuffin took another sip of champagne. "So, when do we start filming my final scene? I can't wait to take this make-up off. My skin is turning raw from prolonged exposure to spirit gum. It stings from the touch."

"We'll start as soon as you're good and ready," said Crawford.

"Well, I'm *good and ready*, right now."

Nigel smiled. "Perfect."

"All right, then. Let's get this thing in the can. I'm ready to party. Tell me what I need to do. I'm ready for my close-up, Mr. DeMille."

"Right this way, Mr. MacGuffin."

MacGuffin followed Nigel and Crawford onto the set of his final scene: a Poor Man's Process car with a rear projection screen behind it, where McKenzie Banks awaited in character for his arrival.

JIMBO SCOTT'S RED VOLKSWAGEN bug rolled up before the studio commissary and parked at the curb. Jimbo, Hayes, and Lincoln climbed out and walked upstairs to the patio deck where Nuke and Murch waited for them at an umbrella table, drinking cups of cappuccino.

Hayes greeted them with a sense of urgency in his voice, "Great, you're still here! We got some important news!"

"What do you got for us, Billy?" asked Nuke.

"Jimbo thinks he's discovered a link between the Hollywood Spectre's victims."

"It's only a theory," said Jimbo. "Nothing concrete."

"Whatever you have, Jimbo, I'd love to hear it," said Murch. "I spent a year seeking a connection, and I didn't come up with anything useful."

Hayes, Lincoln, and Jimbo each grabbed a chair from a nearby table, dragged them over, and took a seat.

"Enlighten us, Jimbo," said Nuke.

Jimbo removed the list of the Spectre victims' names. "This list of victims goes back some twenty-five years to the early '80s. With such an extensive list, any connection is like finding one specific needle in a pile of needles."

"I prefer a needle in a haystack, but okay," joked Hayes.

"There are names on here of celebrities and non-celebrities. Dr. Lawrence Milner and his fiancée, Theresa Burkhart, for example. Dr. Milner was a plastic surgeon, not a celebrity. Nor was Miss Burkhart. She was only his fiancée. A nobody. An aspiring actress."

"Where is this leading, Jimbo?"

Jimbo frowned, sheepish. "Sorry, Nuke, I'm rambling here. Anyway, excluding non-celebrity names, I focused only on the actual celebrities. The problem is, they've worked for various studios and, in some cases, the same directors and producers. There's too much info to sift through. Finding a solid connection is impossible without a key to unlock it. So, I chose to look 'outside the box' as Hayes suggested."

"Are you saying you found the key?" asked Murch.

Jimbo nodded. "I did. I went with only what we know."

Nuke stood and clapped his hands. "Ladies and gentlemen! A round of applause for my boy, Jimbo, here! He's a genius!" He sat back down.

Jimbo smiled. "We connect through investigating the Milner-Burkhart homicides, Rivers' abduction, and the Calvecchio murder. Of those three connections, which names have anything in common?"

"Christian Rivers and Juno Calvecchio," said Murch. "They both worked on the same movie together."

"Correct. And why were two people from the same movie targeted? Anybody?"

The others appeared baffled.

"No clue, Jimbo," said Hayes. "So, please, acquaint us with your infinite wisdom."

"Thank you, Billy, I will."

"What's the connection?" asked Nuke.

"The connection is the movie they were working on. Or, more specific, the person behind the film: John Crawford, the producer."

"You're saying John Crawford is the Hollywood Spectre?" implied Lincoln.

"No, *he's* not the killer. But, all the actors on this list at one point in their careers worked for Crawford; be it in the movies or on television."

"How does Crawford fit into this?" asked Nuke.

"That's the one question I can't answer."

"So, what do we do?" asked Hayes.

"Let's ask John Crawford," proposed Murch. "See what he knows."

"Do you think he's going to talk to us?" asked Lincoln.

"Do you have any better ideas?"

BACK ON STAGE 28, MacGuffin and McKenzie sat in the Poor Man's Process car, finishing the scene.

Nigel Guest raised his megaphone and shouted, "And... CUT! Check the camera gate! We'll print that one! Good work, everybody!"

MacGuffin climbed out of the driver's seat, walked around, and opened the passenger door for McKenzie. He kissed the back of her hand and hugged her. "Good job, McKenzie."

"You, too."

Crawford grabbed Nigel's megaphone and announced, "Ladies and gentlemen, that's a wrap on Mr. Mac..." He coughed. "...excuse me..." He cleared his throat. "...that's a wrap on Mr. Rivers, everybody!"

MacGuffin clapped his hands and took an impromptu bow as the cast and crew cheered him on. Nigel stepped over and doused him over the head with a bottle of Cristal, which drew more cheers from the crowd.

Crawford handed MacGuffin the megaphone. "Say something."

MacGuffin felt nervous. "For real?"

"Go ahead, son," said Nigel. "*You've* earned it."

MacGuffin raised the megaphone and addressed the crowd, "Wow! This is awesome! I don't know what to say." He wiped champagne from his face. "A towel would be nice right about now."

Nigel whispered something into his ear.

MacGuffin smiled. "Nigel told me to tell you, 'See you at the wrap party tonight. The drinks are on me.'" He laughed. "Hold the phone, Nigel. I don't know about that one. The drink *was* on me, for real."

Nigel grabbed the megaphone and commented, "Of course, he's joking. The drinks are on the studio. But first, we have the big death scene to shoot with McKenzie and George. It's the final scene, so let's get to it. Then, we can go home, get dressed in our Sunday finest, and come back here to party the night away and get shit-faced drunk." He hesitated a moment. "One last round of applause for our boy, Christian Rivers, on a job well done. Until the next picture, that is."

Everyone clapped and cheered as MacGuffin took a final bow, and it was back to business as usual.

As MacGuffin walked to his talent chair to grab his stuff, one of the grips handed him a towel. "Here's a towel, Mr. Rivers."

MacGuffin dried himself off. "Thank you, Ernie." He went to his chair and picked up his jacket. Beneath it, the manila envelope addressed only "C. RIVERS" sat on top of his script. "What are *you* doing here? I thought I left you back in the trailer?"

Suspicious, he turned the envelope over and ripped open the

169

seal. He pulled out a black and white agency photograph of Christian Rivers X'ed out in dried blood. "What kind of contract is this?" He turned the photo over and found a message: "To Whom It May Concern, If you want to see Mr. Rivers have a safe return, G.P.O. Tuesday 8:00 PM. P.S. Bring the fake Rivers."

NUKE, MURCH, AND THE three others sat around the commissary patio table, deep in discussion, as Nuke's cell phone beeped.

Nuke checked his phone's screen. A text message from MacGuffin read: "URGENT. COME QUICK. TRAILER."

"Who is it?" asked Murch.

"MacGuffin. We need to go."

TEN MINUTES LATER, NUKE and Murch stood in MacGuffin's trailer and examined the photo of Rivers, as MacGuffin looked on. Jimbo, Hayes, and Lincoln stood guard just outside and listened in.

"I'm not sure why I felt the urge to open the envelope," said MacGuffin to Nuke and Murch. "Guess I thought it had something to do with the contract I signed. They promised to send a notarized copy for my records."

Nuke turned the envelope over and over as he inspected it. "No address. This letter had to have come from within the studio."

"Whom did you say delivered this to you, Rich?" asked Murch.

"A mailman. He was wearing a postal uniform and rode a bike."

"Was he carrying a mailbag?"

"No."

"What did he look like?" asked Nuke.

"I'd say around age 40, 50. Long black hair. Kind of nervous. Six feet tall. A thin build. Pale."

"Doesn't sound like the Hollywood Spectre. One of his goons?"

"Is it possible he got caught on camera?" asked Murch.

"Nah, the studio surveillance system is still down," said Nuke. "We got nothing to go on other than this letter."

Murch took the letter and read the message on the back again. *To Whom It May Concern, If you want to see Mr. Rivers have a safe return, G.P.O. Tuesday 8:00 PM. P.S. Bring the fake Rivers.* "What's the G.P.O.?"

Jimbo peered through the trailer's doorway. "I'm guessing the Griffith Park Observatory."

"But, what does the Hollywood Spectre want with MacGuffin?"

"A hostage exchange?" suggested Hayes.

"Forget it! No way!" retorted MacGuffin. "That's not part of the deal."

"Don't worry, it's not gonna happen," said Nuke. "We're not gonna let them just have you, Rich."

"Tuesday's not far away," said Murch. "We need to come up with a strategy, a plan, or something."

"Well, for now, let's convene back at headquarters for a briefing," said Nuke. "There's a little more privacy and more security."

"But, what about me?" asked MacGuffin. "I have the cast and crew wrap party tonight."

"Sorry, my friend, but it ain't gonna happen. We got a bigger fish to fry. Someone's life depends on us. And you. We need to place you into protective custody for the time being."

"And where might that be?"

"There's a private security room back at headquarters. You'll be under lockdown with an armed guard on the inside and one on the outside. There are security cameras inside and out, as well. Nobody gets in or out without our consent. It's like Fort Knox."

MacGuffin grinned. "Right. As long as Pussy Galore and her Lesbian Flying Circus don't nerve gas everybody and steal me out under the nose of the LAPD."

Nuke smirked. "Like *that'll* happen. That kind of stuff only works in the movies."

CHAPTER THIRTY-NINE

MACGUFFIN, MURCH, HAYES, AND Lincoln lounged around inside the West Los Angeles Community Police Station's Lockdown Suite, chatting nonsense, eating pizza, and having drinks from the mini bar.

"No way, Billy!" retorted Lincoln. "There's a reason he stands around the skiff like a bump on a log doing nothing. The man is in pain. He can't move."

Hayes sneered. "He doesn't move because he can't see! He's got hibernation sickness! His eyes haven't adjusted."

MacGuffin smiled and chuckled. "You guys don't have a clue when it comes to describing 'hibernation sickness.'"

"Oh, and I suppose *you're* the expert on the subject, boychick?" scoffed Hayes.

Lincoln popped the tab on a can of soda and took a sip. "Okay, Mr. MacGuffin, tell us your theory. I'd love to hear your expert knowledge on the subject of carbon freezing."

Murch shook her head and rolled her eyes. "This I got to hear," she sighed.

"Come on, hotshot," mocked Hayes, "tell us your theory already."

MacGuffin grinned. "All right..."

"*Well?*"

"It's like this: The whole 'he's alive and in perfect hibernation' business is a total load of crap, to begin with. Han Solo is encased in metal. Not one inch of him is exposed. He would have suffocated due to the lack of oxygen, like Shirley Easton in *Goldfinger* from being covered in gold paint; his muscles would've atrophied, and there's the business of blood clots, impacted intestines, and, not to mention, starvation. Han Solo would've quickly become one dead, fuzzy nerf herding space smuggler who always shot first."

The suite's stainless-steel vault door opened, and Nuke and Jimbo entered the room.

"Honey, we're home!" shouted Nuke, sarcastically.

"Thank God," said Murch.

"And," said Jimbo, "we picked up a little friend on the way, so Mr. MacGuffin will have some company during his stay here at the Chateau d'Nuke."

Nuke chuckled. "Good one, Jimbo."

Nuke made a loud whistle, and MacGuffin's dog, Hitchcock, trotted in and ran to his master.

"Hitchcock!" bellowed MacGuffin, surprised. "Hey, there, boy!"

Hitchcock jumped up onto the bed and lay down beside MacGuffin, who gave him a good scratch-over. "Yeah, I bet you missed me, too, didn't you, boy?"

"Thought he might starve without you, Rich, so we stopped by your apartment and picked him up for you," said Nuke. "It's the least we could do to make your stay here a little more pleasant."

"Oh, no, this...this place is great," remarked MacGuffin.

Lincoln noticed the long roll of paper in Jimbo's hands. "What you got there, Jimbo?"

"The complete blueprints to the Griffith Park Observatory. It's fascinating what fifty bucks can get you at the County Recorder's office."

"Oh...great," muttered Hayes.

"Enough small talk, boys and girls," said Nuke, taking the blueprints from under Jimbo's right arm and spreading the roll out on the bed for all to see. "It's time we get down to the business at hand. We need to come up with some plan for this hostage exchange at the Observatory."

"You do realize the Observatory is under renovation?" asked Lincoln. "These building plans might no longer be accurate."

"It's something we'll have to deal with when we get there."

"And, what time is this thing scheduled to take place?"

"Eight o'clock Tuesday night."

"It'll be dark out. That could complicate things. We have no idea how many goons this Hollywood Spectre guy even has."

"The video from the Chateau Marmont shows two men

entering the back of the limo with Rivers," stated Murch.

"Don't forget the limo driver," added Jimbo. "That makes three."

"Okay, so, assuming there's only three henchmen, there's also the Spectre himself," said Hayes. "That makes four."

"Assuming he's not one of the three in the video," said Nuke.

"What are you guys getting at?" asked Murch.

"Yeah, we don't even know if the Hollywood Spectre will even be there," stated Hayes. "What if it's only the three goons plus Mr. Rivers? The Hollywood Spectre or somebody else altogether could be waiting in the shadows with crosshairs pointed at us ready to pick us off one by one like *Ten Little Indians*."

"*Ten Little Indians*? What the Hell, Billy?" retorted Lincoln.

Hayes shook his head. "An Agatha Christie reference, Linc. Forget about it."

"No, Hayes, you've got a point there," stated Nuke. "Somebody could be hiding in wait. We need to take that into consideration."

"Even still, Nuke, there's five of us to their four. We got them outnumbered."

Nuke took a seat on the bed beside MacGuffin and added, "Don't forget Mr. MacGuffin here, Billy. He's coming with us. That makes six. He's the one the Hollywood Spectre wants in exchange for Rivers."

"Yes, but how do we ensure they don't get Rich once we get Rivers?" asked Murch.

"That's why we need to come up with a plan here. That's why we got the blueprints."

MacGuffin grew frantic. "Holy shit!"

"What? What is it?" asked Murch, concerned.

"I remembered something."

"What?" asked Nuke. "You forget to bring an extra change of underwear?"

"No. Tuesday night won't work for me. I'm supposed to attend some stupid premiere in Pasadena. Rivers is the star of the movie. He's contracted to appear on the red carpet to sign autographs and do interviews. I have to be there as Rivers. I have a date and everything. I have to go."

"Forget about it, Rich, it ain't happening. We need your help rescuing the real Rivers. This needs to happen if we're to find the location of the Hollywood Spectre's hideout. It's part of our deal with you, and the Hollywood Spectre doesn't give out rain checks."

MacGuffin sneered. "*What?* If I don't help you, I go to jail? Is that it?"

Nuke looked at the others and grinned. "We're dealing with a genius here, boys."

"You're out of line, Detective," said Murch.

"All I'm saying is, he doesn't have a choice in the matter, darling. The Hollywood Spectre isn't gonna make an exception because of some stupid movie premiere MacGuffin needs to attend."

"Don't forget about his date to the premiere," added Hayes.

"Who is this girl you're to go out with, incidentally, if you don't mind my asking, Rich?" asked Jimbo.

"McKenzie Banks, the actress."

Jimbo smiled. "Ooh...nice."

"No shit."

"I'm sorry, Mac," said Nuke, "but this case takes precedence over anything you need to do that night. Wish it didn't need to be that way, but the cards have fallen. I know how much that girl means to you. Hell, even I'd lop both my balls off for a date with her."

Murch slapped Nuke across the head.

"What the—?"

"Never mind," she said, blushing.

MacGuffin hesitated a moment and became somber. "Fine. I'll go with you on this exchange thing. It's the right thing to do. I mean, a person's life is on the line and all, even though he is a real prick from what I understand. A lot of people could care less if he ever returned. Alas, though, he is a human being."

"Take it easy, big guy. I'm sure you'll be able to work out something with this girl of yours."

"Yeah, how's that, Nuke?"

"You have a background in the special effects business, Rich. You turned yourself from a nobody into an A-Lister using foam latex, glue, and one awful hairpiece. Think about it, Mac. Get creative. In the meantime, we've got a plan to hatch out the details here and only a couple days to do it. Let's focus our energies on that. Okay?"

"Easy for you to say. Your job's the easy part. I have to give myself over to some dude with a face that looks like burnt meat; who wants to rip me open like some stuck pig."

"That ain't gonna happen, my friend. You aren't gonna become the Hollywood Spectre's next victim. Not on my watch."

CHAPTER FORTY

THE HISTORIC RIALTO THEATRE in South Pasadena was one of the last single-screen movie palaces in L.A., featuring Moorish décor, with Spanish-Baroque elements, Egyptian styling, and classical attributes including an outdoor cashier box and a college-lettered blade marquee.

Tonight was the world premiere of Christian Rivers' latest action extravaganza, *Texas Ace Arcana and the Lost City of Atlantis*. The red carpet swarmed with celebrities, security, paparazzi, and reporters. A strict black-and-white-style affair.

While John Crawford stood back and shunned the spotlight, Nigel Guest basked in all its glory. He wore a designer red-velvet tuxedo and supported a leggy, blonde model on each arm.

KLAX-TV News reporter Gloria Cox interviewed him on camera. "... What can you tell us about your next film, *Teenage Confidential?*"

"Well, the movie recently wrapped principal photography and is moving on to post. Expect it to arrive sometime in December to be eligible for award season."

"A little bit of the plot?"

"Um, yes... Christian Rivers plays a high school teacher named James Stark, who comes to the aid of a troubled student—McKenzie Banks in a breakthrough performance—whom Rivers suspects is being abused by her father."

"Wow! Sounds a lot darker in tone than your other films?"

"Indeed," said Nigel, clearing his throat. "Um, scope-wise, the movie's a lot smaller and has a lower budget than our regular fare, such as tonight's *Texas Ace Arcana*. No...um...we're making *Teenage Confidential* between post on tonight's movie and the next *Texas Ace* picture, which we hope to get before the cameras shortly."

"You mind commenting on your choice of attire—a red tuxedo—

while everyone else is wearing black or white?"

"Sure, darling. What can I say? I do like to stand out amidst a crowd of my contemporaries. It helps boost my already inflated ego. I am the director of tonight's movie, after all. I'm wearing red because I am the devil at the helm, sweetheart. I'm demanding on my cast and crew. I always get what I bloody Hell want."

Cox turned her attention to the reclusive John Crawford. "John Crawford, would you like to say a few words about the untimely death of actor Juno Calvecchio?"

Crawford shrugged her off, but Nigel dragged him before Kenney's camera.

Cox shoved her microphone in Crawford's face, as he reluctantly replied, "Well...Juno's murder was a tragic event for us. With the investigation still going, I'd prefer not to elaborate, except to say we've dedicated this movie to him. He was our good friend and co-worker over the last couple of pictures, and we'll miss him. I only hope the authorities find the party responsible."

"Now, one last question for either of you," said Cox. "Why did you choose South Pasadena's Rialto Theatre as the location for tonight's big premiere, when there are many other glamorous locales you could have chosen, such as the Chinese Theater? I mean, if there were a term to describe the Rialto, it would be *decadent*."

Nigel stepped up and addressed the camera, "Darling, to use the word *decadent* to describe this lovely old lady is regrettable, as the term doesn't carry a positive connotation as one would think. It doesn't mean campy, extravagant, or obsolete, but corrupt, debauched, or depraved. Not words I'd use to denigrate any theater."

"I was only referring to the fact that the Rialto is in serious need of repair. Let's face it, it's a place frozen in time; a faded glory from the Jazz Age."

Nigel appeared a bit irked. "That's the reason we're holding the premiere here, as a fundraiser to help restore the Rialto to its original glory."

"Sounds like a pretty hefty price tag to me. Are you going to be able to raise enough money for a complete overhaul?"

"Oh, far from enough, unfortunately. A total restoration would run upward of $1 million. No, the money we raise tonight will only lend a small helping hand, but it'll be enough to help keep the doors

178

open another year and allow for a new Dolby Digital-Dolby Stereo sound system. To start things off on the right foot, both John and I are each contributing $25,000 to the cause."

"Wow! That's quite generous of both of you!"

Crawford stepped up to the mic. "Now, I've been in and around this industry some forty years now, and I've seen a dramatic number of changes. No longer is it the same Hollywood I remember from when I started. Holding a fundraiser to help save this place is the least we could do.

"The Rialto is one of the few remaining pieces of old Hollywood history. I first met my late wife, Victoria, here at a premiere back in 1973. God rest her soul. It's one of the last unadulterated theaters left in the country not controlled by a huge corporation. It still provides the guest with the single-screen charm of a bygone era."

Nigel grabbed the microphone from Crawford and further added, "Yes, this theater has fallen on hard times in recent years. It's survived two fires, countless threats of demolition, and changes in ownership. That was before locals championed to make it a member of the National Historical Society. The Rialto is a cultural, historical monument. She needs to remain a symbol of classic Hollywood."

A white limousine pulled up to the curb before the red carpet, and Christian Rivers and McKenzie Banks stepped out, dressed to the nines.

Crawford motioned to Cox and pointed to the limo. "Now, Miss Cox, there's a couple you need to interview, Christian Rivers and his lovely date, McKenzie Banks. The real stars of the show."

Cox yanked Kenney away to snag an interview. "Kenney, move your fat, tub of lard ass..."

NUKE'S MERCURY TRAVELED NORTH on North Western Avenue in Hollywood. Its six passengers crammed inside like sardines.

"So, Rich, how did you manage to get Rivers out of going to the movie premiere?" asked Nuke, sitting behind the wheel.

MacGuffin sat in the backseat, sandwiched between Hayes and Lincoln. "Oh, Rivers will be there for the red carpet, all right. I won't be the one in disguise."

AT 6:47 PM, MCKENZIE Banks stood in the bedroom of her

second-story, S. Detroit Avenue apartment, dancing by herself before a long, narrow mirror, as she prepped herself for the big movie premiere.

Outside the front entrance to the apartment complex, a white limousine pulled up to the curb.

Soon there was a knock at the apartment door. As McKenzie opened it, she found "Christian Rivers" standing in the hallway in a black tuxedo, dark glasses, and a black ball cap. "Christian!"

Max stood mystified by McKenzie's stunning beauty. "Wow! You look fantastic!" He handed her a corsage box. "I brought this for you. May I?"

"Be my guest."

He removed the corsage from the box and fixed it around her right wrist. "Look at that. The perfect fit."

"Thanks. You okay? You sound kind of...froggy."

"Oh, heh, didn't sleep well last night. I look and sound terrible."

"Huh. You look edgy and mysterious. It works."

"Thanks."

"Would you like to come in?"

"Thank you."

Max stepped inside and closed the door behind him.

"GOOD CALL ON MAX," remarked Nuke.

"Hey, you told me to get creative, so I did," said MacGuffin. "I'll tell you, it wasn't easy convincing the Limey bastard to do it. In the end, though, it turned out great. I only hope he can pull off the required Texas accent. His Scottish brogue is pretty thick."

The Mercury turned east onto Los Feliz Boulevard and soon passed the Fern Dell Drive turnoff to the north.

"Nuke, where the Hell are you going?" asked Jimbo, riding shotgun. "We passed the turnoff to the Observatory."

Nuke rolled his eyes and throttled the steering wheel. "Sorry, Jimbo. You never want to take Fern Dell to the Observatory. It's a long, winding road and gives me a friggin' headache."

"Where are we going, Nuke?" asked Murch, sandwiched between Nuke and Jimbo in the front seat.

"Many roads in life converge at the same destination, darling, and the path we're taking is the path of least resistance; a shortcut:

180

Vermont Canyon Road—it's a short, straight shot to the Observatory."

The Mercury turned north onto Vermont Canyon Road, and, soon, the street sign for Boy Scout Road appeared up ahead to the left through the front windshield.

"There she is kids, Boy Scout Road: The end of the line for Billy and me," said Nuke.

The Mercury slowed and turned west onto Boy Scout Road, which quickly turned into a dead-end. The car pulled to a stop, its engine still running.

"All right," said Nuke, "here's the plan: Hayes and I are gonna jump ship here and hike the trails a quarter mile to the south base of the Observatory. Once there, the two of us will climb the stairs at the southeast corner to the south driveway. From there, we'll ascend to the East Observation Terrace, take the ramp to the northeast corner, climb to the East Rotunda, and take cover by the Zeiss Telescope rooftop dome where we'll set up a sniper's nest."

"In the meantime," said Hayes, "the four of you will continue to the Observatory, about a mile from here. Once there, all proceeds as planned. You'll park the car along the curve in the road by the north lawn and leave it idling. Go to the Astronomers Monument and wait for the Spectre's goons to arrive with Christian Rivers, if they're not already there."

"Yes, but what happens if the two of you don't make it there in time for the exchange?" asked MacGuffin. "We could be walking into a trap."

"I assure you, Mac," said Nuke, "Billy and I will be there by the time you guys arrive."

"We'll signal to you from the roof with three quick flashes from a flashlight," added Hayes.

"What if we encounter security guards or visitors?" asked Murch.

"The Observatory's closed since 2002 for major renovations," said Jimbo. "It doesn't re-open until sometime next year. We shouldn't encounter any problems."

Nuke opened his driver's door, climbed out of the car with Hayes following close behind, and moved on to the trunk, from which they removed a gun case containing a sniper rifle and a canvas bag of supplies.

As Hayes slung the gun case over his right shoulder, MacGuffin stopped him. "You got enough ammo for your big gun there? I don't wanna be a sitting duck out there. You don't need another hostage on your hands."

"Take it easy, my friend. I'm using .50-caliber shells. When you need to get the job done, accept no substitutes. Nothing much remains standing."

"I wish I had your confidence."

"Trust me. I'm an old hand at this kind of stuff. I used to be in the Marines before becoming a detective."

As Nuke and Hayes approached the start of a hiking trail, Jimbo took a seat behind the wheel. He called out to Nuke, "Thanks for keeping the seat warm for me, buddy."

"Remember, Jimbo, we'll signal to you with a flashlight when we see you. Three quick flashes."

"Three quick flashes, gotcha."

"All right, see you there, Jimbo."

Jimbo gave Nuke and Hayes a quick salute with two fingers to his right temple and replied, "Good luck."

As Nuke and Hayes started up the dirt trail, Jimbo closed his door and turned the Mercury around in reverse.

In the distance, the Griffith Park Observatory stood at the edge of a mountainside, overlooking the city to the south.

CHAPTER FORTY-ONE

A GARGOYLE STATUE WITH glowing red eyes sat perched high above the Rialto Theatre auditorium's proscenium. Beneath was an aged, 40-foot-wide, top-down screen adorned on either side by plaster-grilled organ chambers supported by harpies. The grille on the left chamber contained fire damage, while the right chamber appeared intact. Below the stage sat an orchestra pit. A film of the "Star-Spangled Banner" played on-screen.

The auditorium featured Spanish-Baroque architecture and Egyptian-accented interior design. Picture tiles, colorful stenciling, and plaster ornamentations decorated the dark burgundy gold toned walls. And, like the rest of the theater, the auditorium was in pressing need of repair.

Regardless, the main floor was at capacity. Luminaries, studio executives, and media representatives occupied 800 of the 1,200 seats.

The audience clapped and cheered as the silver screen lit up with the vintage animated *Let's All Go to the Lobby* ad, featuring the singing and dancing Refreshments crooning modified lyrics to the tune of the classic folk song "We Won't Be Home Until Morning."

A teaser trailer for *Teenage Confidential* unfolded on-screen. The first image to appear was the MPAA green-band screen, followed in close succession by logos for Paradise Pictures Studios and Haze Films Productions. A series of title cards appeared:

PARADISE PICTURES STUDIOS Presents
In Association With HAZE FILMS PRODUCTIONS
A Film By NIGEL GUEST
CHRISTIAN RIVERS MCKENZIE BANKS
JUNO CALVECCHIO
"TEENAGE CONFIDENTIAL"

In the back row, a trio of stoners lit up a joint and passed around a bottle of Jack Daniels.

A few rows down, McKenzie Banks sat in a middle aisle seat and stared back at the stoners. One of the stoners noticed her and gave her the international sign of cunnilingus.

McKenzie glanced at Max on her right. "Where are the ushers when you need them?"

Max took a quick glance at the stoners and turned back to McKenzie. "They *are* the ushers."

The movie trailer continued on.

Max fidgeted in his theater seat. He tried to pick up his left foot to cross his legs, but the sole of his shoe stuck to the gum- and soda-encrusted concrete floor.

He grinned at McKenzie. "A great theater, eh? Sticky floors, an outdated, crappy sound system, no air conditioning, and springs-in-your-ass chairs."

"You wanna get out of here?"

"Why? Aren't you having a good time?"

McKenzie stood up from her seat and tugged Max's left arm. "I am. It's... Can we go, please?"

"All right."

Max got up from his seat and followed McKenzie up the center aisle. As they neared the exit, he snatched the stoner's joint and whiskey bottle.

"Hey, man, what the—?" groaned the stoner.

"Can't you read?" asked Max, pointing to a sign on the exit door, sneering. "No outside food or beverages and...no smoking! This place is a fire hazard waiting to happen! What's the matter with you?" He extinguished the joint and dropped the Jack Daniels bottle into a nearby trash bin, as he and McKenzie stormed out of the auditorium.

AS NUKE'S MERCURY TRAVELED north up Vermont Canyon Road, it passed an idle black-and-yellow Rolls-Royce Phantom III sedan, parked along the east side of the road. Once the Mercury was a hundred yards ahead, the vehicle followed with its headlights off.

"I can't believe we agreed to this stupid plan," fretted Lincoln from the backseat beside MacGuffin. "It's reckless and crazy. We should be using a hostage negotiator."

"The Hollywood Spectre gave us explicit instructions," said Murch, riding shotgun.

184

"He's leading us on a wild goose chase."

As Jimbo drove, he glanced at his side mirror and noticed something following them. It concerned him. He chuckled at Lincoln. "Linc, you got to remember, a job like this requires the patience of a Jedi or a practicing Buddha. Try to relax a little."

"That's easy for you to say, Jimbo."

MacGuffin sank in his seat, muttering to himself, "Ugh, I'm gonna be sick."

"Better look the other way," pleaded Lincoln. "I don't want no one upchucking on me."

CHAPTER FORTY-TWO

THE RIALTO THEATRE LOBBY featured historical memorabilia, a tiled fountain, and a grand staircase.

Max stood at the concession stand as the teenage concession girl poured him a large drink.

"Four dollars," she requested.

Max handed her a $10 bill, as she gave him the soda. He applied a plastic lid and grabbed a straw from the dispenser. "Keep the change, darling."

"Thank you," she said, smiling.

"No, thank you. Gotta respect the fans. Especially the ones as lovely as yourself." He tipped his black ball cap.

"Aw, thank you." She smiled again.

As Max turned to leave, he stopped as a black cat strolled out from behind the concession stand and brushed up against his legs, affectionately.

"Well, well...hello there, little guy. What are you up to?"

"It's his dinner time," explained the concession girl. "I was feeding him some of the stale popcorn. He likes to lick off the melted butter."

Max pointed to the cat and asked, "Do you mind?"

"Knock yourself out."

Max knelt and offered the cat a friendly hand. The cat sensed he wasn't a threat and allowed Max to pet him. "Hey, there, little fella. Haven't seen you in a while."

Max scratched under the cat's chin and scooped him up in his right arm. He stood and carried the cat to the grand staircase where McKenzie sat waiting.

He handed McKenzie the soda. "Here you go."

"Thank you."

"Don't forget to save some for me."

Max took a seat two steps down from McKenzie and set the cat on the step between them.

As McKenzie sipped her soda, she glanced down at the cat rubbing against her legs. "Who's your little friend?"

"I'd like you to meet the Rialto's mascot, L.A. Smith."

"What kind of name is that?"

"He was named after the original architect of this place, L.A. Smith. The Rialto was one of the last theaters he designed before he died. L.A. here was a stray until Kirby Sweetman, the projectionist, found him in the back alley and took him in. The owners don't care. They let him roam around the theater freely."

"Aw, cute."

"Yeah. Sometimes, he'll roam the aisles of the auditorium, hide under the seats, brush up against people's legs. The best one, though, is when he runs across the stage in front of the screen during a show. If he looks directly at the audience, his eyes reflect the glowing red light from the gargoyle statue's eyes. Freaks the customers out. They think he's a ghost."

"A *ghost?*"

"Oh, yeah. This place is full of ghost stories. The joint's haunted."

"What kinds of ghosts?"

"Some people claim to see an apparition of an old man walking up and down the aisles and sitting in various seats. Bathroom stalls start shaking of their own accord, especially in the women's bathroom. And, abnormalities in photographs, uneasy feelings, whispers heard, you name it."

"I take it you've been to this theater before?"

Max glanced around the lobby and replied, "Oh, Hell, yeah. This place is one of my favorite haunts in the city. Not only has the Rialto appeared on-screen in such movies as *A Nightmare on Elm Street 4, Scream 2* and *The Player*, but it also boasts one of the country's longest midnight runs of *The Rocky Horror Picture Show*. I'm a huge *Rocky Horror* fan. I love dressing up in costume and throwing shit at the screen. Yessiree."

McKenzie cracked up. "I've never been to a midnight screening before."

"Aw, you're a virgin! Well, well...hmm? I'll have to bring you some night."

"I'd like that."

"It's a date, then."

"But I don't have a costume."

"Don't fret. I have an extensive collection."

JIMBO SAT BEHIND THE wheel of the Mercury and fiddled with the rear-view mirror.

"What are you looking at, Jimbo?" asked Murch.

"Do you see a car following us about thirty yards back?"

Murch, Lincoln, and MacGuffin craned their heads, peered out the back window, and witnessed the sedan following at a distance with its headlights off.

"Someone is following us," replied Lincoln.

"You think it's them?" asked Murch.

"Most likely."

"Looks like a Rolls-Royce of some type," remarked MacGuffin.

"Should I lose them?" asked Jimbo.

"No, keep going," said Murch. "Stick to the plan."

BACK AT THE RIALTO Theatre, John Crawford and Janine Potts sat three rows down from the back of the auditorium. Crawford glanced down to the middle row and noticed Max and McKenzie still hadn't returned. He turned to Janine and said, "If you'll excuse me, I need to make an unscheduled pit stop. Nature calls."

He got up from his seat, squeezed past Janine, and walked up the aisle to the exit. He glanced back at the audience before ducking out the door.

As Crawford entered the lobby, he spotted Max and McKenzie sitting on the grand staircase, chatting with fans and signing autographs.

A middle-aged man exited the auditorium and bumped into Crawford. "Oh...sorry. Forgive me. My sincere apologies," he said in a British accent.

"No problem," said Crawford. "It's my fault. I should watch where I stand."

The man patted Crawford on the shoulder and smiled. "No harm, no foul. Excuse me." He continued on his way.

Crawford ran into Nigel Guest and his two girlfriends, all three of them carrying glasses of Cristal. "Nigel!"

Nigel motioned to his two dates. "Darlings, will you excuse me a moment?" He kissed them both on the cheek. "Run along, now. Thank you."

As they walked away, Nigel pulled Crawford aside. "John, where are you off to at this early hour? The movie's only starting."

"Oh, I'm on my way to pay my respects at the Altar of the Porcelain God."

Nigel chuckled. "The *what?*"

"I need to drain my lizard, Nigel. You know, take a leak?"

"You're a funny bloke, John. Funny. Funny." He sipped his champagne. "Well, hurry it up in there. Bleed your willy dry and get your ass to the press room. The reporters want an interview."

"I'll be there in a couple of minutes, Nigel. Talk to them until I get back."

Nigel took another sip of his champagne and asked, "So, John, how's the response to the movie so far?"

"The audience appears to be eating it up. We may have another hit on our hands, Nigel."

"Excellent."

As Nigel drained the last of his champagne, Crawford ambled away and strolled over to Max and McKenzie on the stairs. "Well, well...look who it is." He leaned in and kissed McKenzie on the cheek. "Hello, darling."

"Hi, Dad."

"Lemme guess: You couldn't stand seeing yourself up on the screen–am I right?"

"It's bad enough hearing my own voice on an answering machine. Imagine seeing yourself thirty feet tall and thirty feet wide on the silver screen. It isn't pretty."

Max stood and shook Crawford's hand. "Evening, Mr. Crawford."

"Please, Christian, call me John. You needn't be so formal. This isn't work."

"Coulda fooled me."

McKenzie appeared embarrassed and blushed. "So, Dad, what did you come out here for? Not to ask how we're enjoying the show?"

"No, you're right. I came out here to use the restroom. I've got a bladder like a geriatric, and it's ready to explode. So, if you'll excuse me." He nodded at them and walked off in the direction of the restrooms.

NUKE AND HAYES ARRIVED at the southern base of Griffith Park Observatory and climbed the southeast corner stairs to the driveway above.

JOHN CRAWFORD RUSHED INSIDE the Rialto's Men's Room and shot for the first stall only to find it locked and occupied. "Oh...sorry." He moved to the second stall.

He hurried inside and locked the door behind him. He dropped his drawers and took a seat on the porcelain throne. Atop the toilet paper dispenser, he found a discarded copy of *Daily Variety*, which he picked up and unfolded to the front page. He whistled to himself as he read.

Unbeknown to Crawford, two feet stepped down from the toilet onto the floor in the first stall...

MAX AND MCKENZIE SAT on the grand staircase, chatting with a young mother and her son, Joey.

"You here to see the new movie, Joey?" asked Max, as he autographed a souvenir *Texas Ace Arcana* movie magazine.

"Yeah!"

"You liking it so far?"

"Yeah! Yeah!"

Joey's mother smiled at Max. "He's a huge fan of yours. Huge."

"I can tell."

"He's seen all your movies. He watches them over and over again."

"Well, it's fans like your son here that keeps actors like my friend, McKenzie, and myself employed."

"He'd like to be an actor like you one day."

"Ohhh...don't we all," said Max, ruffling Joey's hair, frowning. "As long as he waits until he's eighteen. This business isn't for kids. It robs them of childhood." He finished signing the magazine and handed it to Joey. "There you go, Joey. One autograph, one black marker."

Joey smiled ecstatically. The autographed message read: *To Joey, My #1 Fan! Best Wishes–Christian Rivers*–along with a drawing of a cartoon bunny. "Yay!"

"What do you say, honey?" asked Joey's mother.

"Thank you."

"You're welcome, little guy." said Max, smiling. "Don't sell it on eBay, or I'll come asking for a kickback."

As Joey and his mother walked off to the auditorium, Max and McKenzie waved goodbye.

Max smiled with glee and turned to McKenzie. "Now, that is what makes this job worthwhile."

"I thought you hated the fans?"

"Only the adult-stalker type. Little kids, on the other hand..."

McKenzie took a final sip of soda and put the cup down on the stairs beside her. A moment of nervous silence followed. "You wanna get out of here? This lobby isn't exactly private."

"What *exactly* do you have in mind, darling?"

She stood and grabbed his right arm. "Come on, let's go upstairs. I want you to show me the balcony."

"But, the balcony is off-limits. It's closed."

"Since when does that ever stop you? You're the king of living dangerously."

"Says who?"

She pulled him to his feet. "Come on! Don't be such a wet rag."

"Oh, all right, if I have to."

"You *have* to."

He took her right hand, followed her up the stairs to a mid-level split landing featuring a large mural, turned right, and took the stairs to the second floor.

CHAPTER FORTY-THREE

JIMBO STEERED THE MERCURY south on East Observation Road toward Griffith Park Observatory and stopped along the curve in the road at the foot of the north lawn. He, Murch, Lincoln, and MacGuffin were the only ones there. A construction trailer sat to the west, and scaffolding and machinery surrounded the building.

Inside the Mercury, Jimbo, Murch, Lincoln, and MacGuffin peered out the windows and looked around the grounds.

"Here we are," said Lincoln. "This is it."

"What do we do now?" asked MacGuffin.

"We wait," said Murch.

Nuke and Hayes watched from the Observatory's East Roof.

Nuke focused on the Mercury through a pair of night-vision binoculars. "Well, Billy, it appears they made it with no problems."

"What about the Spectre's goons?"

Nuke angled his binoculars up and watched the Rolls-Royce arrive. He glanced at his watch. "8:00. Right on schedule."

MAX AND MCKENZIE STOOD by the south entrance to the Rialto's second-story balcony. An iron gate blocked their access. McKenzie rattled the gate and fretted, "Oh, this one's locked, too!"

"I told you," said Max.

"Oh, I wanted to see the balcony!"

"Boy, you sound desperate."

"I am."

Max hesitated for a moment and said, "All right, I'll show you the balcony."

"And how do you plan to do that?"

Max stepped up to the gate and pulled back the metal bolt holding the gate closed. "*Voila!*"

McKenzie smiled. "How'd you do that?"

"Darling, this isn't the first time I've done this."

"Yay!" she squealed, clapping her hands.

Max pulled the gate open and ushered McKenzie inside. "After you."

She walked past him and entered the balcony. Max followed close behind and pulled the gate shut after him. As a final thought, he slid the metal bolt back into place. The bolt failed to slide back into its catch completely.

Max and McKenzie entered the back of the balcony and stood at the top of the left middle aisle beside the back row of seats. It was almost total darkness except for the throw light from the projection booth. The balcony held 400 seats, all of them foam-stuffed and leather-upholstered.

Max motioned to McKenzie and pointed to the projection booth. "Keep your voice down. Don't want the projectionist to hear us."

They crouched and hurried down the back row of seats in the mid-section, past the projection booth, careful not to interrupt the path of the projector's throw light, and stopped at the top of the right middle aisle.

McKenzie plopped down in an aisle seat in the back row of the far-right section. "These seats are nice. They don't hurt like the ones downstairs."

"Padded leather."

They paused to watch a bit of the movie unfolding on the giant screen before them.

McKenzie was quick to realize the film's sound from the speakers at balcony level was horrendous. "Too bad the sound isn't as good up here. I can't imagine why anybody would want to sit up here."

"Well, most people didn't come up here to watch the movie. They came up here to make out."

"Why is the balcony closed?"

"You're sitting in it."

"The seats? What's wrong with the seats?"

"They're a fire hazard."

"What?"

"The foam padding isn't fire resistant."

"Oh, come on. You're kidding me, right?"

"I kid you not, sweetheart. In fact, these seats used to be downstairs, and the downstairs seats used to be up here."

"Why'd they swap them?"

"A while back, the fire department shut the place down due to the main floor's loge seats not being fire resistant. For the theater to stay open, it was cheaper to swap the leather seats with the balcony's fireproof velvet seats. It woulda cost a fortune to rebuild the leather seats with fire-resistant stuffing. As a result, the balcony closed for good not long after. Sucks, eh, not being able to watch a movie in luxury?"

"Is the balcony haunted like the rest of the theater?"

"Oh, I've heard stories. A girl slit her wrists in one of the bathrooms downstairs, came up here, and bled to death in one of the seats. Another, a legend of a man who went insane in the projection booth. Eh...it's all a bunch of bullshit to me. I've never seen anything."

McKenzie got to her feet. "Good. Now that I know it's safe, I want to check it out." She grabbed Max's right arm.

"Check *what* out? There's nothing to see. It's pitch black up here."

She started walking down the stairs but stopped and looked back. "Don't be such a wallflower. Come on..." She grabbed his right hand and pulled him forward.

"Oh, all right," he relented. As he followed after her, he smirked. "A *wallflower*, eh? What the...? What is this, a high-school dance?"

McKenzie smiled. "You'll see."

She led him down to the middle of the aisle, made a beeline down the middle row of seats in the right section, and plopped down in the last seat by the wall aisle. Max remained standing.

"This is a good spot," said McKenzie. "We're safe."

"*Safe* from *what*?" asked Max.

"*Safe* from the prying eyes and ears of the projectionist in the projection booth."

"Why? What exactly do you have in mind?"

She raised a finger to his mouth. "Don't say a word."

In the darkness, she pulled Max down onto his knees in the aisle to her right and started unbuttoning his pants.

"What are you doing?" he asked, bewildered.

"*What* does *it* look like?"

"I don't know. It's dark."

"I want you, silly."

"Now's not a good time. This isn't the place for that sort of thing."

"Now's the perfect time; the perfect place. I want you inside me."

"I don't know about this. What if someone..."

"Relax. This won't take long. Let me do all the work."

"Fine. Have it your way."

She laid him down on the frayed burgundy carpet and straddled him, leaning her head down over his and kissing him on the lips. She pulled her hair out of her face and looked into his eyes. "I want you. I want you hard."

Max blinked. "Be glad to."

They locked lips and made out passionately, while an incredible cinematic car chase played out on-screen below. McKenzie moaned loudly.

"Sshh! Keep it down!" pleaded Max, embarrassed.

"I'm sorry. I can't help it. You touched a nerve."

THE ROLLS-ROYCE DROVE past the north lawn of the Observatory and pulled up to the entrance stairs.

On the East Roof, Nuke and Hayes took purchase besides the Zeiss Telescope rooftop dome. Hayes removed his sniper rifle from his bag and set it up on a mini tripod. Nuke removed a flashlight from his bag and signaled to his comrades below with three quick flashes.

Inside the Mercury, Jimbo saw the three flashes through his driver's side window. "You guys, Nuke and Hayes are in position on the roof."

"It's time," said Murch.

Murch, Jimbo, Lincoln, and MacGuffin climbed out of the idling Mercury and ambled down the sidewalk to the Astronomers Monument in the center of the north lawn. Murch carried a bullhorn.

Igor, Grendel, and Sebastian watched from inside the Rolls-Royce, paying extra close attention to MacGuffin.

"Heh. There *he* is," said Igor. "There *he* is. Heh, heh."

"This will all be over in a manner of minutes," said Grendel.

He ripped Rivers' black hood off.

Rivers appeared sweating, struggling to breathe, his mouth sutured shut. His deformed facial reconstruction, a study in horrors.

Grendel handed him a gun and said, "All right, Mr. Rivers, this is it, your big chance to get even with the guy who stole your career."

Rivers tried to speak, but all he could do was grunt and mumble through his stitched lips.

"Hey, this was your idea," smirked Grendel. "You do this, you're a free man. Once you take care of him, you walk away. End of story. You don't, you're a dead man. Understood?"

Rivers mumbled something unintelligible in response.

Grendel turned to Sebastian. "Did that sound like a *yes* to you?"

"I'm not sure," replied Sebastian, scratching his head.

"Heh, heh," grunted Igor.

Grendel turned back to Rivers and remarked, "I'll take that as a *yes*." He untied Rivers' hands behind his back. "Now, don't screw this up."

Grendel removed a handgun, chambered a round, and re-holstered it.

"So, what's the word, boss?" asked Sebastian.

"Okay, boys, let's go."

The doors of the Rolls-Royce opened, and Igor, Sebastian, and Grendel stepped out, assembled before the right side of the car, and looked toward Murch, Jimbo, Lincoln, and MacGuffin beside the Astronomers Monument.

As Nuke watched things from his position on the roof, Hayes adjusted the scope on his sniper rifle.

"You got 'em in your sight, Billy?" asked Nuke.

"That's a big ten-four, chief."

Below, Murch, Jimbo, and Lincoln drew their weapons. Murch raised her bullhorn and addressed the three goons, "You three stay where you are. That's far enough. Keep your hands out, so we can see them."

Grendel shouted out, "The young man with you, the one who thinks he's Christian Rivers, send him over!"

"The name's *Mr.* MacGuffin to you, shithead!" protested MacGuffin.

Lincoln put a stern hand on MacGuffin's shoulder and gave

him a concerned look. "Take it easy, Rich. You don't want to get yourself killed. Listen to Haley, and do what she says. Don't say anything to provoke them."

Murch addressed the goons with the bullhorn, "Before we hand Mr. MacGuffin over, let's see Mr. Rivers first."

Sebastian opened the Rolls-Royce's right rear door, leaned in, and pulled Rivers out. He nudged Rivers forward and closed the car door.

"There! You see him?"

"How do we know it's him?" asked Murch.

"Believe what you want, sister," replied Grendel, "but I assure you, it's him!"

Rivers' new look mortified Murch and the others. "My God! What have you done to him?"

"The three of us were only responsible for his abduction, not his makeover," explained Grendel. "The Master did this to him."

On the roof, Hayes lined up the three goons in his scope. "Come to Billy, boys."

Nuke removed a .44 Glock, took the safety off, and cocked it. "Locked and loaded."

MacGuffin grew more and more anxious with every passing minute. "Come on, let's get this over with."

Murch again addressed the goons with the bullhorn, "They both go at the same time!"

"No! Your man goes first!" shouted Grendel. "Once we know he's unarmed, then we'll send Mr. Rivers!"

"No fancy stuff from you, either!" added Sebastian. "First, put down your guns and kick them away! Slowly!"

Murch, Jimbo, and Lincoln gave each other a concerned glance.

"What do you think?" asked Jimbo.

"Do as they say," answered Murch.

"I hope Nuke and Billy can handle the three of them all at once," said Lincoln, worried. "Otherwise, we're up shit creek without a paddle."

"It'll be all right, Linc," said Jimbo. "Have a little faith."

Murch, Jimbo, and Lincoln placed their guns on the ground and kicked them away. As they stood back up, they raised their hands and arms and took cover behind the Astronomers Monument.

197

Murch turned to MacGuffin and said, "All right, Rich. This is it."

"What do I do?"

"Walk out to the middle of the sidewalk with your arms up. Let them see you aren't armed."

MacGuffin took a deep breath and stepped forward. "It's now or never." He took another step, another, and another, all the while, his arms raised.

Up on the roof, Hayes lined up the back of Sebastian's head in his scope's crosshairs with his right eye. From his vantage, he watched MacGuffin continue down the sidewalk.

As MacGuffin crept forward, Grendel shouted out, "That's far enough. Igor!"

Igor removed a switchblade knife and cut the sutures binding Rivers' mouth shut. He nudged Rivers forward. "Heh, heh. Get moving. Heh, heh."

Rivers stepped over the curb and walked up the sidewalk to MacGuffin.

MacGuffin turned and looked at the Astronomers Monument where his friends waited, watching.

Jimbo gave him a "good luck" gesture. "You can do it, Mac."

Rivers walked up and met MacGuffin face-to-face. "So... *you're* the one who's been impersonating *me*?"

MacGuffin didn't quite know how to respond, so he stated, "Yep."

"What's your name, stranger?"

"MacGuffin...Rich...Rich MacGuffin."

"Well, Mr. MacGuffin, I don't think I need any introduction. You already know who I am."

"I suppose you wanna kick my ass right now for what I've done?"

"Seeing as I never gave you permission to do so...no, not at all. That won't be necessary."

Rivers raised his arm and offered MacGuffin a friendly hand.

MacGuffin reluctantly accepted. "Nice to finally meet you, Mr. Rivers. I'm a big fan of your work."

"I see that."

"I'm sorry about this whole thing. I–"

"You needn't worry about anything. It's *I* who should be thanking *you*."

"Why is that?"

"Because, if it weren't for you pretending to be me, I wouldn't be here right now being set free. If it weren't for *you*, *I'd* be dead now."

"But why are they letting you go now? Whose idea was it to let you go? What am I worth to the Hollywood Spectre?"

"To be perfectly honest..." Rivers drew the gun Grendel gave him and pointed it at MacGuffin's head. "...nothing." He snickered. "This hostage exchange was all my idea." He forced MacGuffin down on his knees.

Murch and the others at the Monument watched horrified. "Oh, no!" cried Murch.

"This wasn't part of the plan," said Lincoln.

"What do we do now?" asked Jimbo.

As for the three goons by the Rolls-Royce, they chuckled with glee.

"Heh, heh, heh. Kiss the gun. Shoot, shoot, shoot. Heh, heh, heh," cackled Igor.

Rivers pointed the gun at MacGuffin's forehead, and MacGuffin closed his eyes. "See you on the other side, Mr. MacGuffin."

"Tell me one thing. Why do you want to kill me? Is what I did all that bad? I mean, without you, the movie wouldn't have finished. The studio would've scrapped it. I did what I did because I had to. I did it because I could. It was my calling."

"Only if I kill you, am I a free man. If not, I'm a dead one. I'm sorry, that's how it has to be."

The three goons cheered Rivers on.

"Do it!" shouted Sebastian. "Do it!"

Rivers cracked his neck from the tension and cocked his gun. "Say your prayers."

Tears ran from MacGuffin's eyes as he clenched them shut. "Don't do it. I beg you."

"Too late."

Out of time, Nuke gave Hayes the command, "NOW!"

"With pleasure."

Locked onto his target, Hayes pulled the trigger and blew the top half of Sebastian's body clean off. Pieces of flesh, bone, organs, pulp, and blood flew everywhere, the concussion knocking Grendel and Igor to the pavement.

"Nice shot, Billy the Kid," said Nuke, applauding.

Hayes kissed the rifle and smiled. "When you need to get the job done, accept no substitutes."

A barrage of gunfire erupted their way courtesy of Grendel and Igor.

"Time to move!" shouted Nuke.

They tucked and rolled back behind the Zeiss Telescope rooftop dome, out of harm's way.

CHAPTER FORTY-FOUR

TUESDAY, AUGUST THE TWENTY-THIRD
EIGHT THIRTEEN PM

THE RIALTO THEATRE'S PROJECTION booth continued the classic design of the theater with the interior featuring vintage movie posters, film reels, projection equipment, and lots of dust. *Texas Ace Arcana* played out over two old projectors.

The projectionist, Kirby Sweetman, sat at an antique negative-cutter machine and trimmed the "cigarette burn" frame from a film reel, as his assistant, Chuckie, entered carrying a box of light bulbs and the cat.

"Honey, I'm home!" announced Chuckie with bravado. "And, look who I found."

Kirby looked up from his work and saw the cat in Chuckie's arms. "L.A.! Chuckie, you found him! Where was he hiding?"

"By the balcony entrance."

"Next time, pay more attention before exiting the booth, dipshit. That way, he won't be able to sneak out."

"Wah, wah."

"Oh, shut the Hell up. Did you get the light bulb?"

"Yeah. I got you a whole box, in fact."

"Perfect timing. You're a lifesaver. The next reel is almost ready to roll."

Kirby grabbed the box of bulbs, moved over to the on-standby projector #2, and quickly swapped out a burned-out bulb with a new one, as a bell on the projector rang, indicating it was almost time for the reel change.

"You were saying, Kirby?"

"Keep it up! I'll shove this bell so far up your stinker, you'll be whistling Dixie."

"I was referring to the reel change, Kirb."

Kirby peered out the booth's window into the auditorium and saw the first reel-change "cigarette burn" marker in the top right of the movie frame. He hit the #2 projector's change-over switch. Two film reels began to rotate, and the film moved through the projector's gate.

The projector bulb glowed white-hot, emitting a beam of light as the second reel-change marker appeared on-screen. Projector #2 picked up where #1 left off, and the film continued uninterrupted.

"Damn, we're good, Chuckie!" said Kirby. He slid over to projector #1, reset its alarm to ten minutes, turned the projector off, and hit the rewind button. "Now we're set for another ten minutes, or so."

"It'd be even better if the owners forked over the dough for a new modern projector. Then, we wouldn't need to keep making reel changes every ten minutes."

"Yeah, but if they did that, one of us would be out of a job."

"Hell, in a few years, none of this'll matter. This whole theater will close for good, and we'll both be on the unemployment line."

"Oh, ye of little faith, my friend. Ye of little faith. The next reel's ready to go. It needs spooling up once the last one's done rewinding."

ONLY YARDS AWAY, MAX and McKenzie writhed furiously on the floor on the far side of the balcony. There was a bit of moaning and groaning, followed by a loud gasp from Max and a soft thud, as his head hit the floor. Silence ensued.

McKenzie became instantly concerned. "Christian?"

No response.

She shook his body. No movement. She checked and found he was breathing, albeit shallowly. He had only passed out.

"Oh, God," she whispered.

IN THE PROJECTION BOOTH, Chuckie stood beside the table, as Kirby took a seat at the negative cutter. "What's that you're working on, Kirby?"

Kirby picked up a single frame of 35mm film and held it up for his assistant to see. "Another cigarette burn for my collection. Took it from the end of reel one once it finished playing. The negative was still warm when I sliced and diced it."

"Great, screw up the reel change for the rest of us!"

"Oh, please! It's only the first reel. Like anybody in the

audience pays attention during the first ten minutes of a movie. They're all out getting popcorn at the concession stand or pinching a deuce."

"You better have punched a new hole in the negative?"

"No need to get your panties in a bunch, *hombre*. I did. I did."

Kirby removed a dusty black binder from a tote bag under the table and opened it to a page half-full of single film frames. He pulled back the protective cover and stuck his latest addition into place. He scribbled the name of the movie underneath with a marker, replaced the transparent cover over the page, and closed the binder. "There. All set."

"You're a freakin' nutbar. You know that, Kirby?"

"Born and bred in the U.S.A."

"I thought you were born in Vancouver, Canada?"

"Oh, who asked you?"

All of a sudden, a loud scream sounded from outside the projection booth's observation window: McKenzie's cry– "HELP!"

WITH GRENDEL AND IGOR and Rivers distracted by Nuke and Hayes on the East Roof of the Observatory, Murch dove and rolled for her weapon on the grass by the Astronomers Monument. She grabbed her gun and tossed Jimbo and Lincoln theirs.

She shouted to Jimbo crouched on the ground behind the Monument, "Jimbo! Go get Rich!"

"What about Rivers? He's got a gun."

Murch sat up and fired a shot that struck Rivers square in the forehead. He dropped to the ground, dead. "Not anymore."

Jimbo and Lincoln appeared stunned.

"I can't believe it!" said Lincoln. "You killed him!"

Murch scrambled for cover behind the Monument with Jimbo and Lincoln. "This was never about rescuing Rivers, Lincoln. It was an ambush from the start. A distraction."

"Yeah, but why?" asked Jimbo. "For what purpose?"

"I'll explain later, but for now, go protect Rich."

Jimbo raised his weapon and fired several shots, as he ran out to MacGuffin on the open sidewalk.

Murch and Lincoln took cover behind the Astronomers Monument.

As Jimbo neared MacGuffin, a stray bullet struck his left arm.

"Aargh!"

"Jimbo!" cried Murch.

Working through the pain, Jimbo threw himself on top of MacGuffin and held him down.

MacGuffin noticed the blood oozing from Jimbo's arm. "You're hit!"

"I'll be okay. Stay down."

PROJECTIONIST KIRBY SWEETMAN ENTERED the Rialto's balcony and shined his flashlight around. "Hello!"

Although the balcony appeared empty, in the far north aisle, McKenzie hovered over Max's unconscious body in a panic. She tried frantically to stir him by slapping his face. "Wake up, darling. Wake up."

No luck.

As she started mouth-to-mouth resuscitation, a flashlight illuminated the two of them.

"Need some help?" asked Kirby, shining the light in McKenzie's face.

She shielded her eyes. "Oh, thank God!" She motioned to the unconscious Max on the floor and pleaded, "Call an ambulance!"

AS THEY DESCENDED THE East Roof, Nuke and Hayes fired cover shots at Grendel and Igor on the north driveway.

Like the sniveling coward he was, Igor dove into the Rolls-Royce's driver's seat and took cover.

Grendel took cover on the opposite side of the car, managing still to fire off an occasional shot. "Igor! Start the car!"

From his crouched position inside the car, Igor turned the key in the ignition and started the engine.

Grendel waited for either Murch or Lincoln to pop out from around the edge of the Astronomers Monument. Lincoln proved to be the unlucky one. As he fired at Grendel, a bullet from Grendel's gun struck him in the upper chest between his heart and left shoulder.

As Lincoln collapsed on the sidewalk, Murch rushed to his aid and dragged him to safety behind the Monument.

Lincoln lay on his back, clutching his chest. "Uh...Haley..." he called out, straining.

"You'll be fine, Lincoln. The bullet missed your heart."

Leaning over him, Murch placed her right hand over the wound and applied pressure. She checked the back of his shoulder for an exit wound. "Feels like the bullet hit was a thru-and-thru. We need to get you to the hospital ASAP."

"Stay with me, Haley."

"I'm not going anywhere, Lincoln. You go, I go, remember?"

He slipped into unconsciousness.

Murch checked his vitals. "Lincoln?" He was still alive. "Stay with me, buddy. Don't give up."

Nuke and Hayes fought their way to Jimbo and MacGuffin on the north lawn sidewalk. Hayes shielded them, as Nuke checked Jimbo's arm.

"Is it bad, Nuke?" groaned Jimbo.

Blood flowed free. Nuke lied. "I'd call this a flesh wound, Jimbo." He removed a handkerchief from his pocket and tied it around Jimbo's arm as a makeshift tourniquet. He glanced over at Rivers' body on the sidewalk. "Which part of the plan said to shoot him?"

"He was going to kill Rich."

"Yeah, but why?"

"Rivers didn't have a choice, Nuke. It was the only way the Hollywood Spectre was going to let him go free."

Nuke grabbed Rivers' .38 from his dead right hand and checked the chamber. "This gun is loaded with blanks, Jimmy."

"*What?*"

"They never intended to let Rivers walk away alive."

"Yeah, but why?"

"Let me explain it this way: If this whole thing were a movie, Rivers would have been the 'MacGuffin' of the story. His abduction set the story into motion, driving it through to the third act–act two being our investigation–but ultimately, his involvement has proven irrelevant to the overall plot.

"It was never about Christian Rivers. The Hollywood Spectre always planned to kill him. Rivers was used as a distraction to keep us occupied, while the Spectre moved forward with an ulterior motive: his master plan–something elsewhere, elusive."

"Yes, but *what?*"

"I haven't a clue."

Hayes dodged a bullet by dropping to the ground. Seeing an opening between the wheels of the Rolls-Royce, he squeezed off a shot, striking Grendel's right leg.

"Aaargghhh!"

Hayes smiled. "Bullseye!"

Wounded, Grendel climbed inside the Rolls-Royce and collapsed onto the backseat. "Igor, get us out of here!"

"Heh, heh...with pleasure, Master. Heh. Heh."

As Grendel pulled the back door shut, Igor floored the accelerator, and the Rolls-Royce tore like a bat out of Hell down the west side of East Observatory Road.

Nuke jumped to his feet and yanked Hayes off the pavement.

"What do we do now, Nuke? They're getting away."

"We go after them."

Nuke and Hayes made a mad dash for the idling Mercury and jumped inside.

Nuke called out to Murch by the Astronomers Monument with Lincoln, "Haley, darling, I need you to stay here with the others! Call for an ambulance!"

"You're crazy! You're not gonna be able to catch them!"

"We don't have a choice, Haley! With Rivers dead, they're our only chance of finding the Spectre's hideout before he strikes again!"

Nuke hit the gas, and the Mercury tore off after the Rolls-Royce.

Murch shouted after them, "Nuke! Nuke!" Her efforts proved futile, as neither Nuke nor Hayes could hear her.

Lincoln came to and tugged Murch's left arm. "Haley!"

"Lincoln!"

"Let them go, Haley," he gasped. "Nuke and Billy know what they're doing. They've been doing this a long time."

Jimbo and MacGuffin joined them.

"How are you feeling, Linc?" asked Jimbo.

"Like I was hit by a semi-truck. Otherwise, I'll live. How 'bout you, Jimmy?"

"My left arm has a pretty good hole in it, but my right arm still packs a pretty good punch."

Murch looked at MacGuffin. "You okay, Rich? Are you hit?"

"No, I'm fine."

Murch turned to Jimbo. "Would you mind putting some pressure on Lincoln's wound while I call an ambulance? He's losing a lot of blood."

"No problem, Haley."

"Thank you."

Winded, Murch let Jimbo take over, and she removed her cell phone and dialed 911.

A dispatcher picked up almost immediately. "9-1-1. Please state your emergency."

CHAPTER FORTY-FIVE

THE MERCURY SPED AFTER the Rolls-Royce through the two-lane Mount Hollywood Drive tunnel. Hayes leaned out the passenger window and tried shooting out the Rolls-Royce's tires with his Glock. It didn't work. With traffic racing toward them in the opposite lane, the Rolls-Royce was an easy miss.

As Hayes was about to fire off another shot, the Rolls-Royce swerved into the oncoming lane, sending cars swerving left and right, out of its way. Nuke grabbed Hayes by his belt and pulled him back inside the car.

"What the Hell, Nuke? I almost had them."

"This is crazy, Billy. That hunchback can drive. A few more seconds of this is all I can take."

The Mercury kept a safe distance behind the Rolls-Royce on the winding Western Canyon Road.

Inside the Rolls-Royce, Grendel tended to his injured leg by tying a rag around it to stop the bleeding. "Igor, try and lose them. You know what to do."

"As you wish, Master."

As Western Canyon Road merged into Fern Dell Drive, the Rolls-Royce sped up and cut in and out of traffic, passing cars too fast for safety.

Nuke was furious. "Goddammit! That little weasel's pissing me off! If he wants to play, let's play!" He shifted into a faster gear. "Hold on, Billy."

The Mercury cut around cars to keep up with the Rolls-Royce. A car suddenly blocked its path, forcing Nuke to press down hard on the car horn. "Get the Hell out of my way, Miss Daisy!"

The Mercury swerved to pass the car on a sharp curve, barely managing to avoid hitting a Grey-Lines tour bus head-on.

Hayes peeked up from beneath the dashboard. "That was

close."

Nuke appeared frazzled. "No backseat drivers, Billy."

TWO PARAMEDICS HAULED MAX'S unconscious body out the front of the Rialto on a gurney, past the media, paparazzi, and fans, and loaded him into the back of a waiting ambulance.

A grief-stricken McKenzie tried to climb into the back of the ambulance to be with him, but a paramedic stopped her. "Sorry, Miss, but nobody's allowed back here. If you want to come with, you'll have to ride up front."

"Well, can you at least tell me what's wrong with him?"

"Again, sorry. If I knew, I'd tell you. But, for now, we won't know anything until we get him to the hospital."

John Crawford pushed his way through the crowd and approached McKenzie. "McKenzie, darling, I'll ride with Rivers to the hospital and stay with him until I find out something."

"What should I do?"

"Janine said she'd drive you home or to my cabin in the Hills if you'd prefer. I'll call you when I get some information."

Crawford was about to climb into the ambulance when reporter Gloria Cox stopped him. She shoved her microphone and cameraman Kenney's camera in the producer's face. "John Crawford, can you verify the medical condition of actor Christian Rivers? We saw him loaded into the back of this ambulance. Is there any truth to the rumors Mr. Rivers collapsed inside due to a drug overdose?"

Crawford grew irritated. "Miss Cox, please! This is an emergency situation. You're impeding our departure. If you'd like some answers, talk to my associate, Nigel Guest. He's hiding around here someplace. Now, if you don't mind, stick that microphone where the sun don't shine, sweetheart." He pushed her aside and climbed into the front of the ambulance.

"Well, there you have it, ladies and gentlemen. Coming to you live from the historic Rialto Theatre in South Pasadena, for *KLAX Eyewitness News*, I'm Gloria Cox."

McKenzie watched helplessly from the sidewalk, as the lights and siren started up, and the ambulance drove away.

In the back of the ambulance, the two paramedics tended to Max Winston while en route to the hospital.

"These rich bastards," remarked Paramedic #1. "All the fame and fortune in the world, and they have to squander it all for a quick fix. What a waste."

"Drugs weren't the culprit, Ronnie. Look at his medical alert bracelet. My guess he has suffered a bout of Neuroglycopenia and passed out."

"He's hypoglycemic?"

THE MERCURY NAVIGATED A hilly valley road made up of little streets, terraced hillsides, and sharp turns.

Driving slow, Nuke looked around, thinking he had lost the Rolls-Royce. "Where did they go, Billy? We were right on them."

"There!"

"Where?"

Hayes pointed to an auto junkyard: Darnell's Auto Salvage. The Rolls-Royce sat idling at the entrance in plain sight.

"Good work, Billy!"

The Rolls-Royce drove forward and turned down an aisle between two rows of cars stacked high.

As the Mercury turned onto Darnell's lot, Nuke and Hayes craned their heads left and right looking for the Rolls-Royce.

"They picked a great place to hide," said Nuke. "They'll blend right in amongst all these cars."

The Rolls-Royce rolled through the canyon of scrap heaps, as the Mercury drove by in the background, which Igor noticed in his rear-view mirror. "I see you. Heh, heh."

As the Mercury passed the aisle, Hayes glimpsed the Rolls-Royce. "There she is, Nuke!"

Nuke cranked the steering wheel and turned the Mercury down an adjacent aisle. "We'll meet them on the other end. There's no way they can turn around. It's too narrow."

The Mercury sped up.

The Rolls-Royce, on the other hand, continued along at a snail's pace.

Inside, Grendel glanced at Igor and remarked, "Sure hope you know what you're doing, Igor."

"Heh, heh."

The Rolls-Royce slowed and backed into a hollow space

between two cars and a heap of junk above. Camouflage.

Igor killed the engine right as the Mercury turned down the now-empty aisle at the opposite end.

"Where'd they disappear to, now?" asked Hayes.

The Rolls-Royce's driver's door creaked open, and Igor slipped out and snuck away through the back of the breach in the junk pile.

Grendel ducked down inside the car, as the Mercury drove past the Rolls-Royce's hiding spot.

Nuke smacked the steering wheel in frustration. "Blast it! How the Hell did they get away so fast? They were right here!"

"They couldn't have gotten far, Nuke."

Grendel slipped into the Rolls-Royce's driver's seat and turned the key in the ignition.

As the Mercury continued down the aisle, the Rolls-Royce pulled out of its hiding space, turned right, and followed after.

Grendel pulled a knob on the dashboard, and the headlights flared, illuminating the Mercury's interior.

Nuke checked his rear-view mirror and saw the Rolls-Royce closing in on them. "We got company."

Grendel slammed his foot down on the gas pedal, and the Rolls-Royce lurched forward, erratically.

Nuke adjusted the rear-view mirror to block the blinding headlights.

Hayes glanced at his side mirror. The Rolls-Royce gained right behind them and veered wildly left and right. "Looks like he's trying to broadside us into the scrap pile, Nuke."

"Not if I can help it."

Nuke shifted into a higher gear, and the Mercury lurched forward.

The chase was on now; bumper to bumper.

Nuke fastened his seatbelt and turned to Hayes. "Better put your seatbelt on, Billy. It's gonna be a tight turn."

Too late! As the Mercury neared the end of the drag, a bulldozer appeared from the right, and Nuke and Hayes watched in horror as it plowed into them. "Oh, shit!"

At the controls of the bulldozer sat Igor, laughing hysterically, as the Mercury tossed around like an empty beer can. "Hee! Hee! Hee...!"

The Rolls-Royce skidded to a stop, as the bulldozer moved out of its way. As for the Mercury, it tumbled side over side and kept going even after the bulldozer shut down.

Grendel stepped from the driver's seat of the Rolls-Royce and limped toward Igor and the bulldozer.

The Mercury crashed into a wall of junked cars. Grendel and Igor approached cautiously. As they got closer, the driver's door fell open, and Nuke's unconscious body dropped out, still belted in.

Grendel knelt and checked for a pulse. "This one's still alive."

"Heh. What about the other one? Heh. Heh."

Grendel looked inside the car at Hayes in the front passenger seat. With his torso mangled, head caved in, neck broken, and slashed from broken glass, he was dead.

"He's looking a little funky. I'd say he's dead-on-arrival."

A few minutes later, Grendel loaded the two detectives' bodies into the trunk of the Mercury. He reached in and removed Nuke's cell phone from his hip pouch and pocketed it in his suit coat. Finally, he slammed the trunk lid as good as it would close and picked the Mercury's rear license plate up off the ground and walked away.

Igor sat behind the controls of a giant industrial claw grab machine and worked the throttles. The massive crane jerked forward and approached the mangled wreck of Nuke's Mercury. The machine's giant steel claws opened and sank their teeth into the car's body.

In a shower of glass and metal, the crane hoisted the Mercury high into the air and swung it up and over a heap of crushed cars to a giant steel-refining machine called "The Grim Ripper."

The claw grab maneuvered into place alongside the Ripper and hoisted the Mercury over a large smelting pot, bubbling with glowing-red molten steel.

Grendel joined Igor in the cab for the final farewell. Igor noticed the Mercury's license plate in his hands. "Heh. A little souvenir for your collection? For bragging rights? Heh. Heh. Heh."

"Consider it our Christmas card to the LAPD, nearly four months early."

"Heh. Heh."

Grendel grew restless. "Igor, you sniveling little shit, drop the car and finish it, so we can go home and hear all about how the premiere went."

Igor pulled the lever to release the claw's grip on the Mercury. "Heh!"

The front of the Mercury plunged into the pool of molten steel, followed shortly after by the rest of the car. As the claws retracted, the car began to sink into the pit of fire.

Grendel and Igor watched in anticipation from the cab of the crane. Grendel snapped a photo with Nuke's cell phone.

The Mercury sank lower and lower, as its interior filled with molten ooze. The left front tire burst, sending chunks of glowing liquid flying everywhere. Next, the right tire went.

"Snap, crackle, pop!" cheered Grendel.

"Hee! Hee!" cackled Igor. "Pop goes the weasel till the weasel goes pop! Hee! Hee! Hee!"

The Mercury sank deeper and deeper, inch by inch, until only the trunk and rear bumper remained. The back two tires were the next to explode. All of a sudden, the car stopped and bobbed on the surface.

Nervous, Igor chewed frantically on a yellowing hangnail. "Eeh...eeh!" He even tried to will the car to sink– "Heh. Sink, you bloody bastard! Sink! Heh. Heh."–but to no avail.

From within the Mercury's trunk came frantic pounding sounds and muffled cries made by Nuke. Gradually, the sounds faded as the trunk interior filled.

"Heh. Heh."

Miraculously, the car resumed sinking and casually slipped beneath the surface, creating a slurping sound.

Grendel smiled. "All too easy."

He and Igor stepped down from the cab and headed for the Rolls-Royce.

"Where to now, Master? Heh. Heh."

Grendel held up Nuke's license plate and cell phone. "Got to overnight a package. I'm driving."

As the Rolls-Royce sped away in a cloud of dust and exhaust, molten steel poured from the Ripper's giant smelting pot into large block molds which traveled down a conveyor belt, depositing into an extensive collection basin.

BACK AT THE GRIFFITH Park Observatory, an ambulance and a

police car sat parked on the north lawn by the Astronomers Monument. Murch and Jimbo stood by and watched Lincoln get loaded into the back of one ambulance on a stretcher. A paramedic gave him a breath of oxygen through a mask connected to a portable oxygen tank.

MacGuffin sat in the back of the police car, as a police officer questioned Murch, and Jimbo had his wounded left arm tended to by a second paramedic.

"Is Lincoln gonna be okay?" asked Jimbo.

"He'll be just fine," replied the paramedic. "The bullet missed his heart and artery by about an inch. He should be up and out of the hospital within a couple of days."

"What about Jimbo?" asked Murch. "How long's he gonna be out?"

The paramedic smirked. "You're kidding me, right?"

"Sorry?"

"His injury is barely a scratch. The bullet only grazed the bone. No fracture. He should only need to wear a sling for a short time."

Jimbo looked to Murch and asked, "Have you been able to get a hold of either Nuke or Hayes?"

"All I'm getting is a busy signal. His phone must be off."

"Keep trying."

As Murch tried again to reach Nuke by phone, she gazed down the sidewalk and watched as a third and fourth paramedic placed Christian Rivers' body into a body bag and zipped it up. They carried the bag to a second waiting ambulance parked by the Observatory's north entrance and loaded it into the back beside a smaller body bag containing Sebastian's remains. The back doors of the ambulance slammed shut, and the two paramedics climbed into the front and drove away.

CHAPTER FORTY-SIX

WEDNESDAY, AUGUST THE TWENTY-FOURTH
TEN FIFTY-SEVEN AM

AT THE HAZE FILMS Productions building, John Crawford sat at his desk reviewing paperwork, as the door burst open, and FBI Special Agent Haley Murch stormed in, as Crawford's telephone rang.

"John Crawford!" proclaimed an urgent Murch. "I need to speak with you about a matter of utmost importance!"

Perturbed, Crawford stopped her with a stern finger, put his phone on speaker, and spoke into it, "Yes, darling, what is it?"

The voice that replied was Crawford's secretary, but not his usual assistant, Janine Potts. It was somebody else altogether. "Sorry, Mr. Crawford, she insisted on seeing you immediately."

"It's not a problem. That will be all, my dear."

Crawford picked up the phone and dropped it back down in its cradle, terminating the call.

He studied Murch for a moment and smiled. "Sorry about that. You must excuse my secretary. She's new at this. Today's her first day."

Murch closed the office door and remained standing, despite two empty guest chairs.

"Must be something imperative for you to barge in on me like this?" asked Crawford.

"I guess you could say that," said Murch.

"Please, take a seat, Miss...?"

Murch showed her badge and ID to Crawford. "Excuse my intrusion, Mr. Crawford. My name is Special Agent Haley Murch of the FBI. I'm investigating the disappearance of Christian Rivers and several associated homicides. Juno Calvecchio for one."

"Ah, yes. Terrible what happened, indeed."

"I don't think *terrible* is the word I would use. It's a tragedy. Two LAPD detectives got shot last night attempting a rescue of Mr. Rivers. One of them is in serious condition. Rivers, sadly, died in the crossfire."

"I'm truly sorry for your loss, Agent Murch. As for Mr. Rivers, his loss will have a profound effect on this industry and my career. He was one of my prized pupils."

"So *prized* that you felt the need to use a look-alike to finish your movie following his disappearance?"

"That's a sensitive area I'd prefer not to comment on. If word leaked out, it would mean bad PR for my company and the studio; damaging even."

"That's the least of my concerns, right now, Mr. Crawford. That's not why I'm here."

"What exactly is it you need my help on, Agent?"

Murch removed the list of Spectre victims from her coat and showed it to Crawford. "This is a list of celebrity victims. An LAPD junior homicide detective did an analysis and uncovered a connection between them and yourself."

"*Me?*"

"The person responsible is a serial killer the media has come to call the Hollywood Walk of Fame Killer. The killer prefers to call himself the Hollywood Spectre."

"Who says I have a connection to all this hocus pocus? That's impossible. I don't even know who this person is. All I know is what I've read about in the papers."

Murch handed Crawford the list. "Do you recognize any of these people, Mr. Crawford?"

Crawford put on a pair of reading glasses and perused the list. "Some of these names, yes, I do recognize. They've worked in various capacities for me over the years."

Murch took a seat. "How long have you worked in the film industry?"

Crawford removed his glasses and leaned back in his chair. "Since the late '60s."

"A bio sheet we uncovered says you started out as a director. You made many low-budget horror films in the late '60s through the mid-'70s. The last movie you directed went unfinished, but it doesn't state a reason why."

"Oh, yes, I remember that one. There's a simple explanation: We ran out of money midway through the shoot. We overspent it on the lavish sets of a haunted house picture. Unlike Hammer Films, we didn't reuse the same sets and props over and over again. We spared no expense to make it a true fright fest."

"Since then, you've never directed another film or television project. Why is that?"

"My fiancée at the time gave birth to our daughter. It was November of '76. I took a few years off to help raise her."

"You resumed working in 1982 in a producer capacity, something you've continued to do ever since."

"Correct. Being a producer takes up less time than a director. I did it so I could spend more time with my family."

"The Hollywood Spectre has been in the killing business since at least 1980, so something must have happened to set him off around the mid-to-late '70s."

"Again, I'm not familiar with anybody called the Hollywood Spectre."

"Not the Hollywood Spectre, but his real name."

"Do you even know his *real* name?"

"That's what we're trying to figure out. Did you ever have a falling out with any actor or crew member on any of your movies before 1976?"

"This is the movie business, darling. Happens all the time. It goes with the territory."

"Well, that's all the questions I have for you."

Crawford got up from his desk and moved to the door. "Sorry I couldn't be more helpful to you. Let me get the door for you. I'll have my assistant walk you out."

"Thank you, sir."

Murch got up from her seat and moved to the door but stopped. "Oh, one last thing before I go. If I wanted to find out more about some of your old movies, where at the studio might I go?"

Crawford opened the office door, thinking. "Um...you might consider trying Archives. I hear the fellow who works there is a glut of information."

"Thank you, Mr. Crawford. I'll stop by there on my way out."

"Hope I helped? Good luck with your investigation. If you need anything more, you know where to find me. Have a good afternoon, Agent Murch."

Murch stepped past Crawford and left out the door.

As she walked down the hallway to the lobby, Crawford shut the door behind her and grinned devilishly. "Yes. Have a good afternoon, indeed, ha, ha, ha."

Murch exited the Haze Films building and returned to her red Mustang where MacGuffin waited for her. As she walked, she pulled on her sunglasses.

Murch sighed as she climbed in the driver's seat. "Gee, that went well."

MacGuffin didn't hear her, as he was too busy with a cell phone call. "...She's back. I don't know."

"Who are you talking to, Rich?"

MacGuffin cupped his right hand over the phone and replied, "Jimbo at headquarters."

She removed her sunglasses. "Has anyone heard anything from Nuke or Hayes?"

MacGuffin held up a finger as he talked to Jimbo. "Here she is. Let me put her on the phone."

"Any good news?" asked Murch.

MacGuffin solemnly shook his head and handed her the phone.

"Talk to me, Jimbo. What do you got? Any news from Nuke or Billy?"

Jimbo, his left arm in a black sling, sat at Nuke's desk in the Robbery-Homicide department of the West Los Angeles Community Police Station, as he talked on the phone. A bulky manila envelope lay on the desk before him. "I'm sorry to be the bearer of bad news, Haley. A package arrived at the office a few minutes ago."

"What's in it?"

"A license plate."

"A license plate? That's kinda odd."

"It's Nuke's custom plate from the Mercury."

Murch appeared frantic. "You've heard from Nuke and Billy, right?"

"Sorry, Haley, I'm...afraid Nuke and Billy are dead."

Tears welled up in Murch's eyes. "*Dead?* No. No, they can't be *dead*. That's impossible. We were with them last night."

"I'm sorry, Haley, but it appears to be true."

She wiped her eyes on her coat sleeve. "No..."

Jimbo held up a second cell phone and flipped through a file of digital photos. "Besides the license plate, the package also contained Nuke's cell phone with pictures of their bodies in the trunk of Nuke's car. The Spectre's goons lowered the Mercury into a smelting pot and melted it down into bars of steel. They burned Nuke and Billy alive, Haley. Cremated."

Murch couldn't handle it anymore, and she broke down crying. "No, no, no..."

"I'm sorry, Haley."

Murch wiped her eyes.

Jimbo picked up a police report from the desk. "And, that's not all I have for you, Haley. A report came in off the wire. Police discovered an ambulance abandoned this morning in Burbank. They found two paramedics and a driver dead inside with their throats slashed and their guts hanging out."

"What does that have to do with anything?"

"A patient chart found inside listed Christian Rivers as the patient being transported, suffering from hypoglycemia. The police didn't find his body in the ambulance."

"Which Christian Rivers are we talking about? What was the pick-up location?"

"The Rialto Theatre in South Pasadena."

"But, that's the theater where they held Rivers' big movie premiere. Rich's friend, Max Winston, was there with McKenzie Banks. He was posing as Christian Rivers in place of Rich, so Rich could be with us at the Observatory. What happened to Max Winston?"

"Good question. A civilian accompanying him to the hospital also went missing."

"What's the name?"

"John Crawford."

"*Crawford?* But that's impossible. I talked to him only a few minutes ago here at the studio."

"Wait. You're saying you just talked to John Crawford? *The* John Crawford, the movie producer?"

"I'm positive."

"That's impossible. A janitor found him dead this morning along with four others inside a locked storage room at the theater."

"Why only now are we learning this information?"

"The bodies were all horribly mutilated, decapitated, and

stripped of any ID. Their heads were missing. It took the Coroner's office a while to get the results back on their fingerprints."

"Was Max Winston among the dead?"

Jimbo checked the report. "No. He's still missing, as is McKenzie Banks."

"Why?"

"I don't know, Haley."

"Is it the Hollywood Spectre?"

"Your guess is as good as mine. We need to find him, Haley, before he strikes again."

"I know where he is. Can you meet MacGuffin and me here at the studio in a half-hour or so?"

"Shouldn't be a problem. I'll be there as fast as the crow flies."

"Thanks, Jimbo."

"Later."

Murch terminated the call, and she and MacGuffin raced inside the Haze Films office building. Murch had her gun drawn. The lobby was ablaze, and the secretary was missing. A prosthetic John Crawford mask lay on the floor for them to find.

"Dammit!" exclaimed Murch. "He was just here!"

"You wanna explain to me what's going on?" asked MacGuffin.

Murch coughed from the smoke. "The Hollywood Spectre was here. It was him, disguised as John Crawford."

"John Crawford is the Hollywood Spectre?"

"No. Crawford is dead. Him and four others. The Hollywood Spectre killed them."

"Oh, my God!"

Murch and MacGuffin fought their way through the flames, in a crouching position to keep below the suffocating smoke, down the hallway to the executive offices. The place was deserted.

MacGuffin coughed. "Where'd they go? They didn't come out the front way."

"Who the Hell knows?" coughed Murch. "The Hollywood Spectre is a master of eluding the authorities. He's done so for the last thirty years. He's here one second and gone the next. He vanishes into thin air."

"How's that possible?"

"Besides being an expert on stage and make-up effects, he's

mastered the fine art of illusion like a Vegas magician?"

"What do we do now?"

Murch coughed. "For starters...let's get the Hell out of here before we die from smoke inhalation."

A FIRE TRUCK AND ambulance parked outside the smoldering shell of the former Haze Films Productions office building. Nothing much remained, as a group of firefighters worked to extinguish the blaze.

Murch questioned Fire Chief Mike O'Hallorhan, "Did you find any bodies in there?"

"Negative," he replied. "No bodies. Only a ton of melted film stock and equipment, plus whatever's left of the building, which isn't much."

"Thank you, Mr. O'Hallorhan."

"You're welcome, Agent Murch."

Murch let the fire chief get back to work. She approached MacGuffin and Jimbo sitting on a nearby curb while MacGuffin breathed through an oxygen mask. Jimbo's red Volkswagen bug sat beside Murch's Mustang.

MacGuffin lowered his oxygen mask and asked, "So, where do we go now, Haley? Back to the station?"

"Not yet. There's one more place I need to check out."

"A lead?"

"More of a dare."

CHAPTER FORTY-SEVEN

WEDNESDAY, AUGUST THE TWENTY-FOURTH
TWELVE ZERO-SEVEN PM

MURCH, MACGUFFIN, AND JIMBO exited the Mustang and stepped onto the sidewalk in front of the vacant Start Fresh Café storefront on the Paradise Pictures backlot Chinatown street façade.

"Where's this place again?" asked Jimbo.

Murch consulted a map inside a studio brochure. "This is where the map says it should be."

MacGuffin stood by a stairwell leading to a basement-level Laundromat storefront. "Think I found it."

Murch and Jimbo stepped over and saw a large sign that read "LAUNDROMAT."

"This isn't the Archives office," stated Murch. "It's a Chinese laundry."

"*Au contraire, mon frere*," retorted MacGuffin. "Remember, this is a movie studio. These storefronts are nothing but scaffolding and plywood façades. A common practice is to hide offices or editing suites within to make use of limited space. The fake sign above the door might read 'Laundromat,' but the real placard on the door reads 'Archives.' See for yourself."

Murch and Jimbo leaned over the railing for a closer look. Sure enough, the sign read "ARCHIVES."

"Hah! You're right!" exclaimed Jimbo.

MacGuffin motioned to Murch and Jimbo with a wave of his arm. "After you guys."

Murch led the way down the stairs, and the three of them entered the Archives office.

Inside, a rotund clerk sat at his cluttered desk, talking a mile a minute on the phone and examining a film strip, as Murch, MacGuffin, and Jimbo entered.

"What am I doing right now?" asked the clerk into the phone. "I'm...looking at a lost film strip of a young Marilyn Monroe performing–I'm sorry, I'll have to call you back."

He slammed down the phone, smiled, and greeted the three visitors, "Yes...how may I help you folks this afternoon?"

"We have a few questions about the films of director John Crawford," explained Murch.

"Whoa. That's a lot of history there. Can you be more specific?"

Murch dropped her FBI badge on top of the desk, causing the clerk's eyes to widen. "Hell-o!" he wailed.

"My name is Special Agent Haley Murch. I'm with the FBI. I'm serving as liaison with the LAPD on a homicide investigation pertaining to an elusive serial killer, nicknamed the Hollywood Spectre, who's been preying on celebrities."

The clerk swallowed hard. "You had me at the badge."

"Good," smiled Murch. "Now that I've gotten your utmost attention, we're trying to find info on a movie from 1976, directed by John Crawford. Nobody seems to know anything about it."

The clerk's face brightened, and a huge smile appeared on his face. "Lady, where have you been hiding the last ten years?"

"Excuse me?"

"I have been waiting ten years for this moment to arrive. Ever since I started working here."

"Sorry?"

"Never mind. Private geek moment."

Jimbo gave out a subdued snerk.

Murch nodded. "Got it. So, you've heard of it, then?"

"Oh, yeah. The reason you haven't been able to find anything on it is because the studio worked very hard to cover up any trace of it. The only people who know about it are the ones who made it, and most of them are either dead or refuse to talk about it. Here, let me go and get what I got for you..."

He lurched up and disappeared down a row of shelves.

MacGuffin looked at Murch and commented, "Odd fellow."

"You don't say..."

"Aha! Yes!"

Murch could have sworn she heard a pig squeal.

Shaking his head, Jimbo looked at Murch and MacGuffin. "Wow, that was quick."

"Not surprising..." replied Murch.

The clerk returned, brandishing a dusty film reel. "And here we go! This footage should answer many of the questions you may have."

He continued the conversation while setting up the showing, pausing to rub his hands together in glee more than once.

"You're saying you have that so-called *lost* movie in your possession?" asked Murch.

"Not the complete picture, *per se*–some of the raw dailies I happen to find very incriminating."

"And, just how did you happen to come across this information?"

"Do you think I work at the studio to be a dull desk clerk? Hell no. My name is Harry J. Ackerman. I do it to dig up the Hollywood dirt for my website and to pad my memorabilia collection. I know everything there is to know about Paradise Pictures Studios. Hell, if they knew what I knew, they'd have me killed. Ask away. I know it all. I have a photographic memory."

Harry turned to MacGuffin and prompted, "Mr. MacGuffin, if you would, please, hit the lights."

MacGuffin flipped off the light switch.

Harry continued, "Now, what I'm about to show you is something the studio has tried keeping a secret for thirty years. It's raw footage from an unfinished movie called *Curse of the Wax Phantom*, or, as the film can says, *Grave Robbers from Outer Space*."

"Isn't that the original title of Ed Wood's *Plan 9 from Outer Space*?" asked Jimbo.

"Correct. And, that's why nobody knows this footage exists. You see, I was snooping around the Archives one night, bored out of my mind. I'm a huge sci-fi geek, and I like to watch the classic sci-fi movies from the '30s through the '60s. I'm also a huge Ed Wood fan. So, when I found a film can labeled *Grave Robbers from Outer Space*, I thought I found some lost footage from *Plan 9*. Now, I've snuck tons of stuff out of the vaults over my years at the studio, mementos for my collection, so I figured nobody would miss some footage from a movie deemed 'the worst ever made.'

"So, I bring the footage home, spool it through the projector, flip the switch, and *voila!*, it's footage from an unfinished sequel to the classic 1967 horror movie, *The Wax Phantom*, starring the late British actor, Anton Leach. I know because there was a production sheet inside the can. The footage was for a 1976 movie called *Curse of the Wax Phantom*, directed by John Crawford, shot in March 1976."

"Why was the project scrapped by the studio?" asked Murch.

"It would cost too much to recast Leach's role and reshoot his scenes. They didn't have the top-notch CGI effects like we do today. They couldn't replace the lead actor with a computer double. No, the footage I'm about to show you is Anton Leach's last known footage."

"Anton Leach?"

"Yeah. He was a popular British character actor. Made a ton of horror movies from the mid-'60s to 1976. Fans regarded him as the next Lon Chaney, Boris Karloff, or Vincent Price, because of his incredible make-up skills."

Murch looked at MacGuffin and Jimbo. "Matches our killer's profile. We found pieces of a prosthetic mask at Juno Calvecchio's murder scene."

"Oh, yeah, and it gets even more interesting," said Harry. "Let's roll 'em." He flipped the switch on a vintage film projector, and it roared to life, projecting the footage onto a small screen suspended from the ceiling.

On-screen: Anton Leach appeared as "The Wax Phantom," resembling Lon Chaney, Sr.'s "Erick" from *Phantom of the Opera*. He had a skull-like face with a few wisps of black hair on top of his head.

The scene took place on a waxwork set. Leach crept along a narrow walkway over a vat of boiling wax, when the molten wax caught fire unexpectedly and exploded, enveloping Leach and the rest of the set.

"Oops!" exclaimed Harry. "That wasn't supposed to happen."

Ablaze, Leach lost his balance and fell over the railing of the walkway into the burning vat of liquid. Even so, the film in the movie's single camera kept rolling. Nobody in the cast or crew did anything to help Leach for close to fifteen seconds, until eventually the film's director, a young John Crawford, walked in front of the camera and ordered the cameraman to "Cut! Cut!" The raw footage switched to black leader, and the screen went white.

Harry flipped off the projector and prompted, "Lights, please."

MacGuffin flipped on the light switch.

"So, what did you think?" asked Harry. "Notice anything

peculiar about this footage?"

"Well, it's odd that nobody tried to help Leach for such a long time," said Jimbo.

"And, when Crawford did try, he *walked* in front of the camera. He didn't *run*. It's as if he wanted Leach to burn to death."

"The explosion was ruled an accident?" asked Murch.

"Well, according to the report, the police had their suspicions, but there wasn't enough evidence to suggest otherwise. If it was incidental, much of the evidence burned up with the actor."

"What happened to Leach after the accident?"

"From what articles I did find on him, Leach spent the next several months in a local hospital burn unit, before the docs declared him dead in a hospital ward fire that October. He awoke from a seven-month coma, set his room on fire, and hung himself. The Coroner ruled it a suicide."

"Was there an autopsy to verify it was Leach's body?"

"The Coroner's office had a Hell of a time identifying the body. The only thing left intact was Leach's hospital ID bracelet. There was no such thing as DNA testing back then. As for an autopsy, not according to the press clippings I found. The Coroner didn't deem one necessary."

"Leach could've switched bodies with another hospital patient, nurse, doctor, even a visitor."

"He could've slipped out of the hospital, while the fire kept everybody preoccupied," said Jimbo. "I doubt they even had surveillance cameras back then."

MacGuffin nodded. "It has to be him."

"Let's assume Leach survived," said Murch. "Where would he go?"

"No idea," said Jimbo.

Murch turned to Harry. "Was Anton Leach married at the time of his supposed death?"

Harry handed Murch a file folder. "Read for yourself. I pulled a bunch of records I thought might interest you."

Murch and Jimbo scanned through the articles. The folder included resumes, tax records, billing statements, and photographs.

"According to this, Anton Leach arrived in the US in 1967," stated Jimbo. "Paradise Pictures contracted him to a ten-year deal.

Made a bunch of low-budget horror movies."

Murch perused Leach's resume. "He married a young American actress named Victoria West in 1969. They met while working on a picture for American International called *Dr. Death*. It was the last movie she appeared in until after her husband's death; after she remarried."

"Would you say Leach was a controlling, egotistical bastard?" asked MacGuffin. "Is that why his wife never worked during their marriage?"

"Your guess is as good as mine," said Harry.

"Harry, you said Miss West remarried," stated Murch. "Who did she marry?"

"The director, John Crawford."

"John Crawford?"

"Yeppers. Crawford told the media he married Victoria because he felt sorry for her losing her husband."

"Do you know where we can find Mrs. Crawford? I'd like to ask her a few questions about her late husband."

"Ooh...sorry," groaned Harry. "Mrs. Crawford disappeared in 1994. Authorities found her car abandoned by Lake Hollywood with her purse inside and a supposed suicide note."

"Did they ever find the body?"

"No."

Murch removed an agency photo of Victoria West from 1969. "She was quite the looker."

"Yes, she was," remarked Jimbo. "She's the spitting image of her daughter."

"*Daughter?* What *daughter?*"

Jimbo examined a birth certificate. "Says here Victoria West gave birth November 20th, 1976, to a daughter: Michelle. The weird thing, though, Leach isn't listed as the father. John Crawford is."

"Seventy-six? You sure about that?"

Jimbo grinned. "This can't be right. It's gotta be a misprint. If her daughter was born in November '76, that would mean Victoria was pregnant with Crawford's baby at the time of Leach's accident."

"A-ha!" exclaimed MacGuffin. "She was having an affair: The perfect motive to kill her husband."

"That's Hollywood for ya," joked Harry.

Jimbo handed the birth certificate to Murch.

MacGuffin scratched his head. "Crawford? The only daughter John Crawford has I know of is McKenzie Banks. Not Michelle."

"Yeah, McKenzie Banks, that's who I'm talking about," said Jimbo. "She's the spitting image of her mother." He held up a photo of Victoria West for MacGuffin to see. "See?"

MacGuffin appeared shocked. Jimbo handed him the photo for a closer look.

"I bet you didn't know McKenzie Banks isn't her real name," added Harry. "It's a stage name. Come to think of it, Victoria West's real name is Victoria Grayson. Go figure."

Murch took a closer look at Michelle West's birth certificate. "According to this, Michelle West's middle name is Kensington."

"Maybe she had the nickname Mickey? Mickey Kensington or McKenzie for short?" implied Jimbo. "Who knows where the name Banks came from? Most likely to distinguish herself from her parents."

A brief pause.

"So, this Victoria West was cheating on her husband, Anton Leach, with John Crawford, the film's director, and Crawford got her pregnant?" queried MacGuffin.

"They must have conspired together to get rid of Leach to be together by staging the accident during filming," suggested Jimbo.

"But, Leach didn't die in the accident."

"Leach must have found out about their affair and her pregnancy while in a coma," proposed Murch. "A comatose person can sometimes hear what people are saying, but they can't respond. When he awoke after seven months, he must have faked his suicide to escape and began plotting his revenge."

"He's trying to destroy anybody associated with Crawford," said Jimbo.

MacGuffin appeared horrified. "McKenzie!"

"What, Rich?" asked Murch. "What's the problem?"

"Leach might be after McKenzie."

"Hold on a second," said Jimbo. "When we investigated the Cielo murders, Dr. Milner's fiancée was missing her ring finger and her engagement ring. They were getting married."

"What are you implying?" asked Murch.

"Maybe Leach is out to reclaim his lost love from Crawford?

He's planning to marry McKenzie Banks...the spitting image, as I said, of his former wife."

MacGuffin grew agitated. "We have to find her!"

"But, we don't even know where to find Leach," stated Murch.

"Remember the limousine used to abduct Christian Rivers?" asked Jimbo. "Traffic cameras tracked the car to the studio gate before it dropped off the radar. I'm betting Leach is hiding somewhere in plain sight on the Paradise Pictures lot."

"Yeah, but where?"

"The movie."

"What *movie*?"

"*Curse of the Wax Phantom*."

"The sets for *Curse of the Wax Phantom* still stand on the abandoned section of the backlot," interjected Harry. "The movie filmed in and around the studio's old Sunset Tower Hotel. It opened in 1925 and became quite popular with celebrities working for the studio and also for tourists wanting a taste of Hollywood glamor. It closed in 1936 following the deaths of several guests during a freak lightning storm. A bolt of lightning struck the hotel's west wing and set it on fire. The place was shuttered shortly after that, until the mid-1950s when the studio reopened it for use as a practical film set."

"Where do we find it?" asked Murch.

"I have a bunch of old studio brochures from the early 1970s, which feature a map inside that still shows the hotel on it. Following the *Wax Phantom* accident in 1976, the studio changed the map to exclude the hotel's location. The area remains a ghost town. Even the studio trams don't go there during tours due to rumored sinkholes."

"We need you to show us the location, Harry."

"But, how are we gonna get inside?" asked MacGuffin. "I'm sure they got that place guarded pretty tight. It's not like we can drive in, walk up to the front door, knock, and say, 'Hi, we're here to arrest you.'"

"Again, I'm here to save the day," stated Harry. "I snagged a bunch of the old blueprints from several of the old sets."

"Do you have them here?" asked Murch.

"No problem."

CHAPTER FORTY-EIGHT

WEDNESDAY, AUGUST THE TWENTY-FOURTH
EIGHT FIFTY-TWO PM

IT WAS DUSK WHEN the Maximum F/X van pulled into a heavily weeded area on the north bank of Paradise Pictures' Sand Pond where the remains of a ferry dock lay sunken in the mud.

The bow of a rusted ferry boat stuck out of the water about twenty feet offshore. Teetering on the edge of a high cliff overlooking the southwest corner of the lake stood the decrepit, towering Sunset Tower Hotel, with ravenous vultures circling overhead.

As Murch and MacGuffin climbed out of the van, MacGuffin remarked, "Hard to believe this place once thrived with celebrities flocking to get away from the paparazzi and over-adoring fans. Looks like Norman Bates has been here. I'm betting that lake is full of old cars and dead bodies. It's like a sump of shit waiting to swallow something down."

Murch handed him a Beretta handgun. "Here, you might need this. You know how to use a gun, right?"

"Oh, yeah, plenty of experience. Max and I, we...we fire off a lot of rounds of different sized ammo to make blanks for movie shoots. I've become quite a decent shot if I do say so myself."

"Good." She handed him a mag of ammo, which he packed inside a pocket of his olive-green cargo jacket.

MacGuffin checked the gun's chamber and stuffed the gun in the front of his jeans' waistband. "Locked and loaded."

Murch pulled her Beretta from her coat pocket and stowed it in the back of her waistband. "Okay, let's do this and get it over with. This place gives me the creeps."

MacGuffin opened the back door of the van to reveal an inflatable raft inside with two wooden paddles. "Wish we had a motor. It's gonna suck rowing through this overgrown mud hole."

"We need to remain silent to ensure the element of surprise. Besides, a motor would jam up from all the weeds."

"Good call. Grab an end."

Murch stepped on over, and together with MacGuffin, they hauled out the raft and portaged it down to the lake.

Murch pointed to the birds circling the hotel. "If the fish don't get us first...*they* will. Those vultures will eat anything with a heartbeat, including us, so keep your eyes peeled."

They lowered the raft into the water, climbed aboard, and grabbed a paddle.

DEEP IN THE BOWELS of the Sunset Tower Hotel, Anton Leach sat at a small pipe organ in his private living quarters, playing the haunting symphony "Don Juan Triumphant." He stopped and turned to look at the captive McKenzie Banks, lying on the concrete floor in drug-induced slumber, chained to a marble pillar, wearing a simple, nondescript, white wedding dress.

Leach motioned to Grendel and Igor, standing guard nearby. "Grendel; Igor—leave us."

"As you wish, Master," said Grendel, bowing.

"Heh, heh. As you...heh...wish...heh...Master. Heh, heh."

Grendel and Igor disappeared behind a red velvet curtain.

Leach turned to Caroline, who occupied herself with housekeeping chores, garbed in a trashy maid's outfit. "Caroline?"

"Yes, sir?"

"Go fetch the impostor Rivers and bring him to me."

"Right away, Master."

With a polite curtsy, Caroline departed through the curtain, leaving Leach and McKenzie alone in the room.

Leach stepped from the organ and approached McKenzie. He removed a vial of smelling salts from his pocket and held it under her nose to awaken her. Her eyes fluttered open, and she coughed.

"Time to rise, Princess. You've slept long enough already."

As her vision cleared, McKenzie saw the hideous face of the figure kneeling over her: his skull-like face, his rotted yellow shark's teeth, and his bulging eyes. She screamed, hysterical, "Aaacccckkkkk!"

Leach mimicked her, "Aaacccckkkkk! Hee, hee, har, har!"

McKenzie jumped, startled.

"Ha, ha, ha!"

"Who...who are you?"

"After all these years, you don't recognize your old uncle, Anton?"

"My *uncle*?"

"Your mother didn't show you pictures of me? I was married to her for seven years."

McKenzie scowled, mortified. "My mother *married* you? B-but, you're a monster."

"Trust me, darling, I may not look like much now, but thirty years ago, I was quite the looker and ladies' man." He removed and showed her a black-and-white agency photo of himself as a young man around the age of thirty.

"What *are* you?" whispered McKenzie.

"I'm Jack the Ripper, I'm Mr. Hyde, I'm Frankenstein's Monster, I'm the Impossible Melting Man from Dimension Z. I'm all those things and more. Much more."

"If my mother married you, why didn't she ever mention you?"

"You've never heard of me because your parents chose to murder me to be together. They were the ones responsible for turning me into the monster you see before you. Their plan almost worked, but I survived. My soul was too strong for the grave. I've worked too long and hard to see my plans for revenge go up in a plume of smoke."

"You need serious help."

MURCH AND MACGUFFIN ARRIVED by raft at the sewer drain at the base of the cliff upon which loomed the Sunset Tower Hotel high above. All that stood in their way was a rusty grate covered in weeds and moss and a six-foot boa constrictor.

MacGuffin tied the raft to a submerged fallen tree as Murch dropped waist-deep into the water and waded up to the grate, carrying a wooden oar from the raft.

The snake made a big splash of its own and slithered away under the water.

Murch smashed the rusted padlock holding the grating in place with the butt end of the oar. The fastener broke away and dropped into the water. "See, Rich? Easy peasy."

"Some security guard that snake turned out to be."

"Don't piss it off. It might give you a little squeeze for good measure."

MacGuffin climbed over the edge of the raft, dropped into the water, and waded over to Murch who pried open the grate, which broke off and fell into the muck. "Oops," she smirked. "They sure don't make 'em the way they used to."

Murch lifted herself into the drainpipe and crawled inside, followed close behind by MacGuffin.

CHAPTER FORTY-NINE

WEDNESDAY, AUGUST THE TWENTY-FOURTH
NINE THIRTEEN PM

IN THE REDDISH GLOW of the sunset, Murch and MacGuffin stood up inside the sewer pipe. Murch removed two flashlights from her coat pockets and handed one to MacGuffin; she said, "Harry's blueprints showed a maintenance hatch near the end of the sewer tunnel. There should be a ladder to climb up to the next level."

MacGuffin switched on his flashlight and turned toward the darkness ahead of them. "I hope so. I hate these cold dark places. Especially the ones that smell like dirty diapers."

They moved forward down the tubular passage. It was wet and dark and hanging with plant life. Their echoing footsteps intermittently overpowered the sounds of loud dripping, whistling air drafts, and scampering claws. MacGuffin hummed to himself, nervous.

LEACH STOOD OVER MCKENZIE, studying her as she tried to free herself from her restraints. "Try all you want, my dear, there is no escape. You better get used to your surroundings. I'm afraid you'll be here for a long time."

"What do you want with me? I didn't do anything to you."

Leach ran his fingers down her face. "It's you I want, my darling McKenzie. You are the spitting image of your mother, Victoria. You're the same age now as she was when she left me for your father, John Crawford. I've waited twenty-nine years for this moment."

"Have you been stalking me?"

"I've watched you from the shadows ever since you were young. Watching, waiting..."

"*Watching, waiting* for what, you sick bastard?"

"Waiting for you to be old enough to replace your mother as my wife. She was your age when she left me, and now, you will replace her. It will be like she never left me."

"You want me to marry you?"

"I dressed you for this special occasion."

McKenzie peered down at the wedding dress she wore.

"The dress belonged to your mother," continued Leach. "She wore it at our wedding back in 1969. You both wear the same size. A small price to pay for your continued survival. If you refuse to take my hand in marriage, you will end up like your parents: dead."

"My father *isn't* dead. I saw him last night."

Leach removed a prosthetic Crawford mask and threw it in McKenzie's lap. "You sure about that?"

"Wha...what did you do to my father?"

"I cut his head off along with the heads of that other idiot, Nigel Guest, and the three women. I then took your father's place on the red carpet. It was me you saw get into the ambulance. I needed to ensure Mr. Rivers never made it to the hospital. He's become a real thorn in my side as of late. And, *you*? I couldn't let you go home all by your lonesome self. My assistant, Caroline, gave you a lift...to my home. And, now, you're all mine to do with as I so choose."

"Sorry to disappoint you; I'm not my mother. I don't love you."

"Do you even know what happened to your mother?"

"I saw her suicide letter. She killed herself because she couldn't deal with the pain caused by cancer."

"No... *I* killed her. That's why the authorities never found her body." Leach stepped away. "It was a cold September night in 1994. I took her from your family home in Laurel Canyon. It was quick and easy. I ditched her car by the shore of Lake Hollywood with a fake suicide letter inside saying she had cancer, when, in fact, she didn't."

"H-how did she die?"

"I held her head under the water until she stopped kicking, and then I brought her body here and turned her into one of my trophies. I have a lot of trophies. Remind me to show you sometime. It's what will happen to you if you refuse my bidding."

"Screw you. I'm not going to marry you. You're insane."

"So be it."

AS MURCH AND MACGUFFIN moved forward in the sewer tunnel, MacGuffin brushed aside a wall of thick cobwebs blocking their path.

Murch shuddered. "Boy, I'd hate to see what kind of creature made that."

"I bet its name is Shelob," smirked MacGuffin.

"I'm sorry. I don't know what that means."

"You've never seen *Lord of the Rings*? Read the books?"

"I'm more the academic type. I don't get out much."

"Of course not."

"Keep moving."

"Right."

MacGuffin moved forward a few steps and halted.

"Why are you stopping?" asked Murch.

MacGuffin sniffed at the air, grimacing. "What's that smell?"

Murch took a whiff herself. "Smells like blood."

"Never mind, I don't want to know."

As they crept forward, MacGuffin fell into some type of pit and disappeared under what appeared to be water.

"Rich! Rich!" screamed Murch.

She knelt, shining her light on a pool of rusted water. No sign of MacGuffin. She splashed her hands around. "Mac! Mac!" In her flashlight's beam of light, the water churned red with chunks of bone, flesh, and blood. "Oh, my God!"

In a geyser of sewage, MacGuffin bobbed to the surface. "Help! Help!" he croaked, choking on water.

"Rich!"

Murch grabbed under his arms and hoisted him out of the watery pit, along with the remains of a skeleton.

Horrified, MacGuffin exclaimed, "Augh!"

"I don't think this drain is used for sewage," said Murch. "It's a body dump."

"Well, whatever was in there, it didn't taste good."

"Next time, pay more attention to where you're walking."

"Well, in that case, you better lead. I lost my flashlight somewhere down there."

"Good call."

Murch trudged forward, shining her flashlight in all directions. MacGuffin followed close behind, reluctant.

They soon came to the end of the sewer tunnel where a ladder led up to an opening in the ceiling.

MacGuffin appeared amazed. "Would you look at that? A ladder, like Harry said there'd be." He hesitated. "Wonder what's in store for us up there."

"I'm counting on nothing," replied Murch. "I've seen enough weird shit already."

She tucked her flashlight in the front of her waistband and grabbed onto the ladder. Before she got one foot on a rung, a large industrial machine whirred to life high above them on the next level.

"What the Hell is that?" asked MacGuffin.

"I haven't a clue."

The machine made a grinding-shredding sound, followed soon by a shower of blood, bone fragments, organs, and God knows what else, pouring down on Murch and MacGuffin through the opening in the ceiling.

Nauseated and furious, Murch wiped the goop from her face. "Goddammit."

The gory remains caked both of them.

"What are they serving for dinner up there?" asked MacGuffin. "Steak tartare?"

"I'm not waiting around to find out what's for dessert," groaned Murch. She drew her gun from the back of her waistband and handed MacGuffin her flashlight. "Here, hold this. I'll be right back." She climbed the ladder for a look above.

Murch poked her head up through the ceiling, gazed up an inclined run-off chute, and witnessed Grendel and Igor feeding a black plastic body bag into a woodchipper. Beyond that were a half-dozen more body bags strung up to a wooden beam by meat hooks, ready for disposal. The room was dim, illuminated solely by three burning torches on the far wall beside an iron door.

Murch again received a blood-and-guts shower from the run-off chute, causing her to lose balance on the slippery ladder and fall backward onto the ground by MacGuffin's feet. Her gun flew from her hand.

"Haley!" bellowed MacGuffin. "You okay?" He helped her to her feet.

"Only my wounded pride," she grunted, holding her back.

"What'd you see up there?"

"Leach's two remaining goons disposing of evidence."

"So, what's the plan?"

"The light isn't too good up there. We can sneak in without

them seeing us. I'll take the left; you take the right. Make sure the safety's off on the gun I gave you. And, watch your step along the way. The blood makes things kinda slippery."

She snatched her gun off the ground and climbed the ladder. As she neared the top, Grendel and Igor fed another body bag into the woodchipper, and, once more, she took a blast in the face with a shower of blood and guts.

Again she slipped off the ladder, but she managed to grab hold of a rung to keep herself from landing on her back. She grew infuriated. "Oh, that does it! No more Mr. Nice Bitch!"

In a rage, she raced back up the ladder, did a quick barrel roll onto the floor above, and fired an entire magazine of ammo toward Grendel and Igor. She also managed to take out Igor with shots to the forehead and heart.

But, as she started to switch out ammo mags, Grendel lunged toward her. "Little slut! How dare you intrude upon the Master's domain!"

He grabbed her by the elbows and jostled her violently, causing her to lose her gun and ammo mag.

"Crap!"

As Grendel folded her arms back and doubled her over, Murch stomped on his foot and broke free from his grasp. She delivered a series of punishing punches and kicks, keeping Grendel on the defensive. He managed to catch her off guard by knocking her down with a steel chain, which he wrapped around her neck as she tried to stand.

"RICH!" she cried out.

MacGuffin poked his head up through the floor, as Grendel began choking the life out of Murch. Gasping, she cried out again, "RICH!"

MacGuffin attempted to squeeze off a shot with his gun, but the gun jammed. "Ah, crap!"

By now, Murch was near unconscious.

Frantic, MacGuffin looked around in the dim light for Murch's gun. He soon spotted it and dove for it. "Hee! Hee!" He checked the gun's ammo mag. Empty. "Dammit!" He spotted the second ammo mag on the ground nearby. "Oh, yeah, baby! Come to Daddy Mac!"

Seeing this, Murch gained a second wind. "I've had enough of you!" With a heroic effort, she flipped Grendel over her head, wrapped the chain around his neck, and hurled the loose end into the woodchipper.

"AAAACKKK!" wailed Grendel as he hurtled toward the spinning blades, but the wrenched chain jammed them, sparing his life. The coiled chain around his neck grew so tight, he slipped into unconsciousness.

Winded, Murch stood and muttered, "Take that you bastard!"

As she turned away, Grendel came to for one final scare and grabbed her by the hair and yanked her back.

MacGuffin shot Grendel in the forehead with a bullet from Murch's gun. "Boo-yah!"

As Grendel dropped over, dead as a doornail, MacGuffin blew away the smoke from the gun's barrel and cheered, "Yippee-ki-yay!" He handed Murch the weapon and helped her to her feet.

Exhausted, she gasped, "What took you so long?"

"My gun jammed."

She tucked the gun away in the back of her waistband. "Thought I told you to check the safety?"

"I did. The safety was off, but it still jammed. It got clogged up with blood and bone chips when I fell into that hole back there."

"Well...good work anyway."

"Thank you."

Right on cue, the woodchipper blades whirred back to life and sucked Grendel in, turning him into mulch.

"Ee-ew!" grimaced MacGuffin.

"Come on, let's go," said Murch. "Your friends, Max and McKenzie, have to be around here somewhere. They need our help. Still got my flashlight?"

MacGuffin removed the flashlight from the front of his waistband and tried to switch it on, but to no avail. "Nope." He tossed the flashlight away. "Great! Now, what do we do for a light?"

Murch remembered the torches on the wall by the exit. "Grab a torch."

CHAPTER FIFTY

MCKENZIE SAT ON THE floor of Leach's living room, tied to the concrete pillar, with tears streaming down her face, while Leach played a somber tune on his organ nearby.

The red velvet curtain moved aside, as Caroline returned with the unconscious Max Winston strapped to a stainless-steel operating table. "Master, I have returned with the trophy you requested."

"You have done well, Caroline. Leave us now. See if Grendel and Igor need help."

"Yes, sir."

With a polite curtsy, Caroline turned and exited the way she came.

Leach stepped from his organ and approached the unconscious Max Winston, who appeared beaten, bloody, and bruised.

McKenzie looked at Max, horrified–to her, he was still Christian Rivers. She screamed at Leach, "What have you done to him?!"

"Don't act so frightened, my dear. I haven't done anything to him...*yet*. He looks this way because of the ambulance crash."

"What do you want with him? I thought this was about me?"

"Mr. Rivers here was an unfortunate detour in my kidnapping plans. You were to be the only one abducted from the theater. He wasn't supposed to be there. My three henchmen were to be taking care of him at the Observatory. Instead, the authorities got wise and sent a decoy to the premiere in Rivers place."

"What do you mean, a *decoy*?"

Leach leaned over Max and grabbed onto a peeling edge of his facial prosthetic. "I mean, *he* isn't Christian Rivers. *He's* an impostor." He ripped the mask off, exposing the truth to McKenzie.

Max's head bounced up and smacked back down hard against the table, but he didn't awaken.

McKenzie shrieked as Leach threw the prosthetic mask in her face, "Aacccckkkkk!"

"As you can see..." said Leach, sneering, "...*he's* somebody else entirely."

McKenzie stared in disbelief at Max. "I... I've seen him before."

"Indeed, you have, my dear. I saw you talking with him and a friend outside the soundstage. They claimed to be Rivers' make-up artists. Make *him* up *they* did, indeed. The question you must ask yourself, though, is, how well did you know the real Christian Rivers?"

"I've known him for at least five years. We've made three movies together."

"Did you now? Hmm...? It seems their ruse was much too good. They fooled everybody, including you. But, they didn't fool me because I already had the real Rivers in my possession."

Leach removed the bottle of smelling salts and held it under Max's nose. "Wakey, wakey."

Max's eyes fluttered. "Oh...did anybody...get the license plate of that truck that hit me? Christ, what a headache." His eyes opened and focused on Leach's gruesome face. "Sheesh, aren't you cute. Who did your facial?"

"Mr. Winston, I don't think an introduction is necessary. You know who I am. I'm sure your friend, MacGuffin, told you all about me."

"Sorry, dude, never seen you before in my life."

A long pause.

McKenzie broke the silence, asking Max, "Why were you pretending to be Rivers? I told you intimate secrets about my life that I would never tell anybody. I even made love to you. How long has this charade been going on?"

"Since the movie premiere–the rest of the time it's been Rich. This ruse has only been going since the real Christian Rivers went missing."

"*Missing?* Where'd he go?"

"I'm sure you saw the newspaper articles. Rivers was abducted on his way to the studio one morning..." He motioned to Leach. "...I'm guessing by this freakazoid, and he was never seen or heard from again." He turned to Leach. "Why is that, by the way? What'd you do with him?"

"Celebrities like Christian Rivers are a thorn in my side. They're given all the money in the world, the keys to the kingdom, but they don't know how to use it to benefit others. All they do is throw it away on frivolities and flaunt their egos. They disgust me."

"What did you do with him?" asked McKenzie.

"I gave him one of my personal makeovers–a cut and a slash here; a nip and a tuck there–to ensure nobody in this industry would ever hire him again. Needless to say, I buggered him up real good. Not even his own parents–God rest their pathetic souls–would ever recognize him. I made him one of my prized trophies for a time, but I grew tired of his whining–always whining–and agreed to let him go. Alas, his freedom was never meant to be.

"My henchmen informed me he was shot down in cold blood by the same people who were trying to rescue him. Blame his senseless murder on the LAPD and the FBI; not on me. Hmp. Well, I have a pressing matter to attend to. Why don't you two *catch up* until I get back? Hmmm?"

Leach left.

McKenzie turned to Max and asked, "Why did you and your friend choose to impersonate Rivers if you knew *he* was missing?"

"All Rich and I knew was that he had gone missing."

"But why did *you* do it?"

"Rich came to me for help–to transform him into Rivers–and I did. All Rich wanted was to help finish the movie Rivers was working on. He saw it as the opportunity of a lifetime. When Rich learned how much finishing the film meant to you, he couldn't walk away. He never would've guessed he'd fall in love with you. Hell, even I fell in love with you the first time I met you."

Max expected McKenzie to rip him a new asshole, but she said nothing. For a while, at least. When she did speak, she murmured, "Thank you." Sincerity.

"*Thank you?* For what?"

"If it weren't for the two of you, the movie would never have wrapped."

"Well, I... you're welcome."

"And, I will never miss the *real* Rivers, believe me. He was such an asshole to everyone, including me. Your version of Rivers was way nicer, funnier, and more...romantic."

"Sorry I passed out at the theater during our little balcony hayride. My hypoglycemia was acting up. It does that at times of high stress."

"I hope when all of this is over, we can still be friends?"

"Sure thing."

"No more rubber masks, though. You don't need to pretend you're someone else to be with me. My star doesn't shine that bright yet."

"I'm sorry about your father. Nobody should have to lose a parent in such a horrible way."

"I've lost both parents to horrible deaths."

"Well, if you need anything, both Rich and I are here for you."

CHAPTER FIFTY-ONE

WEDNESDAY, AUGUST THE TWENTY-FOURTH
NINE THIRTY-TWO PM

DEEP BENEATH THE SUNSET Tower Hotel, Murch and MacGuffin climbed a winding staircase, using two torches to light their way.

"If this part of the backlot has been abandoned all these years, I wonder how this derelict manages to retain its power?" asked MacGuffin.

"Batteries and generators?" guessed Murch.

They came to an arched doorway with a tall door controlled by a wooden lever instead of a doorknob. MacGuffin grabbed hold of the bar, forced it upward, and the door lowered by metal chains. "What kind of door is this?"

"It's some sort of drawbridge."

She led the way into a small room that appeared to be the inside of a well. MacGuffin followed close behind.

The room stood twenty by twenty feet and thirty feet high. Mortared stone made up the walls. In the middle, a concrete pedestal, serving as a median between two drawbridges, stood ten feet off the ground and surrounded by water. A steel cage suspended from a ceiling pulley by a rope hung only feet above the water. The half devoured-half decomposed remains of a man decorated the cage floor. An arm dangled through the bars at an unnatural angle, the hand skimming the surface of the water.

Murch and MacGuffin appeared mortified.

"What the Hell *is* this place?" she asked.

"I don't wanna know."

Something small moved under the surface and grabbed onto one of the dangling corpse's fingers and took a nibble. Then, something else moved in the water. Then another. And another. Soon, there was a frenzy of motion in the water, and the corpse became their lunch.

"Is that...?" asked MacGuffin.

"Yep," replied Murch. "Piranha."

"A shitload of them."

The piranha jumped, tugged, and chewed at the corpse, pulling it free from the cage. As the body dropped into the water and became consumed, an attached wire triggered the drawbridges to close.

"This room is a trap!" shouted Murch. "Move!"

She shoved MacGuffin forward, and the two of them raced across the second drawbridge into the adjoining room.

The drawbridge closed, sealing them in a dank, musty cellar full of gigantic oak barrels and wooden crates. Unlike the first drawbridge, this one had no lever to open it back up.

Murch moved her torch around, examining the area. "Well, that's that. There's no going back that way."

AN ALARM SOUNDED, SENDING the returning Leach into a frenzy. "INTRUDERS!"

He turned on a closed-circuit television. A black and white image soon appeared, showing Murch and MacGuffin inside a small room full of crates and barrels.

"Aww...your friends have discovered my hideaway. Tsk."

"Thank Christ," said Max.

Leach scowled. "Thank *Him* all you want. It won't matter. Your friends will never find their way in here. They've reached a dead end, I'm afraid. Once they figure out how to escape the room they're in, it'll be too late for them."

Helpless, Max and McKenzie watched the grainy images of their doomed friends on the screen.

MURCH AND MACGUFFIN FELT their way around as they moved, as the only light in the tiny cellar came from their torches.

Murch shined her torch off the walls. There appeared to be no other doors besides the drawbridge entrance.

Murch examined another side of the room. "I'm afraid I don't see any other way out of here."

"This floor sure feels strange," remarked MacGuffin.

Murch held her torch low and glanced down at the black substance covering the floor. "It's dirt."

MacGuffin waved his torch across the barrels and crates. "This room must be a wine cellar."

"Look around. See if you can find a door or something that'll get us the Hell out of here."

CAROLINE ENTERED THE SUBTERRANEAN room housing the woodchipper and body bags. She grabbed the lone remaining torch off the wall and searched around for Grendel and Igor.

As she waved the torch around, she spotted Igor's bullet-riddled corpse laying on the ground by the drain opening. A moment later, she found a pile of shredded clothing and shoes covered in blood and fleshy sinew.

BY TORCHLIGHT, MURCH AND MacGuffin searched the underground wine cellar for hidden doors amidst stacks of crates and barrels.

"You finding anything, Rich?"

"Negative. Nothing but crates, barrels, and tons of cobwebs. If there's an exit in here, it has to be invisible. These walls are solid."

"Check the floors. Maybe there's a trap door."

"Seriously, I kind of doubt it."

"Keep looking." She pushed a pile of crates out of the way for a better look at the floor.

MacGuffin uncorked a barrel to sample the wine. "Come to Papa Rich, sweet nectar of the gods." Instead of wine, he imbibed a mouthful of black powder; the same black powder all over the floor. He spat it out. "Ugh...whatever fermenting techniques used to make this wine didn't work. This wine has gone bad. It's turned into powder."

Murch uncovered the edges of a hidden trap door in the floor. "Think I found our ticket out of here, Rich."

"Thank God."

As MacGuffin worked to clean the residue from his mouth, he unwittingly backed into a pile of crates, toppling them over. The top crate broke open as it fell, spilling out all sorts of exotic, squirming insects and bugs.

MacGuffin panicked, screaming, "AACCCKKKK!"

"Rich! You okay?"

"NO! GET THEM OFF OF ME! THEY'RE ALL OVER ME!"

MacGuffin dropped his torch and batted and swatted at the insects. The flame ignited the black dirt, and the fire swept across the floor.

Murch stopped dead in her tracks. "Oh, my God! What was in that barrel?"

"Wine! It's turned into powder it's been sitting here so long!"

"Rich, wine doesn't turn into powder if it ages! It doesn't start on fire!"

"Then, what the Hell is it?"

"It's gunpowder!"

"Augh! The barrels are full of it! It's all over the floor!"

"This room isn't a wine cellar! It's one giant powder keg, and it's about to blow sky high!" She yanked open the trap door in the floor and shouted, "Through the door, Rich! NOW!"

Ignoring the giant bugs crawling all over him, MacGuffin scrambled to his feet and dove through the opening in the floor. He tumbled down a flight of wooden stairs and landed face down on the floor of a sub-cellar with a resounding thud.

Murch jumped down and yanked the door shut, as the room exploded above her in a giant fireball.

As the trap door in the ceiling flopped open and closed, Murch jumped on top of MacGuffin and shielded him from burning debris raining down on them.

The trap door slammed shut for good, as a heavy crate landed on top of it.

CHAPTER FIFTY-TWO

WEDNESDAY, AUGUST THE TWENTY-FOURTH
NINE FORTY PM

LEACH, MCKENZIE, AND MAX watched via closed-circuit television, as Murch and MacGuffin picked themselves up off the sub-cellar floor, as the fire spread.

McKenzie cried, "Stop! Let them go! I beg you! They're gonna burn to death!"

"And, what if I let them go?" asked Leach with a hiss. "What do I get in return?"

"Try a nice tiny prison cell for you to rot away in," retorted Max.

"It's me you want!" cried McKenzie. "Let them go!"

"Tell me that you love me, or you'll forevermore be only as beautiful as you are dead," chastised Leach. "I will kill everyone and myself if you do not consent to be my wife."

A large explosion ripped through the underground tunnels, causing the living room to shudder.

"There isn't much time left," noted Leach, with a wry chuckle.

McKenzie watched the television monitor, horrified, as Murch and MacGuffin became cornered by flames and smoke.

"Will you be my bride or not? That is the question," jeered Leach. "If not, everyone will be dead and buried beneath the ruins of this hotel."

"All right!" bellowed McKenzie. "I'll do anything you want! Let them go, okay?"

MURCH AND MACGUFFIN COWERED on the cellar floor to avoid smoke suffocation.

"I'm sorry to get you involved in this, Rich," said Murch. "This whole ordeal was never your fight."

MacGuffin chuckled. "Not like I had anything better to do on my schedule."

ACCEPTING MCKENZIE'S PLEA, LEACH untied her from the concrete pillar and dragged her across the room to a Spanish chest.

"What's *this*?" she asked.

"A choice," explained Leach.

He removed a key from his pocket and unlocked the chest to reveal a mechanical device. Upon a piece of plate glass were two objects, a grasshopper and a scorpion, made of Japanese bronze. From each of these objects, a rod ran down out of sight. Coming up through the glass was a liquid, watery light effect.

"A *choice*? What *choice*?" asked McKenzie.

Leach flung aside a large rug to reveal a hatch in the living room floor with a small observation window peering down into the bottom cellar. "If you turn the scorpion around, it will mean you have said *yes*. If you turn the grasshopper around, it will mean you have said *no*. Be careful of the grasshopper. It hops, and it hops jolly high."

Leach stepped aside and resorted to his organ. He took a seat and resumed playing "Don Juan Triumphant" as if he were a skeleton gone mad.

Without hesitation, McKenzie hastily put her hands on the grasshopper, but Max urgently stopped her before she could turn it. "McKenzie! Don't do it! It's a trick! This whole set-up is straight out of *Phantom of the Opera*! It's a trap! If you choose the grasshopper, the hotel blows up, and we all die! If you choose the scorpion, you'll save our friends from burning alive by drowning them! Either way, we all die!"

Leach leaped to his feet and rushed to Max on the operating table. Drawing his stiletto knife, he sliced Max's left nostril and stabbed the blade through Max's left shoulder, pinning him to the table. Blood sprung up like a geyser.

Max screamed out in pain.

"You little prick!" shrieked Leach. "You have meddled in my plans for the last time! Now, I'm going to finish you off once and for all!"

As Leach reached for the knife in Max's shoulder, McKenzie shouted, "I love you!"

Leach turned and faced her. "*What?*"

"I'll marry you if it's what *you* want," replied McKenzie, in earnest. "I'll marry you if it means my friends can all walk away unharmed."

Leach hesitated, thinking. "The scorpion! The scorpion is the one to turn!"

McKenzie contemplated. "But, he said it's a trap no matter which I choose?"

"If you want your friends to live, turn the damn scorpion!"

She chose the scorpion and rotated it 180 degrees to the left.

"NO!" screamed Max.

A PIPE IN THE sub-cellar wall near the ceiling burst open, and water from Sand Pond poured into the room, extinguishing all the flames.

Murch turned to MacGuffin. "Great. We won't burn to death, but instead, we'll drown."

"Out of the frying pan, into the fire."

"Try the hatch to the wine cellar. Once the water rises high enough, it'll flow into that room and put out the fire. Then we can escape through there."

MacGuffin climbed the blind wooden staircase to the cellar hatch and tried pushing against it with his back. No use. The heavy crate fallen over the hatch wouldn't budge. "Uh...oh...for...forget it! It's no use. It won't budge."

Murch glanced around for another way out but didn't see one. "That was the only way in or out. Dammit! We're trapped."

"Don't give up yet," encouraged MacGuffin. "Keep looking. There's gotta be something..." He spotted a small window in the ceiling with a hint of light shining through. "Look!" He pointed. "Up there! A window!"

Murch saw it, but she seemed curious. "Why would there be a window in the ceiling? Unless–"

"Somebody's watching us," concluded MacGuffin.

ANOTHER EXPLOSION RATTLED THE lower levels of the hotel. Sensing imminent danger, Leach rushed to McKenzie's side, grabbed her arm, and cuffed himself to her.

"What are you doing?" she asked. "You said you were going to free them?"

"Change of plans, darling," replied an eager Leach. "This place is coming down faster than I anticipated. We only have enough time to free ourselves. We need to get up top if we're to make our escape."

McKenzie motioned at Max on the operating table. "But what about him?"

"He was never part of my plan. Only you. He was merely in the wrong place at the wrong time. He's on his own."

Leach dragged McKenzie to a heavy red velvet curtain and pulled it aside to reveal a hidden door. "Come on. We must go, now."

"No! You promised!"

Max raised his head and looked into McKenzie's eyes. "McKenzie! Don't worry about me! I'll be fine! Save yourself! You must go before this place comes falling down! Go! Go now!"

Leach pushed open the secret door and dragged McKenzie into the darkness beyond.

"No...!," she screamed.

The door closed behind them.

Max fought to free himself from the leather tying him to the table, straining with all his might, but it was no use. The straps were too tight. "Uh...goddammit!"

MURCH AND MACGUFFIN STRUGGLED to reach the window in the ceiling as they floated atop the surface of the water.

MacGuffin noticed the outline of a hatch door around the window. "Looks like a trap door."

"Pray it opens," replied Murch. "Otherwise, we'll find out which one of us can hold his breath the longest."

LEACH AND MCKENZIE ASCENDED a smoke-filled stairwell which entered the main floor lobby where they ran into Caroline.

"Caroline!" shouted Leach. "Where are Grendel and Igor? It's time to leave. Soon this whole place will be at the bottom of the cliff."

"Grendel and Igor are dead at the hands of the FBI agent and her companion."

"Pffft. No tragic loss. They were near useless from the start. It will be easy to find suitable replacements."

Caroline blinked. "Where are you going?"

"We're making our getaway. You may join us if you'd like."

"Very well, then."

Caroline docilely followed as Leach dragged McKenzie to the

service elevator. He pulled open the heavy outer stainless-steel doors and the inner doors, before the three of them entered.

"Where are we going?" asked McKenzie.

"Well, my dear, there's two choices. One: We could take the elevator back down to the wee bowels of the hotel, but we'd likely burn to death, or, if the structural foundation has collapsed, we'd drown in the incoming lake water. Or, two: We could go to the tippy top of the hotel and float away on the winds. The second idea seems like the obvious choice." He pulled the elevator doors shut and pressed the button for the 12th floor. "And, away we go! Ha, ha, ha...!"

SCARCE INCHES OF BREATHING space remained before the water consumed Murch and MacGuffin. Floating beneath the ceiling hatch, their breath on the window showed their disparity.

"The hatch won't open!" shouted MacGuffin.

"It's locked from the other side!"

Another explosion struck as the water filled the sub-cellar to capacity. Murch and MacGuffin managed one final lungful of oxygen and grabbed onto each other.

LEACH'S LIVING ROOM BEGAN to fill with smoke as Max worked to remove the stiletto knife from his left shoulder. Covered in blood from the cut to his left nostril, he clenched the knife handle with his mouth and teeth and yanked up with all his might, wincing in pain, as he freed himself.

He closed his eyes in concentration and hurled the knife with his mouth toward his right hand. Miraculously, he caught it.

"Oof."

Palming the knife handle with his right hand, he cut himself free.

Liberated, he jumped down off the table, rushed to the hatch in the floor, and pulled the sliding bolt lock open. A gush of water blasted him, as he flung the trap door open. Yet, he stood firm.

By reflex, he shoved his right arm beneath the surface of the water. "Rich! Rich!"

The floundering and waterlogged Murch and MacGuffin swam upward toward the open hatch, reached for Max's arm, and pulled themselves up through the opening.

Max fell backward in pain onto the floor, as the two collapsed on top of him.

"Rich!"

"Max!" sputtered Rich.

"You all right, man?"

MacGuffin vomited up a lungful of water and replied, "Another minute..." He coughed. "...and the two of us would've been floating tits up."

MacGuffin and Murch stood and shook themselves off.

Murch noticed Max's shoulder and facial wounds. "You're bleeding pretty hard. Your nose should be okay, but you should put some pressure on your shoulder."

Max smirked. "Believe me, it looks worse than it is."

MacGuffin shook the water from his ears and glanced around the room. "Hey, Max, where's McKenzie?"

Max motioned to the door at the far end of the room. "That hamburger-faced freak took her through there a few minutes ago. He was babbling on about how McKenzie is the spitting image of his dead ex-wife and how McKenzie is to take her place by marrying him."

MacGuffin grimaced. "*Marry him*? Who'd want to *marry* that monster?"

"Did he say where they were headed?" asked Murch.

"The top floor," replied Max. "He's taking McKenzie to the top floor."

"What's on the top floor?" asked MacGuffin.

Murch removed her cell phone. "One way to find out."

"Do you even know if your cell phone still works after being submerged in water?" asked Max.

"It should work. It's waterproof."

Murch turned on her phone and dialed Jimbo's number.

With the hotel blueprints spread out beside him on the passenger seat, Jimbo sat in his Volkswagen bug, parked in the vicinity of the Sunset Tower Hotel. He picked up and answered his ringing cell phone, "Hello?"

"Jimbo!"

"Haley! What can I do for you?"

"What occupies the top floors of the hotel? Leach is trying to make his escape. He's got McKenzie."

Jimbo picked up the blueprints beside him and flipped to the upper floor plans. "Lessee...floors two through ten are occupied by hotel guest rooms; that sort of thing. However, the hotel continues higher by another three levels."

"What's up there?"

"A ballroom and a restaurant. The highest level is storage space. A belfry." He hesitated, thinking. "Um, Agent Murch, if he's trying to escape, why wouldn't he go through the front door of the lobby?"

"The lower floors of the hotel are on fire. Leach strategically placed large barrels of gunpowder to explode from the bottom up."

"Sounds to me like he's trying to cover his tracks."

"Still doesn't make any sense, though. How would you escape from the top floor of a burning hotel?"

"Well, considering the hotel is around two-hundred-feet tall—one hundred ninety-nine to be precise—plus the cliff and foundation beneath it—add another fifty feet or so—I doubt they'd jump to the lake below. I mean, they'd probably survive, but the impact with the water would hurt like Hell."

"What other way is there off a roof?"

"Some sort of aerial escape."

"An aerial escape would make capture by the authorities more difficult. Especially at night."

"I have to agree."

"Thanks, Jimbo. You were helpful."

"No sweat. Give me a call if you need anything else. I'll be here."

Murch hung up her phone. She drew her gun and motioned to Max and MacGuffin. "Let's go. Leach is getting away."

"If we follow them upstairs, how are we gonna get down?"

"We'll worry about that when we get up there. If Leach gets away, we're never gonna catch him, and McKenzie will become another name on his Hollywood Walk of Fame."

They moved to the door into a stairwell full of flames and smoke. The stairwell forked up or down. The way up was full of fire and smoke, while going down had only smoke.

"The fire is moving upward," stated Murch. "We can't go that way. We'll have to go down and find another way up."

254

"Fine, it's settled then," replied an anxious Max. "We go down. Let's move."

"Cover your mouths, so you don't inhale the smoke. I don't want anybody passing out on me."

And, so, they took the left fork in the stairwell and hoofed it downward.

CHAPTER FIFTY-THREE

THE STAIRWELL DESCENDED TO the basement catacombs. The labyrinth of tunnels and dungeon cells flowed with a shallow stream of water about six inches deep along the floor.

"Mr. Winston, do you recognize any of this?" asked Murch.

"Not that I recall. I don't remember much of anything on account they had me drugged out."

MacGuffin peered into one of the dungeons along the tunnel walls and observed numerous skeletons in varying stages of decay shackled to the walls in sitting positions. "Appears as though this hotel has a few guests that forgot to check out at the mandatory time."

Murch took a look for herself. "God, how many people has this guy killed? And, for what purpose?"

"I don't think he *has* a purpose," said Max. "He likes to torture people and see how long it takes for them to break."

With that, the hotel began to quake and rumble, followed by a loud suction sound and a gust of wind.

Murch's eyes went wide. "Get down!"

She grabbed MacGuffin and Max and pulled them under the water, as a horizontal wall of fire exploded down the tunnel, causing a section of the dirt and rock ceiling to collapse only yards away. Once the firestorm subsided, the three of them popped their heads out of the water.

"Holy smokes!" exclaimed Max.

"What the Hell was that?" asked MacGuffin.

"A backdraft," explained Murch.

"Christ, I'm getting sick of this place!" shouted Max. "It's a house of horrors!"

"Then, let's not spend another moment wasting our precious time," proposed MacGuffin. "Let's get the Hell out of here."

"Right, but do we go back the way we came or continue this

way and have the rest of the ceiling collapse down on us?"

"Let's keep going this way," suggested Murch. "There's gotta be an exit somewhere."

They picked themselves up out of the water and continued moving down the only accessible tunnel.

LEACH, CAROLINE, AND MCKENZIE made their way across the Moonrise Ballroom and stopped at the foot of a stone stairwell leading to the 13th floor, as Leach uncuffed himself from McKenzie and turned to Caroline. "Caroline, take McKenzie to the belfry and get the balloon ready for takeoff."

"What are you going to do?"

"Create some interference. Time to release my trophies. They are no longer any use to me."

Leach walked away in the opposite direction, stepped inside the elevator, and pulled the doors shut.

Caroline forced McKenzie up the stairs with a knife to her right side. "Move it, sweetheart."

MURCH, MACGUFFIN, AND MAX made their way upstairs from the catacombs to the burning boiler room and took a second stairwell up to the hotel lobby, which was now a raging inferno. There was no escape as the flames were too intense around the exit. Only then did they start feeling the heat of the situation.

MacGuffin groaned.

"Yeah, so much for getting out that way," added Max.

They exited the stairwell and cautiously made their way to the service elevator at the north end of the lobby.

Murch pressed the "UP" button and remarked, "Let's hope this still works. I don't feel like hiking up a dozen flights of stairs."

"Please, show a little optimism," scoffed Max.

MacGuffin sneered. "Easy for you to say, Max. We could be hitching a ride to our deaths right now."

"Hey, we all gotta go sometime, *hombre*."

The elevator arrived. Murch slid the double set of stainless-steel doors open, and they all climbed aboard. She closed the doors and pressed the button for the 12th floor. The elevator rose.

The hotel rumbled as an explosion raced up the elevator shaft, causing the three to collapse to the floor, as the elevator car slammed to a jolting stop.

MacGuffin threw up his hands. "Great! What else can go wrong?"

The elevator dropped a good three feet before coming to rest at a precarious angle, its doors facing down and hanging partially open, allowing smoke and heat to enter.

"Sorry, I spoke too soon. Now, how do we get out of this mess?"

LEACH WALKED DOWN AN aisle between rows of cylindrical tanks containing his celebrity trophies, all unconscious.

He ambled over to the control panel and pushed a button allowing him to speak over intercoms embedded within each tank. "My children! Hear me!"

Inside one of the glass coffins, the eyes of a male trophy popped open.

"The end is nigh!" continued Leach's voice. "You will all be set free!"

He turned the dial which activated a drain mechanism in the bottom of each tank, allowing the translucent bacta suspension fluid inside to empty out rapidly.

Once the tanks were empty, he pressed another switch to unlock the door to each tank.

Inside one of the tanks, a trophy fluttered her eyes and gasped as she began to breathe on her own.

"Arise, my friends! Free yourselves! You are being liberated!"

The half human-half zombie trophies ripped the tubing from their faces, arms, and legs and took their first awkward steps back into reality, as they climbed out of their glass coffins. Some appeared more animated than others. Some didn't move at all, as they were long since dead, remaining suspended in their tanks.

MURCH, MACGUFFIN, AND MAX climbed through the top of the service elevator and scaled a maintenance ladder as high as the shaft went. The elevator car was on fire, teetering perilously from its suspension cables.

At the top of the shaft, MacGuffin worked to open a pair of

steel doors to escape the smoke-filled passage, while Murch and Max dangled from the ladder below him.

As MacGuffin found the door release lever, an explosion far below hurled an intense fireball up the shaft which slammed into the elevator, jolting it violently side-to-side.

With a loud crack, the suspension cables snapped, sending the elevator plummeting to the ground. The severed cables zipped upward and pulled out of their pulleys at the top of the shaft, right above MacGuffin and the two others.

"Yikes!" screeched MacGuffin.

"Hurry up, Rich!" pleaded Max. "This place is rocking and rolling!"

"I'm working as fast as I can!"

"Well, work faster!"

As MacGuffin managed to slide the doors open, another fireball raced up the shaft toward them.

"Move! Move! Move! Go! Go! Go!" shouted Max at the top of his lungs.

MacGuffin somersaulted through the opening into the 12th-floor hallway outside the Moonrise Ballroom. He turned and helped pull his companions up and out of the shaft.

He was a moment too late with Max, as the fireball caught up to him and ignited the back of his pants and shirt on fire. "Help me up! Help me up! I'm burning! I'm burning! Ouch! Ouch! Ouch!"

MacGuffin and Murch leaned down in the elevator doorway, grabbed hold of Max's right arm, and yanked him up and out of the shaft with all their might.

Once on solid ground, Max dropped and rolled on the carpet to extinguish the fire from his clothing. Only his back suffered any burns, albeit nothing severe.

MacGuffin and Murch knelt over him as he laid face-up on the floor. "Max, old buddy, you okay? Can you move?" asked MacGuffin.

Max groaned. "Unh...I'm like a toasted bagel: crisp on the outside; chewy on the inside."

"But are you okay?"

"Fine and dandy. Nothing a little Silvadene® cream can't cure."

They helped Max to his feet, and he brushed himself off. "Now that's what I call a special effect! Christ Almighty, what a rush!"

MacGuffin glanced around the room. "Where do we go from here?"

Murch spoke up. "This must be the entrance hallway to the ballroom Jimbo was talking about. According to the blueprints, there's an observation deck and belfry directly above that. We're almost there. Look for a stairwell, a door, something."

With a foul smell and awful squelching sound, the doors to the Moonrise Ballroom burst open, and a throng of Leach's zombified trophies filtered into the room.

"We've got company!" hollered MacGuffin.

"Who are these guys?" asked Max.

"More of Leach's aborted experiments, I guess."

"I thought he only kidnapped around twenty people?"

"Only the confirmed cases," clarified Murch. "I'm betting that number goes much higher."

"That doorway is our only way out," said Max. "How do we get past them?"

"Look at them," replied Murch. "They're zombies. It's like they're lobotomized. They're alive but have minimal brain activity; some worse than others. They don't know which way is up."

"In other words," added MacGuffin, "they're the kind of zombies that don't eat people."

"Go through them it is, then," suggested Max.

"I'll accept that," replied Murch.

As the three of them moved to the doorway, the zombies passed by on all sides with no awareness.

Max smiled. "See, no problem. Easy peasy."

The words were no sooner out of his mouth than one of them grabbed Max around the throat and began to strangle him. "Ah! Why is it always me that gets the short end of the stick?" he gasped, pulling on the zombie's hands around his neck. "Trot out!"

Murch grabbed her gun and shot the zombie in the head, and both the zombie and Max went down. "Max! Need a hand?"

He pulled the dead zombie's hands off his neck and got to his knees. He took Murch's hand. "I swear, this is the last time. Already I've been drugged, sliced, stabbed, toasted, and now strangled. The next one's yours."

"Bring it on," she smirked. "I'm armed, dangerous, and

menstruating."

Once Murch pulled Max to his feet, the three of them continued through the open doorway into the ballroom and searched for an escape route.

CHAPTER FIFTY-FOUR

IN THE HOTEL BELFRY, Caroline prepped a silver hot air balloon for departure. In the basket, McKenzie sat handcuffed to a support cable beside two propane tanks.

Leach entered the room carrying a bulky burlap sack and shouted, "Caroline, fire up the burner! We leave immediately."

"As you wish, Master."

Leach climbed a step ladder and dropped down into the woven willow basket. He gazed down at McKenzie, cowering on her knees against the floor of the basket. "And how is my bride to be? Hmm...?"

She said nothing in reply and turned her eyes away in disgust.

Leach frowned. "Nothing to say, eh? Must be the pre-wedding jitters?"

"Screw you!"

Leach smirked. "Oh, you will, once we arrive at our new hideaway; to seal our nuptials."

"I'd rather be dead than be your wife."

"Be careful what you wish for, my dear, you might get it."

Leach increased the amount of fuel to the burner, and the balloon's envelope inflated at a faster rate. He released sandbags from outside the basket to gain some altitude.

He gazed down at McKenzie again and smiled. "I may still get a rise out of you yet."

As the balloon filled, the rotted roof timbers above the balloon's envelope broke apart under stress, exposing the night sky beyond.

As the hot air balloon cleared the roof, Leach severed the mooring lines tying the balloon to the ground. As the ropes and chunks of roof dropped back down inside the belfry, Murch, MacGuffin, and Max arrived.

They dusted themselves off and watched the balloon float

away.

"We're too late!" shouted Max. "They're getting away!"

McKenzie, hearing Max's voice below, stood up in the balloon and screamed out, "HELP!"

Leach grabbed her and shoved her back onto the floor of the basket. "Quiet!"

He primed the burner and further inflated the balloon to make it rise higher.

Another thunderous explosion rocked the hotel's structure, as the fireball tore up the stairwell to the belfry.

Murch snared the one remaining mooring line left dangling and not anchored to anything and yelled to the others, "Grab on!"

"This is crazy!" shouted MacGuffin.

"Would you rather be dead?"

"No!"

"Good! Now hold on, and don't let go! Don't look down!"

The slack in the mooring line drew taut, and the three of them soared through the gaping hole in the roof.

Max made the mistake of looking down. "Yep. Now's a good time to be scared of heights."

MacGuffin groaned, sick to his stomach, "Oh, nertz!"

Beneath them, the Sunset Tower Hotel exploded in a brilliant flash of light, flames, and debris. It toppled over the cliff upon which it perched and fell to the lake below, creating a massive scrap pile.

The maelstrom subsided. Leach pulled out a black felt ring box and opened it before McKenzie's eyes to reveal Theresa Burkhart's severed finger and the attached diamond engagement ring.

Leach removed the ring with ease and discarded the withered finger over the side of the basket. As he roughly forced the ring onto McKenzie's finger, the silver band cut into her flesh and drew blood.

"Ouch!" she cried.

"Sorry, my dear. I didn't have time to get it resized. It'll have to do on such short notice."

Leach grabbed the burlap sack and dumped the severed heads of Crawford, Dr. Milner, Janine, Nigel, and Nigel's two dates into the floor of the basket. McKenzie wailed, mortified at the sight of her father's severed head.

Leach grinned, nonchalant. "Sorry you have to see your father and friends in such a manner, my dear, but we need to have a few witnesses present at our wedding; otherwise, it won't be official. Even if it's only their heads."

Leach pulled McKenzie to her feet and turned to his assistant. "Caroline?"

Caroline stood to attention and served as a makeshift wedding minister. "Do you, Anton Leach, take McKenzie Banks to be your lawful wedded wife, to have and to hold, in sickness and in health, till death do you part?"

"Ha, ha, ha...I do."

Caroline turned to McKenzie and asked, "Do you, McKenzie Banks, take Anton Leach to be your lawful wedded husband, to have and to hold, in sickness and in health, till death do you part?"

"Screw you, bitch!"

Leach put a hand over McKenzie's mouth and gave her a tight squeeze. "Yes, Caroline, she does!"

McKenzie freed herself and shouted, "You're mad!"

Leach squealed with delight. "Mad as a Hatter!"

Below, Murch inched her way up the mooring line, grabbed onto the base of the basket, and drew her gun.

Caroline continued her ministerial duties and stated to Leach and McKenzie, "I now pronounce you husband and wife. You may kiss the bride."

Leach smiled. "With pleasure."

Caroline restrained McKenzie's arms as Leach leaned in and planted a kiss on the girl's lips, oblivious as Caroline secretly unlocked the cuffs binding McKenzie to the basket with a tiny cuff key.

A voice shouted from below the basket, breaking the moment, "It's over, Leach!"

It was Murch.

Leach pulled away from McKenzie, his eyes wide with surprise. "*What?!*" He peered over the edge of the basket and saw Murch and the two others dangling.

"Give it up, Leach!" ordered Murch. "This sick game of yours is over!"

Leach hissed. "My pretty, you ain't seen nothing yet!"

Without hesitation, Leach pulled out a wireless detonator box and pressed the switch.

From the air, everyone watched as Paradise Pictures Studios exploded in the distance, one building at a time, domino-style. Four hundred fifteen acres worth of hideous, raging inferno.

The concussion wave shot up and knocked Murch, MacGuffin, and Max loose from the mooring line, and they plummeted to the lake below.

Leach laughed maniacally.

Murch, MacGuffin, and Max surfaced.

"Augh! It's *Apocalypse Now!*" shrieked Max.

McKenzie backed up against the rail of the basket as Leach again kissed her. With her arms now free, she pushed him away and kicked him solidly in the crotch. "Kiss this, sucker!"

"Unh...!"

As Leach keeled over in agonizing pain, McKenzie dropped backward over the edge of the basket.

Leach lunged over and tried to grab her, but he was too late. "NO! NO! AAAARGH!" A single tear rolled down his right cheek.

Seconds later, McKenzie hit the water below with a tremendous splash.

Leach turned angrily toward Caroline and noticed her holding the cuffs and the key in her hands. "You little traitor! I should have killed you long ago! You've meddled in my plans for the last time!"

He drew his sword from the scabbard on his belt and stabbed Caroline in the abdomen. She dropped to her knees.

Leach raised the sword for the final death blow. "It's all over now, baby blue!"

Caroline chuckled, spraying blood from her mouth and nose. She pulled open her coat to reveal a belt of dynamite strapped to her chest and a detonator box which she armed. "How about one final kiss for your 'Sweet Caroline?'"

She pressed the detonator switch.

The hot air balloon exploded high in the night sky against the backdrop of the silvery moon.

Flaming debris rained down as the balloon dropped slowly into the water below. The shredded remains of the basket and canvas smacked the water and sank below the surface from the weight of the burner.

In the meantime, Murch was the first of the survivors to make it to shore and climb out. "Christ, what a workout!"

Max was right behind her. "You're telling me."

Murch helped Max to his feet and put pressure on his bleeding left shoulder. "You better get that looked at. You have no idea what kind of crap was on Leach's knife. Most likely blood-borne bacteria."

Max smirked. "You have no idea what kind of crap's floating around in that lake."

Murch laughed. "My guess is crap and lots of it."

A moment later, MacGuffin made it to shore and helped McKenzie out. Together, they collapsed on the bank in each other's arms.

"Ouch!" he muttered.

"Sorry," she apologized.

"Don't be. It's all right."

They shared a healthy laugh.

Out of breath, McKenzie looked around. "Who are you people?"

"It's kind of a long story, and I'm not sure you want to hear it."

"Try me." She grabbed his face and pulled it toward hers. They kissed.

"Why did you do that?" he asked. "Aren't you pissed at me for what I did."

"I'm not sure I'll ever get another chance to. If you're as good a kisser as the times you made out with me disguised as Rivers, you're as good in my book. Even a little better."

She kissed him again, and they lost themselves for a moment.

Max protested, "Get a room, will you?"

MacGuffin gave Max the finger, as he and McKenzie continued to lock lips.

CHAPTER FIFTY-FIVE

WEDNESDAY, AUGUST THE TWENTY-FOURTH
TEN THIRTY-SEVEN PM

AN ARMY OF POLICE, fire, and other emergency vehicles descended upon the burning Paradise Pictures Studios, with more en route. Sirens filled the air like buzzing mosquitoes. The entire studio lot was ablaze and appeared leveled.

A boat of rescue workers searched Sand Pond for the remains of Leach and Caroline with flashlights and a giant spotlight. One of the workers spotted a tattered wide-brimmed black hat floating on the surface: Leach's hat. "I got something."

A second worker approached. "Another piece of hot air balloon. The lake is full of it."

The first worker fished the hat out of the lake with a pole hook.

"Anything human?" asked the second worker.

"Negative. It's an old hat."

"Toss it. We're only looking for human remains. Keep looking."

The worker threw the hat back in the lake, and it sank out of sight. He shined his flashlight elsewhere and kept looking.

On the north shore, MacGuffin stood and watched a team of paramedics load Max Winston, his shirt cut away and his left shoulder bandaged, into the back of an ambulance on a stretcher.

MacGuffin called out to the paramedics, "Please note: He's hypoglycemic. Don't let him pass out."

As the ambulance doors shut, MacGuffin took a seat beside McKenzie in the back of a police car.

Murch flashed her FBI badge and ID to the officer behind the wheel of the car. "Nobody questions them, let alone touches them, without my authorization. The FBI is in charge of this case now. Detective Scott and I will be along shortly."

As the police car drove away into a haze of smoke and flashing red-and-blue lights, Murch approached Jimbo leaning against the hood of his Volkswagen nearby, and the two of them walked away, becoming two more faces amongst the gathering crowd.

CHAPTER FIFTY-SIX

OUTSIDE THE HOLLYWOOD KINGDOM Hall Church, a mob of cars filled the curbs on each side of the street, as an overflow of uniformed police officers, friends, and family members lined up to pay their respects to deceased LAPD Homicide Detectives Christopher "Nuke" Bonaduce and Billy Hayes.

Inside, mourners filled the wooden pews to capacity. Murch, an arm sling-laden Lincoln, and Captain Dreyfus sat up front beside the families of the departed. A few small children ran around and played on the floor by their parents' feet.

Two easels were set up at the front of the church: one with a portrait of Nuke; the other with a portrait of Hayes. A folded American flag sat on a small stand before each easel.

Jimbo stood at the podium, finishing his eulogy to his two fallen partners. He too sported an arm sling on his left arm. "...I've only served alongside Nuke and Billy for the last couple years, and never once did I witness either of them stressed-out by the workload. They never brought along any outside baggage into the job. I can't vouch that they were always professional, but they still managed to make the job exciting. A few penalties along the way never made much of an impact. They took punishment in stride.

"Anyway, to keep this short, I'd like to finish by playing a song Nuke demanded for his memorial service in the event he ever died in the line of duty. It's kind of an odd choice, but that's the type of person he was. Happy-go-lucky. I suppose he wanted everybody else to feel the same spirit he had."

Jimbo pressed a button on a remote. "To Nuke and Billy."

The Beastie Boys' "(You Gotta) Fight for Your Right (To Party!)" erupted from the speakers.

Everyone in the audience gave a strange look to their neighbors but soon loosened up.

Murch and Lincoln each laughed, while Dreyfus appeared mortified.

Jimbo walked up to Murch and offered his right arm to her. "Care to dance, milady?"

Murch blushed and took his hand. "Your lead."

She joined Jimbo in an awkward waltz at the front of the church, and the crowd cheered them on.

As they danced, Murch noticed FBI Deputy Director John Kimble watching from the rear of the church. As a gesture of quiet pride, he held up his fists and gave her a power salute. She smiled back.

FOLLOWING THE FUNERAL SERVICE, a reception took place downstairs in the church's banquet hall, with food, drinks, music, and dancing.

Murch stood at the food table having a glass of punch, as John Kimble walked over and stood beside her.

"Haley!"

"Mr. Kimble."

He handed her a plate of cake and dug into his own. "Thought you might like some cake before it's all gone."

"Don't mind if I do." She took a bite of cake. "You mind telling me why you came all this way to Los Angeles?"

"I dropped in to pay my condolences to the departed and to compliment you on solving the case. It's one that's been on the books for close to three decades. Splendid work, Haley. Well done."

"Thank you, sir."

"So, what are your plans for this evening? Care to join me for dinner and a concert? The Los Angeles Philharmonic is playing at the Hollywood Bowl."

"Sorry, sir, but I'm flying back to D.C. later this afternoon. I'd like to catch up with work on a prior case by Monday morning. The BAU is having a briefing."

Kimble nodded awkwardly. "Yes, your BAU team uncovered the body of another missing co-ed abducted last Spring."

"How awful."

Kimble finished off his cake and shook Murch's hand. "Once again, good job, Agent Murch. Congratulations. I hope to hear many great things from you in the future."

"Thank you, Mr. Kimble."

"Pleasure's all mine. If you'll excuse me, I could use a drink."

He walked away, leaving Murch alone once again.

CHAPTER FIFTY-SEVEN

SATURDAY, AUGUST THE TWENTY-SEVENTH
ONE THIRTY-SEVEN PM

HALEY MURCH STOOD IN her room at the Highland Gardens Hotel, packing her belongings into a suitcase. Her FBI credentials, badge, and holstered gun lay on the bed nearby.

There was a knock at the door. Haley opened it. To Haley's surprise, Jimbo and Lincoln stood outside in the hallway. Jimbo carried a large cardboard box.

"Knock! Knock!" said Lincoln.

Murch smiled. "Hey-ee! Wow! What a surprise! Elvin!" Instead of a hug, she shook Lincoln's hand, as he still wore an arm sling.

He smiled back. "Haley. Nice to see you again."

Murch turned to Jimbo and laughed. "Jimbo!"

As she leaned in to hug Jimbo, he grimaced and grabbed his left shoulder. "Oh-uh."

"Oh, Jimbo, I'm sorry," she apologized. "I forgot it was your left shoulder."

Jimbo grasped her hand with his right. "No, no... don't worry about it. It's fine, really. It's all stitched up and ready to go." He swung his arm sling. "See? All better."

She kissed him on the cheek, instead.

He blushed, now sheepish. "Erm...thank you."

"What are you guys doing here?"

"Well, we thought we'd drop by and say goodbye once more before your flight took off."

"But, that's not the reason we're here, Jimbo," said Lincoln.

"Oh, right...um..." Jimbo placed the cardboard box on the floor and removed a package wrapped in tissue paper. "We were going through Nuke's stuff at the office yesterday, and we found this in his locker."

He tore off the tissue paper and presented Murch with a custom blue pearl-flake chopper gas tank with an airbrushed caricature of Murch on the side as a big-breasted, raven-haired superhero. "I think he was making it for you as a gift."

"We thought you'd like to have it to remember him by," said Lincoln. "I mean, he *clearly* had the hots for you."

Murch smiled wistfully. "You don't know the half of it." She accepted the gas tank and inspected it carefully. "It's beautiful. I like the pearl flake. Bet that cost a lot."

"I think it runs roughly a thousand dollars a pint or something."

"It ain't cheap," said Jimbo.

Murch checked out the superhero caricature with its embellished features. "Nice rack. Do I look sexy?"

Jimbo swooned. "Oh, yeah. Definitely!"

Lincoln smacked him across the head. "Jimbo!"

Jimbo looked at Murch, blushing. "Sorry. You do look quite sexy."

"Well, thanks for the compliment, Jimmy. Say whatever you like in front of me. We're all adults here. Don't let Lincoln bully you."

"Thanks."

"Please, come inside," she offered. "I was packing my stuff." She stepped aside and allowed the men to enter. Lincoln closed the door behind him.

Murch placed the gas tank atop her open suitcase. "Well, thank you both much for this. It's a lovely parting gift. I'll continue to treasure it and Nuke's memory forever."

Lincoln smiled. "It's our pleasure."

A brief pause.

"So, did they ever recover Leach's body from the lake?" asked Murch.

"Not yet," said Jimbo. "But, they did fish out a bunch of piranhas yesterday morning, though, with inconclusive forensic tests on them, so far."

"Huh. Damn things were in schools all over the place, I guess."

"Yeah, but they found the girl, though...or, what was left of her. According to Max Winston and McKenzie Banks, her name was Caroline. Other than that, we couldn't find any other information about her. In all regards, she might as well have been a ghost."

"The explosion made a mess of her," added Lincoln. "She was

mangled up pretty good. Some parts were even missing. Food for the fishes, I guess. It's safe to assume Leach met the same fate but washed away."

"There is a chance he survived," said Jimbo. "The case remains open."

"At least you'll be there to stop him if he does turn up again," said Murch.

"Hopefully, not for a long, long time," said Lincoln.

Murch got up from the bed and pulled on a gray suit coat over her black shirt. "There's a bar in the hotel restaurant. Care for a quick drink before you go?"

"Why not?" replied Lincoln. "We're off duty. Right, Jimbo?"

"But I don't drink. Remember?"

"Well, I'm pretty sure they can conjure up something for you," said Murch.

"Can I get chocolate milk?"

Murch laughed. "A chocolate milk it is." She grabbed her purse and led them back out into the hall.

"As long as it doesn't culminate in another bar fight," mocked Lincoln.

Murch was flabbergasted. "Why? You don't think Jimbo could win in a bar fight?"

Jimbo smirked. "No. Not at all. No."

Murch closed her hotel room door and started walking away. "Come on, boys. Let a lady show you how it's done."

THE END

ABOUT OUR AUTHORS

ROY C. BOOTH hails from Bemidji, MN where he manages Roy's Comics & Games (est. 1992) with his wife and three sons. He is a published author, poet, journalist, essayist, gag writer, and optioned screenwriter with over 1,000 publication credits, and internationally awarded playwright with 57 stage plays published (Samuel French, Heuer, et al) with 875+ documented productions worldwide in 30 countries in ten languages.

Roy has won various writing awards in horror, science fiction, and fantasy, including over 50 Preditors & Editors/Critters Awards, most notably for Best Young Adult Novel (*The One: Children of Destiny*, w/. Paul Copeland, 2013); Best Book Editor (w/. Jorge Salgado-Reyes, 2014); Best Steampunk Short Story (*Sherlock Holmes and the Man-Made Vacuum*, novella, w/. Nicholas Johnson, 2014); Best Poem ("Deconstruction," 2014); and Best Poet (2014 and 2017).

Roy is also known for his presence on the regional convention circuit, often being an Invited Participant or a Guest of Honor. He also likes to collaborate as a form of paying forward in the writing industry. See his entry on Wikipedia, his Facebook pages, his publishers' sites, and www.amazon.com/author/roycbooth for more.

JOHN F. MOLLARD (1976-) was born in Virginia, Minnesota, to a schoolteacher/hospital volunteer coordinator mother and millwright father. Graduating high school in 1994, he attended Mesabi Community College, Bemidji State University, and Mesabi Range Community & Technical College, earning degrees in Liberal Arts, Mass Communications, Creative Writing, and Carpentry. In his spare time, John is a hardcore movie geek, collecting movies and TV series. He even appeared as a featured extra in the films *North Country* and *The Day Lufberry Won It All*. John, with collaborator Roy C. Booth, is also an optioned screenwriter. John's writing credits can be found at www.amazon.com/John-F.-Mollard/e/B00OYUO3GY.

AFTERWORD

WE WOULD LIKE TO personally thank you for buying and reading this book. Writing this novel has been and continues to be fulfilling for our authors, and we hope that it is enjoyable for you to read.

Please consider taking a little extra time to help others find this book by leaving feedback where you purchased it. Your opinion about this book truly matters, both to other readers and to us.

If you have any questions, comments, suggestions or just want to say hi, please visit our website on www.salgado-reyes.com and follow our publisher's twitter: @Indie__Authors

~Indie Authors Press~

www.ingramcontent.com/pod-product-compliance
Lightning Source LLC
Chambersburg PA
CBHW070854180626
46817CB00003B/773